iUniverse®

The Faults of the Owens Valley

iUniverse books may be ordered through booksellers or by contacting:

iUniverse
1663 Liberty Drive
Bloomington, IN 47403
www.iuniverse.com
1-800-Authors (1-800-288-4677)

ISBN: 978-1-4401-7793-4 (sc)

Print information available on the last page.

iUniverse rev. date: 03/09/2015

The past is never dead. It's not even past.
William Faulkner

PART ONE:
THREE EVIL PLACES

CHAPTER 1

The note was lying on Undersheriff Howard's desk in a plastic cover. Howard shoved it over to her, and Liz Nolan read *The first body is at the first evil place. The evil will be expunged at the three evil places, and this defiled Valley will be cleansed.*

A few minutes before, Howard called Liz in, using the intercom, saying only, "Nolan, get in here, we have a problem." Liz checked the clock as she headed for Howard's office. It was 8:45 on an early May morning, and they had just come on shift at the Owens County Sheriff's headquarters in Independence.

Liz looked up from the note and said, "Somebody is a little hung up on evil. Mentions it three times."

"Yeah. Looks like we have a body out there somewhere," said Howard with a very unhappy look on his weather-beaten, fifty-five year-old face.

"Where did the note come from?"

"Found it on the front door when I came in this morning. Just taped on, looked like no prints on the tape. Tech guy is checking the original."

"Calling the Valley defiled. Maybe some kind of religious nut?" Liz said.

Howard said, "Or some kind of Indian religious nut. They used to worship the Valley, didn't they? What the hell does 'three evil places' mean?"

"Maybe a prank. Wait for the call," Liz offered.

It didn't take long. An hour later, the guard at the front gate of the Manzanar National Historic Site was on the phone. The Park Service patrol had found a body at the Site, white male, no ID yet. Liz and Howard climbed in his personal vehicle—a Suburban he had driven forever—and headed south from Independence on 395, the main north-south highway that bisects the Valley.

Liz Nolan had been assigned to work with Jack Howard in the headquarters two weeks ago. She had just received a disciplinary review, and was still trying to sort out whether she had been demoted or just re-assigned to headquarters so they could keep an eye on her. All Howard had told her when she began the assignment was that she would report directly to him, which was fine with Liz. Howard's reputation was tough, fair, and blunt with his deputies.

Howard's Suburban was a perfect complement to his work ethic. It was a 1998 four wheel drive monster, old, but reliable. Howard told anybody who questioned his choice that it would take him anywhere, anytime, in any weather. The deputies quietly made fun of it because the Undersheriff was entitled to a new vehicle every two years, but Howard was totally committed to the Suburban, and it had become his trademark.

As they rode south into the bright sun, Liz watched the mountains on both sides of the road. Off to the right, the sun was full on the Eastern Sierra, but was still erasing the shadows on the Inyos to the east. She had lived in the Valley for almost twenty years, but she had traveled away from it often enough that she never took the mountains for granted.

The Sierra was the unforgettable feature, an outrageously bold part of the landscape, sweeping up in the steepest rise of any mountain range on the North American continent—the stark, eastern side of the mighty Sierra Nevada. And then, as the Suburban got closer to Lone Pine and Manzanar, the rolling Alabama Hills came up in the foreground, the backdrop for more than a hundred Westerns and TV shows from the 20's through the 50's.

Liz sensed the vehicle slowing, looked up, and saw a huge SUV passing them and then swinging erratically back into its lane after passing three cars, missing their front fender by only a few car lengths.

"*Fuckingflatlanders,*" Howard said, in a phrase Liz had heard from a few of the oldtimers in the Department. Few of the younger deputies used the phrase, but the older ones always pronounced it as a single word, full of disgust. Owens County had the kind of love-hate affair with tourists endured by every resort and vacation area: love the cash, hate the customers. And in the Valley, it came with a second layer of a high-tension relationship with Los Angeles, the Valley's part-owner and sometimes desecrator, and, some would even admit, benefactor.

Liz smiled at the thought of the rapid justice that would have followed Howard's pursuit of the SUV, with a certain ticket and a scorching lecture if they hadn't been en route to a homicide scene. Howard had instinctively reached out to turn on the light bar, and then pulled his hand away reluctantly. "Next time," he muttered.

Liz glanced out the window as the Suburban passed over the Aqueduct, and noticed for the hundredth time or so where the Los Angeles Department of Water and Power had blanked out the letters identifying it as the Los Angeles Aqueduct. She could never figure out whether the DWP was trying to confuse prospective terrorists—or the Valley's residents.

When they got to Manzanar, the sun was climbing toward a late morning glare, yellow tape was needlessly staked around an empty piece of desert, and the forensics crew was standing by waiting. They pulled into the parking lot next to the Administration building and walked over to the taped–off area in the dirt at the far edge of the parking lot. As Liz approached it, she could see that the male body, which was naked, had white clothesline rope wrapped around the waist, with one arm lashed to the body and the other outstretched. The first finger of the hand that wasn't tied down had been rigged to point east, toward the Inyos, which began to rise from the Valley floor five miles from the front gate of Manzanar.

Liz knelt close enough to see the man's face, carefully making sure she didn't disturb the ground next to him. It had been quick—a single shot through the temple.

Howard straightened up slowly from his own examination of the body, years of driving and desk work having taken their toll on his lanky frame. He turned to the head of the forensics team, Willard Korper, and told him, "Work out from the body. There have to be some footprints, and a vehicle. Find them. And check the tape on the fingers."

Korper was a heavyset, older professional with an improbable head of blondish hair who had told everyone he was "months from retirement" when Liz first met him a decade earlier. He nodded, and then motioned his two-man crew forward.

As Liz and Howard walked back to the cruiser, she looked over at the slanted roof of a small building at the front gate, and asked, "Do you think this is about Manzanar—what happened here?"

"Maybe. Funny place to leave a body unless you're trying to say something about the relocation. He wasn't killed here, that's for sure."

Liz figured the statement was a kind of test, and she responded. "I could see that. Blood dried, looked like the face had even been wiped clean. No splatter on the sand. We need to figure out what he's pointing to. Killer arranges a scene like that, he may be trying to tell a story. Wonder what the story was."

Howard grunted, seemingly satisfied with her read of the scene. Then he shook his head. "I'll tell you what it means. Dumping the body here means we are going to have to deal with a small army of feds. They are going to be all over us, and if there really is more than one victim, the FBI will probably get into it, too." He frowned as they neared the Suburban, already irritated at the red tape parade awaiting him.

Manzanar was in the middle of a lengthy renovation. Liz had visited the site a year ago with her husband Paul, a high school teacher in Bishop, and their two daughters. The Site had been the first of ten relocation centers for 110,000 Japanese citizens and foreign nationals—90% of them American citizens—who were forcibly moved to these camps from coastal areas of the western U.S. beginning in February 1942. The renovation projects had restored the guard house at the front gate, which had a small, swooping roof, and had repaired a large building that was a processing center. The cemetery at the Site had also been cleaned up and a white fence around it had been replaced.

Off to the north, next to the highway, a new two-story guard tower had been built to specifications from the original plans for the camp. It looked exactly like every guard tower in every prison camp movie from the World War II era, and it was chilling. The tower lacked the machine guns and searchlights of the original, but it was still an ugly intrusion on the high desert floor.

Manzanar remained a controversial site for some oldtimers in the Owens Valley. Some resented the reparations and formal apology by President Reagan to the Japanese in 1988, and if you asked them they would frown and say "We had to do it—what's the big deal?" The renovations were part of the agreement. Last year, Paul and Liz and their two girls had attended the annual ceremony of remembrance conducted by hundreds of Japanese-Americans from all over Southern California, who came to the site each year in April.

Back at the OCSD headquarters, Liz went to work on the dead man's prints. Within half an hour, the Cal–ID system yielded a match. She took the printout into Howard's office. The office was spare, with bare walls except for a relief map of the county and a view of the dry, brown Inyos out a small window.

Like a number of older law enforcement officers, Howard was long divorced. Liz had heard some vague rumors about Howard and Natalie Reston, a tall, attractive widow who worked for the County Health agency, but had never seen him with anyone at any of the OCSD events Liz had attended over the years.

"Jack, he's a fed, works for the National Park Service. Name is Edward Washburn. I called the Park Service and they confirmed he was missing. He was part of the group out here from D.C. working on the restoration. He's been here for two years on a detail. Park Service is handling NoK notification."

Howard pushed back from his desk and put his boot up on his desk. "A fed, killed at 'the evil place.' So it's some kind of Japanese group still pissed off about the relocation sixty-five years later. Make sense to you?"

Liz was slow to answer, though she immediately thought Howard had made a bad guess. "Maybe, but a lot of Muslims have been raising the same issues lately. Calling the round-ups after 9-11 'relocations' and trying to stir up bad feelings."

Howard shook his head. "Bullshit!" He reached in his pocket and pulled out a small cigar, biting off the end of it and spitting it in the general direction of his wastebasket. His efforts to chew them and not smoke them were well-known—since he usually failed after a minute or two, to the great displeasure of the County's environmental health officer when she came through on an annual inspection. He continued, "We relocated everybody Japanese on the Coast in '42; today, there are three or four million Muslims in this country and we locked up maybe 2000 of 'em. Prosecuted a few dozen. Convicted maybe two or three so far. Big deal."

He sat down and swung around to look at his computer screen. "Look at that! Five emails from the feds in DC in the last fifteen minutes. They are going to be all over this, and we are going to have a jurisdictional pissing contest worse than when that Marine shot the DWP guy in the bar in Big Pine three years ago. What a pain in the ass this is going to be!"

Liz said calmly, "I enjoy your precise language, Boss," knowing that he would shift his irritation to her and away from the feds, which was probably safer at the moment. Risky for her, but safer for the case.

Liz Nolan was thirty-five, stood five three and a half, and had joined the Owens County Sheriff's Department thirteen years ago. She was a light brunette, hair worn short, who gave up trying for blonde a few years ago with her second child and the approval of her husband. Paul Nolan had taught in the Bishop schools for ten years, and his family had been in the Bishop area since the 1880s.

Paul was crazy about Liz and had been since they had been students together at Bishop Union High School in the seventies. Liz had transferred from Van Nuys, and the second day she was there, a group of older students teased her about being a Valley Girl, which stopped when Paul shoved one of the guys so hard he broke open four lockers. Liz and Paul were inseparable since that day.

Liz didn't think she was pretty and secretly thought her husband was weird because he told her so often that she was. A more objective observer would say she was probably the third best-looking girl in her class, and easily the best–looking woman that had ever worked for the OCSD. She had the kind of figure that was acceptable for a cop, neither bulging out of a too-tight top, nor boyishly flat. Her green eyes, emerging somewhere out of her dark Irish past, were easily her best feature. A lot of the time, they studied people. Some of the time, they glared. And every now and then, they crinkled in a first-class smile, and those few who caught the glow saw a different, warmer Liz.

Liz went after police work for reasons she mostly understood. At the core were three certainties: she had two brothers who were LAPD cops and a father who spent his life in private security work; she hated bullies since she had been picked on by one in the second grade; and she had learned while playing high school basketball that being small and fast and mean could get you places in life.

But she had always had what her father carefully called "a slight problem with authority," which had earned her two suspensions since joining the OCSD. She was "working on it," as she told her husband and her father.

The man who called himself Avenger rode across the high desert, knowing his first kill had been successful. He had already planned the second, but he was going to hole up in his lair for a few days, waiting for the fear to spread among the hated people of the Valley. His long-awaited revenge was falling into place, and he felt his pain subside.

CHAPTER 2

The first thing to understand, if you are trying to understand the Valley, is that the Owens Valley really isn't in California. This makes its connection with California, especially Southern California, all the more complicated.

All the road signs say California, the maps say California, but the geology points east to the Great Basin. There is almost nothing of the Pacific here, nothing but the sparse, stingy rain, the little bit of water picked up offshore, surviving its trip over the coastal range and across the Central Valley, blown up into the foothills and over the 14,000 foot peaks, and then dropped on the Owens Valley floor. A few inches a year in most parts of the Valley, no more. A fine writer, Mary Austin, lived in the Valley in the early 1900s, and wrote a book about it called *The Land of Little Rain*. Right.

But if you counted the snow—then it was a different story. For there was snow in some parts of the Sierra all year round, dropped in swirling storms, snow that sometimes roared down in blizzards that exploded out of Alaska and the North Pacific in the deepest parts of the winter, and at other times dropped softly at the end of a storm that still had some punch left when it got to the Eastern Sierra. And if you counted all that snow, then the residue of the magically lifted and transmuted Pacific and Arctic Oceans was always there, freezing, then melting from the peaks and the back country, running down the tiny creeks and streams and rivulets, making the Valley green—but only in those places where the long hand of the City had not diverted these streams of shifting colors, colors first falling white, then melting into blue-green, green-making, fast-flowing treasure.

So what Mary Austin might have called her book, to be accurate, was *The Land of Little Rain—But Sometimes a Hell of a Lot of Snow.*

CHAPTER 3

Rudy Warland had a bad feeling about the call from Jack Howard. The killing at Manzanar—or wherever the killing had actually taken place—didn't make sense yet, and Rudy was wary of anything that didn't make sense. As a Paiute, he was also wary of anything with a hint of racial or cultural overtones, and leaving the body at Manzanar was full of those overtones.

Rudy had been a deputy for four years. There had been two or three Paiutes in the deputy ranks over the years, but Rudy's hiring was something new. He was the first Owens Valley Indian who had gone to college, majored in criminology, and come back to the Valley. He had grown up among the Big Pine reservation people, which made him a more neutral figure than if he had come from the dominant Bishop reservation or one of the southern Owens Valley groups in Independence, Lone Pine, or further south. Since the Sheriff patrolled the reservations, except in Bishop where the City had its own police force, most of the time an uneasy truce prevailed when the line had to be drawn between the County, the City, and the reservations.

Rudy liked being a deputy. He had always been big—tall and stocky, but muscular, not the tubby fat some Paiutes slid into so easily. He had learned to be cautious about his size, but never took any abuse about it, either. The guys who had wanted to test him in high school—and there were always a few, Paiute, Mexican and white alike—learned that Rudy had two basic responses: the first was to invite them to play football, and the second was to carefully pick his hangouts around the school buildings where teachers and staff were most likely to walk by. He had developed a trick of seeming hard of hearing, so that when someone insulted him, he would ask *what did you say*, and get the antagonist to repeat himself louder, which usually ensured that a friendly witness would hear what was going on and back Rudy up when he needed it.

A few times, away from the school and separated from the other Indians he usually traveled with, he had been cornered, and had to go at it. He won two, which were fair fights, and definitely lost one, which had turned into a four on one when Rudy started winning. The other one was a draw, unless you looked at the other's guy's face.

Rudy was an unusual student at Bishop High for several reasons. The coaching staff at Bishop had never recruited outside the city, but the coach stayed in close touch with the Paiute players after they graduated, encouraging them to scout the eight-man teams in the smaller schools in the Valley, as well as the junior high-aged players. Growing up in Big Pine, Rudy had been outstanding in peewee football games as early as the sixth grade, and when his parents divorced and his father moved to Bishop, it was not difficult for the coach to persuade him to try out. Rudy's mother had never wavered when the decision came up, telling her son that she was only 15 miles away and that his chances to go to college on a football scholarship would be far better in Bishop.

Rudy loved football, because it satisfied a deep aggressive streak in him and allowed him to work it out by the simple expedient of being encouraged by adults in authority to run into and through and over other people. Once Rudy figured out that was how it worked, he gave himself up to the game, going both ways, getting all-conference fullback and second team linebacker. He was good enough and big enough to play at Fresno State, and when he decided to come back to the Valley to work, his criminology degree had made him an easy hire.

His instinctive sense of the role of the rules in football was part of what led him to law enforcement. He valued fairness—having seen a lot of unfairness in his life. And he saw that the rules, and by extension, the law, usually made things fairer. Not always, but usually. He knew there was a great gap between Paiute ideas of rules and those in the larger society outside the reservation, and he instinctively knew he could sometimes be a good interpreter of the rules, as any referee has to be.

But after the first year, Rudy had trouble figuring out why his assignments had been a mix of community relations and real deputy work. Just as he began to feel useless and token, they gave him a good assignment. It was as though they could read him and sense when he was getting pissed off—which pissed him off all the more.

Driving down toward the station in Independence, Rudy thought about the call from Jack Howard. Howard hadn't said much, just told him there had been a homicide at Manzanar that might have a racial angle. That was the part that had bothered Rudy the most.

Rudy was certain that he wouldn't have been detailed from the Bishop sub-station to work on the Manzanar killing unless Jack Howard had already cleared it with the Sheriff. And he knew the Sheriff's agreement meant they had both seen a role for a Paiute deputy that might be useful in the case. He wondered what that role would be.

He got on the patrol radio and asked the dispatcher which deputy was handling the investigation for Howard. When she told him it was Liz Nolan, Rudy clicked off the radio and muttered to himself, "Strike two." He knew Nolan, had worked with her as part of a team a year before. She was a good cop, but he had found her very hard to read and sometimes on the rude side of abrupt. He had heard through the deputy grapevine that she had recently been suspended for an incident in which she had mouthed off at a lieutenant, who was widely regarded as an officious ass, so that counted as a plus with Rudy. But it also made him wonder if he might get splattered by the spillover from one of her outbursts.

Rudy had met Paul Nolan in a parent workshop at the high school and liked him. Paul had been around a while, and was comfortable holding the Indian kids accountable without either feeling guilty about it or targeting them unfairly.

But Liz, he wasn't sure about. Her explosions were well-known among the deputies. And he knew now that they would be teamed up to work on the case, with Howard watching every move they made.

CHAPTER 4

Elaine Carpenter was working on a sermon, and she was trying not to yield to temptation.

The temptation was at her fingertips, only a few inches away: downloading one of the pre-canned, smoothly written 15-minute sermons from an online website she had used more often than she felt she should. She supposed, out of her limited experience with sexual adventure, that the emotional cost of the vice she was considering was something like the aftermath of an afternoon sneakaway special at a motel: a good feeling at the time and a lasting, guilty ache after.

She pushed away from her desk and walked into her kitchen—facing other temptations that she had become much better at resisting, once she had realized that there was no other place for her study than the parsonage's renovated back porch adjoining the kitchen. It was not a formal parsonage, but a rental house that one of the parishioners had let the church use, four blocks away from the sanctuary. Elaine had grown to love it, with all its quirks and mixed memories. It had been the house she and Ed had moved to when she was first called to her church in Bishop eleven years ago, and after he died, it was a place that comforted her, even with all of its echoes.

Elaine's collie padded in from her nest of blankets on the porch, hopeful for a walk, a biscuit or some other treat. The dog had been Ed's, a beautiful purebred collie that the school kids all called Lassie when they walked by the house. Ed had named her Dulcinea, after Don Quixote's love, and Elaine shortened it to Dulcie. She was getting old, but still had all the grace of a longhair collie, was great company, and gave a piercing bark when anyone came to the door that she didn't know. Elaine was a tall brunette who kept her hair long and her body slim. When she walked Dulcie, the effect was two elegant ladies swinging down the sidewalks with long strides and classic lines.

Sipping a cup of tea, Elaine looked out the window, framing a panoramic view of Mount Tom and a sweep of the nearby Sierra. A small bit of snow clung to the barely visible northeastern face of the peak. Horsetail clouds brushed the light blue sky above the mountains. Elaine offered silent thanks for where she lived, set the cup down in the sink, and went back to her desk.

Ten minutes later the phone rang. It was Jerome Nadeau, the minister at the Lone Pine evangelical church she had gotten to know through some of the inter-church council work she had done in the Valley. "Elaine, have you heard about the shooting?"

"No, Jerry, what's happened?"

"One of our members, Ed Washburn, was shot and killed out by Manzanar. I'm calling you because you know Liz Nolan and it looks like she's handling the case."

Elaine made a face, and then was glad visual phones had never caught on. Jerry Nadeau was a good preacher, though his politics differed widely from Elaine's. But he was a terrible gossip, and was not above using his church ties to track down nuggets of information. She marveled at how much he had already learned about the case.

"Haven't heard from her, Jerry, but I suppose I'll see her and Paul this Sunday. Though not sure she'll tell me much," she quickly added, to forestall his calling Monday morning if he thought Elaine would have some fresh news.

CHAPTER 5

"Less than twenty thousand people and more than ten thousand square miles. What am I?"

Paul Nolan used quiz questions at times to see if he could wake up the sleepers in his senior history class. It worked fine for the core of academically solid students he had in most classes, but it rarely got the sleepers.

When he began teaching, he was genuinely curious about the sleepers. Were they out all night partying and drinking? Were they hung over? Were they just staying up watching mindless television, or satellite TV porn? Or were they so besotted with the live-action, fleshly offerings of their equally sleepy members of the opposite sex that they were sleeping off the glorious excitement of sex at 2 am? Were they holding down a night shift job to help their family, or to buy the consumer *stuff* and electronic goodies they craved?

But after a while, he no longer cared. He had concluded that it was all of the above, augmented by pure laziness for some of them. He also admitted with some chagrin that in too many cases, they slept because what he had to say had far less appeal than sleep. And his treaty with them, unspoken but rigidly enforced, came to be that if they did not disturb the class and sat in the back, and remained a minority of four or five of his class of thirty, he would not disturb them.

He kept a pitcher of fresh water on his desk because at the end of the day his voice sometimes started to fade, and sipping water helped it. Several years ago, he had dumped a pitcher of fairly cold water on a sleeper who was snoring loudly. The rumors had quickly exploded across the school, assuring newcomers that "he always does that." The pitcher became a visible guarantee that the sleepers stayed in the back, and got poked by someone when they got too loud. Paul could live with that.

The classroom was on the second floor of the east side of the building, with windows giving a wide view of the several large trees on the front lawn of the school. Like some of his students, Paul had vivid memories of late summer evenings under those trees, conducting pre-Liz experiments in his own self-directed physical education course, full of murmured talk, adolescent negotiations, and, for some, fervent, hurried explorations of young bodies in bloom.

Paul looked more like a mountain guide than a teacher, with a deep, year-round tan from his outdoors activities with his daughters. His craggy features usually attracted two or three of the more impressionable seniors until they noticed Liz picking him up after school in her OCSD cruiser.

On the wall, Paul had hung a set of maps of the Valley, both current and historic, along with its waterways, earthquake faults, and hiking trails. He had several of the classic Ansel Adams posters of the Sierra, along with some photos he had taken and three color shots by the great nature photographer Galen Rowell. The class began at 8 am, so morning sun coming through the wide windows sometimes lit the photographs as brightly as if the ceiling held recessed lights.

And sitting in the front, or sometimes off to the sides, were the ten or fifteen kids he was really teaching for, those who were there for learning. Some of them stood out: the brightest kids, the straight A students who were going to go off to the UC at Berkeley or UCLA or Irvine or Santa Cruz or to the Cal State campuses. He had a sizable chunk of the forty kids who would graduate in the top quarter of their class, the kids who would go to the University and Cal State campuses, a few who would make it to the private colleges. Those kids were always challenging, because even with their ability, only some of them wanted to work hard, instead of just sliding by with memorizing. And the goal with these kids was to get them to think, to think harder than they wanted to or needed to in order to rack up the As. Not all of them saw the need, because their trophies were already lined up.

And so he saw his job as pushing the ones who were on the edge, the ones not sure they wanted to make the extra effort, not sure they could push beyond rote mastery of the facts to what the facts *meant.*

The class was an elective, so he got these kids as well as others who wanted a class they thought they could get through easily because it was about the history of the Valley, and, hey, how hard could that be—that was where they *lived.*

Then there were the ones who were the most fun of all, the ones he called "The Maybes." There were nine or ten of them in most classes, kids who maybe would get an A or B, maybe would see the point of some of what he was trying to tell them, maybe would get out of the Valley for college and then come back with something of value, maybe would escape the easy life if their parents had money or maybe would somehow rise above the hard, thankless $12 an hour life if they didn't.

But they were maybes, because their cards were not all filled in yet. They had a shot at it, but it would take work and character. And some of them would go their whole lives and never recognize character in themselves or the people around them. Some of them would never know what it was to believe enough in themselves to want to do something, just because some jerk of a parent or teacher or first boss had told them they *couldn't* do it.

But some of them, he knew, would catch fire from a spark of his or someone else's, or just by the grace of God. And they would come back to the Valley or live in a place like it, small, less metropolitan than most of California. And they would sometimes think about their life, and want it to be better. And one day, they might trust themselves enough to try to make it better, marrying a person who would challenge them, divorcing someone who was pulling them down, doing a better job of raising a difficult kid, taking a class at the community college, pressing for a promotion they deserved because they had worked hard and gotten good at what they did.

But today, he had only one taker for his question. The boy was sitting quietly, his hand half-raised but not waving, waiting to see if anyone else would try to answer. He was one of the headed-for-UCs, Mitchell McLellan, a boy who had always been one of the top students in his class, coming from a blue-collar family, whose dad worked for DWP.

"Mitch, what say you?" Paul asked.

"Owens County, Mr. Nolan."

"Yep. Not quite twenty thousand people and ten thousand square miles, give or take. Lots of land. And that's what we have been talking about in this course—the land, and the water, and the people. And I sure do wish more of you had remembered that basic little set of numbers, because we started with them in January when we got this course going."

Paul recalled the first session of the course with pain and a bit of pride. The kids who walked in prepared to be bored were bored, but he knew he had prodded a few of them into listening.

Liz teased him sometimes—though she was at least half-serious when she thought he was bringing too much of his work home—that he had trouble locating the line between passionate and pedantic. And he supposed he *was* pedantic at times, fueled by his passion for the Valley and what it could mean to inspire these students.

But most of them knew surprisingly little about where they lived. So his first lecture had to get them to begin thinking about the Valley differently. The first part of the course was numbers and facts, but now he had come to the payoff sessions, which were the core of the course: the geology, the water, the mines, the Indian wars, Manzanar, and how their own futures were a part of the Valley's future.

But back in January, the introduction had been difficult.

Paul began, "We're going to talk about the water, but the Owens Valley is not just about the water. The water is what people out there have heard about most, but the story is more than the water, much more. If you just tell the story about the water, about Fred Eaton and Mulholland and LA stealing the water and the dynamiting of the Aqueduct, you get some of it, but it's not the whole story of the Valley, not by a long shot.

"The Valley is about the people who have been here for ten thousand years and the ones who got here last week. And it is about the crimes committed here and the decency and goodness that sometimes accompanied those crimes. The miners and the train robbers and the little churches and the fishermen and the skiers and the farmers and the Mexicans and the Chinese and the Basques, and of course the Paiutes.

"These were tough people. There was not much milk and damned little honey when they got here, and they had to make a living and raise kids on land that was not that fertile. And the weather was fierce, it was wet, sometimes, and cold in the deep winter. You all know it's 4000 feet up here, and it gets mighty cold, even though it's a desert out there. These were tough people, without air conditioning or central heating. The ones that weren't tough went south.

"And part of the story we'll talk about in this class is about the rest of the geology that isn't the water: the desert and the mountains and the quakes and the volcanoes and the vast inland sea that once covered it all. And it is about the empty spaces and the ones that aren't, the ones that fill up with people, but not too many people, people able to live lightly on the land because there is so much of it and because the land is so much stronger than we are. And when we forget that, the land shakes us up"—he threw his arms out and gave a quick shake of his whole body, getting a few laughs—"and it sends up steam and hot water and kills a few thousand tress, and just casually reminds us that we are not really in charge here. However many gas stations and outlet stores and casinos and fast food places we stick on top of the land, we are not in charge here.

"Frost said it about New England, but it is true here—the land was ours before we were the land's. I think that means that we have to grow to appreciate the land, because it is so ancient and we—some of us, anyway—are so new here. Just standing on the land, just sticking a house on top of it, isn't enough. We have to work to understand the land, and what happened here on that land. Just owning it is not enough."

He stopped, wanting to emphasize the next part. "Any place that ignores or tries to forget its history is in trouble, because its people have no idea where they came from. And when you don't know where you came from, you may have a lot of trouble figuring out where you're going."

Paul turned to the topographic map of the Valley that covered a large part of the side wall. "Now it is possible to think of this county as a strip four or five miles off 395 in both directions, and forget about the rest of it. It is possible, but it would be a big mistake, because you'd be leaving out a lot.

"This course focuses mostly on the Owens Valley, but the Owens Valley is not Owens County—not by a long shot. In fact the Owens Valley makes up less than 15% of the County. The Owens Valley can be defined, stripped to its essentials, as a 100-mile long by 6-to-20-mile wide drop in the earth's crust between two large faults at the eastern base of the Sierra Nevada and at the western base of the White-Inyo range.

"If you want to identify the County with a valley, it's Death Valley, not the Owens Valley. Because the Death Valley National Park has 3.4 million acres and the county has about 6.5 million acres. So the Park is nearly half of the county, once you subtract the parts that are in Nevada and San Bernardino County. But we're going to focus on the Owens Valley, because it is where we are.

"Now, there is a theme in this Valley's history, probably several themes. But it's my course, and I get to choose the one I think makes the most sense. And so I choose freedom as the theme—taking it, giving it, taking it, earning it, fighting for it, losing it, winning it back. It's a very Western thing, and as we'll see, sometimes it's really the freedom we here seek to take money from the rest of the country while we are proclaiming our independence from them. 'Stay away, leave us alone, keep sending money.' Quite a message.

"One more thing: I'm not going to go over these topics chronologically, people, because what we're going to be discussing can be better understood if we take them out of order. Each of these sessions will review a kind of conflict over something valuable—water, land, gold and silver, and freedom. So we're going to go from the water wars to the Indian wars and relations with the tribes, then we'll talk about mining in the Valley, and then Manzanar, and then politics as it affects the Valley today."

As he wrapped up the lecture in January, Paul had thought that he had maybe half of them tuned in. But now it was May, and Paul forgave them a lot in May. They were six weeks from graduation, most of them, and they were counting the hours. They had either gotten into college or hadn't—or hadn't tried. And for some of them, it was the last summer before they sank into the slow quicksand of their lifelong balancing act between work and family, and they knew it but did not yet want to face it. So his numbers and his questions were a long way from the forefront of most of their brains, and he understood why.

The course was new and Paul had lobbied for three years before the principal allowed him to offer it as a senior elective. There had never been a course about the history of the Valley—pieces were chunked into American history and California history, but there had never been a semester-long course focused just on the Valley.

But although he'd gotten the approval he needed, Paul still had to be careful with these lectures, because sitting out in his class were a dozen or so adolescent land mines, set to go off when he crossed an invisible line of religious or cultural or racial tolerance. There were three Paiute kids, four Baptist fundies, two DWP employees' kids, and a smattering of kids from families with cops—like his own—Sheriffs' deputies from two counties, and even a beautiful, brilliant girl who was the daughter of the editor of the local newspaper. So he sometimes felt like he was walking on very thin ice, sure he would offend someone as he tried to tell the tangled stories of the Valley's complicated history.

And yet he saw it as a duty, an almost sacred duty, to tell these stories and to try to get them right, to try to help his students think harder than they normally would about the history all around them. His job, he thought, was to help them see and feel beyond themselves and their *stuff*, the material things they possessed or longed for. He wanted them, a few of them, at least, to understand that there had been and still might be ideas and values in the way people lived in the Valley that lasted longer than their stuff—ideas that people had lived for, fought for, and sometimes died for.

Being married to a tough guy wife and having two daughters could have neutered some men. But Paul knew who he was. Part of it was loving teaching, and part of it was being rooted in a family that had been rooted in the same community for well over a century.

Paul's dad had always worked his own land east of Bishop, raising cattle and working hard to keep a large grove of fruit trees in water. His family had been one of the ones that had sold part of their original spread to LA , and Paul's dad had gotten tough and crusty over the years enduring the remarks of other landowners. Paul's interest in history grew out of his father's stories about the early days of the Nolan family in the Valley, and how hard his parents and their parents had worked to make their farming and cattle business succeed. When Ted Nolan saw how bright Paul was, and that he wanted to teach, he had done all that he could to support him. He had sold off some of the family land to pay for Paul's education at Occidental, wanting him in a first-rate college that was still in California.

When he first started teaching, Paul was depressed at how little most of the kids knew about the history of the Valley where they lived. Two-thirds of them had lived there all of their lives, and those kids had less of an excuse. The rest were in and outers, with parents who had been transferred by Caltrans or the Highway Patrol or the DWP. Some had tired of LA and moved to the Valley without knowing much about it except the tourist attractions and that it wasn't LA. Some of the kids from those families loved it, coming to see how much they were amazingly lucky escapees, while others acted like they were deprived, because there were no real malls within 200 miles. They all gradually learned the code of joking to each other and their younger siblings with the ancient Owens Valley phrase, embodying an imagined revenge: "Be sure to flush; LA needs the water." But few of them knew the real, tangled history, and so Paul accepted the challenge of doing some of the untangling, as a good fisherman knows he will sometimes have to untangle a messed-up line.

Paul worked hard to make his lectures easy listening. He used his summers to polish the class, taking his notes with him everywhere, drawing on a keen sense of when he could fit writing into a good day's pleasure. Some of his best sections were written and re-written during the mind-numbing drills of his two daughters' soccer practices. Kick, kick, miss—go chase the ball. Repeat endlessly. All presided over by the patient coaches and assistant coaches, men and women Paul would gladly have elected to sainthood on the first ballot.

And while the kicking cycles went on, his head was lowered to his notes, bobbing up regularly over the dashboard or a picnic table to see what the girls were doing. He had mastered the art of absorbing just enough of their triumphs and mishaps to be able to converse sympathetically with them as they drove home, while getting a respectable amount of work done during the practices. The eternal blend of parenting and work, for Paul, became this careful balancing between the needs of the older children in his classrooms and the needs of the two he had fathered.

CHAPTER 6

Fred Bancroft was sitting in the Bourbon River Bar with his sales associate, Will Sawyer. They had finished their sandwiches and were on their second beer, chairs pushed back from the table, expansive, avoiding going back into the real estate office.

"What do you make of this latest environmental crap about the River, Fred?" said Will.

"I'm a green/green," Fred said with immense self-satisfaction. He looked like the prosperous businessman that he was, dressed casually but expensively, with a conservative haircut showing his mostly brown hair to full advantage, and good enough looks on a nearly six-foot frame to enable him to catch the eye of most waitresses.

"Meaning what?"

"Meaning I'm for the environmental BS if it helps my bottom line—if it brings me more green stuff. If tourists come and want to buy quarter acre places up here, I'm for it. If some damn windmill guys come up here and need land to stick their three-armed whirling power plants on, I'll sell it to them. The river renewal will probably be good for real estate over up against the Whites—so I'm a green on that one." Then he leaned forward and lowered his voice. "Will, I need to explain some of this to you, because I need you to understand that our business is about to take a major leap ahead. Let's schedule a trip out to the River next week, because I want to show you something."

Fred had come to the Valley thirty years ago, after graduating from college, in the classic pattern: fished and camped and skied here, decided to live here. There had been good years and lean years since then, but he had quietly assembled a portfolio of rental properties and real estate ventures that had made him one of the wealthiest people in the Valley.

Over the past ten years, Fred installed solar panels on all his apartment buildings and long-term care facilities, and had gotten some good publicity for it. He had branched off into long-term care at a point when the Valley's age profile showed how profitable this could be, serving younger families who wanted their parents near, but not under foot.

Fred attended the Presbyterian Church, respectability and making contacts being his goal. But he was a bit out on the edge on the respectability front, due mostly to his wife.

Fred's wife Dale grew up in Arizona, and had been a cheerleader for the Arizona Cardinals in her younger days. She worked hard at staying trim, well-dressed, and presentable, and mostly succeeded. If you could use the word chipper for a fifty-two year old woman, Dale Bancroft was chipper. Even perky, some would say. She had an easy smile, and kept her hair short and blonde. The best facials money could buy and occasional trips to Beverly Hills left her looking much closer to early forties than early fifties, and she still got plenty of appreciative glances from Fred's male friends and associates.

But Dale had a secret vice, and it took only a short drive into Nevada to indulge it. Dale loved high-stakes poker. Taking a run at a hand worth $10,000 gave Dale a sexual tingle that Fred had rarely sparked. Once, maybe twice, as Dale counted out her years with Fred, had sex been as thrilling as watching the cards turn over for a win on a big hand.

Dale had signed herself into counseling for her gambling addiction twice, and had been pronounced cured both times. But the call of the green tables was far more powerful than anything she had ever gotten from therapy.

She never gambled at the Paiute casino in Bishop—too local, too likely to be seen by someone she knew. So she took their late-model Mercedes out onto 395 or, when she wanted smaller games, Highway 6, heading for Nevada, and when she got there she happily gave in to her addiction. And Fred tried to ignore it, but worried about what was going to happen when she went past the invisible line he had drawn in her bank account.

Fred looked up, as Will droned on about some lot sales up in Round Valley. He saw the manager of the Bourbon River lean over and whisper intensely with a uniformed officer whom he recognized as one of the Sheriff's deputies. The look of shock on the manager's face was all Fred needed to see.

"Will, hold on, something's happening. Let's go check it out."

CHAPTER 7

Cecelia Flores had opened her restaurant at 8 am, catching late breakfasters who wanted a serious burrito or *huevos rancheros* that tasted better than the cardboard tortillas from the fast food places. She had stayed busy, but by 10 it had slowed down, and she was working on bills for her suppliers.

The restaurant on Main Street was small, but brightly decorated with paintings and weavings from Oaxaca and the Huichol areas of Northern Mexico. Dominating the back wall was a large poster of two eagles—the United States eagle against the American flag and the Mexican eagle from the Mexican flag, atop a cactus with a snake in its hooked beak. The poster and the idea behind it had given the restaurant its name: *Dos Aguilas*.

The front door chimed, and she saw her daughter walk in. "Hello, Mama, no classes this morning so I thought I'd stop by and help out." Her tone was cheery, telling Cecelia that Rosa had decided to ignore the blow-up they had gone through two nights before when Rosa came home at 3 am and woke Cecelia.

Rosa was 20, a sophomore at Cerro Coso College outside Bishop, and was planning to follow in the footsteps of her famous cousin, Maria Chavez, by going to UCLA. Rosa often reminded Cecelia of her cousin, who was still in Mexico after leading a march of hundreds of thousands of people across the border at San Diego. Maria had the same quiet certainty that Rosa displayed at times—but, Cecelia sighed to herself, Maria was far more comfortable with celibacy than Rosa seemed likely to be in the years just ahead.

Rosa was a good five inches taller than her mother, with the same wide eyes, flowing dark hair, and easy smile. Rosa's curves were the effortless gifts of late adolescence, while Cecilia had kept most of hers by doing the hard work of running a restaurant that was open sixteen hours a day.

Cecelia quickly decided that no replay rules were in force, and the 3 am incident was closed. She said to Rosa, "Thanks, chiquita. I need refills on sugar and the pink stuff, and then some new coffee ready to go for the lunch people. That would be great."

Rosa began the refilling, humming softly, and Cecelia stayed quiet as long as she could, and then gave in. "Why so happy? You get a good grade? Car running good? New boyfriend?" —hoping that it would be one of the first two.

"None of the above, Mama. Just a good day. Thinking about UCLA and moving down there." Then, realizing how that sounded, she quickly added, "Not that I want all the traffic and being away from here. But it will be so *different*. I kind of like that part. Something new."

Cecelia felt a tug, and turned away so Rosa would not see her frown. For generations Valley youngsters had been heading south,.and most of them came back only for the holidays, once they realized how much wider the rest of the world was. For all its downside, Southern California had lots of jobs, lots of money, and lots of distractions. Among them, she feared, were lots of men who would be chasing after her beautiful, brainy daughter. And she hated the thought. And she missed her husband.

Rosa's father had died when she was ten. Esteban Flores had been a construction supervisor who worked in the mines in the foothills above Keeler, down by Owens Lake. He was very proud of being a descendant of Pablo Flores, the miner who had worked Cerro Gordo in its earliest days in the 1860's.

With the price of silver at a temporary spike in the late 90's, an investment company had tried to reopen three of the old silver mines further up in the hills, and they had come to Rosa's father to head up the job. But Esteban had died in a cave-in three weeks after the mines were re-opened. When the old mine walls gave way, Esteban had pushed two of his workers out just before the collapse. What Rosa remembered of him was warmth, the smell of cigars and *Dos Equis*— and a conversation they had when she came home from third grade with a report card full of A's. As she sat on his lap, he had shown her his hands, scarred and gnarled, and then repeated words used by fathers in the New World for centuries: "Baby, I work with these hands so you can work with your head." And then he added his own postscript: "But don't forget to work with your heart, too."

CHAPTER 8

Jim Scott was driving into Lone Pine in his pickup, thinking about two of his favorite things: baseball and women's breasts. He had read somewhere that someone said those were two of the three proofs of the existence of God, and he could never remember the third. The Beatles, maybe, he wondered to himself as he walked into the Alabama Saloon.

Jim was 33, going on 17, and had reached an age where he realized that he was probably going to have to decide fairly soon what he wanted to do when he grew up. Jim had gotten through high school in Lone Pine, tried Bakersfield Community College for a semester, and came back to the Valley to spend some time fixing cars and trucks, working as a contract mechanic for the Highway Patrol and the Forest Service, and pursuing women and girls in his own low-key, highly effective manner. He had spent two years in Kuwait with the Army in the mid-1990s, part of the post-Gulf War cleanup, learning to hate the foreign sand and the women-fearing culture with all of his might.

Jim thought of himself as many men in the Valley did—a native good old boy—a basic GOB. He had fished and hunted and driven all over the hills and mountains and offroad corners of Owens County. He loved the Valley, and he loved being outdoors in it with other men like himself, able to let go and enjoy the weather and the scenery and feeling like he was always home.

And yet Jim was also totally at ease in the company of women. One of them had once accused him of being a closet feminist, and Jim thought it might even be partly true. He had been raised by a mother who died of cancer in her early sixties but not before impressing upon him that he was always to treat women *right*, and that she would return to haunt him if he didn't. And it was that fundamental respect for them that made him nearly irresistible to a large percentage of the women he sought—and a considerable segment of those he didn't seek, including a few who were attempting to work out creative compromises with the institution of marriage. It helped that he had an off-blonde head of semi-curly hair and a look of strength well-distributed around his six-foot frame. In a moment of passion, one of his more intimate female friends had confided that he reminded her of the early Robert Redford—and Jim could live with that.

Sitting at the bar, Jim began the process of sipping his beer. Jim liked to drink, but he hated being drunk, so he had learned over time—the hard way—how to be a world-class slow drinker. He waved at a friend, Bill Solomon. "Hey, Bill, what's playing?"

Bill Solomon, a short, balding man who was almost always smiling, had retired from a career editing film for Hollywood studios for many years. When he was starting out, he had worked on the last of the Alabama Hills Westerns in the late 50's. He loved the Hills, and after he retired he had bought a place west of 395 in Lone Pine and turned his whole house around to face the Sierra and the Alabamas, with picture windows across the entire front of his house.

Jim had been out to Bill's house to watch movies several times, once or twice connecting with his dad, Ernie Scott, who was an old friend of Bill's who drove down from his place outside Big Pine. Whatever the movie—and Bill had a secret source for the latest films that was the delight of his close friends—the first show was always the sunset over the Sierra. People sat in his huge living room facing west, or, in summer, on folding chairs set out on the lawn in front of his house, and as the sun went down, the group fell quiet, hushed with the spectacle. Even on a cloudy day the show could still be a slow-motion explosion of color-shot sky.

Jim had spent some of those evenings thinking about colors. The display was beyond his ability to put into words, so he tried to think about it in colors. He wondered about the reds and the blues, especially. Because when the mountains are shading into early night's softest blue, with the sun behind them sliding lower and lower, while still casting reddish streaks across the blue sky, the two colors spill out of the sky and onto the mountains, and then they become, he thought, with the words of the song slipping easily into his thoughts, truly purple mountain majesties.

In the daytime, Bill Solomon was a slow, mellow drinker, who had also apparently mastered the dangerous art of drinking for hours and staying mostly coherent. Jim supposed Bill was an alcoholic, but he was among the roughly two-thirds of all alcoholics who could hold a job. As he saw it, Bill's job was telling stories about movies at the Alabama Saloon, the well-named bar in Lone Pine that had been the legendary hangout of the Hollywood cowboys. The bar's front wall was well-lit, in contrast to the rest of the bar, with recessed lighting displaying hundreds of signed photos of the movie cowboys and dozens of posters from those films.

Whatever happened in the Valley, Bill Solomon could recall a movie that made some point about it. People who didn't know him well called him "the movie guy," because he simply could not carry on a conversation for more than fifteen minutes without saying "that reminds me of…" and go on to connect the latest Valley or world news with some movie. Usually it made sense.

"Hey Jim," Bill said, moving two bar stools over. "How's cars and trucks?"

"Still running, I guess."

Bill, hearing his cue, said "That reminds me of the movie *Top Gun: I feel the need for speed!* Those trucks ever get up any speed out there, Jim?"

"Never. We build 'em for durability, never speed."

Jim looked up, and saw a sometimes friend and more, Allison Gray, the newscaster for the Bishop cable station, headed his way with a very promising smile.

"Hello, Jim," she said, throwing her arms around him and nestling him for a few fine moments against her ample bosom, letting him smell the faint perfume given off by her definitely blonde, shoulder-length hair. "You don't get up our way enough lately, pal—what have you been doing?"

"Fixing trucks, patrol cars and beat-up old jeeps, and not much else, I swear, Allison. What have you been up to?"

Allison was in the news business, and had the looks and the brains to be headed up out of the Valley sometime if she wanted it. But what Jim liked most about her was that in a bar already full at noon, she wasn't doing the media hounds' or politicians' pathetic, room-sweeping gaze, looking over his shoulder trying to see who was more important than whoever they were talking to at the moment. She looked at you, straight at you, and it was a look that had some serious interest behind it—or at least that was how Jim read it.

"I'm down here covering a homicide. Jack Howard got called to Manzanar this morning—they got a note from some guy who said there were going to be more killings, and then they found an NPS employee who had been drilled in the head and dumped at Manzanar."

Jim leaned back on his stool. "Whoa. Homicide? In our quiet little valley?"

Allison said, "Yep. Right here in River City. And more to come, if you can believe this guy's note. It says there's going to be three killings. So we're down here to do a standup out at Manzanar and see if we can get Howard to go on camera on our way back up when we stop off in Independence."

Jim said "Three killings. You might be busy. Better watch out for yourself. Hey, I saw the feature you did on the Owens River last week. I really liked that."

"You did? What did you like about it?"

Knowing that he was being tested to see if he had thrown her an easy compliment or in fact liked the program, Jim smiled and said "I liked what you said and what you showed about LA's side of the story. I hate most of those DWP bastards, but you made the good guys credible because you let the LA PR people tell their side. Which is a crock, but you let them tell it and then anybody watching could hear what a crock it was instead of you telling them." Watching her smile broaden and seeing her shake her head with amazement at his critique, he anticipated her next remark, "and now you're about to say Jim Scott, you aren't as dumb as you look."

"No, I'm not. But you sure as hell aren't dumb. And that review is about the best I've gotten in the last year. I might just buy you a drink at Bourbon River next time you are up." The emphasis she put on the last word was too subtle for anyone but Jim to hear, but he heard it. And filed it away.

Allison got up, leaned over and touched Jim's lips with her finger, and said "Gotta go. Came in here to see if Howard was hiding out in here, which he does sometimes. Glad to run into you, pal—see you in Bishop next time." And then she gifted him with a softly swinging exit, which Jim enjoyed, knowing she knew he was enjoying it every step of her way out the door.

CHAPTER 9

Liz Nolan was tired of digging the details of Ed Washburn's life out of the personnel files sent over by the NPS office, she was tired of Jack Howard sticking his head in every hour and asking her if she had any leads, and she was tired of listening to the stupid country songs that passed for background music in the station.

She looked down again at the pictures of Washburn's body. A question rose to the top of her mind, where it had been headed for an hour and had finally arrived. Walking into Howard's office at a pace slow enough to keep him from getting excited, she said, "Jack, he was pointing east, to the Inyos. We never figured out what was he pointing at—what's out that way?"

Howard pulled a folded-up map from his bookshelf and spread it out on his desk, looking from it up to the relief map on his wall.

Liz looked up at the clock, realized she should call Paul about what time she would get home, and then stopped. Paul. Maps. Paul was a nut about maps—he would have had a map on every wall of their house if she'd let him. Old maps, mostly. "That's a map from today, Jack. Manzanar is about history; maybe the map is too new. What *used* to be out there?"

Howard frowned, thinking. "Manzanar—means apples in Spanish. Used to be apple orchards, used to be the river and irrigation ditches that watered the apples, used to be mining towns." He pulled out a copy of *The Story of Inyo*, the classic 1933 text of the Valley's history. There were old maps in the front and back of the book. "Out that way it would have been Owenyo, Reward, Kearsarge, the little village of Manzanar. So the guy was pointing to an old mining town—how does that make sense? The river?—lots of politics about the river, but what does that have to do with the Japanese and the camp?"

Liz said, "Let's look at the note again." She pulled the copy out of her file. "'*The body is at the first evil place. The evil will be expunged with evil. Go to the three evil places, and cleanse this sacred and defiled Valley.*' So Manzanar is the first evil place, and he's pointing to the second one?"

"The defiled Valley. The killer thinks the Valley is defiled. Why? Manzanar means the wrong people got locked up. The river means LA took the water. The mining means they took minerals out of the ground. All those could be defiling the Valley." He shook his head, impatient with it all. "Not sure we're getting anywhere, Nolan."

A soft knock at Howard's door broke their focus. "In!" bellowed Howard, his impatience rising. Liz wondered who was going to get the brunt of his frustration, but was glad to be able to share some of it.

CHAPTER 10

It was Rudy Warland. He came in and nodded at both of them, waiting for Howard to explain the call.

"Rudy, you're just in time. You know Nolan. Sit down. We're trying to figure out what this picture means—the guy who was shot and tied up was pointing east to something, we think, and we're trying to figure out what the killer is teasing us with here."

Rudy saw that there was not going to be a smooth, opening explanation of his role, and that he was expected to dive right in. He had worked with Howard before and he knew it was Howard's way of throwing things at him to see how he'd react. He picked up the picture of Washburn's body and studied it carefully.

Liz knew Rudy a little, knew Paul liked him, and wasn't yet sure how she felt about working with him, which seemed to be where Howard was heading. So she joined Howard in waiting him out. Rudy wore his hair long, but not pony-tail or braided-long, more like early John Travolta long. Liz wondered what he would look like if he grew it as long as some of the younger Paiutes in high school who had taken to wearing braids. His height, broad shoulders, and his hair gave him a look that was impassive and gave off a message that *I can handle whatever you've got.*

After taking more time than Howard was comfortable with, Rudy looked up and saw the map. "Looks to me like he was supposed to be pointing to the river or the Inyos, right? No, wait"—he looked at the picture again. "Wonder if the killer knows about Winnedumah?"

"The rock or the hotel?"

"The rock—what the hotel is named after. You probably know the story." Howard nodded, but Liz looked puzzled. "There's a rock straight up into the Inyos east of Independence, which he could have been pointing to from Manzanar. It's an 80-foot granite slab, looks like a finger, way up on the crest of the Inyos. Some people call it the Paiute Monument. The old story is about two brothers and a battle with a San Joaquin tribe who came over the Sierra on a raid. Winnedumah was one of the brothers and he was turned into this stone." He looked at the picture again, then looked up at Howard. Seeing the Chalfant book on Howard's desk, he picked it up, flipped through it, and pointed to a page. "There—page 63. Tells all about it." He stopped, looked out the window at the Inyos. "Maybe this is a guy who believes all that archeological stuff about how we came across the Bering Strait and we're cousins to the Japanese. Maybe that's the connection."

Howard and Liz stood silent, trying to see if Rudy was pulling their leg or serious. His face showed nothing, absolutely nothing, so they didn't know how to react.

He broke the tension, finally. "Joke. I think."

Liz was irritated, and she wanted to get on the road to Bishop. "Rudy, this isn't too helpful." Turning to Howard, she asked "What do you want us to do, Jack?"

"Talk to people. See who this guy was. Maybe the killer knew him. Start tomorrow first thing; Rudy, stay down here and look over the file, make copies of what you need. Work as a team, and check in with me at noon and tell me what you have."

As they walked out together, Rudy held down his desire to snap back at Liz about her comment. Just what the hell would be helpful, then, since she had been on the case all day and he had just gotten there? But he buried it. There would be lots of time to figure Liz out, if he needed to, and figuring out the case was a lot more important, anyway.

"So I'll see you in the morning," Liz said as she headed for her car.

"Right. I'll get the file—see you then."

After her drive home, Liz came in the door, hung up her jacket and locked her sidearm in the safe in the front hall closet. Paul had fed Jessica and Jeannie, who were 9 and 6, both fully pre-teen in their worst moments, and adorable in their best ones. They were still up, but pajamed and ready for bed. The faint odor of cookies told her that Paul had succumbed to their pleas for an after-school baking treat.

Paul slipped out into the entry way as the girls stayed glued to the TV, and gave Liz a better-than-average hug. He stood back and looked at her, saying in a lowered voice, "I see no signs of patrol-car spread, but more detailed inspection would be required."

Liz, tired but with some leftover energy for intimate joking, responded with a smile, "We welcome inspections, sir, we prepare day and night for inspections."

As they entered the living room, the girls' greetings were loud but brief, since they had one final half hour of the Tivo'd show Liz allowed them to watch. Liz and Paul had invested in a Tivo for the girls, as a means of controlling the TV they were bound to watch, pushing the kids toward quality and away from junk as often as possible. Negotiations were ongoing about how to define quality. Liz's votes went for Seventh Heaven reruns and the Discovery channel, while Paul permitted the full range of Disney and Nickelodeon pre-teen "buy-me shows," as Liz thought of them.

The house they lived in on Fowler Street a few blocks off Main had been moved from its original location a few blocks over when an expansion of the city's parking lot forced the house out. It was a two-story home, about two thousand square feet, with a warm living room that flowed into the eating area and a kitchen, two bedrooms downstairs and two smaller ones upstairs. The furnishings were bright-colored and light wood, revealing both an eye for good fabrics and an earlier Ikea/Salvation Army phase. Four pictures of Eastern Sierra sites, taken by a local photographer and framed in Sierra-cut pine, were the major decorations on the walls in the living room, with a large expanse of the wall in the eating area filled with pictures of the girls, separately, with each other, and with Liz and Paul and their grandparents.

Liz worked at being a working mom, but she sometimes felt she wanted Paul to apply for the job. She would watch and listen to them, feeling at times like an eavesdropper, hearing the softness his voice eased into when he was with them, gentle, coaxing them to begin to think, and then just settling back, letting them say whatever emerged from their blessed, growing minds, listening carefully to what they said. She once told him he was wasted on high school aged kids, that he should have been working with fives and sixes in the primary grades, and he laughed, and then said "But that would probably be too much fun."

She had read somewhere in a pedantic parenting book that parents should praise their children on a four to one ratio—four positives to one negative. She thought it was a good, but tough standard, and admitted to herself that it was much tougher for her than for Paul. She once said to him "You would praise them for just waking up in the morning," and he said "Of course," and then went off onto a long riff on what they looked like when they were just waking and how beautiful they were.

He was hopelessly sentimental with them. When the movie *Polar Express* had come out, he took Liz and the girls. Toward the end, Jessica tugged on Liz's sleeve and whispered "Why is Daddy crying?" Paul had read the book to them over and over when they were younger, and Liz knew he was deeply moved at how well the film and Tom Hanks' voice-overs had captured the special feeling of the story.

Paul had a ritual at the dinner table that had been part of his own family, and so Liz was reluctant to suggest a change. Each night, he asked the children two questions: "What did you learn today and who were you kind to?"

When he had first started doing it, once Jennie was old enough to get at least part of it, Liz had felt mildly embarrassed. But then it settled into a ritual, and she loved seeing what the kids would come up with. With Jennie, she had once told a friend, we could just ask the questions and then take a nap—she starts talking and won't stop until she gets hungry again. As their answers shifted from what Paul called "the Mimi answers—all about me," to stories about other people, she marveled at how the questions took them out of themselves, moving away from pure ego to some sense of others and the rest of the world.

There had originally been a third question: "what did you see or hear that was beautiful?"But the girls had learned quickly that if they just said "the mountains," it would always get a nod. So that question was dropped, and the surrounding beauty was, at least at the dinner table, always taken for granted.

But then came the summer when Jessica turned nine, and everything changed. Out of nowhere, Jessica had become fiercely irrational, exploding in frightening emotional peaks and valleys. They had taken her to specialists in Southern California, and the diagnosis had been pediatric bipolar disorder, which Paul immediately read up on and Liz wanted to dismiss as psychological mumbo-jumbo.

But the symptoms the doctors had told them to watch for were unmistakable. She would be fine, and then something would set her off, a disagreement with her sister or either parent, just being told to pick up her things, or an argument about what she should wear. She started talking fast and loud, waving her arms around, and within minutes was screaming or sobbing. After trying different medications that the doctors had recommended, they found a dosage that seemed to help, but each afternoon around 4 or 5 she began slipping out of control and sometimes didn't come out of it until she fell asleep around 8 or 9.

They had been lucky to find an older woman, Marilyn McGill, who stayed with the girls in the afternoons after school. She was a former special education teacher from Orange who loved the mountains and lived in the most up-scale of the area's mobile home parks, getting by on her pension and what Liz and Paul paid her.

They tried everything with Jessica—they changed her diet, they watched out for sugar and processed foods, they talked with her teachers about what was happening at school, where thankfully the meds usually kept her stable and under control. In the afternoons, when she came home from school, she could sit at the kitchen table for an hour at a time and just draw picture after picture, not finishing most of them, but achieving swooping, graceful shapes that she called "my singing clouds." And while she was doing it, she would sing in a soft melody of her own invention, with words that she sometimes added, even rhyming them perfectly on occasion.

When the mania rose to its angry, screaming highs, which usually happened at night, Liz had sometimes tried taking Jessica out for a drive. They had read that parents of irritable infants often put the child in a car seat and go for a long drive to quiet the baby. One night that year, after a long episode of mania, Paul suggested trying a drive. So Liz loaded her up and just drove around the streets and the near foothills for a while. Jessica was chattering away in the harsh, 3-year old voice she adopted when she was in mania, and Liz reached down and turned on Paul's satellite radio. He sometimes set it to the classical station, and what began playing was Faure's *Requiem*, a piece Jessica had heard when Paul chose evening music for their bedtime. Liz waited until the *Pie Jesu* came on, and turned it up.

Jessica was silent for a moment, listening, and then Liz heard her start singing with the radio, and as she listened, the miracle came. Out of the mouth of the child who had seconds before been angrily babbling nonsense, came a sweet, perfectly pitched duet with the soprano, with such crystalline purity and emotion that Liz had to slow the car because tears had filled her eyes. Just then the car passed the church the family attended, and Jessica reverted to the baby voice and said "that's where Jesus lives." Then she returned to the *Pie Jesu*—Lord Jesus, and then the *Dona eus requiem*—give us peace. And peace descended, for a few blessed minutes.

Liz felt at that moment that Jessica's singing was a pure gift of grace, along with the other artistic things she had always done, drawing and painting and singing softly in the house when she was well. And for Liz, the sorrow and fear and joy were all mixed up—the sorrow that Jessica had gotten so sick in the past few months, the fear that she would lose her artistic center of balance, and the joy that her heart-lifting voice could sing those notes with such rich beauty. And she prayed, *Thank you, Lord; help her, Lord. Help all of us to help her.*

CHAPTER 11

By the end of the next day, Liz had worked ten hours, doing five interviews of Washburn's friends and associates with Rudy, four by herself after they had split up. Ed Washburn checked out as a quiet, decent bachelor with a religious leaning and a love of the mountains. He had no known enemies, and no one had given either Liz or Rudy any reason to think Washburn had been stalked by anyone.

Liz and Rudy sat in the outer office at the Independence station, waiting to see Howard. Liz reviewed where they were. "It was random, or it was just because he was a fed. What scares me about the note is that the killer sounds like a serial. And that means we're going to have the bloody FBI profilers in here, with the serial angle and a dead fed."

Rudy looked at his notes. "We track Washburn up to 4:30 when he leaves work in Lone Pine. He gets into his car in the NPS parking lot, heads north to where he lives in Independence. Car found in the park in Lone Pine, no signs of a struggle, no blood. So he doesn't even get out of Lone Pine before someone gets to him. Who? Why would he stop for someone in the park?"

Liz grunted, suspicious. "Bachelor? Maybe he runs in cheerful circles. Maybe he met a special friend."

Rudy shook his head. "We didn't get a whisper of that from anyone we talked to, and the church people said he had transferred membership from a church like theirs in Virginia. Fundie church like that in a small town is pretty hard on gay stuff. I don't think so."

He went on. "The killer wanted to leave him at Manzanar, and it looks like he wanted it to be a fed. So Washburn was tagged because he was the easiest to knock off quietly and then transport back to Manzanar, probably in the guy's trunk, a van, or a covered truck bed."

Liz added, "Korper found no tire tracks that stand out, just dozens that came in and out of Manzanar over the last few days. It's dusty, so stuff blows away. Nothing to track the vehicle. The body is clean, his history is clean, the site is clean. So where do we go?"

Rudy grimaced. "If it's serial, we get the next bad news soon. Howard wasn't happy when we called in at noon, and he's going to be even less happy when we tell him where we aren't."

As if summoned, the door to Howard's office swung open and they could see his secretary scurrying out, motioning for them to go in, as they heard Howard yelling on the phone and smelled the residue of his cigar's victory over cleaning fluids. "I don't give a damn if the FBI wants to take the original copy of the note—tell them to call our forensics guy directly and deal with him. They don't need to hold the frigging paper in their hand to do a profile!" He hung up the phone with a violence that must have boomed on the other end, and turned to Rudy and Liz. "What do you have?"

Liz had agreed with Rudy that she would start the briefing because she had been on the case longest. So she went for blunt. "We've got next to nothing, Jack." She summarized what they had found, as Howard's face got darker and darker.

Finally he exploded. "You are *not* telling me we are just going to wait around until this guy kills somebody else and hope he makes a mistake this time. You are *not* telling me that!"

Liz tried to stay calm. "No, sir, we are not. We are saying that we have to work as many leads as we can get on Washburn and keep waiting for some kind of break."

But after four more days, the break had not come. And everyone who knew about the note and the threatened new killings was very, very worried. The Sheriff had gotten some calls from LA DWP headquarters, people nervous as always about the Aqueduct. But he waved them off, telling them that they didn't yet have any leads that seemed to point to the River as a problem.

CHAPTER 12

"This should probably be a class in geology. Which you'd probably hate a lot more than history. But it all begins with the land. The water begins with the land, the Indians begin with the land, all of us began with the land. The Owens Valley is about the land, and the land began with fire and ice."

Paul paused, checking to see how many were still with him. Looking quickly across the faces he could see, the ones that weren't nestled into their elbows already, tucked away like migrating ducks snoozing out on the pond with their heads under their wings. He guessed maybe half were listening.

"Here are the four most interesting facts about our geology:

"Number one: If you were skiing at Mammoth in the morning, it is geologically possible to be on the slopes at Alta, in Utah, the same day. But you'd have to do it the hard way. Since Mammoth Mountain is an active volcano, if you are on top when it blows the next time, some very small vaporized bits of you could land as far away as Utah. Messy—but cheaper than flying. That's what all that steam is about that's coming out of the ground along 395 by the Mammoth turnoff—there's molten magma under there, and it's going to come up fast some day. That's what the dead trees up at Horseshoe Lake are all about—there's acid under there in the stresses between the rocks. Some people think there's more energy under our valley than there is oil in Alaska, but no one has figured out how to get to it—yet.

"Second. The whole valley was underwater for millions of years. It was a huge lake, an inland sea, long before it was a valley. They've found seashell fossils 3000 feet up from the valley floor in the White Mountains.

"Third fact: The ice was last here in serious amounts only 10,000 years ago, when the Sierra was still covered with the last glaciers, and the Valley was mostly a fast-moving river from the foothills of the Sierra to the foothills of the Inyos. That river drained south into what we call the Mojave Desert but was then Mojave Lake. Some people think that this ice is what forced the first people in the Valley to come here from the north.

"Last one: Ice carved out the valley, and then earthquake faults dropped it. The Valley is called a graben in geological terms. You live in a *graben*—pronounced grah-bin. Not 'grabbin', which is what some people think LA did to our water. *Graben* is the German word for ditch or depression; we live in a ditch made by Mother Nature.

"And here's a bonus fact: if all geological time was reduced to a one-year calendar, humans came on the scene at about 7:15 pm on December 31. Lots of changes out there, long before we got here."

Then he remembered, just as the four hands were going up from the window side of the room where the inseparable Baptist clan sat. And he quickly added, "And I should also say that there are other concepts that good people believe to be true, which is that the earth is not in fact four billion or so years old, but should be dated from the events set forth in the Bible."

He said that not so much to stay out of the headlines and the minutes of the school board, but also because he liked the Baptist kids and wanted them to stay in his class. They were easily the best-behaved kids he had. He glanced over and saw the hands go down, but noted the glares still coming in his direction from two of the four kids.

"We are a rift valley, like the valley of the Jordan River and the valleys in Africa where," he paused, "some people say man first appeared as a human-like creature." Paul avoided using the e-word, since it was the idea of evolution more than its facts that tended to set people off. And then, as he wound down the final section of the lecture, even though he had been careful, he started to worry what the kids were going to report back home.

After class, Paul stopped off for a beer at a local restaurant with Mike Paulsen, a classmate from high school whom Paul hung out with occasionally. Mike was both a parent of one of Paul's former students and their insurance agent, and Paul enjoyed shooting the breeze with Mike. He could talk to him openly, and Mike was willing to let Paul unwind sometimes after class. But this was a tough day to explain.

After Paul had gone over what had happened with his tiptoeing around evolution, Mike offered an opinion he'd shared before: "I've told you, Paul, you ought to be writing about history instead of teaching it."

"Oh come on, Mike, you know why I teach. You've heard me talk about this before. The teachers in little towns like this are our only hope. If they just go through the motions, then our kids are either going to be stuck in these places or get the hell out as soon as they can and go sell cars in some bigger city.

"But if our teachers can get across a little of our history, and a little of the biology and geology that makes this such an amazing place to live, and teach them how to read and write and how to ask the computers questions when the answers are all in the walls…"

"The answers are in the walls?"

Impatiently, irritated at being interrupted, Paul said, "Yeah, the technology people say that in a few years we won't need anyone to do basic or second-level math because you'll just turn to the wall and ask the question and some built-in computer with voice recognition software will tell you the answer."

"Wow. Wish to hell that had been around when I did sophomore geometry."

"But hear my point, Mike. It's the teachers that matter. They send out a hundred and fifty kids who graduate every year from this high school"—he jerked his thumb over his shoulder in the direction of the school, "and fifty more up and down the Valley. And some of them got some sparks lit during the four years and the eight years before that—and most of them didn't. And that's just so damn sad, to me, that some kid who could have gotten lit up instead had a teacher who was just going through the motions, and didn't much care if the sparks were there or not."

"Lots of the kids were lit up when my kids were going through."

"I don't mean high, you dolt—oh, forget it." He sipped his beer, then started up again. "The granola-eating, ramen-slurping rock climber teachers, they aren't into it for the kids or the learning—they're into it for the damned rocks they can climb. This is just a place to park their trucks, so they don't have to do the five hour drive from LA. They figured teaching was easier than being a cop or fireman or salesman—and it came with a pension. There's a handful of them who work with special ed kids, or have a gift with words or math, and they're golden. They're godsends for some of these kids with special needs. But most of them are here for the scenery, not the kids or the teaching."

"Careful, pal. Some of them might hear you."

"Let 'em. Look, I gotta get home, Liz will kill me if the sitter has to stay late with the girls again. See you, Mike."

CHAPTER 13

Nobody much liked Arnold Finnerty. As a professor at Cerro Coso Community College, he did his work, taught his classes, had earned tenure a decade back, and would probably retire at the college. Arnold was 57, looked older, and was between his second wife and a vague hope for someone new who could put up with him.

Arnold's problem was his face and his attitude. And his attitude fed into his politics, which were also hostile—at least to some of the Valley residents.

Some people's faces are set in smiles, and some in frowns. And it may not directly affect their personality, at first, but after a while, it matters. Over a lifetime, when thousands of people think you are happy because they see your face set that way, it affects them as they react to you. And so it becomes easier to be happy, because you look happy, and people treat you as if you were happy.

It is unfair that a few millimeters of flesh and bone—a mouth that turns up here, an eyebrow that goes off that way at a quizzical angle, or looking "mean"—could make all the difference in the way the world reads a face. Unfair, but almost final, in the traces that people's quick judgments can leave across a life.

Arnold Finnerty was a frowner. That is, his face was set in a look that was more scowl than smile. Once you got to know him, you knew that was not all of who he was, and other facts registered: he was tall, and balding, and acerbic. But the frown was what you saw first, and it came with an attitude that said loud and clear *I am really a hell of a lot smarter than everybody else.* As a result, he ended up with very few friends.

Because he taught history, he had run into Paul Nolan at several Valley historical society events. Paul was pretty easy to get along with, but he had never been able to figure Arnold out, and didn't much want to try after the first few encounters.

Arnold was a prolific writer, and sent op ed pieces off regularly to several newspapers and online blogs. He had basically one theme: that casino gambling and the special status of tribal lands as semi-sovereign were destroying both Indian and white lifestyles. Since his thesis resounded with a sizable backlash against both the casinos and the tribes, he got a ready audience for a lot of his diatribes.

A week earlier, he had been in the local spotlight even more than usual.

Arnold Finnerty seated himself behind the interview table, leaning back and completely at ease as he prepared for the "debate." It was not a real debate, but a two-person panel discussion on the future of Indian gambling set up by the cable TV station. The panelists were Finnerty and a tribal spokesman, and when the tribal vice-chair had agreed to participate, the temptation for the station to promote it as a debate was irresistible. The vice-chair, Sarah Mendoza, was a fiery health educator who had fought many battles for the tribe over the years, and was widely known as someone who would not back down from a fight.

Allison Gray was the moderator, and after a brief introduction, she began by asking Sarah to explain the history of casino gambling in California. Sarah reviewed the Supreme Court decisions beginning in 1987, when the Court ruled that the government of California had no right to regulate bingo and card-game operations on reservations. Federal legislation on Indian gaming followed the next year. Within ten years Indians across the country had built casinos bigger than any in Las Vegas or Atlantic City. In 2005, total national gambling revenues from all sources were $85 billion, with $23 billion of that going to 424 tribal casinos. Of that total, about $8 billion came from California.

Sarah was careful to add the local angle, pointing out that the Bishop casino and the other gaming in the Valley operated on a much smaller scale than the larger casinos around the state. Proposals to expand gaming in the Valley had come up from time to time, but none had yet been taken seriously.

After she did the numbers, Sarah glared at Finnerty, knowing what he was about to say and deciding to make her own pre-emptive strike. "Those that say that tribal gaming is bad for the tribes have never come up with any alternatives that would create as many jobs or produce as much revenue. They criticize the gambling industry as addictive and harmful, without ever proposing what industries they would put in its place. For a population as poor as our tribes, the casinos have been a critical new source of revenue and jobs. Our critics need to answer that question: where are the jobs going to come from if not from the casinos?"

Finnerty began slowly, looking at the moderator and ignoring Sarah. "Tribal gaming is unquestionably a big industry. Some studies say it has grown 25% a year in California in the last several years—a growth rate matched by very few industries." He leaned forward, talking now to the camera, drawing upon many years of lecturing and speaking. "But what that growth represents is a growth in addictive behavior and a get-rich-quick mentality that has undermined all the talk of Indian self-determination. When families sit around and wait for monthly checks from their gambling allotments—where is the self-determination? Where is the development? In some tribes in other states, young men have three cars, because they can barely spend all their gambling revenues in tribes so small that all its members are millionaires.

"And here's the key point—the numbers that Sarah has used and the numbers that I have used are all estimates. Because nobody really knows how much money tribal gaming produces. The accounting is a joke. Sure, they're supposed to spend half of it on economic development, but where are the independent audits that prove it? The tribes claim sovereignty when anybody asks for audits, which works perfectly if you're trying to conceal where the money comes from and where it goes. Too bad for Al Capone that he couldn't claim sovereignty when the feds came to audit *his* books."

Seeing that the two of them could go back and forth endlessly, Allison tried to regain control of the session. "Sarah, why don't you describe what you see as the benefits of gaming for the tribes?"

Sarah responded, "Part of every nickel going into those machines pays for scholarships. In some tribes all of the kids who qualify for college can go tuition free because now the tribe can pay for it."

Finnerty shot right back, "Yes, and in other tribes—most of them, in fact—in states where kids can drop out of school at 16, the kids start getting their gambling dividends at 16. Which creates a huge incentive for those kids to drop out. Pretty easy to promise scholarships when so few of your kids even graduate from high school," Finnerty taunted.

Sarah said, "That may be how it works in other states but you need to do your homework, Arnold—kids have to stay in school here until they are 18."

Finnerty's smile was malevolent, since she had walked into one of his traps. "That's a great law—but then what explains the fact that a third to a half of all Indian kids don't graduate from high school, according to the state of California?"

Ignoring Finnerty, Sarah went on, "Let me respond to your question, Allison. Funding also helps the tribes in other ways. It is paying to preserve our language and culture, and we use some of it for education programs in tribal classes." Then, turning to Finnerty, she added, "Gambling has been part of our culture for centuries—we always play the hand game at gatherings of the tribe, which is an ancient form of gambling. It's been part of our culture for a long time."

Finnerty shot back, "No one ever lost their house because they were addicted to the hand games. But the seniors you have in there pumping those slots are gambling away their Social Security checks, and you're picking their bones as clean as the vultures over in Death Valley. How could a people ravaged by addiction think they could make things better by preying on another kind of addiction? And let's talk about the jobs. The jobs that tribal members do in the casinos are emptying trash and busing dishes, because the service staff and dealers all come from Vegas or New Jersey."

Allison tried a second time to get back into it. "Dr. Finnerty, can you summarize your case against the casinos? And then Sarah, could you respond?"

Finnerty smiled, in his unkind way, his face betraying his enjoyment of the verbal combat. "Sure. Let me summarize the three basic reasons I oppose casino gambling. First, we have no way of knowing whether the economic benefits promised are being achieved, since the tribes refuse to account for the money. I can only assume that if they had the evidence, they would use it—so it must not pay off. Second, gambling is addictive, and lower-income people tend to gamble more than higher-income people. So the money that does go to the tribes comes from the people in society least able to pay. Not a very good way to end poverty, with money taken from the poor. Finally, the uses of that money that we *can* identify subsidize people who don't work, to a large extent—they reward not working, without any link to personal responsibility. That's bad for anyone, but especially for an ethnic group that says its pride and self-determination are a big part of its heritage. There is no evidence that the gap between Indians on reservations and the rest of the population has been reduced. And let me respond to something else that Sarah said. She said there is no alternative to casinos, but tribes all over the country have launched economic development efforts in energy, water use, and green-oriented sustainability projects. Why not devote resources to exploring those instead of counting on the casino so heavily?"

Sarah nodded, warming up for her response. "Arnold, I'm surprised but delighted to hear that you're concerned about our tribal heritage. And I welcome your support for our other economic development efforts to create good jobs—I look forward to getting your formal endorsement of those programs."

Then she turned her attention to Allison, away from Finnerty. "As you know, economic development in a region like the Owens Valley is extremely complicated, with land in this county owned by the federal government under the Bureau of Land Management, the Park Service, the DWP, the Navy—and small portions of it owned by our tribe. We have had discussions with all of these agencies about development projects, even a small business incubator for energy projects, and some have led to commitments—but most have not. These agencies are not yet at a point where they want to part with any of their land for the benefit of tribal or wider communities." She turned back to Finnerty. "So if you will add your voice to the tribes in seeking that land, we'd welcome your support."

Then she leaned forward, dropping all the civility she had shown moments before. "But Professor, there is one part of this that you just don't seem to get at all. We live on *sovereign lands*, declared sovereign by treaties and legislation for centuries in the nation and by agreements signed before this nation even existed. The courts have endorsed those agreements over and over. Simple justice and common sense make it clear. And so when you say we shouldn't use our land as we please, you don't have a quarrel with us, Professor—you just don't agree with your Constitution or the law of the land."

Allison knew she had finally gotten to a confrontation that might yield up a good sound bite, asked Finnerty, "How about it, Dr. Finnerty, can you support those land requests?"

Finnerty's face was even sourer than it had been at the opening of the show, and he blurted out, "Send me your proposals and I'd be glad to review them. Beyond that, I can't commit to anything without seeing what you're proposing."

Allison wrapped up the show with a predictable "only time will tell" closing, and Finnerty left as soon as he could.

The Avenger turned off his television and sat thinking. As he had worked out his deadly plan over the past three years, he gradually saw the possibility of a more devastating effect than anything he could do by himself. He had read the Valley's history for years, and knew well how fierce some of its battles had been, and how many of them still continued beneath the surface of the communities of the Valley. If he could trigger a new outbreak of some of those old wars, the hated residents of the Valley would be doing some of his work for him. The trick was how to get them to do it. He began making some notes.

A week later, Arnold Finnerty left the college late at night, after grading some tests he had given at the end of the semester. He walked out to his car, one of only two left in the parking lot that looked out over the Valley from its site on the edge of the foothills west of Bishop. If he had lifted his eyes, he would have seen perhaps the most astounding 360-degree view from any college campus in America: the lights of the town below, the winding course of the river marked with green curves of willows and cottonwoods, the Whites twenty miles across the valley floor, and the Sierra rising up behind him in the moonlight.

But Arnold did not look up, because he was thinking with great self-satisfaction about the TV show, which in his mind had been a complete triumph.

As he walked, he noticed a van pulling up, and wondered who would be coming to the college this late at night. As the van slowed and pulled into a slot two spaces over from his, he looked up just in time to see a muzzle sticking out of a window, with a ski mask-covered face looming behind it. But the sound of the shot did not register, since the bullet had already gone through his right eye and silenced his angry brain forever.

PART TWO:
THE FAULTS OPEN UP

CHAPTER 14

"Rudy, you're not going to like this one. We got the second killing. They found Arnold Finnerty's body this morning—the guy who teaches up at the college. He'd been shot and left at the Bishop Creek battle monument off Line Street."

Liz and Rudy had just arrived at the station in Independence when Jack Howard came in with the latest bombshell.

"I know Finnerty. One of the most anti-Indian people I ever met." Rudy swung his fist against an invisible wall, with a furious look on his face. "This sucks, man. That monument is where the battle between the Bishop settlers and the Paiutes happened in 1862. This is going to look like it was anti-white, pro-Indian, and makes it look like the first killing at Manzanar was anti-fed, anti-racist. Messages blazing out all over the place: leftie, Indian, civil rights. This is going to piss some people off big-time."

Liz waved her hand, "Come on, let's get past that to push the case harder, now that we've got two killings." She pointed at the map they had tacked up on the wall. "OK, the first evil place was Manzanar, where ten thousand people got locked up, and today, most of us agree that was wrong. Evil place two was the battle monument, and folks in the Valley are a lot more divided on what happened in the Indian wars." She paused, thinking about the flow of Paul's history lectures. "What's the biggest historic controversy in the Valley, bigger than Manzanar and the Indian wars?"

"The Aqueduct. LA taking the Valley's water." Howard saw where she was headed. Rudy was looking out the window at the Inyos coming into full sunlight.

"Right!" Liz had gotten excited. "I know where this guy is going now. I just don't know why. Somehow he's pointing us to the history of the Valley and leaving his victims in these places, these evil places, as he calls them. But what the hell is his point? Bad stuff happens? Duh. What's his agenda?" She looked over at Rudy, trying to get him engaged again, knowing they needed him for the next phase.

Rudy, turning back from the window, thinking about what she had said, answered, "The note said the Valley had been defiled—meaning these bad things had harmed the Valley itself, not just the people living here. So he's a crazy environmentalist—it's all about the land? But that makes no sense in terms of the first two killings. Looks like somebody's trying to give us a history lesson."

Howard turned and gave Liz a very hard look. "Your husband teaches history, doesn't he?"

"Yes, but you aren't thinking...?"

"No—but maybe he could give us some help. Maybe he knows somebody who takes this stuff seriously and is twisted enough to try to make his point by killing people."

"I'll talk to him."

"All right. But you'd better tell him that some people are going to start wondering what all this history stuff is about." He shook his head. "Funny, if Finnerty hadn't been killed we probably would have had *him* on the suspects list."

Rudy was looking at maps again. "Sir, if he's transporting bodies from where he kills them to wherever he puts them to make his point, he may be using a truck. We need to go over every inch of ground between the college and the Monument. The Monument is only a little over a half mile from the college. Is the crew doing that?"

"Yep, they were out there this morning after they got the call. Some tourist who was visiting all the historical monuments found him. Looks like Finnerty had been dead for at least a day. All they found was what looked like mountain bike tracks. No tire tracks, nothing recent from a car or truck anywhere near the Monument."

Howard paused, and sat down across from Rudy, trying to work out how to say what he needed to say next. "Rudy, you know better than we do that this is going to get ugly because of who Finnerty was.

People are going to focus on the Paiute angle and less on the note we got here. It looks a lot like somebody took him out for what he has been saying and writing, and leaving him at the Monument makes that seem even more likely. The TV show he did last week doesn't help much, either." He stopped, watching Rudy's face as all signs of his reaction disappeared, and he began to look more like a statue than a person. "So what do you think?"

Slowly, Rudy responded. "As an Indian, or as a deputy?"

Unintimidated, Howard answered. "Both."

"You're right. It's going to be ugly," Rudy said. Getting up, he added, "I'm going to go try to get in touch with the tribal council—if they'll talk to me. See how they read this—that's what you want from me, right?"

Howard pushed back, wanting to be clear. "Yes. It is."

CHAPTER 15

It *was* ugly. The reaction to the second killing was quick, angry, and dangerous. In small towns, an event like a homicide is at first treated like a terrible aberration, an occurrence that cannot be explained, so it must have come "from outside."

But these two killings were unmistakably local, in their ties to local history. As word got around that the second body also had a link to Valley history, it became much harder to project the cause southward, as so many Valley residents tend to do when bad things happen. And so its local roots could not simply be covered up, and blaming an imported evil for what happened in the Valley would not work this time. It may have been done by an outsider—but it was about what had happened here.

The local TV coverage played up the Paiute angle, running the "debate" with Sarah Mendoza repeatedly. For filler, the station added clips of Finnerty's testimony in Sacramento a year earlier, arguing that the casinos had done great harm to the native way of life without any real economic benefit. At the time, the reaction from tribal lobbyists from all over the state had been swift, fueled by their massive campaign donations. So the TV station ran these outraged statements from pro-casino forces in response to Finnerty, with the result that the story became even more polarized.

Even worse, the LA media had gotten hold of the story. Someone had leaked the angle that there might be a third killing, and it was Page 1 news in the *Times* and was all over the glitzy 6 p.m. entertainment spectacles that passed for news in Southern California. "Is someone killing people all over the Owens Valley and leaving their bodies at historical monuments? Tune in at 11!" was one of the more restrained teasers. Speculation about terrorists bombing the Aqueduct to cut off LA's water supply also figured into the TV coverage, and someone even managed to find old film on the 1924 dynamiting of the Aqueduct which ran over and over on the "news."

With the second killing, as Howard had predicted, the feds wanted in at an even higher level of involvement than the Manzanar killing had allowed. Both bodies had been dumped on public land, the Finnerty killing seemed to have obvious racial meaning, and the publicity had moved up to a level where local politicians' interest was also rising. The Sheriff handled most of the flak, but the county Board of Supervisors was also in the crosshairs.

Howard met with the Sheriff after a briefing session with the Supervisors, and he later briefed Liz and Rudy. The Sheriff had been forced to set up an elaborate interagency briefing process, with every conceivable state and federal agency at the table. "I'd rather brief the bastards every hour on the hour than let them come in and screw up the investigation itself," the Sheriff had said to Howard. "And I negotiated hard for Navy recon flights, which could help us later on."

Sheriff Terry Michaels had been in office for twenty years, and was a very savvy politician who was easily re-elected every four years. He was six feet, four inches, and tended to remind older people of Gary Cooper, both of which helped him do his job. Michaels knew his way around the tricky inter-jurisdictional politics of the County, the DWP, and all the feds with a claim to some piece of the Valley. Even the Navy got into the act, since their aircraft flew over the Valley from their bases in the Mojave. Plus all the state agencies, with the California Highway Patrol and various agencies in Sacramento who always wanted to second-guess the small counties. LA DWP owns 4% of the County, the state owns 2%, the feds own 92% of it, and the politics of those claims were Byzantine.

So the Sheriff had his hands full, and Howard told Liz and Rudy that he wasn't sure how long Michaels could keep the state and the feds from taking over the case. But he was going to do his damnedest to keep them out as long as he could.

It wasn't the outsiders, but the local reaction that was concerning Liz and Rudy, in different ways. Liz talked to Paul, who was fascinated by the historical tie-ins, but had no idea who might be doing it and no leads on where to look. After an hour of frustrated questioning of Paul, Liz felt as though she had run into another brick wall on the case. Meanwhile, Rudy was getting more frustrated with each phone call and drop-in on tribal leaders, where he was encountering nothing but resistance and suspicion.

Two days after Finnerty's body had been discovered, Liz and Rudy met with Howard for their daily review.

Howard asked Rudy for an update on his talks with the tribes. Rudy frowned, and began. "Nobody from the tribal council would even agree to meet with me. So I got in touch with a few people I respect and kicked it around with them. They all said that the leaders of all three tribes in Bishop, Big Pine, and Lone Pine are worried about what's going to happen next. They've seen outsiders' trucks cruising through all three reservations, and the tribal leaders are trying like hell to keep the lid on, and not give anyone an excuse to start shooting."

Howard grunted. "Yeah, but we all know that everybody in this Valley has at least one or two guns, and I'd bet a case of cold beer that most of them were taken out of closets and gun racks and cleaned in the past week."

Liz, impatient as usual, pointed at the now-familiar map spread out on the conference table. "Look at where the two killings were. Lone Pine area, then Bishop at the other end of the Valley. He's moving up and down 395 all the time, just like the rest of us. So what if we ran a road block two or three times a night and see who turns up? Anyone doing this is traveling at night more than in the day. What do you think?"

Howard looked at Rudy, who seemed skeptical. "I don't know. This guy looks like he knows the back roads as well as he knows 395. He may have used the back roads at Manzanar, and the Bishop Creek Monument is off Line Street. If he's not local, then he sure has spent a lot of time here."

Liz fired back. "But those places are 40 miles apart. No way he used back roads all the way from Lone Pine to Bishop."

Howard surprised Liz by his quick response. “Do it. Tell the team I authorized it. See if CHP will let us have some extra patrol cars to help with it. I’ve got to brief the Sheriff in an hour, and I’ve got to tell him we’re doing *something*. Give me a plan for road blocks starting tonight, north and south of Manzanar, at the Alabama Gates, and north and south of Bishop. And get it to me by 10.”

CHAPTER 16

Fred Bancroft was talking to Dale in their kitchen, as they finished breakfast and prepared for the rest of their day. Fred was talking and Dale was pretending to listen, and Fred was pretending not to notice that she wasn't really listening. A marriage as far along as theirs in years and compromises was full of such little, unspoken bargains.

"What this is, is bad for business," said Fred with a frown and a stab at the paper with his fork. "And that is bad for Bancroft Realty. Customers get the idea that homicide goes on up here as often as it does down South, and they'll stay down there, frightened of the wild people up here who are killing each other off."

Dale looked up from her laptop and the online version of the *Arizona Republic*, which she had never gotten out of the habit of reading, and said "Sure sounds bad to me, hon." She then clicked over to the sports section, wondering if any of the Diamondbacks' coaches she had known were still there.

"One killing is random, and no one gets very worried. Two killings are a big problem, and the talk going around is that this note the killer left says that another one is coming. I hear that LA DWP has hired some more ex-cops and gotten the FBI involved because it's all Reclamation land. Those cops and feds and rent-a-cops are going to be falling all over themselves. And the TV people—that Allison what's-her-name with the hair and all—are already playing it up on the cable and that's getting picked up by the LA stations. And my time share deal for a fall opening will head straight for the toilet."

Dale looked up from her laptop and said, "Yep—sounds bad, Fred." Then, realizing this was an inappropriately mild response, she added, "What are you going to do?"

Fred heard the vague disinterest in Dale's voice, and was irritated by it. He tossed his coffee in the sink, and said, "I'm going to work, and I'm going to try to figure out how this affects my plans."

At his office, Fred reviewed sales patterns for the few condos in the Valley. Fred knew the real estate of the Valley better than any one else. He had studied its patterns and its geography, and had used his Internet skills and Will Sawyer's technical support to create a monthly pattern of every sale and listing in the Valley for a decade. As he prepared for his own efforts to expand his sales in the Valley, he went over the information he and Will had compiled on the current housing stock and how it affected the communities of the Valley.

The layout of the towns varied with their size. The smaller places—Olancha, Cartago, Pearsonville—were spread out along 395, with a few side streets rolling out into the desert or up into the foothills. Bishop and Lone Pine, the two larger towns, were wider, and Big Pine and Independence extended only a few blocks on both sides of their Main Streets. Housing close in town was varied, with a few surviving Victorians, a lot of post-World War II ranch-style houses, and some smaller bungalows dating to the 20s and 30s. A few apartment buildings in Bishop and Lone Pine loomed among the smaller homes along side streets.

But the further one moved away from 395, the more the streets and the landscape were dotted with mobile and manufactured homes, ranging from rusted-out, ancient trailers to luxurious doublewides that were as big as medium-sized houses. The census said there were 2,500 mobile homes in the County, which was more than a quarter of all the housing—higher than all but one of the state's 57 other counties. Up toward the foothills, and on the reservations, the ratio was more like three mobiles to every built house.

Some of those mobile homes were surrounded by well-kept fences and yards, with flowers, hedges, and trees, pines and aspens, all softening the hard angles of the metal and plastic structures. Others, sadly, looked as if a giant hand had just dropped them down in the dirt and left them, untouched by any adornment. They were as out of place on the desert floor as a herd of elephants—and a lot uglier.

But even in the lower-cost economies of the Eastern Sierra, the hard realities of housing finance led inexorably to these structures. The choices were easy: you could pay a mortgage for over $1500 a month on a $250,000 house in town, or pay rent and finance charges on a singlewide further out toward the hills for around $400 a month—or less. Older trailer-style homes could be picked up for $10,000 in some of the towns.

Then there were the million-dollar homes, with lots of acreage, streams running through them, and fish ponds. Professionals, doctors and dentists, and retired government employees who had invested well and retired comfortably had watched homes they had bought for $200,000 as they started their careers in the 1970's and 80's steadily march up past seven figures.

These differences marked the boundaries of the class system, which in the Valley was more like a housing hierarchy, with far more people nearer the bottom than the top. Living in those semi-houses was a rough, uphill road. Most of the people squeezed inside their plastic shells had backed into that lifestyle without ever intending it, ending up with $10 an hour jobs and a single-wide because that was all that was left for them.

Fred continued his work, looking for an angle, worried about the effects of the killings, and vaguely worried about Dale as well.

CHAPTER 17

For a minister in a small town, shopping at a local grocery store was both rewarding and difficult. Drawing on her own experience and talks over the years with friends in the ministry, Elaine felt that the good part was having some members of the church smile and stop and talk, and the bad part was having other members of the church smile and stop and talk.

Elaine had several fantasies about inventions that she suspected would come along just when she ran out of time and life-extending technologies. One of the more benign inventions she imagined was a mind-diverter, with a button that could be surreptitiously pressed to move a conversational pest on to another topic.

But here she was in the Big Market, the plainly named grocery store in the middle of town, sweeping the aisle ahead with the *who's up there and who's over there* look that now came to her naturally. And sure enough, around the corner with her 3 year-old in tow came Rebecca Barton, a member of the church whose husband worked for the City in the public works department.

"Elaine, hi there!" Rebecca had one of the high-volume, cheery voices that child care and kindergarten teachers often use with adults because they are so used to aiming it at children. With Rebecca, the voice came from her unending pursuit of her own stairstep-aged offspring, including three of preschool age. Rebecca was short and bouncy, which Elaine assumed were both helpful characteristics in keeping track of her children.

"Hello, Becky. How are things?"

"Oh, Elaine, I am so frightened. Have you heard about all these killings? What are we going to do? Doug says the Sheriff is going to call a meeting with all the towns in the Valley. Did you hear about it? Are you going?" As she talked, her voice got louder and louder, and her toddler was by that time standing up in the shopping cart, nearly jumping out of it as she heard her mother's voice getting more and more shrill.

Elaine decided first things came first, so she ignored Becky's barrage of questions and moved to pick up the little girl, to make sure she didn't end up on the floor. Naturally, the child had been eating something with peanut butter, which ended up smeared on Elaine's blouse. Elaine also smelled an odor she preferred not to explore further, as she carefully handed the child back to Becky.

"Oops. Sorry about that," said Becky as she applied a wet wipe to the stain on Elaine's blouse, managing, Elaine noted, to smear the peanut butter around an area about twice the size of the original mark. Then, undeterred, Becky went back to her inquisition. "What have you heard?" as if Elaine had an inside track to the latest knowledge about crime in the Valley.

"Not much. It's terrible, isn't it?" asked Elaine, knowing that she would thus trigger another round of Becky's exclamations. She needed the time to try to develop her own answer to at least one of the questions in Becky's rambling interrogation.

Since getting the call from one of the Sheriff's staff that morning, Elaine had been thinking of little else beyond the killings. She was very worried, not as much about the next killing, if any, but about the effects of the first two.

Elaine had made her own compromises with living and serving a church in the Valley, and with its sometime conservative values and politics. And she worried greatly about anything that jeopardized the cautious balance between the more reactionary members of her congregation and the fewer, but vocal, progressive ones.

Whoever did the killings clearly had a political agenda, and Elaine worried that the uncertainty about that agenda only worsened the odds that the outcome would be to divide forces in the Valley more starkly than they already were. Elaine saw her job, in part, as keeping a community together, and anything that threatened that community's consensus was a threat she had to take seriously.

She said a few of the appropriate things to Becky Barton about how she hoped they would catch the guys doing this and moved off with her bag of groceries to check out and get home as quickly as possible. She had some ideas about a sermon on the killings, and she wanted to get to work on it. Sermons that were topical were always risky, but pretending nothing had happened seemed even riskier to Elaine.

CHAPTER 18

The restaurant had filled for lunch and then mostly emptied, and Cecelia was catching a break while her afternoon waitress took care of the only customers left from the noon rush. Her cell phone rang, and she saw that it was Rosa. What did people do, she wondered for the hundredth time, when phones rang and you had no idea who it was?

"Hola, baby. How are you?"

"Hey, Mom. Heard the latest about the murders?"

Cecelia shuddered, not yet used to the idea of killings in the Valley. She had overheard some rumors from some of the lunch crowd that there could be more. As always, her first reaction was to worry about Rosa getting caught up in whatever cross-fire was likely to develop. "They were talking about it at lunch. What did you hear?"

"They got that jerk Finnerty, did you hear that? I hated him, but it was terrible, Mama, they just drove up to him and shot him in the parking lot. I heard it from a guy whose brother is a deputy."

Cecelia had heard Finnerty's rant at a community meeting a year before, and was far from one of his fans, so she quickly tried to calm Rosa. "Yes, baby, I heard that. Not a good guy, but no one deserves that kind of wipe-out—almost like a gang thing." In a lighter voice, she asked "Where are you, and what are you doing? Coming by here tonight?" she added, hoping for a peaceful evening.

Rosa answered carefully, a 20-year-old trying to be respectful and declare her independence at the same time, "I'm going to stay at the college and catch up on some papers that are due. Then I'm going up to Mammoth with some friends to see a movie. We should be back before too late."

Cecelia's "too late" and Rosa's varied by several hours, so she replied "Please make it early. You know I worry about you coming down the Sherwin Grade in the night with all those damned LA turistas out there driving trailers."

Rosa giggled. "Mama, what are you going to call me when I'm from LA?"

"You'll never be from LA, baby. You've heard me tell you over and over that our folks have been in this Valley longer than any of the Anglos. Be *careful.*"

CHAPTER 19

Rudy sat in his office—his cubicle, to be more accurate—in the Bishop sub-station, trying to sort out how he felt about the case. Sorting out his feelings was not Rudy's favorite pastime, and he wasn't enjoying it.

Rudy's workspace was less than 75 square feet, and he could touch the walls at the narrowest point of the room. A computer monitor, keyboard, and phone were on top of the desk. A file cabinet with three different fishing magnets stuck near the top was up against one wall. On the longest wall opposite the opening to the cubicle he had the well-known poster that had come out after 9/11: "*Homeland Security: Fighting Terrorism Since 1492*," with a picture of five elderly Indians, including Red Cloud, seated and holding rifles.

He had received several mildly negative comments about the poster, but none went over the line. He suspected the Sheriff or somebody near the top of the OCSD had made some kind of decision about the poster and what license Rudy was going to be allowed, and the poster seemed to fall within those boundaries. "What's that supposed to mean?" was the least objectionable comment he'd received. "So you're saying *we're* the terrorists?" was the most pissed-off, from the Northern Division lieutenant who supervised the Bishop office. Rudy's answer was "No, sir—those guys were upset about Custer, not us," delivered in the most expressionless voice he could achieve. The near-total lack of familiarity of most non-Indians with the history of Indian wars usually worked for Rudy.

On the other wall, over his desk hung a tapestry made by weavers from one of the Nevada tribes. He had a shelf high on that wall, carefully made of local cottonwood and polished to a deep brown shine, which held four intricate baskets made by local artisans from the Big Pine tribe. Rudy had long ago decided that was what he would go for first if there were a fire. The wall also included a picture of his parents at a family gathering when they were still together, a photo of his high school football team that had gone to the CIF Small Schools playoffs, and his diploma from Fresno State.

Rudy had made five phone calls that morning, again asking tribal officials if they had heard anything about the Finnerty shooting. He had gotten stonewalled until he got to the last person on his list, one of the elders from his own tribe in Big Pine. Carefully, without mentioning any names, the elder had suggested that Rudy call a woman who was working out of the Attorney-General's office in Sacramento. A Yurok from Klamath, she was apparently the lead investigator on casino gambling issues, according to the elder. He had been tipped off by a relative who had married into a Yurok family.

The call to the state investigator was painful, and as he hung up, Rudy wondered if there was any connection between the killings in the Valley and the investigation he had just been briefed on. The cautious language used at first by Janet Fourtrees, the investigator, made clear that she didn't yet trust him. What she had told him was that she had been working with state tax board staff to look at six separate casino operations alleged to be skimming funds that were supposed to go to the state for economic development projects. Without divulging sources or the likely outcome of the investigation, she told Rudy that the cases were looking solid. In the next round, the casino in Bishop was going to be included. She said they had found nothing yet, but they were still looking at it.

Deciding he would take the initiative to try to learn more about the case, Rudy said, "You have a tough job. Lose many friends over this stuff?"

She was silent, and he thought he had upset her. "Most people don't ask—thanks for asking, I guess. Yeah, I've lost some friends. But I hate gambling—my old man went under twenty years ago and it pretty much wrecked our family. So I do this work. People running clean operations don't have anything to worry about." She stopped. "You really interested? I go on about this stuff too long."

Rudy quickly said "Yeah, go on. I don't much like the setup here, but I keep my mouth shut, mostly."

She went on. "You know how it works. There are at least two Indian gaming problems, maybe three. The first is the big casinos. They compete with Vegas and online gambling, and they're where most of the money is. They've got the lobbyists in Sacramento, and they make the big campaign contributions—more than anybody except the prison guards union and real estate.

"The second problem is the smaller tribes' casinos that mostly have slot machines, and the third problem is who gets the money from all of these. By federal and state law, half of the money is supposed to go to economic development on reservations. But no one has ever come up with enough data to prove that this is or isn't happening—because the states don't monitor gambling closely enough and each tribe has its own accounting system."

Rudy interrupted, trying to let her know he was sympathetic. "I did a paper on that when I was at Fresno State. Nobody can add this stuff up—the numbers are all over the place. I was never convinced tribal gambling was a good thing, because the real numbers are buried so deep. Everyone agrees we need more economic development, but you'd think sovereignty would help us make something happen besides gambling."

Fourtrees said, "Exactly. What we do know is that in California there are 58 casinos, and they admit that total revenues add up to nearly $8 billion a year—$1.6 billion more than Las Vegas. So the real total is more than that. A California appeals court has revived a lawsuit that claims tribes with casinos owe more than $330 million to the state. So somebody thinks the books are being cooked. But applications are still pending for 29 more casinos, and another 67 tribes are seeking federal recognition that would make them eligible to apply.

"Some tribes get it, though. The Navajo Nation voted twice in referenda to reject gaming, and so did the Hopis in their own referendum. But most of us fall for it. Most tribes want the quick bucks. Some are so greedy it makes them stupid, and not just about gambling." She laughed, without humor. "There's a tribe of about 125 people in Utah that has been working for years to get 44,000 tons of nuclear waste dumped on their reservation—because it would make them all millionaires. Even the federal government figured out that was insane!"

Her voice had dropped into a lower, sadder register. Rudy was struck by her passion, and wondered what she was like as a person. He thanked her, hoping he would talk to her again, and hung up.

As he thought about it, and after a few more calls, the connection became clearer. The tribal leaders were aware that the skimming investigation was coming, and they were afraid that the Finnerty murder would somehow get caught up in the story that was about to break on the casinos. Whether they were clean or not, it would complicate things. He knew he would have to brief Howard and the Sheriff on this angle, which meant he had something new to worry about. And for the first time in several months, he recalled his first conversation with the Sheriff.

After Rudy had been on the job for two years, the Sheriff had called him and asked Rudy to stop by his office in Independence. Clearing it with his supervisor at the time, Rudy went to the meeting wondering if he was in trouble.

The Sheriff came at Rudy as soon as he walked in the room. "I hear you're pissed off about the assignments you're getting."

"I'm not wild about some of them, sir, no. I signed up to patrol, not to do school fairs."

The Sheriff looked at Rudy for a long time, and then leaned forward and said, "Son, you are going to get middled in this job. It is who you are, and sometimes it is going to be what we need. I promise you we will do less of it, and we will give you more line duty. But you are going to be the guy in the middle. And you will learn from it, and you will get better and better at this, and you will preserve your standing with the good people in the tribes. And one day, you may even have a shot at my job if you do it right. And whether you get the job or not, you will make things easier for your tribe if you do your job well, and that will be a good thing in this Valley.

He went on. "You may not like this reference, Warland, but have you ever heard the story about Branch Rickey and Jackie Robinson?"

Rudy smiled, on more familiar ground. "I had a coach at Fresno who knew Jackie. I know his side of it, I guess."

"When Rickey ran the Dodgers organization, he told Jackie that he was going to have to be strong enough to take a lot of crap. This isn't the same thing, exactly, but you *will* take some crap. So listen—if anybody inside this Department treats you in a way that's unfair—not just tough or old-school discipline, but unfair, you come straight to me. You ignore your chain of command and you come straight to me."

He stopped and sat back in his chair, trying to read Rudy's reaction. Then he went on. "It's this simple, Warland—I don't want to lose you, and you don't want to lose this job, because it is the best chance you have to be somebody very important. I think you're tough enough to do this. I think it's in you, but you're going to have to wade through some deep water to get there." He paused again, and then he asked, "Do we have a deal?"

Rudy wanted to say that he wanted to think about it, and he heard more than a small note of condescension that he wasn't thrilled about. But he knew that delay would be taken as a turn-down by the Sheriff. And so, with some misgivings, he answered, "Yeah, we have a deal. And thanks for being telling me where you stand, sir." They shook hands.

Thinking back on the session, Rudy realized that the Sheriff was taking almost as big a risk as Rudy. If Rudy bombed out, it would look like the Sheriff had picked the wrong guy. And Rudy was far from certain that he had picked the right guy.

CHAPTER 20

Paul saw that most of the class was ready, and he got under way. "Today we need to talk about what is missing from the Valley. Because in our part of the West, it's what's missing that's most important."

"Why can't we talk about the killings, Mr. Nolan? They're happening all over the Valley, and people are saying it's got something to do with our history?" It was one of the fundie kids, a girl who had dipped into the mainstream culture enough to have adopted the sentence-ending upswing that was a tic for about half of the young females in the country, based on Paul's limited sample.

Paul liked challenges, usually, but this one he had to resist. No parents wanted their kids talking about local homicides in class, much less what part of local history might be involved.

"I'm going to pass on that one, Jolene. We can do that on our own time, and we should leave that up to our highly competent local law enforcement folks." He knew they all knew what Liz did. "They can solve the crime; here we need to look at the curriculum. So what's missing?"

"What is *missing,* Mr. Nolan?" asked a bored-looking kid. He was one of the "B's could be A's" gang, underachievers who had the brains to do better but were either too lazy or too intimidated by their peers to make the effort. "How can you find what's missing?"

"You use your senses, especially hearing and seeing." Then, pacing again, warming to one of his favorite topics, he said, "Who knows who Sherlock Holmes was?"

"Some kind of British detective?"

"Right. A famous character in fiction by Sir Arthur Conan Doyle. And Holmes solved his most important case based on something that didn't happen. Anybody know what?"

Talk about silence. Not a head moved, not an eye was aimed in his direction. Paul gave up quickly. "He solved a case based on a dog that didn't bark. And that was the clue that broke the case, because it meant the dog knew the person who committed the crime."

Summarizing quickly because he knew he was at risk of losing most of them, "And so sometimes what matters most is what *doesn't* happen. Life works that way," he added, watching their faces for comprehension. "The call you don't make, the date you don't go out on, the assignment you don't complete"—that got a few random chuckles—"what is missing from life, what doesn't happen, can be more important than what does happen." He waited, than asked again. "So what is it about our landscape and our history that is missing?"

Betty Reynoso answered, a pretty girl who was smart enough to undermine Paul's secret prejudices against cheerleaders. "Water?"

"Prize for the day, Betty. Yes. We are defined by our lack of water. Mary Austin—do you read anything by her in Lit classes?" Blank stares. "Lady who moved to Independence about a hundred years ago and wrote a fine little book called *Land of Little Rain*—she got that right. But a funny part of the story is that her brother-in-law was the one who first invited Fred Eaton to come to the Valley. Eaton was the former Mayor of LA who was one of the people who helped LA DWP secretly buy up land all over the Valley for the first Aqueduct."

He went over the highlights, not going into all the detail that he knew so well, because he feared losing them. But he gave them the outline: "1903—that's when it began. The federal Reclamation Service was planning a series of dams that would have saved the water in lakes spread up and down the entire Valley. But then somewhere between Washington and Los Angeles, a deal was struck that the dams would never be built, and that the water needed for LA's growth into the San Fernando Valley would be taken from the Owens Valley. Fred Eaton, who had worked for the federal Reclamation Service, was buying land, and the story told by Chalfant and others is that everyone thought he was working for the federal government on a massive dam and reclamation project. But by July 1905, the LA Times published a story that the purchase of water rights hadn't been for dams for the Valley, but for a scheme to bring water to Los Angeles' northern regions.

"But when it came right down to it, it took that great conservationist"—he spoke the words as though he were saying *slimy bastard*—"President Theodore Roosevelt to sell the Owens Valley down the river, so to speak. It all happened in the Roosevelt White House, as Remi Nadeau tells the story in his fine book *The Water Seekers*—though he tends to favor LA more than us plain Valley folk. When it came down to choosing between an irrigation project for the Valley and giving the water to LA, Teddy Roosevelt completely went along with Mulholland and Eaton and Otis from the *LA Times* and the rest of the LA gang."

He paused, hoping some of them would see the irony. "Get this: a President remembered for saving Yosemite Valley signed off on the act that spoiled *this* Valley. On June 11, 1906, Roosevelt signed a bill transferring title to Yosemite from California to the U.S., which started the process of making Yosemite a national park. Great move—a real good deed. *Twelve days later*, with Senator Flint from California sitting in his office, he dictated a letter saying that LA needed the Owens Valley's water and the interests of 'a few settlers...must unfortunately be disregarded in view of the infinitely greater interest to be secured by putting the water in Los Angeles.' The President giveth, and the President taketh away.

"The great Teddy Roosevelt, beloved of all progressive Republicans—a now-extinct species. He also said that if it wasn't true that the only good Indian was a dead Indian, he believed it was probably true of nine out of ten of them, and you wouldn't want to look too closely at the tenth one. *Teddy Roosevelt*!"

Paul knew he might have gone over the line with the crack about Republicans, but he hoped that the idea of progressive ones would seem implausible to any of the students who were listening—somewhat like pocket-sized dinosaurs—and not worth reporting to anyone. Paul could tell that he had at most a dozen of his class listening at that point, in one of those painful realizations a teacher sometimes gets that he has lost most of the class and has to decide whether to press on for the sake of a few students who wanted to learn something. He pressed on.

"The Aqueduct built by William Mulholland and his work crews was finally opened in 1916. Farms and orchards began going under because the water was all diverted to the Aqueduct. Then from 1924 to 1927 dynamite was used at least sixteen times against the aqueduct and wells of the LA DWP. LA came in with more security, local law enforcement went along with DWP ownership, and the state leaders in Sacramento lost interest. And the Valley's decline really began to accelerate.

"In 1932, Will Rogers wrote in his national column

> Ten years ago this was a wonderful valley with one-quarter of a million acres of fruit and alfalfa. But Los Angeles had to have more water…more water for the geraniums to delight the tourists, while the giant cottonwoods here died. So now this is a valley of desolation.

Paul finished his summary and began his wrap-up. "So 'LA stole the water.' And that's how we usually tell the story." He stopped, and watched to see if they were ready for his curve ball. "But there are other ways to tell the story—not only LA's side of it—" he waited for the predictable hisses and snorts to die down, "but a different story."

He leaned forward, making sure he had the listeners, at least. "And that is the story of what some people still call 'the traitors.' Now I am not going to use any names, because you will recognize some of them. Some of these families are still living here. But there were people who sold their land and banks that financed the purchases and knew what was going on, and did everything they could to make their own best deal with LA. And some of what they did *helped* LA, while it hurt the Valley and some of the people living in it then. There were bankers who embezzled from their neighbors, there were irrigation ditch owners who made secret deals with LA, there were informers who told the LA agents everything the Valley organizations were trying to do to stop them."

Paul stopped, because a girl in the middle of the class had just picked up her books, stood up, put her head down and walked angrily out of the room. Knowing that her last name was one of those he was deliberately not using, Paul wondered how soon he would get the phone call—or if he even would. He had the history ready, just in case, but he suspected the family would be less anxious than their daughter to call attention to the facts that were on the record.

"So LA not only stole the water—they also bought it. And at the end, they bought it from sellers who lived here and who knew exactly what was going to happen. And one of the saddest things about our history is that there was never a leader in this Valley who rallied enough people to a single battle plan. We were too busy fighting among ourselves most of the time, and we never pooled our resources to fight the common enemy. My own family sold some of our land to LA—after trying to sell it to a land trust that never got enough people signed up to make a difference."

He stopped again, seeing the frowns, certain that most of them had never heard the story told this way before. Which was exactly his goal in telling it that way—not to change their minds, but to show them how to *use* their minds to think about the familiar story differently.

And so he plunged on. "And there is another way to tell the story—even more upsetting to some of us, maybe. And that is to stand back and ask what the Valley would be like if LA had gone away after the first dynamiting or the first court case, and left us with our water. We'd have all that water. What else would we have? Hands?"

The answers came back from all over the room, faster than he could call on those with raised hands. "Traffic. Better fishing. More tourists. *Smog*. Green spaces and parks. A river we could kayak on all the way from Crowley to Owens Lake. More expensive houses." And finally, from one of the sons of a staunch conservative who was headed for Pepperdine, "Higher taxes."

Paul smiled. "All probably true. Now who would trade the good parts of that for the bad parts?"

"Wait, Mr. Nolan—so you're saying LA saved the Valley—something like that? That doesn't make sense." This from one of his more frequent tough-question kids, a likely escapee to a UC campus whose family had moved to the Valley two years ago.

"No, I'm not saying that. But I want you to think hard about what this Valley would be like if we had won any of the early battles of the water wars. And we also need to remember that there are at least three separate water wars—the one about pumping and irrigation in the Valley, the one about Owens Lake, and the one about Mono Lake.

The pumping battle is about how much water LA can take from the water table below the surface, the Owens Lake battle is about putting water back into the Lake to keep the dust storms down and restore the ecosystem down there, and the Mono Lake one has gone on for years since they discovered the Lake was disappearing. All three of them have been in the courts, and all three are far from over. The front in these wars has shifted from bombing the Aqueduct to battles in the courts. The weapons aren't dynamite any more—they're environmental laws and the technology that allows us to put sensors in the ground that shut off the water pumps when the plants and trees begin to die off. And lately LA has been losing more of those battles than they win."

He turned to the LCD, and brought up a new slide. It was a picture of a short man standing on top of a concrete wall turning a handle. "Who knows what this is?"

After too much silence, he answered his own question. "It's a picture of the Mayor of LA turning on the water in 2006 to send water back into Owens Lake. And it did not happen because LA had a change of heart and decided it liked all of us after all. It happened because people fought hard in the courts and because a judge fined LA *$5000 a day* until they put more water back in the Lake, because lake dust was killing people. Who knows what chemical they found in the lake dust?"

Blank stares. Paul wanted to pound the desk or somehow let them know this was not a small thing. With as little irritation as he could let through his emotions, he said "It's what some of your grandparents had to breathe every day the wind blew. It was *arsenic*!

"In February 2008 the Mayor came up again and turned some more valves to let more water into the Lower Owens and gave a pretty speech. He said in the beginning you were an oasis and we were a desert and we came up here and made you a desert so we could be an oasis. And he said now we are going to do things differently. And the head of DWP came up and made some more nice speeches. And we are supposed to believe they are all our friends now and we are going to sit down and sing Kumbayah together.

"So should we? Should we assume they are our friends? Or should we assume they are lying through their teeth? Or is there another way to see the story? Maybe they have run out of options—the courts have set them back and the weather has set them back and the voters have set them back, and they have to be nicer to us now because we still have one-third of their water and without it, they are going to have to pay a fortune every month for someone else's water.

"There are many different ways to tell the story. Let me tell you another story, about Lyndon Johnson, who was president during some very hard times in the 1960s. When he was first starting out in Texas, he was a school teacher. And he used to tell a story about an earlier teacher in a very rural district. The teacher was being interviewed by the school board, and he knew that they were very traditional, very religious people." Paul did not look over at Baptist corner. "And after a few early questions, one of the school board members leaned forward and asked him, 'Young fellow, do you believe the earth is round or flat?'

"And the would-be teacher gulped, and then blurted out "I can teach it round, or I can teach it flat."

Paul let the light laughter die down. "There are two sides to many stories. *But sometimes, only one of them is right.* And it is up to you to be able to put the facts together and talk to people who know the facts, and then decide what is round and what is flat. That is what I hope this course helps you do—to put the pieces together for yourselves—to learn to think critically, not just to repeat the facts. Because for the rest of your lives you are going to hear two sets of facts, and if you only choose to believe the people who are like you—you will miss a lot.

"Yo, Mr. N. Do you think that guy they killed down by Manzanar had something to do with the LA water thing?" The kid asking the question, Robby Jerson, had almost never spoken in class before, so Paul assumed he was into the true crimes genre of TV. Realizing that he had just lost the class entirely, and looking up at the clock, he said "No, but we'll all probably know more about that in a few days. We're dismissed."

CHAPTER 21

Jim Scott had decided to visit his father. He had finished working on a truck at the DWP repair yard in Lone Pine, and was cleaning up with his partner, Ollie Thurgood. They had swapped out three aging engines for new ones, and Ollie had once again proven that he knew truck engines like Picasso knew painting. Ollie had worked with Jim since he had gotten back from Desert Storm in 1991. He commuted up to Lone Pine from his home in Ontario, usually staying with Jim during the three days a week when they worked together. But he'd never met Jim's father.

"So you're going to go see the old man?" Ollie asked.

"Yeah. About time. I haven't been out there for a couple of months."

"Want company? He'll probably like me more than you."

"Sure. That doesn't say much, though. Not sure he likes me all that much."

"What is your problem with him?"

"He's just weird."

"Weird how?

"Weird about lots of things. He's nuts about opera, for one."

"Opera?"

"Yeah. Years ago he bought an old DVD of the movie Moonstruck, the one with Cher and Nicholas Cage in this thing about a bunch of Italians in New York? It's a good movie, but that wasn't what Pop loved. It was the friggin' opera."

"What about it?"

Jim shook his head, wondering how to explain. "See, in the movie they go to see the opera. Cher cries. So Pop likes the movie, and he likes the music, so he finds out which opera it is, and he buys it. And then he goes nuts, and now he owns practically every opera ever written by this Italian guy. Or sung or whatever they do with opera. He had to move his doublewides further out into the desert because he has these huge speakers that blasted out everyone for half a mile around his old house. They used to call the Sheriff on him, but it turns out the Sheriff likes opera too. So they sit out there in the sagebrush on the front deck of the doublewide and smoke cigars and drink a little bourbon and crank the amplifier up as far as it would go."

"Sounds great. What opera was it?"

"What opera? Who knows?"

"You doofus—that's the whole point of the scene—which opera they go to."

"You mean you know which one it is?"

"My ex-wife loved that movie. I forget the name of the opera, though—something about some flower girl who dies and a bunch of artists who live in an attic in Paris. I forget the name. Good movie, though."

"Ah, crap. Now *you're* starting it." Jim went on, shaking his head. "He lives up there outside Big Pine. He's got two doublewides, built 'em side by side. All of the first doublewide is bookshelves—and half of the second one. He had to build a special foundation for it. He must have three thousand books in there. History, politics, art, science, novels—and he reads the damned things."

"I'd like to meet your dad."

"He's not a bad guy—you'd like him, Ollie. Grew up here in the Valley, our family has been here forever. He was in Vietnam, worked for the government for a while, and then traveled all over the world with the government, doing some secret stuff. My mom was his second wife—she died ten years ago. He always had books, but after she died, he just kept buying more and more."

"Did he ever try to write one?"

"Oh yeah. Three years of agony for all of us, my sister and brother. It turned out it was about all of us, it was awful, and we made him throw it away." He paused and frowned. "At least he *said* he threw it away."

Jim went on. "After he plays that opera stuff, he puts on the Highwaymen albums with Willie and Johnny Cash and all of them and cranks that amplifier up even higher and plays The Last Cowboy Song and Desperadoes Waiting for a Train and songs like that. He says it cleanses his palate."

"Pretty interesting guy."

"Yeah. Pretty weird, too."

"Why do you keep calling him weird, Jim? Man who's lived a lot, didn't do too bad by you from all I can tell, sitting out there, getting ready to ease peacefully out of his life with the things he loves. And staying close to you instead of going off to some killer rest home down South. That doesn't sound too bad to me."

"Yeah. I don't know, I've just always had a hard time getting used to his ways."

When they got out to Jim's dad's place, they found him sitting on the front porch that had been built onto the doublewides, with a hunting rifle across his knees. The sun had gone down over the Sierra, but there was still plenty of light on the front of the house, which faced west into a classic postcard view of the Valley floor, sparse brush in the foreground, the track of the river visible from the trees lining its banks, and the Sierra peaks rising beyond.

Jim got out of his truck, holding his hands up. "It's me and Ollie, Dad, don't shoot."

Ernest Scott stood up on the porch and waved them in. He was heavy-set, with a full head of white hair and a trimmed beard. He was wearing a Janis Joplin T-shirt that was either a collector's item or a fine replica. "Come on up and have a beer. Things have been getting a little crazy out here."

When they got inside and found a place to sit in the middle of all the books, Jim asked "What's with the rifle, Dad?"

"I was sitting out here last night trying to catch a breeze." Pointing to the desert east of the trailer, he went on, "I had the music off, just listening to the desert. Then I heard an engine out there. Sounded like a motorcycle, but very quiet. So I got the 1000-watt flashlight, went around back, and shone it out there. Next thing I know two rounds are fired at the house, but high, like the guy was trying to get me to turn the light off. So I did. Later I checked the top of the house. Look." He pointed to two small holes right at the roof line, within three inches of each other.

"Whoa. Guy can shoot. Think it might have been this killer?"

"That's what I wondered. I waited, but didn't hear anything more. So I called the sub-station in Bishop, and told them what had happened. I asked them not to send anybody but promised that I would call if anything else went down." He frowned. "Kind of pisses me off, guy rides by and shoots at me just because I turn a light on. He sure didn't want anyone to see him."

Ollie said "I was talking to one of the deputies last night at the Alabama. He said they have no real leads on this guy, and they're getting ready to let the DWP and the feds come in, as much as they hate that, because they just haven't got the manpower."

"Want me to stay out here tonight, Dad?" Jim asked.

"Suit yourself. I've got some steaks and plenty of beer. Wouldn't mind the company." The phone rang from inside the mobile home. "Hold on."

When Ernie came back out, he was smiling. "That was an old friend, Sam Leonard. He says he's headed up this way and wants to drop by. Good guy—maybe you could come up and meet him."

"Maybe that would work. Dad, you still got those Havanas?"

Ernie frowned. "You mean you'll only stay if I have good cigars? Yeah, I still have a guy who knows what Cuba is good for, and he keeps me in a solid supply. Here." He reached up to the top shelf of one of his bookcases, and opened up an oversized book that was labeled *Encyclopedia Cubano,* which turned out to have a hollowed out shell with an entire humidor built into it.

Jim and Ollie stayed, but the night was quiet, except for Jim and his dad getting into a low-grade argument about the Dixie Chicks and whether they were true country any more. His father was pro, and Jim was con. Ollie stayed out of it, enjoying the meal, the cigars, and the argument.

The Avenger rode silently along a dirt trail up against the Whites. He had been surprised when the porch light went on down by Big Pine, and had shot too soon, out of fear that someone would see him and report his method of moving up and down the Valley. He knew he needed to be more cautious, because his plan was still in the early stages. He did not care what happened to him at the end, but he needed to be free to carry out the killings and the other parts of his plan. Now he needed supplies, so he decided he would head down to Independence to stock up some of his hideouts.

CHAPTER 22

Liz and Rudy were back at the station in Independence poring over the details of the two killings, trying to find patterns that might help in spotting the next one predicted by the note. By this time, DWP and federal Reclamation officers and rent-a-cops were all over the Valley, according to Howard, at least fifty of them at last count. But there was no coordination and they were all starting to bump into each other.

The road block had gone uneventfully the night before, except for several dozen irate fishermen and families all set for their annual spring camping trips who resented being pulled over and asked a few questions. The three DUIs they caught were a small bonus, but hardly worth the manpower it had cost.

The two deputies leaned over a map table that had been set up in the conference room, which had been converted into an ad hoc war room. Pins in the map marked where the two bodies were found, where the two victims lived and worked, and where Ernest Scott had been shot at. But none of it yet added up, and they were getting frustrated with the map, the repetitious talk about the two killings, and each other.

Liz finally sat down, tipped her chair back, and said, looking thoroughly tired and cranky, "Feels to me like we're wasting our time."

Rudy heard the unspoken *and you're wasting mine*. Looking straight at her, he said. "You got any better suggestions?"

Liz deliberately paused and said, "Yeah, I do. What more have you heard from the tribal leadership? I'm not saying that Finnerty was killed for what he said about Indian gaming, but a lot of people are coming to that conclusion."

Rudy had sensed that was where Liz was going, and he decided to stop being polite and start being direct. "So let's round up some of the usual suspects off the rez and push them around a little and see what happens?"

"Lighten up, Rudy. You have the contacts, we don't. So use them."

Rudy laughed, with nothing funny in it. "You have no idea what contacts I have—or used to have. This uniform burns a lot of bridges, Liz. And why don't you get it that a Paiute would be the last person to take out someone like Finnerty? It's just too obvious—it's what this guy wants everyone to think. And you've fallen for it."

"Well, that's a hell of a compliment. I'm the kind of dummy the killer wants to sucker into thinking a Paiute did it?"

"I'm not in this work to give compliments."

They were both getting angry about the case, frustrated by the brick walls they were running into, and beginning to run into each other. Rudy felt it first, perhaps because at this point he had more to lose.

"Look, Liz," he said in a softer voice. "You know how this works. You had to get through some stuff to make it as a deputy, and so did I. You're a good one. I heard all about the time that guy came after you in Riverside. You handled it. And I've had to handle some stuff too. When I started out here, they had me doing fourth grade classes on Officer Friendly duty for months. The top brass still sees me and thinks 'Indian guy'—have him handle the Paiute stuff. So if I go around sniffing at all the hot heads on the reservation, doors are going to shut. And some of them already have."

She could see he was trying to defuse it, and she went along. "All right, I get it. But what about this? What if we went to them and asked the tribal leaders to run their own patrols, voluntary, but coordinated with us. Ask them to recruit some volunteers. It'll let them know we don't suspect them on the Finnerty killing, and maybe give us a few more eyes and ears out there watching for the guy. And tell them that the note we got at Manzanar said this guy is going after a trifecta—that makes it clear that Paiutes have nothing to do with this."

"Patrols. Like John Wayne and the Indian scouts, huh?"

She smiled, knowing he was trying for a lighter tone. "Something like that. Track the bad guy. Watch close around the edges of the reservations."

"Not a bad idea. I've been thinking of something like that myself. Let's go try it out on Jack."

They did, and Howard bought it. And so did the tribal leaders, after some tense phone calls and a session with Rudy and the tribal leaders up in Bishop that afternoon. Liz was right, the tribal leaders cooled off once they heard Rudy tell them that none of the current suspects were Paiute, based on the note left at the first killing. By nightfall, the first patrols were out, covering the areas surrounding all three reservations in the Valley, with the Sheriff's teams and the CHP and the DWP officers all notified who was covering which area.

All those watchers, trying to pick up one good lead, one good sighting, but with ten thousand square miles to watch.

Driving home, Liz turned down Home Street past the high school football field, and saw that the spring football workouts had begun. Football in the Owens Valley was not as fundamental as in those legendary Texas towns where football is life, but football was pretty big. A game is a social occasion for several hundred people, watching the kids playing and watching the kids watching and watching the ones just parading around in their bizarre *look at me* clothes and hair styles.

Liz pulled her cruiser over to watch the practice team for a while, remembering what it was like to run or play a sport outdoors in the Valley. All you had to do was lift your eyes from the field or the track, and you got for free, the kind of spectacular view that people all over the world paid a fortune to see. The mountains rose around the Valley's edge, so close to the playing fields it was as if an outer row of grandstands had been erected for a race of giant, hill-dwelling spectators.

But last year in the fall Liz had seen something new, and was still trying to sort out how she felt about it. At a game with Paul and the girls, she looked down the list of junior varsity players, and she saw a Sarah and a Charlene and a Dakota. Three girls with the guts to sign up to play, whose lithe frames were easy to pick out from the freshman and sophomore boys lined up along the sides of the field. Their weights were listed at 120 and 125, but Liz looked at them and knew that was hype.

She looked out at the field and thought she could see at least two of them, or their successors.

Liz had heard some of the deputies talking about it, some disapproving, some suspending judgment until they saw whether the girls could play well enough to be competitive. Word was that no girl had ever made it through the season, and Liz felt a vague hope that one or two of them would. Last year, she could see them standing together along the sidelines for a few minutes as the JV game moved on, then separating with an unspoken agreement that they would not be seen hanging on to each other, that they were alone in this, except when they suited up and showered, and that the rest of the time they had to fit in. She knew that was the deal—they had to fit in. And Liz marveled at the guts it took for them to go through the rest of the week, and wondered whether they hung out together before classes. Remembering the ache of wanting to belong, she thought how lonely it must be to try to do what they were doing. And she wondered how those girls' parents were handling it—whether they were pushing the girls or bothered by it.

And as she pulled into her own driveway, she resolved to keep trying to let her own girls know that they were going to be backed all the way by Paul and Liz—no matter what they tried to do.

CHAPTER 23

Fred Bancroft walked into the *Dos Aguilas*, noticing Cecelia's wary look as he sat down at a table. They had gone through a serious disagreement several months back on what Fred thought was a simple business dealing and Cecelia had seen as exploitation. But Fred knew that the restaurant, as the only source of decent Mexican food for several hundred miles, was a great place to meet people he needed to bump into, and the food was spectacular, so he kept coming there for lunch.

Cecelia finished with the table she was at, and walked over to Fred. "Hello, Fred. Thanks for coming in. What can I get you?"

Fred answered, "Number 3 with a Carta Blanca, Cecelia. Thanks."

Five minutes later, as Fred finished a cell phone call in a lower voice than most of Cecelia's customers managed to use, she brought him his lunch. "Here you go."

Fred, trying to keep up the spirit of at least pretended friendliness, pointing at the back wall, asked, "Cecelia, I've always wanted to know—what does that poster mean? Why two eagles?"

"It's because the artist wanted people to notice a very curious thing—that both countries use the eagle as their national emblem. Maybe trying to say we have more in common than we think."

Fred, unerringly putting his foot into it, chuckled and said "I see the American one is on top."

Cecelia, more irritated than she was going to let Fred know, smiled as sweetly as she could, and said "That's just because it's further north. Not because it's on top."

Fred missed the cue and thought he would try for some more conciliatory talk. "Cecelia, I want you to know that I went ahead and used those workers we disagreed about—but I paid them full wages and even took care of their disability. They did a good job."

Cecelia answered quickly, "Of course they did a good job, Fred. They're construction workers and you have a big share of construction work here in the Valley. What I objected to when you asked me about hiring them was that you were talking about paying them under the table so you wouldn't have to pay their taxes."

Fred waved the comment away. "Oh, come on, Cecilia, you know that a lot of them have fake Social Security cards and don't want anything taken out of their wages. They want to send it all home. I was doing them a favor."

"Not really." Cecelia sat down and lowered her voice because she knew it was a sensitive subject in the Valley and she sensed some of the customers might be listening. "Paying taxes is one of the things they need to do to show they've been trying to be legal, whether they have papers or not. But if they need the work, they are going to take the pay any way you give it them. I'm just saying you shouldn't take advantage of them. They come in here, a lot of them, and we talk. They use the computer in the back to send email to the village internet cafes back home." She paused, wondering if it was worth the effort to make him understand. "They aren't dumb, Fred, just because their English is bad. They know if you don't pay the taxes for them, they will show up illegal if they are caught."

She looked at him, remembering a letter she had gotten from her cousin Maria last week. "Ever hear of the suspense files, Fred? It's where all the Social Security taxes go that are paid on phony numbers. Know how much it is? Over 50 billion dollars now. It goes up several billion every year, and everyone knows most of it is paid in by workers without papers. Fred," and now she laughed at the absurdity of it, "your only hope of Social Security being solvent for your kids is by raiding the money paid in by those people you call illegals. The Social Security Administration calls them saviors."

Fred was swimming in numbers he'd never heard of, and was hugely irritated at Cecelia. "We don't have any kids," he glumly said.

"Well, I do, and you ought to obey the law when you hire workers. Enjoy your meal."

CHAPTER 24

Rosa Flores drove down Line Street from the college humming a tune she had heard on the Tex-Mex station she sometimes picked up at night as it broadcast over the Internet from Laredo. The polka beat and the smooth Spanish lyrics were just right for her mood, the improbable German-Mexican blend working its magic. Her mood soured when her Corolla backfired twice as the grade leveled off, and she wondered again how well it was going to do on the freeways around UCLA.

As she got closer to Main Street, she replayed the discussion in her last class, which was held in a classroom only a few feet from where Finnerty had died. It was a sociology class, her favorite subject, and her professor, a woman on an exchange fellowship from a community college in England, had gone into the theory of crowds, how mobs and large groups of people sometimes act like a single organism. Rosa disagreed with the professor's point that crowds were rarely responsive to single leaders, since the woman had used the example of The March of over a million Mexicans across the California border that had taken place two years before.

It was a subject very close to Rosa and Cecelia, since Cecelia's cousin Maria Chavez had led the March. But then the professor launched into her own diatribe about how the leadership of the March involved had "sold out," in her phrase. At that point, Rosa decided that saying she personally knew the woman who had led the whole thing was going to focus more attention on her than she wanted, so she remained quiet.

Her cell phone rang, and Rosa quickly flipped on her hands-free device. *Private caller.* "Rosa here—Quien?" Her Spanglish greeting was deliberate, trying to identify herself, whoever was calling.

It was her friend Dawn Scott, who was inviting her to a party that night. Rosa accepted, and then began plotting her approach to Cecelia.

The party was medium-sized, about forty or so, at Dawn's house out among the fancier homes on McLaren Drive. Rosa had gotten to know Dawn in high school playing basketball. Dawn had much more class than ability, looking great in a uniform but rarely scoring more than two or three points a game. Rosa was a fast-shooting forward who never let an elbow go unthrown when it would help her game, which resulted in her fouling out of a number of games. The fouls, and the fact that she made a third of her shots—which was high-scoring in the league Bishop played in—had given Rosa a kind of semi-celebrity status that wasn't hurt at all by her long dark hair and her faint resemblance to a young Salma Hayek. So Dawn occasionally invited Rosa to parties, even though Dawn's future was clearly going to be working for her father's car dealership while Rosa headed off for UCLA.

Rosa arrived and saw that the usual group of recent graduates and older high school kids were still drinking and smoking weed with the same false sophistication that they had always had. She went looking for someone to talk to who wasn't drunk, high, or pretending to be. A lot of the talk she overheard as she moved through the group was badly informed speculation about the killings and what would happen next. Rosa was tired of hearing people who knew nothing about it try to talk about what it meant.

As she came around a corner, she bumped into a man with a cowboy hat tipped back on his head, a blondish head of hair that curled over his collar, and a wide smile. She smiled back at him, realizing that he was in his early thirties or so, and watched him sweep off his hat with a gesture he could get away with because he was so good-looking.

"Ma'am," he said, "I'm Jim Scott, Dawn's uncle, and I want to thank you. You are the first person who hasn't looked at me like I'm a senior citizen. I was in town buying some stuff for my car, and Dawn asked me to stop by and meet some of her friends. She's worried that I'm going to become a monk. And I am talking too much because I am nervous," and then he leaned forward, careful not to touch her and lowering his voice to a whisper, "and because these kids are so young and you are so pretty. So please tell me your name."

Rosa vaguely remembered Dawn talking about her uncle, who lived in Lone Pine and worked for the City or somebody. "Rosa Flores," she answered, "thank you, and you have no reason to be nervous, Mr. Scott, because you could pass for one of us."

"You lie well, Miss Rosa, but when you call me Mr. Scott, I know I am ancient and in my final days here on earth. But can I get you a beer anyway?"

She asked for a Mountain Dew instead, found it in her hands within seconds, and wandered out into the back yard with Jim. It was a classic late spring night, with vast fields of stars and enough moon to see the outlines of the Sierra to the west and the Whites to the east. Jim looked up, turned and looked at the Whites, closed his eyes for a second, and then said "I apologize, but this reminds me of the first time…" He stopped, and fell silent.

"If you are going to tell me a story of sexual conquest, Mr. Scott, I am not interested."

"Jim, call me Jim. No, no, that's not where I was going." And so he told her about his love affair with the mountains. He loved being in the Whites and the Inyos more than the Sierras, but part of why he loved the east side mountains was that they were the best place to see the Big Ones—the highest Sierra peaks, dropping a breath-taking five thousand feet from their tips down to the higher foothills, and then another five thousand down to the valley floor, the high desert, still four thousand above sea level.

He censored some of the story as he told it, remembering the first time he had fallen in love with the Whites, coming up after a dance at the high school with his girl friend, who lived in Bishop. It was a hot summer night, perfect for only t-shirts and cutoff jeans, sitting out on the hood of their car, necking, touching, then pulling away, half scared of what the next step toward real sex would mean, half wanting to watch the free light show. The moon was three-quarters full, and softly lit the jagged hulks rising up across the valley floor. On other nights, with less moon, he saw the Milky Way in all its vast glory, not believing what he was seeing, unable to take it in fully. He never again saw, anywhere on the planet, in his visits to twelve countries and four continents, anything like that immense expanse of stars, so many points of light brushed across the sky that it dwarfed his ideas of what he was for a few moments, took him out of himself and into a sense of creation beyond anything he had ever thought or felt.

He remembered the girl, but he remembered the mountains and the stars a lot better, and a lot longer.

He ended his musings, knowing he had not been able to tell her all of it with his words. He had been careful, talking mostly about the stars, and only a little about the girl. He looked at her. She had an expression he could not read. He smiled at her and said, "Old man's memories not all that exciting, eh?"

She looked at him, trying to figure what part was man, what part boy, what part romantic, and what part repair guy. And then she remembered a piece of advice from her mother, given with a stern voice and a twinkle in her eye, "Keep them off balance, whatever you do. Keep them guessing, even if you have to get a little bossy."

She touched him lightly on the chest, a half-tap, half-poke. "Jim, you and I are going to get to know each other a bit better. I'd like to take you to dinner in Lone Pine Saturday night. Pick you up about 7?"

He recovered from the shock fairly quickly, but not without showing her both how surprised and pleased he was. "7. Saturday. Lone Pine. Uh, know where I live?"

"I'll find it." She waved at him over her shoulder and hurried out the door to her car, knowing that she had made a great impression but wondering, as she drove home down Line Street, what she had gotten herself into. And what Cecelia would say. Cecelia wasn't exactly a bigot, but she had her preferences lined up very clearly, and Anglo guys in their 30's who worked with their hands weren't high on the list. She had a design for Rosa's life that was far more specific than Rosa's, and she knew who should be part of it—and who shouldn't.

CHAPTER 25

The Avenger maneuvered down the hillside on his stomach until he could see the Aqueduct three hundred yards away. He had practiced with the launcher over and over until he could put a 1-pound packet in the middle of a target 90% of the time from a half mile away, adjusting for the slope of the hill and the wind.

He had picked a point where the Aqueduct was twenty-five feet across, so he had plenty of room for error. He waited to make sure there were no foot patrols or aircraft that could detect his shot. He had become very good at waiting, able to remain still for long periods of time. He went into a kind of trance, replaying the good times with his father over and over.

After ten minutes, he knew he was clear, and he rose to a kneeling position, removing the launcher from his backpack. Within a minute, he had it assembled with the packet in the carrier. He made the slope and wind corrections, and quickly launched the packet, watching it curve up to about 100 feet above the desert before it descended and dropped with a splash right in the middle of the Aqueduct.

In seconds, the blue-green water began turning red downstream from the splash. He had experimented with the colors and knew that the high-concentration dye would continue to spread to cover more than a mile of water. Five miles downstream the monitors at the Alabama Hills station would see the dye and panic. The message he wanted to send was clear: this is what I can do for now, but your whole water supply is in danger.

CHAPTER 26

Elaine was tired, and it was 7 pm, and with no sense of guilt at all she walked over to her liquor cabinet, opened it—and pulled out her satellite radio. It was time for Dodger baseball.

Shortly after Ed's death, Elaine had been befriended by a remarkable woman whose main form of therapy was sitting quietly with Elaine on the front porch of her cabin on the shore of Lake Mamie, listening to Dodger baseball games. Leona Steinway was a former kindergarten teacher who had become single through the painful events around her husband's sudden disappearance from their small community in Riverside County. Leona, coming from a long line of strong women, toughed it out, and had semi-retired soon after to her cabin, which she had bought with money from her family. She tutored students in the Mammoth Lakes school district in English and history, and had been responsible for getting several students into the UC system. Elaine had met her in a district church council, and enjoyed her wry sense of humor and ability to talk about almost anything without rancor or meanness. Leona was a lifelong Dodger fan. So they fell into a habit of listening to the games together when Elaine visited her, and it was a habit Elaine had imported south to Bishop.

At one time, Dodger baseball had been a near-subversive activity north of the Vin Scully line, which ended around Ridgecrest where the Bishop radio station began to come in, carrying San Francisco Giants games, who were widely known to Dodgers fans as "the little fellas." But the move of more Angelenos into the Valley and the expansion of radio coverage had meant the Dodgers were now as local as the Giants had once been.

Elaine had come to love the rhythm of the games, brought closer by Scully's marvelous voice and his knowledge of the game and the English language. Sitting with Leona, silent through the innings and then adjusting their conversation to the 90-second commercial breaks, became some of the most restful times she had ever experienced with another human being.

Leona had first shown Elaine the wonders of satellite radio, and Elaine was thoroughly addicted. Dulcie had adjusted well to sitting at Elaine's feet while the game droned on. When the crowd noise signaled something good happening at Dodger Stadium, Dulcie's ears pricked up in a sign of solidarity with the Blue. Elaine even imagined that from time to time when the Dodgers were playing the Giants, Dulcie growled when Vin announced the Giants lineup.

Two years ago she had had her first serious suitor after Ed's death, an old friend from divinity school who had looked her up and come to visit her in Bishop. But he had been completely unable to understand why she couldn't go out to dinner or even cook much more than oatmeal for dinner from April through September when Dodger games were on in the evening. And Elaine had come to realize that she depended very much on her ability to control that part of her life and her nights during those months. She kept up with all her night meetings at the church, usually missing Sunday afternoon games, but taping some of them for playback later in the day.

The game was in the fifth inning, the Dodgers were sitting comfortably on a three-run lead, the pitching was holding, and Elaine felt content.

And then the phone rang. She debated letting the answering machine take a message, and then her sense of duty took over and she picked up.

"Elaine, it's Jerry Nadeau." Her pastor friend from Lone Pine, full, she was sure, of the latest gossip.

"Hi, Jerry. What's up?"

"I just wanted to ask if you are hearing any of the rumors up there."

"What rumors?"

"There's a lot of talk down here about some kind of organized response to the killings. A citizen's patrol or something like that." He lowered his voice, "Someone saw a group of Indians riding around in a pickup with guns."

Elaine had heard from Liz Nolan, as she dropped off some used clothes at church, that there was a patrol of some kind organized by the Paiute leadership. "Jerry, I'm pretty sure that they're cooperating with the Sheriff on that, trying to help find this guy. It's pretty farfetched to believe they'd be waving guns in trucks. They're an unarmed patrol, from what I heard."

"That's not what people down here have heard." Jerry often tended to hide behind the phrase "people down here." It boiled down, in Elaine's experience, to three or four of his own congregation, whose speculations Jerry loved to repeat as general public opinion, trying to enhance his own reputation as being at the center of everything that happened in the southern part of the County.

Elaine decided to stop being one of Jerry's enablers. And in the background, the turned-down game sounded like it was getting interesting. "Jerry, I sure hope you're doing everything you can to head this crazy story off. A bunch of vigilantes is not what we need now with this guy still on the loose. Everybody and his dog has a gun here, and having more armed people riding around just means that sooner or later someone gets shot."

"Well, I don't know. If the Indians are riding around with guns, I know people down here are going to want to keep an eye on things."

Elaine felt for a moment as if she had been time-transported back to the 1860's. *The Indians have guns now so we should get more*, without any clue that the Indians got guns because whites with guns were shooting at them and because other whites had been happy to sell them some rifles. Another Owens Valley arms race, Elaine thought, just what we need.

She rang off with Jerry as quickly as she could, assuring him that there were no rumors flying around that she had heard, but wondering just what counter-actions were under way that she hadn't heard about yet. There had been a very ugly incident in 2005 after a grocery store clerk had been shot and killed by a Paiute—who happened to be the brother of the tribal chairman. Then a letter was found at a day care center serving Paiute children threatening to dismember Paiute girls, signed "KKK." It had calmed down when members of both the victim's and the assailant's families had come together to ask for peace. Elaine hoped that those memories were well-faded by now. But she worried that it might not take much to re-ignite those tensions.

CHAPTER 27

As Sam Leonard pulled into Ernie Scott's driveway in his beat-up Highlander hybrid, Ernie Scott watched him from his front porch and thought back to the forty-plus years of their friendship. Ernie had first met Sam Leonard in Vietnam. Ernie had been doing something mysterious with "an American firm" which Sam always thought was the CIA, though Ernie never admitted it. They were both in-country during Tet 1968 and both had been involved in the defense of the U.S. Embassy in Saigon when it had been briefly occupied by Viet Cong guerillas. Coming through a bloody day that rang in history for decades had become another bond they shared.

They had stayed in touch, as people sometimes do who have been under fire together, and Sam came up to visit Ernie in the Valley from time to time. Ernie had followed all of Sam's dispatches from Mexico during the period of what came to be called "the March," and admired his friend greatly, delighted that he had received the Pulitzer for his broadcasts on National Public Radio covering the events of that year. Two years before, Sam had moved back to LA from Mexico to be near his two grandchildren in Orange County.

As a serious student of American history, Ernie valued Sam's journalistic sense of what was happening to the country, and welcomed his visits as a chance to catch up on Sam's latest ideas from his journalism and his writing. Ernie had realized over the years of their talks that Sam had some bedrock beliefs, far starker than his own shaded views acquired from years of covert work in government warrens. Ernie had worked the gray territories, while Sam's outlook was much more black and white.

Ernie had kidded him over the years that Sam's former life as a Franciscan novice had left him "a raving moralist," while Sam responded in kind, calling Ernie "the gray man." But for each, the other was one of the few people he could sit with for hours talking about their country and the world without lapsing into slogans or cant, drawing on their decades of living through history.

Sam belonged to the "three strikes" school of American history. The first strike, he told Ernie when they first had this conversation soon after getting back from Vietnam, was slavery. The second was genocide.

The first time they talked about it, Ernie protested that genocide was too strong a label for the Indian wars. Sam had said "Then I've got two factoids for you, Ernie. General Philip Sheridan was the first SOB who said 'The only good Indian is a dead Indian.' Teddy Roosevelt and a million or so others repeated it or modified it a little. Second fact: Ever hear about the Pequot Wars?"

"Connecticut, somewhere in the 1600s?"

"Right—1637. The English settlers from Massachusetts decided to burn down Indian villages and killed about 400 Indians doing it—mostly women and children. Arguably the first genocide in the New World involving Anglo-Saxons, brought to you by those smiling black-hatted stars of our Thanksgiving drama: the Pilgrims."

"Pilgrims? Genocide? Whoa, Sam, are you sure?"

"The historian who studied the Pilgrims for years said that in the Pequot War, New England was introduced to the horrors of European-style genocide. That doesn't get much emphasis in the fifth-grade pageants." He added, "Along with the benefits brought by the Spanish missions to the California coastal tribes a century or so later. At least it was pre-statehood California. But it was as close as you can get to slavery without calling it that."

And for Sam, the third strike was immigration: who gets to live here and work here. Sam was clear about it: America would either keep the door as open as it had in the most welcoming eras of American history, or it would cease to be America. For him, it was that simple. And he feared that America was already at the plate, looking at the third strike as it sailed on by.

Sam had a deeply religious streak in his background, dating back to his Franciscan years. So his politics was built on a foundation of his religious outlook on life. He was hopeful about some of what had happened in Mexico and at the border, and the settlement that Maria Chavez had reached with the Governor. The sight of a million or so marchers coming peacefully across the border all at once, led by US citizens, created a crisis that had forced clearer thinking about immigration. But he wasn't at all sure that the rest of the country got it. And the yahoos were out there fanning the flames on immigration all the time. Immigrants had become the new communists, wrapped up with fears of terrorists, and the country sometimes seemed like it was just waiting for its next McCarthy. Ernie wasn't quite as pessimistic as Sam, but he recognized that he was also a lot further away from the worst of the yahoos in Southern California.

But he still teased Sam when his moralizing became angry, telling him "you're still looking for Assisi, St. Francis." To which Sam's occasional response was, "No, but I'd sure like Sister Clare to show up."

Occasionally in these discussions, Sam used a phrase summarizing the last two and a half centuries of California's history that Ernie warned him against ever repeating locally: "California—built by the Chinese, maintained by the Mexicans, and just waiting for both of them to come back and claim it." Sam argued that a careful reading of California's history would justify both statements, but agreed that he probably shouldn't go around quoting the slogan freely.

After Sam brought his suitcase in and stashed it in Ernie's guest room, they moved back to Ernie's porch and watched the sunset over the Sierra. They were seated on the end of the porch, sipping their beers, with a view of the Whites behind them. Sam, who was about six feet tall and still lean, stretched his long legs out on top of the porch railing. He gestured over his shoulder and asked, "What are those lights over there against those foothills—all in a row?"

"That's the Radio Astronomy Observatory, huge antennas arrayed so they can hear signals from way out in space. They're listening for the Big Bang."

"The what?"

"The radio signals that go back to the beginning of time."

"Oh. I thought that was a reference to your social life."

"Very funny. I wish."

As they turned back to the Sierra, the view reminded Ernie of a similar setting further south where he had watched sunsets.

"Sam, you like movies, don't you?"

"Sure. Rather see a movie than listen to you any day."

"There's a guy I'd like you to meet down in Lone Pine. Should be fun."

"Let's go down there tomorrow."

"Done."

As they drove down to Lone Pine the next afternoon, Ernie started telling Sam about his sister's kids, who lived in Reno and whom he saw often.

"You know, Sam, uncling is a great job, maybe the best job you get if you're in a family where most of the people like each other most of the time. You can go to football games and track meets and plays and weddings and cheer and clap for the stars, and you're not doing it because it's your own kids—it's because you really like and admire the kids. And some of them realize that, and see an adult who's known them all their life cheering for them."

Sam nodded, but went on to disagree. "Uncling is good, but grandparenting is the best. It's huge fun to see your genes out there walking around in the world. You give them whatever you want, and then you hand them back to their parents and drive on home. Grandkids *have* to pay attention to you. With nieces and nephews, it's more optional, so you've got to pay attention to them in a different way. With both, if you're lucky, you catch them listening to you, and sometimes paying more attention to you and your stories and ideas than they sometimes do to their parents. You see, they don't have to rebel against you, because you never tried to run their lives or set their boundaries. And so you want to be useful to them, to do or say something they can take away and recall some day when it may help them make a good choice."

Ernie broke in. "That may be why some people write books."

"Maybe. And every now and then, you get this terrific bonus. You spot a gesture that your mom or dad used a thousand times, a move or phrase that has passed down to a third generation, and the echo rings sweetly in your head for hours."

"That's immortality. You get that as a grandparent, too."

"Immortal? What do you mean, immortal?"

Sam said, "Well, not immortal. But if your daughter, and then your grandson or grand-daughter, or a niece or nephew, says something you first heard from your father, or likes a book or a piece of music your mother and you loved—then something of you stays alive. I've got a nephew who roots for his football team with exactly the same words my father used: '*knock 'em into next week!*' And so a few of those traits and phrases pass on down to two or three more generations. That's damned near immortal, in a world when famous people only last fifteen minutes or so."

Ernie shook his head. "I just wish that damned son of mine would find someone he could start producing kids with."

"Give it time. And for God's sake don't *tell* him to do it, or he'll slow down even more, just to piss you off." Sam continued, "Tell me about your kid. He's what, 30 now?"

"Uh, 33. Good kid." He pulled on his cigar, letting the smoke waft out through the half-open window, and looked out across the Valley to the Sierra, then frowned. "I embarrass him, though."

Sam said, "Makes sense to me. Who wouldn't be embarrassed by an old fart like you?" He was quiet for a minute, then asked, "What embarrasses him?"

"Oh, the opera, and the books I guess."

"You're into opera now?"

"Yeah, sort of."

"And he isn't?"

"No."

Sam was silent again, and then said, "I saw a great sticker on a radio somewhere, Ernie. 'It's not that I don't understand your music—it's that your music sucks.'"

"Good sign. About *his* music."

"He probably thinks the same about yours."

"When his has lasted two centuries, he'll be right. Until then, I win."

They had arrived in Long Pine, and Ernie was negotiating the turns to get to Bill Solomon's house on the west side of town. He picked up the thread of the last conversation."He has this new girl."

"Oh yeah? Who?"

"Cecelia Flores' daughter Rosa."

"Cecilia from *Dos Aguilas*? I know her. Knew her cousin very well in Mexico.

Great people." He was silent for a while. "I'll bet her daughter is a great kid."

"Jim wouldn't talk much about her, but he sounded different about her than he has about other hotties he chases after—or the ones who chase him."

"I'll bet she's a keeper, Ernie. Her cousin Maria is one of the best people I ever knew."

"How close were you to her? All that stuff you wrote about her?"

"Closer than physical, man, if you can get that." He stopped, remembering. "I kept her from getting killed once."

"I remember your coverage about that, when she got shot, down by Pendleton when you were covering her for NPR. Must have been a terrible thing."

"It was, but she came through it OK. Had a million people praying for her, right there spread out along the 5. She had this amazing hold on people—for good, mostly. If Rosa is anything like that, you'd better tell Jim she's very special."

"Right—that would ruin it for sure. *You* tell him."

"Maybe I will."

They pulled in the driveway of Bill Solomon's house. Ernie had called ahead and told Bill he was bringing a friend down. Bill knew Sam's writing, and was anxious to meet him.

After greeting each other, and moving out to the shaded part of Bill's yard with their beers, and settling into the chairs and the view, they started talking about Southern California, because Sam had just finished a series of articles about population growth. As they talked, Bill's famed sunset show began, living up to its billing.

Sam explained, "Down there, all those people, they're erasing history. They live in tracts on the old Spanish land grants, but only one in a thousand people knows how the land changed hands, from the Indians to the Spanish to the Mexicans to the Californios to the Americans and the Persians and the Koreans and the Chinese and all of them. They don't know their own history—they don't know anything about the land they live on. And maybe that's why they don't know how to get along very well with each other. They all just think they're moving on eventually, no place is permanent, so why get to know anything about it?"

It was a long diatribe, even for Sam, and Ernie let him cool down a bit before he answered.

"Yeah, but what makes you think that folks up here spend a lot of time thinking about history and where the land and the people who live on it came from? They move up here, get out of their cars, the moving van pulls up, they move in, and they talk about the mountains and the weather a little more than people down south. But they don't know where this Valley came from or who used to live here, any more than a kid in Dana Point knows that Richard Henry Dana used to throw cattle hides off the cliffs to the ships anchored down below."

Bill joined in. "You know, that's what's so weird about this killer. He's either a local or he's read a lot of the history of this place, to be leaving the bodies in what he calls these 'evil places.' It's like he hates us, and wants to rub our noses in the worst of what happened here."

Sam had a funny look on his face. "What if we helped find the bastard?"

"Who, us?" asked Ernie.

"Sure—why not?" said Sam. "You two know a lot about this place, this is your home base. I've done a spot of investigation here and there. I could say I'm working on a story and want to see what the locals know. Could be fun working with you old farts, and we might even do some good, keeping it quiet and out of the media."

Ernie laughed and said, "Could we call it Old Farts Undercover Company?"

Having worked with government agencies' bureaucratic acronyms all over the world, Sam quickly answered, "Not for publication."

They quickly agreed to meet the next day at Ernie's place and begin their "investigation."

CHAPTER 28

Paul looked out at his mid-May class. "Now let's talk about the Indian wars in the Valley. Where did the biggest battle between Indians and whites occur in the Valley?"

He deliberately did not look over to the back corner of the class where the three Paiute students were sitting, but the answer came anyway, in a steady, deliberate, female voice. Brenda Warland said "Out Line Street past the college, turn left half a mile after the college turnoff. There's a monument there. The battle was fought in 1862." She paused and said, "It's where Professor Finnerty's body was found."

Brenda was a tall girl who seemed plain until you saw her move. Paul had heard that she might be attending UCLA or Berkeley on a dance scholarship, and to watch her walk was to behold near-feline grace.

Paul knew Brenda's uncle Rudy, and he knew she would have the answer. He also knew she would probably be able to go on for a long time about what had happened in 1862. Brenda's remarkable poise and knowledge of history had both been on display in his class, and he enjoyed watching and listening to her.

Sadly, Paul realized, she might be the only one of the three students who knew the history. Paul had talked with Rudy once about the lack of knowledge of local history among the Paiute students. Rudy disagreed mildly, saying some of the kids talked with their parents and grandparents about it, but he agreed that there was little basic knowledge of the facts. Rudy tended to blame the school district for avoiding the subject, and Paul agreed. But Paul was also frustrated at how little of the story was carried on through the Paiute community itself.

Paul's course had included an earlier unit on the history of the Valley's earliest people, the Nuumu, the Paiute word for "the People." He had pointed out the great irony, for those who see the Valley as a dry place today, that some scholars translate Paiute as the Pah-Utes—the Water Utes, distinguished from the other Utes in the Great Basin by their nearness to water. Paiutes, Paul pointed out, live all over the West, including some very arid lands.

But this session was about the armed conflict in the 1860's. And Brenda's reference to the Finnerty killing had caused a stir in the class, so Paul knew he was going to have to tiptoe through this lecture more than he had some of the others.

"Exactly right, Brenda. I'm going to ask one of the tribal elders to come next week and tell us about the Fort Tejon march that happened a year after the battle at Bishop Creek. How many of you have ever heard of the Trail of Tears?"

"Was it a movie?" asked one of the maybes, hoping to get some credit for trying.

"Yes, it was, a movie made in 2006 that was endorsed by the Cherokee Nation. Never made it into theaters, but you can get the DVD. It tells how Andrew Jackson forced the Cherokees from all over the Eastern United States onto reservation lands in Oklahoma. And guess what convinced Jackson and Congress and the State of Georgia to exile the Cherokees—they had found gold on the Cherokee homelands."

He couldn't resist adding, just to nail the point home, "Historians of World War II tell us that Hitler studied Andrew Jackson's Indian removal policy in preparing for his attempts to exterminate the Jews in Europe.

"So the Trail of Tears was a sad piece of American history. And here in the Valley, we had our own trail of tears. "The Indian problem—which is what Californians who came here after 10,000 BC called it—was the subject of some of the dumbest ideas in our history. In 1862, a state senator proposed moving all 16,000 of the Indians in the entire area of Southern California up here to a new reservation in the Owens Valley."

A hand went up in the back, and immediately Paul knew there was going to be trouble. It was Jack Latham, the son of Earl Latham, the arch-conservative treasurer of the local Republican Party. "Maybe that's dumb, but what could be dumber than letting a tribe with only sixteen people run a casino and pay no taxes on their land?"

He heard desks scraping, but looking around at the Paiute group, he gladly saw that none of them had risen—yet. Quickly he responded, "I guess you're talking about some of the proposals for Southern California tribes to set up new casinos down there—that's unlikely, given where the legislature is. We'll talk about casinos later in the course, but today we're back at the wars of the 1860's."

Jack Latham kept his hand up, even though Paul had never called on him. "But you were talking about dumb ideas…" he smirked. A few muffled laughs went up from those seated near him.

"Later—we're going to talk about it later, Jack!" Paul spoke strongly enough to draw a line he knew the Latham boy wouldn't cross, while carefully avoiding any statement for or against the plan for new casinos, which he happened to think were a mistake.

"Now, where were we?"

Brenda Warland, smiling this time, cued him. "On Bishop Creek about three miles out of town."

"Right. April 1862, the Battle of Bishop Creek. In a way, you see, we had our own civil war here in the Valley, at the same time as the big Civil War back east."

Paul continued on through the basic facts. "In August of 1861 Sam Bishop—who left the Valley soon after and died in San Jose—set up what he called San Francis Ranch out on Bishop Creek, where today there's another historical marker. It's not the one Brenda mentioned, but one right on Line Street. This was the first settlement that could properly be called 'Bishop.' Sam Bishop and several other cattlemen had driven herds into the Valley as part of a plan to sell the beef to the mining settlements in and around Aurora, east of Bodie.

"The winter of 1861-62 was a bad one, and the Indians in the Valley were low on food supplies. So they caught a few of Bishop's cattle and drove them off to be slaughtered for their families. Eventually this led to gunfire and an Indian was killed southeast of Bishop. Then a miner from Aurora was caught by the Indians and killed. A treaty was drawn up with Chief George, the leader of the Paiutes around Bishop, and signed at San Francis Ranch on January 31, 1862. But southern Mono area Paiute bands didn't sign it, and they began their own raids.

The Bishop settlers started getting reports that miners in Aurora were selling weapons to the Indians, which made the tension worse.

"Soon the Paiutes escalated by inviting warriors from tribes in Nevada and in the San Joaquin Valley to join them. On April 6, 1862, a battle was fought on Bishop Creek near the San Francis Ranch in which three of the white settlers and eleven Paiutes were killed. The whites retreated to Big Pine. At the moment of the battle, a group of fifty soldiers from Nevada was camped on Owens Creek a few miles away, having been sent by the Governor of Nevada after getting word of the fighting in the Owens Valley. But the unit had no way of knowing the Bishop group was under attack." He looked up at the class. "No cellphones."

"By May 1862, the Indians were described as being 'in possession of the entire Valley.' The white settlers sent for help from the army, and a battalion was sent from Los Angeles to the Valley, establishing what they called Fort Independence on July 4, 1862. On July 5 the commanding officer of the troops met with the Paiutes who had drawn up the original treaty with Sam Bishop, and both sides agreed to a truce.

"The Paiutes from the Valley blamed the Mono tribes for starting the fighting, and this was believable enough to convince the army leadership to allow the summer to pass without launching any new campaigns against the Paiutes. But plans were quietly drawn up for a reservation near Big Pine to hold as many as 2,000 Indians.

"That summer, more gold was discovered in the Valley, near Independence, and the flow of new cattlemen and new miners continued. In the long run, it was the gold and silver mines that made all the difference. First the mines to the north in Nevada had made the Valley a passageway used regularly by hundreds of miners and those who wanted to sell them supplies. And then the discovery of gold and silver in the Valley brought more miners and settlers. The isolation of the Valley was over, and the gold rush that had swept over the northern California Sierra had come to the eastern Sierra as well, and to the Paiutes. And it changed their lives forever.

"By spring of 1863, reinforced army units were fighting around the Big Pine area and in Independence. Another battle ended up on the shores of Owens Lake, with at least thirty Indians reported killed.

Negotiations resumed with Chief George in May, and another treaty was concluded in June. Hundreds of Paiutes came into Fort Independence to be fed, because they were running low on food due to the deliberate destruction of their food supplies by settlers, miners, and soldiers.

"Then on July 11, 1863, the trail of tears began in the Owens Valley. Nearly a thousand Indians were marched out of Fort Independence toward Fort Tejon, two hundred and fifty miles south. Chief George accompanied the group of men, women, and children. Only four hundred made it; the others either ran off during the forced march or died.

"Yet the Mono bands, led by a Paiute called Joaquin Jim, continued their guerilla raids on white settlers and miners in the area around and north of Big Pine. Several bands of settlers were caught and killed by the Indians in late 1863.

"But by then, the gold and silver strikes had increased the flow of settlers into the Valley, along with army reinforcements, and as the numbers of armed whites increased, the Indian attacks decreased. By 1864, the Visalia papers reported that so many settlers and miners had come into the Valley that the legislature was being petitioned to form a new county west of Tulare. Finally, in 1866, the new county was formed.

"Will Chalfant's account of all this, published in 1933 in *The Story of Inyo*–in language far from our early 21st century ideas of political correctness—summed it all up:

> That the Indian should resist trespass on his hereditary domain was but natural. Some white men proved themselves as savage and ruthless as those they fought. But the white domination, and its ability to make use of resources which to the Indian meant far less than the comparative comfort the conquerors have brought to him, were as inevitable here as they have been elsewhere as civilization advanced.

The class was quiet. The sleepers were at their task, the maybes were watching to see if the disagreement with Latham would start up again, and Brenda and her band were watching Paul to see how he, not Chalfant, would sum it up.

As Paul looked out over the class, he realized that another part of the lesson was sitting in front of him. Among the students there were two sets of matching names, showing the tangled history of Valley families. In a painful echo of the genealogy of African-Americans, many Paiute families adopted the names of the families they worked for. The local phone books also told the story, with the names of long-resident families alongside the names of their former Paiute employees, who adopted "American" names when their own names proved to be unpronounceable by the early settlers.

He began slowly, hoping that some of them would get it. "The gold and the silver in the 1860s were as powerful in changing the Valley as the lure of the water was fifty years later in changing the Valley again. Later, at the end of this course, we'll talk about all the takings—the taking of Paiute lands, the taking of water, the taking of freedom from those imprisoned at Manzanar. But here we see the takings of the ancestral lands of some of you to build ancestral lands for others of you. What happened, and what continued to happen, was not fair. It *is* not fair.

"We can look back over a century and a half and say what happened in the 1860's in the battles with the Paiutes was wrong. But that does not mean we can set it right by easy answers in which one side is all wrong and the other is automatically all right. And that is what I want you to learn how to do—to gather the facts and the opinions of people on both sides of a debate like this one, and draw your own conclusions on who was right and who was wrong. And often, it will end up a 60-40 balance. Rarely will it be 100-0 or even 90-10. Your job, when you work and vote and try to be citizens and neighbors as you go out in the world, is to learn to weigh the evidence, and then to make a judgment—not to be ruled by ancient prejudices of the past."

He had talked too long, but he wanted to preview his final and most important lecture, and so he had laid out the first part of his wrap up, the conclusion that was only a few weeks away. And both sets of students who cared most about this chapter—the Paiutes and Jack Latham and his buddies—were quiet for the moment.

CHAPTER 29

Howard was briefing Liz and Rudy on the latest developments. "The Sheriff called an interagency meeting for tomorrow morning at 7. He's fed up with having to make eighty phone calls a day to find out what everyone is doing. I want the two of you to report on what we've done, and then we can let the rest of the group spout off about how they're going to do what we local yokels can't do."

So they prepared a ten-minute briefing on the two killings and their follow-ups. At the end of their dry run, Liz and Rudy both knew they still had far more questions than answers. They weren't looking forward to 7 am. They knew the Sheriff would back them if they came under fire, and they knew they probably would.

By 6:50 the Sheriff's conference room was full. More than forty uniformed officers and various other agency types were present, twenty or so around the long oval table and the rest were seated along the sides of the room. At the front a screen was lowered and a large map of the County was fastened to a display board.

The Sheriff quickly convened the meeting at the stroke of 7, and asked for introductions. The attendees included the Highway Patrol, the Bishop PD, the LA DWP, the feds from Interior's Park Service and Bureau of Reclamation, along with Agriculture's Forest Service, a Navy representative from the China Lake Naval Air Station, and two aides from the Governor's office.

Liz glanced over at the Governor's staff, whom she instinctively disliked. The two aides were talking with the Sheriff in whispers, ignoring the introductions still going on, and missing the obvious message that Michaels wanted to hear what was being said. In Liz's experience, hot shots from state agencies were nearly always ignorant of law enforcement realities. And being from the Governor's office made it even worse, since they'd be trying to protect him at all costs.

Once everyone did their introductions, Liz and Rudy ran rapidly through their slide show. As they wrapped up, Liz could see frowns on at least half the faces in the room. The first question said it all, and came from the DWP operations director for the Valley: "So you don't have anything on this guy yet—no leads, no tips, no tracks away from the scene? I've got a supervisor down at the Gates who wants to take early retirement—he thought that red dye was blood and it scared the hell out of him."

With a quick look at the Sheriff, who nodded to him, Howard stood up and said, "That's right. And the road block last night got us nothing. So we'd like to talk about who is covering what area tonight. Sooner or later—if this guy goes through with the third piece of his puzzle—he's going to run into one of us. We need to be clear where we are going to be patrolling."

The DWP guy shot back, "That's obvious—we're going to be all over the Aqueduct. If he's continuing this insane history lesson, that's the obvious next one."

The Sheriff said "We appreciate that, but there are a lot of other targets. We'd like to watch the fifteen historic markers in the Valley, because we think this guy is trying to make a point about the monuments. Who wants to help us with that?"

What followed was a classic BOGSAT, Liz realized, having heard Howard rage after such meetings—a bunch of guys sitting around a table, getting nothing much done. Everyone wanted to cover their own turf and their own ass, so everyone said they didn't have enough manpower to assign staff to a team effort. Each agency made its own little speech about how important the task was and how great it was that they were all cooperating with each other. And as happened at nearly every meeting like it ever held in the Valley, the representatives from DWP found an opportunity to point out that they paid 80% of the property taxes in Inyo County.

But then DWP overplayed their hand.

The head of the DWP team from the central office was an LA-based vice-president for security, Miles Holland. Holland had said nothing during the meeting, but had been glaring at the Sheriff from the moment he sat down. He finally chimed in, starting out with an imperious attitude that seemed well off the mark, given the mostly informal tone of the rest of the meeting.

"Sheriff, our property has been threatened, and you've done nothing about it. This guy shot dye into our water, which could have been deadly to millions of people. You leave us no choice. We're going to go to the Governor, and we're going to tell him that local law enforcement just can't handle this guy or group or whoever it is. And then you're going to—"

He stopped in mid-sentence because Sheriff Michaels had stood up, leaned forward on the table, and in a low, menacing voice said, "You do *not* come into my county and tell us what to do, or threaten us with the Governor. I will tell the Governor you are disrupting local law enforcement with your rent-a-cops and your reckless tactics, and then we'll see if he over-rules me or you. Now, I will work with you, and I will run joint operations with your people. And I will do briefings for your people every damned day if you want—the way I have been doing for a week already." He paused, and then pointed at Holland. "But you go over my head, and I assure you I will run your asses out of here. And I'm pretty sure I'll get help from most of the twenty thousand people who live here. We're going to catch this guy, with or without you."

Then he smiled, looking like a man who held most of the good cards. "You guys tried this a few times before, and you ended up with the water. But it isn't going to work this time, because you can't pick us off one by one the way you did a hundred years ago."

Then he played another big card. "Miles, your mayor has been coming up here lately, making nice, telling us we're all friends now. So are you repealing all that?" He waited long enough to embarrass Holland, then repeated, confidently, "We are going to catch this guy, with you or without you. But do *not* come in here and threaten us ever again." Then he sat down and waited.

The Sheriff had called his bluff, and Holland knew he either had to follow through on his threat or back down. His face-saver was not long in coming. "You have a week. We'll meet here then, and we want daily reports." And he pushed his chair back, rose, and left, with all his minions scurrying out the door with him.

After the DWP gang left, it was all the Sheriff could do to finally get fifteen people to agree to be part of a team that would try to cover the most important monuments. Then the meeting degenerated into side conversations, and most of the attendees began drifting away from the table.

As they were leaving, Liz overheard one of the Governor's aides mutter to the other, "About what we expected from the rednecks up here."

As the group broke up outside the conference room, Liz walked up to the aide, close in, making sure she was violating the hell out of his personal space, and hissed at him, "Rednecks? You have a problem with rednecks? Rednecks fight your stupidass wars, pal. Look around the next time you get to an army base or walk in a Marine Corps bar—as if. Those are rednecks, and you'd better be damned glad of it."

The aide was backing away, and she pursued him, "Know George Orwell, hotshot? Know what Orwell said—big English leftie who wrote *1984*?"And she quoted it from memory, jabbing her finger at him: "*People sleep peaceably in their beds at night only because rough men stand ready to do violence on their behalf.*" She lowered her voice, and got even closer to the guy. "Those rough men are the rednecks, and you should pray every night that they stay out there, ready to do violence and protect wimps like you."

The aide looked furious that he had been called on his comment, and snapped, "Thanks for the history lesson, Deputy," as he hurried off to his car.

Liz knew that she had lost it, and she hated to let them see how much she cared. But she had cousins and too many friends who had shipped out and come back screwed up, shot up, or, in two cases, in a body bag. She knew that in Owens County, the total percentage of veterans was more than one-third higher than in the rest of the country. And somewhere along the line she had decided she would not let anyone run down those she thought of as "the rough men."

Rudy had been watching, and over his shoulder, Liz saw with a sinking feeling, so had Jack Howard. Rudy was smiling broadly, but Howard walked up to her with a frown on his face and said "Next time,

Nolan—" he paused to make sure she heard him, "next time, you be sure to tell them how you feel." And then he broke out one of his rare, huge smiles and walked off to his car, shaking his head.

Rudy came over to her and said "Way to go, deputy. As a true redneck, I salute you."

She was too angry and too relieved at Howard's reaction to be able to sort out Rudy's comment, but she managed to say "Thanks, Rudy."

CHAPTER 30

Fred Bancroft frowned, looking down at a map spread across his desk. Will Sawyer pointed to a thin ribbon of blue on the eastern side of the Valley, and said "There's where the new river is spreading out into what used to be the marshes. Cottonwoods are growing new branches, tule is springing up—it's going to be a whole new landscape out there in another two years or so. I spent half a day out there with the photographer last week. I got the pictures on the computer," he motioned to the desktop, "and it is something to see."

Fred nodded, and said, "Yeah, but that new growth may bring out every greenie in California, wanting to protect that land from development, land that was useless ten years ago. And that's right where our riverfront condos are going in," he jabbed at the map, "if the DWP and the Reclamation people can get over panicking over a little grass."

"It's a lot more than grass, Fred. That whole area for thirty miles south of the diversion point is going to be completely different. When we picked up the option from BLM five years ago, they told us the River diversion was going to make a big difference, and it sure has. But no one knew the water was going to make these changes so fast. That land was thirsty, but it started growing stuff that hasn't been out there for seventy years or more."

Fred nodded. "The other piece of the puzzle is the airport in Long Pine. If the plans for these new regional short-hop planes go through, it wouldn't take much to pour a few thousand feet more of runway, and then all of a sudden you're less than an hour from Burbank to your weekend condo." He shook his head, losing the thread of his sales pitch. "But if this bastard keeps killing people, we won't have to worry about the greenies. Who the hell would want to buy a condo in the middle of a blood bath?"

Will pointed at the map again. "Here's where he left the body at Manzanar." Then he pointed to a spot on the map forty miles north. "And here's where he left Finnerty's body. I was over at the Alabama in Lone Pine last night, and that guy Bill Solomon—the old duffer they call 'the movie guy'—was talking about how this all reminds him of the part in Jaws where the townspeople try to cover up the shark's attacks. He said this was the same—that everyone who has a stake in the tourist business is going to try to pretend nothing happened."

Fred asked Will to do some research on the water patterns that DWP had collected and uploaded to the Internet. As Will began, Fred wished he had some earplugs. Because Will was a hummer. He could not work for longer than five minutes at a time without humming an approximation of a tune that only he could decode, which sounded to anyone else like an aimless, melody-free noise with the irritation quotient of fingernails on a blackboard. Usually a loud "Will!" was enough to bounce him out of the mental track of his humming for at least a few minutes, but soon it would return, lower in volume and then rising as he got deeper into his work, staring at his monitor, fingers flying across the keyboard, with the humming rising in decibels up past the pain threshold of everyone else in the office. But Will was a computer whiz, largely self-educated, able to put together graphics and find sites on the Internet that would have taken Fred hours to locate. And when he was most immersed in his work, the humming inevitably increased.

Fred had finally given Will his own inside office, but he rarely closed the door. Fred was worried enough about his productivity that he liked to have the door open enough to see what Will was working on. And so the humming continued, and Fred longed for the day when it would blend into the office sounds and become unheard. So far, the day had not come.

Fred had his own office, with a long window offering a great view of the Sierra. Other than Will's small inside office, the rest of the area was divided into cubicles used by Fred's clerical and sales staff. He usually had four or five other people working for him, mostly part-time, assembled from bored housewives and recent high school graduates.

He employed a financial officer, Dean Bannerman, who doubled as a sales associate. Dean had grown up in the Valley, gotten an MBA from USC, and returned to the Valley when Fred recruited him through a friendship with Dean's father.

After a half hour, Fred stood up and reached for his coat. "Will, let's go out and look at that land along the river again. I don't like the photos that guy took for the brochure—let's take some shots ourselves."

As they drove out to the site in Fred's Lexus, Will asked Fred what he had heard about the possibility of a third killing. Nearly everyone in the Valley had picked up the rumor that the original note left by the killer had mentioned three killings, and the speculation was widespread that it would have something to do with the Aqueduct. They were driving on one of the back roads to the east of 395, out toward the old ghost town of Owenyo, where a narrow-gauge railroad had run up the Valley to Laws until 1960.

Fred said, "All I've heard is what you've probably heard. They think the guy will do something connected to the Aqueduct, and the DWP cops are all over the place. But nobody's seen anything. One of the deputies in Independence told Dale the other day that they think it's a local guy, and another one told Lew Wilson at the post office that they're sure it's some guy from down South. Nobody knows, so they're all putting out these stories to make it look like they know something."

"Lying as usual." Will had run into the Bishop police force a few times on DUIs, and wasn't much of a fan of local law enforcement.

They got to the site, and Fred swung the SUV over and parked under a cottonwood tree. As he got out of the car, he could see that the tree, which looked dead at the top, had green shoots coming out of the base of the trunk. "Look at that. We're a half mile from the river here, and it's already bringing some growth all the way out here." He looked west, over toward the river and the Sierra beyond, Whitney and Williamson and all the higher peaks thrusting up into the afternoon sky. "That's the shot I want—the Sierras and the green along the river. We'll shoot it so it looks closer than we are."

"Don't want to exaggerate too much, Fred."

As Fred moved to get closer to the trees and the camera angle, he said, "Will, people have been lying about water and land in this Valley for over a hundred years. Hell, Fred Eaton was the Mayor of LA who set up the original DWP, and he's the one who hired agents to start buying up the land in the first place. Told people it was for a reclamation project that was going to irrigate the Valley. Right—only it was the San Fernando Valley. And his buddies who owned the LA *Times* in those days made a bundle. That movie Chinatown got some of it right. Another movie."

He smiled and said to Will as he maneuvered his camera, "With all this growth, we are going to have to play some new cards, Will. It's time to turn on the hot water."

As Fred was taking pictures and recalling history, Dale Bancroft was driving back from Hawthorne down Highway 6, her mind working hard on two tracks. The first was replaying the last five hands she had been dealt in a poker game that had gotten a little out of control. Dale defined out of control as what she was going to have to tell Fred about, because he would notice it in the bank account. One, two, three thousand was not a problem. Twenty thousand was definitely a problem. So the other track of her mind was working through how she would tell Fred about the losses.

Early in her gambling days, Dale had spent time with a professor from Arizona State who once likened her to Fitzgerald's Daisy Buchanan, telling her "your voice is full of money." But Dale never figured out whether he was complimenting her or feeling sorry for her. And she had never sorted out for herself whether the wins and losses were about the money or about the thrill when she scored big.

Dale had painfully learned the language she needed to tell herself that she was addicted. She had been to one of the best gambling treatment centers in the nation, in Las Vegas, of course, and had picked up the vocabulary quickly enough to be able to convince most of the therapists that she was able to control herself "next time." But there was one counselor, Al Goldman, who just sat and watched her in group sessions with a faint smile. He had tried to talk with her once but just walked away when Dale started her happy talk routine about being cured. Al had been a high stakes player in Europe, came back to

Nevada, and crashed so badly he had been living on the streets begging for nickels for the slots. He worked the program carefully, and Dale knew he could see straight through her façade.

The AA people used the pungent phrase "a dry drunk," meaning someone who wasn't drinking at the moment but had not dealt with any of the issues beneath the craving. And Dale knew when she was not gambling, she was a dry gambler, and knew that Al knew it too. As soon as she could, she got out of the treatment center, and tried not to think of Al's knowing smile.

What she *was* thinking of as she drove her car into their garage was Fred, and how much was on his mind with his new developments, and the murders in the Valley. She knew he was preoccupied enough to give her a little time, and she wondered just how long his leash would prove to be. She knew Fred was getting closer to his own economic crossroads, with deals he needed to succeed, and she worried about what would happen if those deals fell through.

As he dug in the sandy soil, the Avenger remembered how his father and he had sometimes dug shelters into the banks of the creeks where they had fished up and down the eastern slopes. When the sun had gotten too hot for them to fish without shade, they would use his dad's folding shovel to hollow out a two- or three-foot indentation in the bank. His father let the boy dig some of the time, and some of his best memories were seeing the hollow cut into the bank grow larger as they worked. When they finished, they would put up a tent cover, lean back against the bank, and rest in the shade.

He stopped digging and stood up, watching and listening for anyone or anything that could see what he was doing. A hawk was circling a half mile or so to the south, waiting for something small to make a mistake. He felt for a moment as if he too was poised in the sky over the Valley, waiting for something to kill. Then he returned to his digging.

CHAPTER 31

"The Finnerty killing is so sad, in some ways. It brings up to the surface so much that is usually buried."

Elaine was talking in her study at the church with her part-time associate, a young man a year out of seminary who rotated among several of the churches on the eastern side of the Sierra. Frank Mather had grown up in Connecticut, and was having some difficulty getting used to rural California. He had come west to escape an exclusively New England track that his father and grandfather had worn deep in the Methodist Church. But Elaine was becoming frustrated even beyond her usual tolerance with the need for repeated New England-Eastern Sierra translations in interpreting the Valley to Frank. So her penance was to try to explain things clearly the first time, whenever she could.

"This tension between the Paiutes and the rest of us…it's one of those things that's so deep hardly any one ever talks about it. It's unspoken, full of what we believe about each other and how much we distrust each other. It goes into the land itself, their land, our land, DWP's and BLM's land. Who took what and when they took it and how they took it."

She paused, watching Frank struggling to tune into her Western broadcast with his Eastern receiver. "As bad as it is between us and LA, we can talk about that. It started in 1903, it goes on today, it's part of the landscape, we see the Aqueduct and the river and all the fences around LA's land. But the other walls, with the Indians—they're invisible most of the time, unless you drive through the rez. And some people can bridge it, can build up the trust, slowly, over time, but most of us can't and don't try. So the stereotypes grow deep roots on both sides. Paiutes call us money-grubbers who never keep promises, and I've heard people in the congregation fall back on the old Digger myths about how primitive the Paiutes were—and we both stay on the safe side of those dumb prejudices. And you look out at that congregation on Sunday, and over the years I've been here, maybe five families that had any ties to the Paiutes have walked through that door. If that many."

Frank said "Churches in New England are pretty segregated too, but it seems worse here. And I'm still trying to understand the differences between the Paiutes and the Pequots—the wealthiest tribe in the nation."

"Different planets," Elaine agreed. "But maybe in the end there's more justice on that side of the country than this one, given the history of how badly the Pequots were treated—by the Pilgrims, unfortunately for our national myths."

"Yeah, though for a tribe that had died out, that one came back pretty strong, thanks to a lot of intermarriage and a lot of gamblers." Elaine and Frank had talked about New England and California Indian tribes before, and the differences and similarities were a favorite topic. But Elaine knew it was still a shallow conversation until local leaders of the tribes themselves were brought into it. And so she and Frank talked further about how to do that. Elaine had chaired the Valley inter-church council during the difficult times after the child care incident, and some useful dialogue had begun—but had soon died out. They talked about how to revive that, and how to keep it alive this time.

After Frank left, Elaine moved her study chair around to her favorite spot, where she could watch the sunset over Mt. Tom. Elaine did not meditate in a formal way, but she thought of her late afternoon, early evening mountain watching sessions as a close substitute.

Elaine had spent some serious time in her life, off and on, thinking about God. She wasn't obsessed by it, but she felt she owed it to herself and her congregation to be as clear as she could on what God was all about. She had spent most of her life, since seminary, in an elaborate, private little balancing act between thinking of Her and making sure she never used the feminine pronoun in public. She'd tried a sermon once on God as Mother, and several people had made clear that they thought she had gone over the line.

Elaine's ideas about God had evolved—which in itself made clear how unconventional her ideas were about Her. Elaine had been greatly interested in science since her high school days, when she discovered that girls could do science, too, and Ed's interest in geology had deepened her understanding of what it meant to work on a time scale of billions of years. But Ed had looked at the earth, while Elaine's eye had been drawn upward. She'd bought a decent telescope and had set it up out in the hills at a friend's house up near Lake Sabrina, in a basin at 8500 feet into the Sierra. Some early mornings she would drive out there just to see what the naked eye already told her about the vastness of the sky above. One of the things she liked most about living in the Valley was that you never forgot how big the universe was, because the stars were a visible, nightly reminder that something else was going on out there, far beyond the day's petty strife.

But reconciling a loving, personal God with all that vastness brought her back to her balancing act. Elaine had days, when she was most missing Ed, trapped in the minutia of running a church, seeing the most venal side of her community, when she suspected that a more clockwork God existed than the One she liked to believe in. A warm and mothering Spirit was what Elaine wanted to believe in, while a clockwork God who worked out the laws of nature and sat back seemed little inspiration for a species that appeared to need inspiration to live up to its best instincts.

Yet Elaine found other evidence for her ideas about a personal God in humor and sex. Ed and she had enjoyed each other's bodies greatly, and had gotten to the point just before Ed's accident that sex had become both fun and funny. Elaine had come to believe that sex was God's best joke on Her creatures, and she and Ed had some of their best moments together laughing before, during, and after both serious and lighthearted sex.

Having an important daily bond to a canine also helped Elaine, because she knew there were facets of her life that Dulcie would simply never understand, and would never need to. Actions and motives that were real to Elaine were eternally incomprehensible to Dulcie, and

Elaine had a hunch that God's motives and operating style were just as incomprehensible to her.

CHAPTER 32

The Avenger was locked in a memory that went back fifteen years.

The boy sat, disconsolate, on a large rock at the side of the dirt road, staring off at nothing. From time to time he raised his head and listened for a car headed uphill from the valley below, but heard nothing.

Immediately after the accident, three hours before, he had run back and forth trying to see a way to get down to the rocks at the base of the steep cliff that dropped off from the edge of the winding dirt road. But he had finally given up, sobbing, after an hour or so, seeing no movement from the body far below.

Maybe somebody could help him. Maybe he's just unconscious. Somebody will come along, somebody has to come along soon. Then they can lift him up and take him to a hospital. Then he'll be OK. Why isn't anybody coming? Where are all those people we saw down there at the campgrounds, why doesn't anybody come up here?

The boy wore jeans and a t-shirt, with a backpack thrown beside him at the bottom of the rock. He was thin, with a face neither appealing nor unattractive, nondescript, like his clothes. He had a broken off branch from which he had stripped the twigs and leaves to use as a walking stick. Now he was randomly swinging it at the road, kicking up clouds of dust each time the branch hit the fine dirt.

Above him loomed the mountains west of Independence, lying at the end of the road switchbacking up to Onion Valley, which had been their destination before the accident. When he looked up there, to see if he could spot a car or truck coming down the road, the mountains seemed immense and unforgiving. He wondered how soon it would get dark, and he listened for a car, and longed for someone to come and tell him what to do. And his anger grew at all the people out there who weren't coming

CHAPTER 33

Rudy and Liz were back in the war room in Independence, going over the deployments of the several different patrols. No one had seen anything yet, and none of their leads had panned out.

Liz pushed back from the table and leaned back in her chair. "I'm sure tired of this case. Tired and scared what we're going to find at the end of it. Some sick bastard who hates everyone and everything and thinks killing is going to solve it."

"You ever go to the FBI training on profiling?"

"No—you?"

Rudy said "Yeah, three years ago. Pretty rough, listening to all the talk about these serial killers they study. Makes you wonder who's walking around out there with all that pain and hate locked up, waiting for something to set off the explosion."

He went on, "The history stuff is weird." And then he stopped, looking at her, and asked, quietly, "What does Paul think?"

"He's worried about it. He says whatever this guy is trying to do, he's picking away at some of the worst scabs in the Valley. 'Three evil places.' Paul says if you wanted to, you could find *thirty* evil places in the Valley."

Rudy was silent. Then he said, walking slowly over to the window and looking out at the evening shadows on the Inyos. "Yeah, but you could find some good places too, if you were looking."

He kept looking out the window. Then he went on, "That Mayor from LA didn't have to come up here and turn on the water running back into the River after they lost the court case—he could have sent a flunky. That was a good thing to do. Some healing." He smiled. "We're big on healing.

"And out on the football fields in the Valley, some good things happen there sometimes." He paused, remembering his own days. "Didn't matter what color you were out there or who your people were. It was how fast you were and how hard you hit and got hit. The old coaches' cliché: there is no I in team."

Rudy continued his recitation. "And over at the elementary school, there was a superintendent back in the '50s who got the first grant for enrichment funding for Indian kids. Never had been done before, anywhere in the state. Didn't do a thing for him, made more paperwork, really. But he went after that grant for our kids, and he got it. There's no historic marker over there, but over the years, hundreds of kids got a little better education because of what that man did. I didn't know about that when I was in school, but we studied it in a class I took over at Fresno State."

Tentatively, Liz said, "I would think you'd see the bad stuff that happened here more than those kinds of things."

Rudy shook his head. "I know. The bad stuff is there, and you can never forget it if you come at it from the Indian side of what happened. But if you take the long view—" he chuckled, "five or ten thousand years worth of long view—you can see some good things, too. We're still here, almost two thousand of us. Some of the historians say that's as many of us as ever lived in the Valley." Wanting to lighten it up, he added, "And now we've got NFL football on big-screen TV. And a K-Mart."

Turning back to the map, he said, "So there are some good places, along with the evil places." He turned and looked at the markers they had pinned up showing the victims and the two 'evil places.' "But this guy, this killer is obsessed with the bad stuff, like the Valley itself did something to him. He can't see the good places. He's blind to them." He was pacing now, intense, trying to put the pieces together.

"Bear with me, Liz. Sometimes, it helps if I can think about stuff like this from an Indian point of view. You know, we make a big deal out of things being in balance, about harmony. The land, the sky, the people, all in balance. The evil comes when things lose their balance. This killer is out of balance—he lost a piece of his life somewhere and he lost his balance. So he hates all of us and is trying throw us off balance, too. If he just left a body at one place, it would be about that victim or that place. But three places, if that's what it ends up being, that's about the whole Valley. He hates the whole Valley. But why?"

Slipping into a kind of brainstorming session, they began throwing ideas at each other.

"He got kicked out of schools up here?" Rudy asked.

"He got lost here as a kid?"

"He got beat up here by townies?"

"His wife divorced him here?"

"His wife died here?"

Liz pounded her hand lightly on the table. "Something—something bad happened to him here—that much sounds right. But what, and where, and when? How many thousand guys come through here, or grew up here, and had a rough life or got a bad break that wasn't their fault?"

"Yeah, but they didn't end up killers."

"Right—so what turned him into one?"

They slowed down, having exhausted the options, and Liz said, "Let's keep kicking this around. Maybe I'll talk to Paul about it and you could talk to people you know."

Then Liz deliberately moved off the topic, hoping that other ideas would come later. "Paul says your niece Brenda is doing very well. Where is she going to college?"

"Berkeley or UCI—if she goes."

"If?! She's bound to get in. Paul says she's the best in his class, and I saw her dance at the spring show—she's fantastic."

"Yes, she is. But she's got to decide to go, and she isn't getting much encouragement. My brother isn't much into college."

"So talk to her. You went to Fresno State—talk to her."

"I can't do that. It violates non-interference."

"Violates what?"

Rudy frowned, and looked away. "It's hard to explain to a non-Indian. No offense. Most Indians still hang on to the idea of letting people find their own way, not interfering with what people choose for themselves, waiting for consensus to build and taking a lot of time to let it happen. People try not to tell other people what to do. Kids are supposed to learn by watching, by models. So the idea that a parent—or an uncle—would tell a kid what to do with their life is just not something that we feel comfortable with. If I push her to go to college, I'm going the white man's way, and it doesn't stay true to our ways as it would if I let Brenda and her family come to the decision themselves."

It was a long speech for Rudy, but he was trying to get the idea across and he knew how foreign it sounded to Liz. A native idea, but he knew it sounded foreign to her.

"But what if a kid makes a bad choice?"

"Then they learn. And they didn't have good models."

"They learn the hard way."

"Maybe. But sometimes it's better than feeling you're only doing something because somebody else tells you that you have to. Then you don't own it, it's not yours."

"Non-interference, huh?"

"Yeah."

She laughed, shaking her head. "Would have saved my dad a lot of trouble if he had gotten a little of that. He was from the 'my way or no way' school."

"Lots of dads are."

"But then why did *you* go to college?"

He laughed softly. "My mother pushed me from day one—somewhere she picked up the idea that I had to go, and she pushed hard. She wanted me to escape." He shook his head, still smiling. "She never understood my coming back here from college. But she balanced out non-interference by coming down on the pushy side about going to college. Worked for me, I guess. "

"Seems like that non-interference stuff would be a problem in law enforcement where we have to arrest people and lock them up."

Rudy nodded. "You have to do it differently when you work under different laws."

"Compartmentalize, huh?"

Rudy nodded, but with difficulty, Liz felt. "Something like that."

It was the longest conversation Liz had ever had with someone about a culture other than her own, and for a moment she was grateful to Rudy, while feeling somehow less a part of the world she lived and worked in. She'd gotten a glimmer of just how much she didn't know about Indian life in the Valley. And she wanted to try to respond.

"See, for us—some of us, anyway—the competition is so powerful, you gotta be first, or try to, or accept that you will be second to someone who is way out there in front. Sometimes there is somebody else who is so much better than you that all you can do is admit it and use them to measure your progress. There was another trainee at the Academy—" she stopped and frowned. "Marianne was so good at everything she did, all I could do was watch her and try to figure out which one or two things I could maybe do as well. I didn't let her intimidate me—but I sure as hell knew she was ahead of me. She could run—she beat all but three of the men when we raced—she could outlift anyone there for her weight, and the worst of it was she looked like a million bucks."

Liz stared into space, remembering the Academy. "Marianne wrote a report once for a class in report-writing, and it was like a novel, it was so good. You just didn't want that report to end—it was that good. At one point toward the end of training, she started to talk to me about looking for a job in the Eastern Sierra. She was from Mariposa and knew the western side and thought she might want to come over here. I thought I was going to be sick. Competing with her would have been hopeless. But then she got an offer in Sacramento and went back over there.

"But you know, I measured myself against her every day. I knew she was better, but in my gut I wanted to try to rise to her level because it meant playing the faster game. You know what I mean?"

Rudy nodded and said, "Sort of. Sounds driven—but I know what you mean."

The door opened, and Howard walked in, with an expression that Liz read as trouble. He motioned to her, closing the door, and said, "Rudy, stay. You need to hear this, too."

Howard was blunt. "Liz, that guy you chewed out from the meeting went back and told somebody in the Governor's office that you had a real attitude problem and didn't seem like someone who could work with the other agencies. He made it about your briefing, not the run-in you had with him afterward. Sheriff is going to back you, but we want to keep you out of the cross-fire for a few days. The DWP guy the Sheriff butted heads with last week has started leaking stuff to the LA papers about how we can't handle the case, and the Sheriff is feeling more heat than usual. So take some time, patrol over on the east side away from all of this stuff. Rudy will handle things here, check in with him. This will blow over, but stay low for a while."

Liz walked over to the map and stared at it. "Liz, did you hear me?" Howard could tell that she had taken it hard, but she seemed to be frozen.

She spun around. "Got it. Stay out of sight. Can do. I'll call Rudy a couple of times a day, and check back with you in a couple of days. I'll log out now." Her face was stripped of what she was feeling, which was equal portions of anger at herself and at the Governor's wiper.

She had mouthed off when she could have just stayed quiet. There had been no need for her remark, nothing got moved any further down the field, and she had cost the team some time and herself a lot of credibility. Her anger had launched a perfectly aimed missile, but it had bounced off the target and come straight back at her.

And at that point, she had no idea what to do about it but drive home as carefully as she could. And try not to think about the other person she remembered from the Academy.

Fourteen years earlier, by the last week of her training program at the Riverside Sheriff's Academy, Liz was nearly certain she was going to make it. She had aced the classroom work, gotten through the physical testing with the 80% marks she needed, and had done better on the firing range than all but five of the class of fifty trainees. The years of hunting and target practice with her father had paid off.

The only thing she still worried about was the instructor ratings, and the only instructor she had any doubts about was Joe Bonds, a thirty-five-year-old instructor with a shaved head who taught hand-to-hand. His nickname among the trainees was "Total PITA," and he was unquestionably a complete pain in the ass.

Bonds' attitude toward all trainees was the same: he saw his sole function as failing anyone who wasn't up to his standards. The problem was that the standards seemed to change for each trainee. His attitude toward Liz was a little different—he wanted to fail her *after* he'd taken her to bed.

At first, he tried to humiliate her on the training mat, but his moves weren't what they must have been when he was first hired. He tried to flip her, but she deftly stepped aside and tripped him with a leg sweep. He bounced up, roaring, "That's illegal, Nolan," to which she responded, "I'm so sorry, Instructor Bonds, I thought the object was to get the guy down."

Then he shifted to vicious comments, usually made under his breath so only Liz could hear them. She was easily able to ignore his sarcastic epithets: "Great move if you're up against a 90-year old lady, Nolan." "Another screwup by Trainee Nolan.""Nice ass, Nolan."

Bonds was Italian-American. Someone who knew someone who'd worked with him before his assignment to the training academy said his name was actually Bonelli. He told the trainees to call him Stallion, which no one did. He was about 6'2", heavier than he would have found comfortable if he'd been in a patrol car every day. His bald head looked more bizarre than tough, since the main feature of the back of his head was two rolls of fat above his neck.

But he was one of five instructors whose ratings made up the final piece of Liz's grades, and she knew he had failed trainees before, because he'd bragged about it on the first day of training.

Liz finished getting her equipment ready for the next day, which she always did in front of her locker rather than at home so she could just step into the trainee uniform when she got to the Academy in the morning. She was working on her shoes when she realized no one was left in the women's locker room. Then she heard a door open. Heavy footsteps came toward the row of lockers, and then Bonds stood at the end of the row.

"Hello, Nolan. Seems like it's just the two of us." His voice was quiet, menacing. He stood with his arms crossed, leaning up against the lockers.

"I'm not sure this is your area, Instructor Bonds," she said.

"I go anywhere I want, Nolan." He uncrossed his arms, took three steps toward her, and put his thumbs in his gun belt. "Think it's time we had a serious talk. Assuming you want to graduate."

"I'd be glad to see you in the morning, Instructor Bonds. Gotta go now." She stood up, shaking her car keys slightly to let him know she was leaving, and in hopes he'd see the self-defense whistle on her key chain.

"Sit down, Nolan. You leave when I tell you." Shaking his head, he went on. "Y'know, you've had an attitude problem from the first day."

Liz decided the exchange wasn't working, so she sat down, staying quiet, hoping he would run out of gas and let her go when he saw she wasn't responding. But she was suddenly sickened, and much more scared, when she saw Bonds reach up and pull his T-shirt out of his pants.

"I'm going to fail you, Nolan, unless you finally get smart and show me you can handle the real stuff."

"What real stuff?"

"We're going to get to know each other." He lifted the shirt off, unfastened his gun belt, hung it on the open locker next to Liz, and slipped out of his shoes. As he bent over and took off his pants, Liz quickly reached over into his gun belt and pulled out his 9.

Bonds' eyes got huge, he froze, and then he started to back up as Liz trained the gun on his crotch.

"Isn't this where I say freeze, asshole?" She stepped toward him, fast, and now the gun was jammed as far into his crotch as she could reach. "So freeze!" She softly asked him, "Can you remember if you have a round in the chamber, you miserable piece of dog shit?"

"You won't do it. You'll never pull that trigger."

And Liz blanked for a second, and then the next thing she knew, four things had happened very quickly. She pulled the trigger, a loud click echoed through the locker room, a soft liquid sound was audible, and a fast-moving stain spread across the front of Bonds' shorts.

Liz emerged from her blank-out, with only one coherent thought left, strangely echoing from her classroom sessions: *chain of evidence*. She reached up and swiftly scratched Bonds' face as hard as she could, held out her bloody fingernail to him, and said "DNA, shithead."

She spun around, almost throwing up, and somehow made it out of the locker room, throwing Bonds' gun into the bushes as she left the building. As she walked out to her car, walking slowly and breathing deeply, she tried to sort out whether it was his attack or her pulling the trigger that was causing the shaking that would not stop.

She pulled into her driveway, the memory fading, and told herself for the hundredth time that she had to get past it.

CHAPTER 34

"He's a *borracho* mechanic, and he's no damn good for you!"

Cecelia was leaning across the front counter of the restaurant shaking her finger at Rosa. Thankfully, customers had left. A few minutes before, Rosa had come by offering to help clean up, trying to regain some of the ground she had lost in the last argument with Cecelia when she told her she was going to go see Jim Scott. That argument ended with Rosa storming out and driving off to Lone Pine.

But now a thunderstorm of another argument had blown up in seconds, as Rosa, trying to calm the waters, made the mistake of telling Cecelia that Jim was polite and respectful, that they had had a very proper date, and then that he had a good job. "They're always polite just before they ruin your lives, Rosa" had been the response to the first claim, and the second was met with the charge that Jim was just a mechanic.

"Mom, how can you be such a bigot toward people who work with their hands?" asked Rosa. This set off another explosion, as vehement as it was devoid of logic.

"Don't you call me a bigot! I respect anyone who works with their hands, as long as they take care of their family and have an education. Your father worked with his hands, all his life. But I have seen Jim Scott in here with five different women, and you are not going to be another trophy in his case! Not if I can help it."

Rosa kept trying to remember the scripture about how a "soft answer turneth away wrath," but she was also getting tired of Cecelia trying to run her life. "Mom, this is going nowhere. This is a nice guy, I am *not* going to marry him and move away to have seven kids and live on welfare, and I *am* going to see him again. I respect you and I love you, but I am going to UCLA in three months and I will meet a lot of people and you will not be there to conduct an investigation on each of them. So let's just let it go."

Cecelia tired of the fight and knowing that Rosa was at least half right, started to agree with her. But as she began to answer Rosa, the front door of the restaurant burst open and three workers dressed in well-worn khakis came running in, the one in the front shouting, "Cecelia, come quick! Somebody shot at our work crew and two of the men have been hurt!"

Two hours later, Rosa and Cecelia slowly walked back into the restaurant, clothes dusty and hair askew. They sat down hard in the first chairs they came to, and as Rosa put her head in her hands, Cecelia began talking slowly.

"I can't believe this is happening. All these years, I knew there was bad feeling and I knew people looked down on us. But this is deep and ugly. Shooting at the workers who are building homes for their parents! What is *wrong* with these people?!"

When they arrived at the work site, which was at a senior citizens' residential area, they found a crew of almost twenty workers milling around, with an ambulance loading a worker who had been shot in the back. Earlier, while the workers were finishing up for the day, two cars had driven by, and the passengers had shouted insults at the workers. Beyond some hand gestures and some colorful Spanish curses, the workers had let it go. But then the cars had spun around at the end of the block, accelerating, and that was when the crew saw that one of the riders was standing up through the sun roof of one of the cars, and was aiming a rifle at them. The first shot dropped a worker who was coming down a ladder from the roof, and by the time the second one was fired, the workers had scattered or thrown themselves flat on the ground. One worker had sprained his ankle badly diving off the front porch of the residence into a flower bed four feet below.

The man who was shot was wounded in the back, but the round had gone all the way through and had not hit anything vital. The Bishop police had rolled on the call, and had taken eyewitness reports from some of the workers. No one had gotten a license plate, but several of the workers described the first car, the one with the rifle, as a black, late model SUV.

The Avenger heard the police broadcast on his portable scanner with pleasure—it had worked even better than he thought. The note he'd left tacked to the wall in the men's room in the bar in Bishop where the Anglo construction workers hung out had been handed around to everyone within 15 minutes of being found. Once they'd read it, the furious workers roared out the back door of the bar and piled into their cars, driving off toward the construction site.

The note read "Hey, Anglo assholes. How do you feel about losing your jobs to us, you pendejos? We work building the old people's home, you drink. Enjoy, lazy cabrons." And it was signed "The Mexican Occupation Army."

CHAPTER 35

Liz had gotten home from her semi-suspension feeling exhausted, and Paul somehow knew from their brief cell phone talk on her way up 395 that she was drained. He met her at the door. Paul was not tall, and so his hands easily reached around her, softly cupping Liz's still-round bottom, and lifting it into himself. It was a gesture they had shared for twenty years, and Liz never grew tired of the feeling of gently melting into his body as they stood in the entry way, slightly swaying and holding each other.

"Bad one, huh?"

"Real bad," she answered. "Let me get into some sweats and we can talk about it." While she changed, Paul checked to see that the girls were watching one of their approved DVDs in the back bedroom, which was sometimes used as "the TV room." The movie seemed appropriate, and he returned to the living room, taking his half of their "talking chairs," two old chairs they usually sat in while they were re-running their days, his rocker and a beat-up old recliner that Liz loved.

While Paul was waiting for her, Jennie came into the living room, looking pensive. Paul thought he knew what she wanted, since TV ads for pet food often led to a recurring conversation.

"Daddy, do fish poop?"

"Yep. Great, gushing quantities of it."

"Fooey." And she headed, frowning, back to the bedroom.

Paul felt mildly guilty, but not enough to change his stated policy. The girls had been told on numerous occasions that they could have any pet they wanted as long it "it doesn't poop." This had led to extensive conversations about the defecatory habits of many different animals. In the meantime, Paul and Liz were very clear about the impossibility of adding an animal to the complications of their lives, although Liz occasionally weakened when visiting her brother's family in Orange County, which featured two badly spoiled Shi Tzus.

Liz walked back into the living room wearing a blue sweat outfit that Paul secretly disliked but knew she wore for comfort reasons, thus rendering it undiscussable. She was frowning. "I screwed up, and I don't want to talk about it yet, so tell me about your day. What did you cover today?"

From long experience Paul knew she meant it, and was not trying to get coaxed into debriefing him. So he picked up the ball. "I did the red and blue states today. Some of them got it, a few of them liked it."

Paul always felt the "red-blue lecture" was one of his most difficult ones, because he had to talk about politics without seeming partisan or even political. He started with a map of the United States, showing the conventional blue and red state division based on voting for Democratic or Republican candidates for president in the last election. Then he superimposed on that map a county-level map, which was far different, showing reds and blue scattered all over the place, with California mostly red, where it had been blue in the first map, because the rural counties took up so much more space than the urban, Democratic areas along the Coast. Owens County, of course, showed red.

Then he asked for reactions.

Brenda Warland spoke up first. "I hate this color stuff, this blue-red state crap."

"All right, Brenda, we get your intensity, but tell us more."

"First, it's just wrong. Look at the map of California—the bluest state there is—it's nearly all red when you look at counties!! Look at Owens County, all red. So there's no blue people here? And how do you sort out the red states and the red*necks* and the red that the *communists* used for all those years? It's *stupid*!"

Since that was partly the point Paul was trying to make, he was delighted she had gotten it. After some more discussion, Paul put up the third and final map, colored in shadings of red and blue according to the percentages of each party's dominance. And that map, predictably, was mostly purple.

Brenda went on. "Red means they don't like the government, right—they want less government? But it seems to me that government has been in the middle of things in this Valley forever. We learned in one of the first classes this semester that more than a third of the people with jobs in the Valley work for the government—the feds, the state, the DWP, our own cities, the reservations, or the schools. And it was government that made all the decisions that made this Valley what it is today. LA City government, Teddy Roosevelt when he killed the irrigation plan in favor of the Aqueduct. And further back, government sent the soldiers to Fort Independence when the Indian wars were going on."

Another student spoke up. "Government set up the reservations, and allows the tribes to run casinos, and then takes some of the money. And government referees the environmental fights and decides who wins in court, making LA put water back in the River and the Lake."

Paul jumped back in. "So just who is against government here? We depend on the government—when we vote, we decide who runs the government. And sometimes the ones we elect in Sacramento and Washington get it all wrong, and sometimes, like putting water back in the Lake—we can agree that they get it right. Or the courts—another part of the government— force them to get it right.

"Somebody once made fun of what they called 'sagebrush socialists,' who have a simple message about government: 'Leave us alone—and keep sending money.' Not so red, but not all blue either. Sounds purple to me—like that map," gesturing to the slide he had left up. "Purple means a mix of anti-government conservatives and people who believe government can get things right if people stay involved and if we elect reasonably competent people instead of narcissistic fools. Think about it." And he dismissed them.

Liz had listened to Paul's replay with nods and smiles at the right places, but Paul could tell that she was still trying to handle whatever had happened at work. He said lightly, "Let's put them to bed and then watch a little TV together." Liz closed her eyes for a second as Paul got up, and then said "Go ahead, I'm just going to sit here for a while. Maybe call my dad."

After her family had moved up to Bishop in her junior year of high school, Liz and her brothers quickly decided they loved living there. But her father had never made the adjustment work for him. Ed Gallagher's security business had never taken off once he moved to the Owens Valley, and the contracts he had hoped to get from Valley companies and the government agencies had been too few and too small to expand his business as much as he had planned when they first moved. Ed had been a strong deputy to a former Army buddy who had set up a security company in LA, but he proved to be too blunt and undiplomatic to be the front man when he tried to set up his own firm.

So when Liz' younger brother finished high school, their parents had moved back to Van Nuys, where he lived in the same house where Liz had been a baby. He had bought it back from the people who had bought it from him. He had told Liz that he liked the backyard garden, but she suspected it was also his aversion to anything new.

Her mother had died of a fast-moving cancer ten years after they had moved back, with Liz and a visiting nurse caring for her at the end so that she could die at home. Her mother was the only person on the planet who called her Elisabeth, and Liz missed her softer touch and all that she could have been for Liz's girls.

After her mother's death, her father settled in to a routine that Liz thought of as lonely, but that Ed seemed to tolerate just fine. He was supposedly retired, but he told Liz periodically that he was worried that when he stopped working, he would "just stop." So he provided security for two senior living areas that were near his home, as well as performing crossing guard duty in the mornings at the nearby elementary school Liz had attended. He was only 65, and Liz's grandparents were both in their late 80's, so Liz expected him to last quite a while.

He answered on the second ring, and Liz said "Your legs holding up well enough now you can get to the phone before it goes on automatic, Dad?

"Hell, yes. I stand up, they creak around for a few seconds, I force them to go to work, and we get where we're going. Usually. How you doing, babe?"

Ed had a knee that had been injured in Vietnam, where he was in the infantry. But he refused to get it replaced, telling Liz whenever she asked "I'll be damned if I'm going to let the government that screwed up Katrina and Iraq stick some hardware in my leg. I need that leg every day."

"I'm not doing so good, Dad. Some more problems with the bosses. And I guess I popped off when I shouldn't have." She told him about the incident with the state guys, and the aftermath.

"Called you rednecks, eh? That must have pissed you off. So you fired the Orwell quote at the little jerk. I remember when you learned that for some high school class. Great quote. Better than slugging him, I guess."

"Yeah, but it was over the line. I should have just shut up."

"Not your best quality, babe, the shutting up part." He paused. "How're Paul and the girls? How is Jessie coming along?"

Liz heard both the change of subject and her father's genuine concern for Jessie, and she appreciated both.

"Good, good, we've got her on some new meds, and it's better, most days."

As with nearly everyone who asked about Jessie, Liz was shading the truth. The truthful answer was so painfully complicated that she almost never came out with it, trusting neither herself nor her listeners to be able to handle the details of Jessie's ferocious traumas and the sheer exhaustion Liz and Paul endured some nights when the mania was raging.

"All right. I think I'll head up there for some fishing, maybe in a month or so. I'll let you know when. Listen, kid, you keep plugging away at it. You can't try to tell every butthead in the world that he's a butthead—takes up too much time." It was his way of cautioning her, urging her to dial down the anger that was her undoing sometimes—as it had been his.

CHAPTER 36

Dale Bancroft was getting ready for bed, with Fred still out at a realtors' meeting. Dale glanced into her dresser mirror, and quickly looked away from the unmistakable signs of time's thefts from around her eyes.

Dale had spent much of her life worrying about her looks, and some of the attraction of gambling was that the power came from her cards, not her looks. Part of her unspoken bargain with Fred, of course, was that she would stay looking good and he would keep pretending that she wasn't—she hated the word, but she had learned to use it—*sick*. He had supported her going into treatment, and he had agreed that she could keep going to Nevada because she "had it under control now."

But now she had run out the string, and the level of losses she had dropped had moved her into a whole new territory of dread. She was afraid that Fred would find out, she was afraid of his reaction, and most of all, she was afraid she would somehow be forced to stop. In treatment, she had learned that denial was part of the disease, and she allowed herself a measure of pride that she had gotten past that stage. She admitted she had a problem, and so, finally, she knew that she was facing a level of consequences more painful and certain than she had ever had to face before.

But although she knew she was sick, like any addict, she was spending much of her time thinking about her next fix. She had gotten past the fantasy of winning it all back—which she had abandoned the third time she bet her car and lost it. That had been the incident ten years ago that had led Fred to take her to Vegas for treatment. But she was still in the grasp of a softer fantasy: that she could somehow convince Fred that she could pay it back and that he would then let her go back to playing with a limit. She knew it was a fantasy, but it was all she had at that point.

And so as she combed out her hair, she began to work out her pitch to Fred to allow her to work in the office, as she had when they were first married, with the understanding that she would put her earnings into a payback fund. She wondered what Fred cared about most at that point in his business, so that she could focus on that part of his interest and show him she cared about it, too. And then she realized that she had no idea what Fred wanted out of the business—she had gotten so used to listening to him without hearing him that she was clueless about his real plans and hopes. She kept brushing her hair, wondering how to have a serious conversation with her husband.

PART THREE:
INTO HOT WATER

CHAPTER 37

"The future of this valley is limitless, Will. Everything is starting to fall into place. Once they catch this killer, it's all going to happen. And we are going to be right in the middle of it. The development along the river that we looked at—that's just the beginning. It's going to go a lot further. It's still about the water, but the serious deals are going to be about the *hot* water."

Fred Bancroft was sitting behind his desk in his office, explaining a new development deal to Will Sawyer. Fred enjoyed rolling out his new ideas with Will, who invariably reacted as a typical Valley resident would. Fred saw Will as his barometer, signaling how warm or cool public reactions to his schemes might be.

At the moment, Will was lost. "Hot water? How do you figure that?"

"Geothermal power. There's already a site at Coso Junction, and another one up at Hot Creek and at the Mammoth airport. Will, this whole valley sits on top of more power than Saudi Arabia. MIT did a report a few years ago that estimated that there was enough heat energy in rocks only three to five miles underneath the United States to supply all the world's current energy needs for 30,000 years. The trick is to get down to it and not blow up most of the surrounding countryside. It's like lancing a boil, if you aren't too squeamish. You could pay for everything green this valley ever wanted if you could produce three or four gigawatts of power and sell it to Reno and Las Vegas. And even LA. That's the same amount of power as two Hoover Dams, Will. It's all down there in the rocks."

"We got a lot of rocks around here."

"Yeah, and a lot of them came up from down below the crust, and they came up very, very hot. Know what country has more geothermal power per person than any other?"

"No, but you're going to tell me."

"Iceland. Know what they got in Iceland?"

"That I know: volcanoes and blondes."

"It's the volcanoes that count. They got as many volcanoes as we have. Mammoth has already been negotiating with a firm from Iceland for geothermal power. This valley could be Iceland West."

"With the blondes?"

"If we had the power, we'd have the big money that attracts the blondes."

"Sign me on," Will said, with a wide grin.

"The thing is, it's still all about the water. You've got to have water to make the steam that powers the turbines. So if this works, the water we have left helps us get the rest of the water back. We sell LA power and they give us back the water—they just shut down most of the aqueduct."

"LA Department of No More Water and a Lot More Power."

"Something like that."

"So how they gonna water their golf courses and lawns?"

"With the power we sell them to desalinate the Pacific Ocean."

"Sounds pretty science fiction to me."

"Not really. Over north of San Francisco, the Geysers geothermal field produces about two thirds of the energy used on the coast all the way between the Bay and the Oregon border. And Israel has used desalination for decades, in deserts a lot dryer than this Valley. They've just started building a new desalination plant down by San Diego that will produce fifty million gallons of water a day."

"Wow. But DWP owns most of the land around here, doesn't it?"

"Only around the aqueduct. The rest of it is federal. And the feds would love to have a way to tell the Arabs and Venezuela to take their oil and shove it, and sell off some federal land at the same time. Read the papers, Will. The feds decided they could fight a trillion-dollar war and cut taxes, and now they seem to have a deficit running upwards of ten trillion dollars. The recession made it all much worse. So they're in a land-selling mood. They've been quietly selling federal land all over the West, around Vegas, especially. DWP has the same problem, and they are going to start to sell land, in some cases side by side with BLM land. They both need the money, and DWP can't get around the courts to get any more water out of us. They'll try to protect what they have, but they're going to lose fights about Colorado water and about Delta water up north and about our water, too. And then they and all the rest of the Southern California water companies are going to have to stop promising people that they can have water wherever they build houses. So they are going to start to sell DWP land up here. And the Valley is going to have 40,000 people by 2020."

"Never happen. The greens and the Sierra Club and the courts won't let them."

"That's where our friends in the other nations are going to help us out."

"The other nations? Like Saudi Arabia?"

"No. The sovereign nations right here—the tribes. Our friends the Paiutes have legal standing in the courts that the Sierra Club could only pray for. They don't always win, but when it's their economic development we are talking about, they have a great shot at blocking anything the greens want to do. The tribes' legal standing and the red ink in the federal budget and in DWP's budget are all going to add up to big time political clout behind more development up here. And we're going to be in the middle of it."

Fred paused, looking out the window at the Whites to the east. He turned back to Will. "Our friends from the tribes are going to help out a lot. You know those homes we built on the reservation for cost last year—the project we did with the tribal leadership in Bishop and Lone Pine?"

"Sure. We could have made a lot more on those than we did."

"We were buying good will, not houses. And now it's time to cash in." Careful to avoid being specific enough to tempt Will to sell what he was hearing, Fred went on. "When I was back in Washington last year, I met with a lobbyist who works with the geothermal industry. He said his people have been looking at the Valley for a long time. They have maps detailed down to the square foot of who owns what. And it turns out when the feds did the big land swap in the 30's with the Paiutes, the tribes ended up with some of the land along the river.

Some of it has very high geothermal potential. There's nothing new about this—the industry leaders have worked with tribes all over the country and with the BIA. Once they got the BIA and the BLM talking to each other, everybody realized that there were thousands of square miles of geothermal areas that were controlled by the reservations, and lots of BLM and Forest Service land close by. That means the tribes can control energy development much more than any of them have yet taken advantage of. And the Paiutes could be in better shape than most of them."

"How so?"

"We work with them to keep it local. Help them set up a development company controlled by the tribes that creates local jobs in the geothermal industry—a hell of a lot more jobs than the bloody casinos ever brought in." He paused, pushing his worries about Dale's gambling out of his mind for the time being. "If we can just get somebody to take out this bastard who is going around killing people, we'll be in great shape here, Will. The 19th and 20th century in this Valley were all about who gets the water; the 21st century is going to be about who gets the hot water. And we're going to be in there, getting warmer and getting richer."

"A few weeks ago you said you were a green green."

"Right—I'm for making money with this environmental stuff."

"But what if it's the right thing to do—and it makes us lots of money?"

"All the more reason to do it, right?"

Will looked at Fred and shook his head. "How'd you figure this out?"

Fred looked smug. "I kept looking at the steam coming out of the ground on the way up to ski. Always there, summer, winter, the steam still comes out. And I realized that anybody who could tap into that would have a lot of power—both kinds of power."

CHAPTER 38

The Three *Amigos Viejos,* which is what Sam Leonard, Ernie Scott, and Bill Solomon called themselves, had begun meeting every few days to compare notes, drink beer, and smoke cigars. Sam was anxious to stay out of sight, as a well-known journalist who might draw too much attention to their highly unofficial efforts. So Bill had been the official face of the "investigation," with Ernie using his ties to the Sheriff as a backchannel to find out what was happening on the official side.

Their explorations turned up little about the killer, but Sam, quietly working his statewide connections in the world of journalism, had found traces of a Sacramento-based casino investigation that seemed serious. Bill had also picked up a report from the county planning staff about a rumored land development project that had something to do with the Paiutes' water rights. But they had not been able to dig out any more useful information, or put the pieces together. So they were taking a break, doing what older men do sometimes, which is telling stories and swapping memories, occasionally getting in the vicinity of the truth of their lives.

Ernie sat on his porch, watching the afternoon sun on the Sierra, and made a long, weary sound. Sam said, "What the hell was that sigh about?"

"Grace Slick, man."

"Grace Slick?"

"Yeah. Just about the horniest looking woman of the last fifty years."

"Grace Slick? Jefferson Airplane Grace Slick?"

"Yeah. Perfect face, sweetest mouth in the world, sweet little bod. And when she sang, she was as far out there as Joplin. There's a picture somewhere of the two of them, Sam. Icons, just sitting there in San Fran somewhere in the 60's. An era in the faces of two wild women. Something made me think of her."

Sam shook his head. "She does benefits now, Ernie."

"Who, Joplin? Joplin is dead."

"No, Grace Slick, I read it somewhere."

"Oh."

"She's about 60, man."

Ernie moaned and then snapped, "Oh, shut the hell up. Why do you have to ruin everything?"

Shaking his head, Sam said, "You need some reality with your prunes in the morning, Ernie."

Sam had noticed Ernie's collection of calendars in the hallway, which included a classic collection of early Playboys. He mentioned it, noting Ernie's out-of-date tastes. Ernie quickly defended his choices as authentic, stressing that most of the pictures were from the pre-saline enhancement era. Warming to the topic, he began expounding his various theories of the breast.

"Sam, you know how much I love breasts? I click everyday on the mammogram site—www.thebreastcancersite.com. Gives mammograms to women who can't afford them. You gotta put your money…you know." He drank his beer, giving Sam a hugely self-satisfied smile.

"You are objectifying women, Ernie. You are pathetic, as well as antiquated."

"No more than God objectified them when She made them."

"She?"

"I figure God has to be female because She got the design so right. God could have had a terrible sense of design—could have made the gorgeous things a lot more functional, stuck the faucet on their elbows or coming off of their chins. Or something like that—would have worked the same for the little ones, but sure would have spoiled it for the rest of us."

"Oh man, you are weird." Sam shook his head, fairly well disgusted. "Their *elbows*?? How much time do you spend every day thinking about that stuff?"

"Not a minute more than an hour a day. I'm not *obsessed* with it, Sam." He managed a minimal amount of indignation, knowing that Sam was onto him, and not caring all that much. "Sometimes," he said, "a fixation is just fine. If you are obsessed by the right thing, it can give shape to your whole life."

And then Ernie got serious for a moment, and once again reached into his bookshelves, finding a small volume and opening it to a turned down page.

"Listen: *'Behold the three blessed curves: the curve of the mother's arm around the nursing child, the curve of the child's upturned face, and the curve of the blessed breast itself. On that sacred geometry an entire religion could be based, resting on the certainty that God is female and that She knew precisely what She was doing when she designed the whole perfect arrangement—aesthetics, function, all of it.*

The message of those three perfect curves is so simple, so clear: we are to care for others, giving them whatever we can, giving them all that they need whenever they need it, from our deepest and most nourishing selves. Nestled within those three blessed curves lie total dependence, total need, and total, loving response to another human.'"

He looked up, and asked them, simply, "What else would you need for a religion? It is enough."

Sam replied, nodding, "You've got a point, Ernie. And it's true that Madonna and Child inspired some of the finest art in Western history."

And Bill added, quietly, "And John Steinbeck got it right, too, in *The Grapes of Wrath.* Only they left that part out of the movie…" He looked at Ernie. "Hey Ernie, who wrote that part you read?"

With only slight embarrassment, Ernie answered, "I did."

Since the conversation had become quieter, Sam tossed in a question he had often wondered about on the long drive out across the desert. "Why do you guys live up here, anyway?"

And Ernie and Bill started in on a refrain that seemed almost rehearsed. Ernie began. "It's the air."

"It's the color of that sky." Bill looked out to the west, toward the Sierra.

"It's that we have real fall and winter up here, there are seasons, and they matter. And they can kill you if you are out in the weather in the wrong time and place."

"It's how close we are to the land."

Ernie said, "It's that we are all imports. We're *all* imports here. The trout aren't native—they're from the other side, where they could originally get to the ocean. The elk were brought from the San Joaquin Valley, too. The Dutch "bakkery" sure as hell isn't native. We all came here from somewhere else, and we all love the land. The only question is how recent the label on the import is."

Bill said, "It's when you get busy in the house, writing or doing something on the Internet. And you forget for a moment where you are. And then you decide to step outside and you lift your eyes up to the hills and the mountains beyond. It's the Psalms: *I will lift mine eyes up to the hills. From whence cometh my help...* "

Ernie was quiet for a moment, then added, "It is that when my kids were growing up, they could get on a bike and ride for ten miles, and I knew they were safe. Until this latest BS with this killer."

Ernie went on, into a kind of reverie. "Each of these little towns is really three or four little towns. And a lot of it is invisible unless you are looking for it. There is the tourist town, the lures dangled to snare passing dollars that you see when you drive through on 395: the outlet stores, the sporting goods stores, the fairgrounds, the museum, the gas stations, motels, the liquor stores. Then there is the town that people live in: the houses that start a block or two behind Main Street, the rez, the mobile home parks, the bars, used car lots, and the churches. And then there's the town the kids live in: the schools, the playgrounds, the park, the streams that run through town where kids can play and the movie house and the high school parking lot and the front lawn where the older ones hang out. And the old folks have their own town, too: the rest homes, the hospital, the long-term care facilities, the senior centers.

"When you put it all together, you get a town that outsiders may sometimes look down on because of what's missing. But outsiders don't spend much time watching little boys and girls run around after soccer balls on a summer evening with a Sierra sunset as background scenery. And the tourists love to come and watch the mules and the rodeos, but damned few of these spectators ever had ancestors like mine, who actually moved goods up and down the valley and across the Sierras using pack animals. Or ancestors like the Paiutes', who could live through the hottest summers or coldest winters and take care of their kids and the land at the same time.

"And so the history and even the geography is invisible, because you can drive through most of it at 70-75 miles an hour, and when you have to slow for the towns, they're small, and the dollar-trapping retail is what's most visible. But there's a lot more that lies behind the main streets. That's what these little towns are all about."

Bill said "Yeah, it's the towns, but it's also the emptiness. Sure, it would be great if it were green from the foothills of the Inyos all the way up through the Alabamas. Orchards again—that'd be nice. But how many hundred thousand people do you think would come up here in the first ten years after we got all the water back?"

Nodding agreement, Ernie said "We are blessed with a great emptiness. Mary Austin did us a favor, even though she ran out on us, when she called that book *The Land of Little Rain*. Puts people right off, a title like that. Thanks, Mary." And he raised his bottle of Sam Adams in a toast.

Bill Solomon laughed to himself. "I always wanted to help make a movie up here that would show how dry and desolate it was, just to keep people away. Was going to call it *How Brown was My Valley*.

Ernie chuckled. "Yeah, good idea, Bill. Or remake *Pale Rider* and call it *Pale Rider, Brown Hills*."

Getting into it, Sam offered, "Or *The Magnificent Seven Dry Years*. Or *Dances with Dust*."

They went on in that vein for several more beats, and then fell silent.

Ernie stood up and rummaged through a foot-high pile of news clippings. "I read something by a guy who seemed to get some of it, let me find it. Guy who used to live up here." He flipped through the files, then pulled a single page out, waving it triumphantly. "Here it is, listen to this."

How does the land insinuate itself into the emotional makeup of the people who live on it? How does it shape and give tone to their politics, their openness, their isolation, their sense of what they owe their neighbor, if anything?

Does the beauty of the land make people more aware of nature's grace, and more inclined to protect that beauty? Or, seeing it so often, do they take it for granted and assume the beauty will always be there?

Does the hardness of the land make the people harder? Or does it make the people more forgiving, because the land itself is so hard and unforgiving? Does the isolation of the place mean the outsider is always the other, easily recognized as not-from-here, and thus suspect as the stranger? Or does it mean travelers are welcome, as they are in some of the vaster deserts of the world, because the land is so harsh that the people have chosen, over the millennia, to offer shelter?

Someone once said the Good Samaritan parable would be incomprehensible to anyone who actually lived in a desert because the code is to offer hospitality to anyone who needs it. The land may not create morality, but it may shape the values underlying the morality adopted by a people as they struggle to live in an unfriendly but beautiful land.

They were silent, and then Bill spoke up. "The Good Samaritan parable—seems like a long way from what is going on here. This whole thing with the killer reminds me of *The Ox-bow Incident*, you know?"

"Never saw that one, Bill," said Ernie.

"Old one, 1943 or so, filmed right here in the Hills. Henry Fonda was in it. A whole town decides to hang three guys for rustling cattle, but they get the wrong guys. It's about mob justice, sort of."

Ernie scoffed. "Great, Bill. So we should look for people getting hanged from now on?"

"No—but we should watch out for people taking things intro their own hands if it goes on much longer."

Sam said, "Maybe that's what's going on here. The people in the Valley are having a hell of a time figuring out how to react to this guy, and the messages he's leaving at these 'evil places.' Brings up a lot of old crap that's been around for a long time."

Ernie said, "Little bit of *To Kill a Mockingbird* in there, too. How the town reacts. Who stands up and who goes with the flow."

Sam said, "Right. But where is our Atticus Finch when we need him?"

For once, Bill had no answer.

CHAPTER 39

The next morning, Liz began patrolling on the Laws road northeast of Bishop, turning south to move along the back roads that paralleled the old train tracks running from Laws to Owens Lake. She knew Howard would cut her a lot of slack on where she was for the next few days, and she had decided that she would try to cover some ground that no one else had worked yet. She had heard a report of shots fired at someone's mobile home east of Big Pine, and wanted to see what she might be able to turn up. At worst, she'd stay out of the way as Howard had ordered, and she might manage to find something useful.

Liz had been able, with some help from Paul and a good night's sleep, to adopt her "on to the next game" routine, drawing on her years of basketball. Liz was a good enough player to have been second team all-league. "Short, good shooter, and tough as hell on defense" was the consensus on her skills. She liked basketball, the flow of it, the marvelous blend of team and individual, where both mattered.

She had once seen Diana Taurasi, the Connecticut all-American who played professionally for the Phoenix Mercury. In women's pro basketball, $15 gets you a seat close enough to the bench and the floor to see the players' facial expressions up close. Taurasi was amazing to watch, a pure spiral of energy, whirling in warmups to give the rest of the team high fives, whirling to break away from a defender and take her shot, whirling on defense to get to the right place before a player from the other team knew that's where she was going. She would stand bouncing in warm-ups and during much of the game, just bouncing, draining off her sky-high energy in constant movement.

Liz never forgot that movement, and the smile, usually broad, sometimes almost feral, as Taurasi saw an opening and moved toward it or made the pass that made the shot open up. Liz coveted Taurasi's ability to see two moves ahead, to keep moving, to keep her opponents off balance with moves too quick to be anticipated. It got Liz in trouble sometimes, but quickness was what you needed as a point guard in women's basketball, and quickness, Liz thought, was what you needed as a woman in police work in goodoldboy territory. You couldn't let someone else force your reaction; you had to keep moving, and you had to get there first.

And yet Liz also knew that she had gone after the guy in the meeting too hard, and it had cost her something she couldn't afford to give up. Taurasi never stopped and argued—she just made the next shot and let her game do the talking.

As Liz came around a turn in the dirt road, she saw a faded blue pickup parked on the road where it ran alongside the river. The river was only about ten feet wide at that point, and two men were kneeling down beside the river, watching something in the water.

She parked her cruiser about a hundred yards down the road where they could see her. She checked her holster, got out, and closed the door loudly enough to let them know she was there. She had learned early in her patrolling days, after a near-shooting incident, that surprising people out in an isolated area was never a very good idea.

As she drew near, they glanced up at her from whatever they were watching, clearly having heard her long before she got near. She saw they were Paiutes, one with a long braid, the other with shoulder length hair hanging loose. "Hey guys, what's up?"

"You work with Rudy Warland, right?" the one with the braid asked. She nodded, and he went on, "We're part of the tribal patrol that's been looking for this killer. See what we found," pointing into the water.

She bent over the steep bank, looking into the river. A tree root jutting out from a curve underneath the bank had caught a plastic gas container, which was bobbing in the current.

The braided one spoke again. "Maybe some asshole fisherman, maybe someone riding around out here who needed extra gas and threw this away when it got empty?"

Liz thought it was probably the first, but said "Maybe. Let me go get a tent pole from my car. I'm Liz Nolan." They introduced themselves as Robin Patricio and Chris Watson.

She walked over, rummaged around in her trunk in the box of camping supplies until she found the extending rod, and walked back while unfolding the pole. Patricio, the braided one, reached out his hand for it, and seeing that he was well over six feet tall, she handed it to him, realizing that his reach far exceeded hers. He poked around for a few minutes and freed the can, managing to hook the handle on the end of the pole and lifted it out of the river, tossing it over on the bank near their truck.

As the three of them knelt to look at the gas can, Liz started to caution them not to touch it, but then realized they hadn't made any move to do so yet and thought she would just assume they knew procedure. She pulled a plastic glove out of her back pocket, seeing that they were waiting for her to handle the can, and was glad she had kept her mouth shut.

Watson grunted. "Four dollars at any Walmart from here to San Diego."

Patricio replied, "Yeah, but why didn't it sink?"

Liz turned the can over and saw on the bottom an attachment that looked like it wouldn't fit into a car. Watson recognized it first. "Nozzle for a motorcycle or something small. Now who throws away a gas can for a motorcycle?"

Then Liz, getting a bit excited, answered "Someone who needs a lot of gas because he can't use stations and is traveling on a lot of back roads like this one. Maybe we've got something, guys. Nice work." Then she realized two things at once: she was supposed to be out of the line of fire for the moment, and it was their find, not hers. "Why don't you call it into Rudy?"

Patricio smiled at her, seeing that she had some reason she wasn't telling them that convinced her to let them make the report, "Sure, we could do that."

Two hours later Rudy called her on her cell, off the department line. "I hear you ran into some of my pals out east of Bishop. Good catch, huh?"

"Very good catch. Those are good guys, too."

"They're the best. Some of their buddies would have started shooting at a can floating in the water just for the hell of it. But Robin and Chris knew it shouldn't have been there. They were glad you showed up to give it a good housekeeping approval." He went on. "We're sending it out for prints, but it was probably in the water too long. But the motorcycle is a good tip—explains how this guy is getting by us. Maybe we'll catch this bastard yet."

Hating that she was having to ask, Liz said "Any word from Howard on the other thing?"

"Your thing? Nothing yet. But we all miss your thoughtful words on our partners from the state."

"Screw you too, pal." She was grateful for his light touch, knowing he was trying not to offer any sympathy while letting her know he thought she got a raw deal.

As she drove back along the dirt roads at the base of the Whites, Liz congratulated herself on her choice of language with Rudy. However minor, she celebrated victories over her foul mouth in the same way a smoker counts cigarettes they are not smoking at that moment. Liz was remarkably foul-mouthed, though she worked on controlling it on the job. Her mother, after many years of persistent trying, had finally given up on her efforts to cure Liz. Her father and brothers, comfortable with the language of the military and law enforcement, had never censored themselves around her, and she naturally competed with them in the vividness of their expressions. At times, she won.

Paul quickly realized in high school that foul language was a bedrock piece of who Liz was, and accepted it as he accepted and adored the rest of the full package that was Liz. After they were married, his only demand was that she not bring it home, and Liz was careful about that rule.

Jessica came to her once with a strange smile on her face, and said "Eddie Jencks said his father the policeman said you swear like a sailor. What does that mean?"

Liz deftly explained that sailors sometimes used inappropriate words and that at her work, people sometimes talked that way, but it was only at work and never at home. Jessica gave her the pre-teen look that says *I know what you are telling me is nonsense, but I won't call you on it—yet.*

Liz drove over a rise in the dirt road and came up on a familiar landmark—the gun club site used by the local NRA chapter. As the area around Bishop became more heavily traveled, the rifle and gun club had used the site in the foothills of the Whites as an alternative to the range that had long existed along Highway 395 just north of Bishop. The newer area was used by most of the local law enforcement officers, and there was often someone shooting at the site. As Liz drove up, she spotted personal cars and cruisers she knew belonged to two of her fellow deputies, two Bishop policemen, and a CHP officer. Five of them were out on the range, popping away with handguns at targets set up against a low rise of hills.

Liz parked and got out of her cruiser, walking over to where the deputies were shooting. She recognized two of them, a young new recruit she remembered coming from somewhere in Southern California, and a veteran who was stationed in Long Pine but lived in Bishop. She watched them for a while, noting that the younger recruit was very accurate with the 9 millimeter he was using.

As she watched, she noticed a faint dust trail rising in the further foothills behind and to the north of the range. She watched it for a minute, wondering idly who was driving in such a hilly area without roads. As the vehicle turned toward the range, she could see that it was a two-wheeled rig of some kind.

The CHP guy had stopped firing and was looking up at the dust. "Who the hell is that? He's going way too fast—he's gonna tip that thing if he isn't careful."

Then the gas can memory clicked in Liz's head, and she started running for her cruiser, glancing at the vehicles parked next to her modified Ford LTD. She yelled back at the shooters, now lined up watching her, "I need 4-wheel drive—that may be the bastard we're after, but he's offroad and I need to go after him *now*."

Telling a group of armed law enforcement officers that a felon may be on the run in their area usually has an electric effect—and Liz's shout worked. All five of the officers ran for their vehicles, scooping up their ammunition bags. Seeing that the most durable vehicle looked like a 4-wheel Jeep, Liz headed for it and found it was the new recruit's.

"Come on kid, you've got the best wheels. I'm Liz—what's your name?" she panted as they jumped in the Jeep, which the kid spun around and headed up toward the dust trail.

"Adam Lucas," the kid said nervously. "We met the first week I came on the job, at orientation."

"Sorry, Adam. Head up toward the dust, but watch out for the dips," Liz said, too late, as the Jeep dove off a deeper-than expected roll in the hill. "Watch out, I said!" Liz cried as she bounced a foot or so off the seat, glad that the hardtop that went with that model was back in a garage somewhere.

By that time, the Jeep had moved out ahead of the other vehicles, which were struggling with the sandy foothills. The dust trail from the bike was still visible, and Liz started clicking on the Jeep's radio, hoping she could get some kind of contact with the rest of the vehicles. She used an all-forces channel that she hoped the others had the good sense to flip on when they started out. "Vehicles in pursuit of suspect in the Whites about two miles up from the end of Line Street. Other pursuit vehicles, split up and two of you head south in case he gets past us by going up higher." She knew they would fumble around until they sorted out who was going to stay on the trail and who was going to peel off, but she saw that two of the cruisers had finally turned away from the chase and headed south.

When she turned around, she no longer saw the dust trail. "Where the hell did he go?" she asked Lucas.

"No idea—all of a sudden there was no trail."

"He must have gone up to a higher ridge, over there," she motioned to the east toward the summit of White Mountain. "Cut back and see if we can pick up his trail."

But after ten minutes of criss-crossing the area, they had lost the trail completely. Furious, Liz told Lucas to pull over."He can't have just disappeared—where the hell did he go?"

As she watched, she heard a ping and then Lucas yelled, "Oh shit, he shot my Jeep!" They both scrambled out and took cover behind the vehicle, as Liz keyed her radio and broadcast "Shots fired, suspect still out of sight." Frantically, she swept the hills with her eyes, trying to see a puff of smoke or dust or some hint of where the shooter was holed up. Within minutes, the two vehicles that had headed south came over a rise and Liz realized they may have opened up an escape route.

Lucas inspected the damage, and saw that a definite hit had gone through the radiator, but it looked patchable. Liz could see that the recruit was clearly worried about how he was going to explain getting his equipment shot up, and she felt half-sorry for him.

She looked up just in time to see a faint dust trail far to the south, "Dammit—he got around us. Let me call down to Big Pine and tell the CHP units down there that he may be headed that way."

After making the call, she turned to the five officers who were waiting to see what she was going to do next. "Thanks guys, sorry we missed him. Maybe they'll pick up the trail further south. I think this is our guy. He must have gotten off a few shots when he thought we were getting close. But I have no idea how he just disappeared like that. I'm going to send somebody up here to see if they can pick up some trail."

The veteran deputy responded gruffly, just as Liz remembered his name—Nathan Johansson. "Some psycho out here blowing people away just makes it that much harder for the rest of us. Glad to help when we can."

And the kid surprised Liz by saying, "I'll drive back up there where we lost him and see if I can find anything. He may have some special rig on that bike or whatever he is riding. If it's the guy, he must have been up to something."

But as Liz drove back into Bishop, she heard the frustrated shouts and curses of the Big Pine area patrols—none of which had turned up any trace of the motorbike. The guy had vanished again.

The Avenger was cursing as he rode south at the motorbike's top speed. He knew he could disappear into one of his nearby holes, but he was furious that he had been spotted and that the cops—he knew what the shooting range was and who frequented it—had chased him. But he had accomplished his purpose in being in this area, and he decided it was time to enter the final phase of his plan. The thought of how brilliant it was soothed him as he sped across the desert.

CHAPTER 40

Rudy drove up to Bishop from Big Pine, thinking about his earlier conversation with Liz, knowing she was going to be all right when she got back. The more he worked with her, the more he saw other facets of her. As tough as she was, she cared about people—some people, anyway, recalling their conversation about Brenda.

Rudy was sure that Brenda could go all the way. She had the brains, she wasn't afraid to speak up, and she had escaped the trap of striking beauty. It was when she moved that she was beautiful, and not everyone saw it, so she might not fall prey to the beauty-stalkers with all their financial lures.

Watching her play basketball, he worried that she lacked a hard enough edge. She'd rather pass off than shoot—no flaw in some spots, but sure to cost her team some points at key moments of some games.

She wasn't exotic because of her looks, but she would still be exotic, by definition, different from the white-bread look of the blonde Barbies or the darker Latinas and Asian girls, different enough for some guy to get the courage to ask her "what are you, anyway?" And when she answered, "Paiute, Indian, native American"—whatever, Rudy no longer cared—she'd become a curiosity from then on, because there were so very few like her.

Rudy remembered the numbers from his time at Fresno State. In all of California, there were nearly three million college students. And among them were fewer than 15,000 Indians from all 100 recognized tribes. And among all of them, in the entire state, there were just 160 Paiutes in college. Among them, only 68 Paiutes from the County showed up enrolled in college in the latest census—43 of them women.

And in the entire county, there were only 39 4-year college graduates who were Indian.

So Brenda would stand out, whatever she looked like, however she danced. She would be an oddity, attractive in the ways she looked and talked and moved, but also an attraction, a novelty for some. And Rudy hoped she would learn quickly how to sort out and reject those for whom that was her major appeal, the diversity trophy-hunters, so different from guys who saw how much else she had to offer.

But first, she had to decide to go. And he was torn between leaving it alone, believing most of what he told Liz, but realizing at the same time what a tragedy it would be if Brenda stayed home.

Rudy's brother Ben was much more of a traditionalist than Rudy, and they did not always get along. Ben was younger by three years, and had decided early on that he was not going to try to compete with Rudy either academically or athletically. So Ben had become a faithful member of one of the tribe's most traditional groups, the Wovokas. Taking the name of the originator of the Ghost Dance, the group was dedicated to preserving Paiute language and customs. Its members spanned most of the Southern Paiute tribes and had made some inroads into the Northern tribes up into Nevada and Oregon and Utah.

And college was far from a priority for Ben. Brenda's dance activities had come at the price of her spending most of her spare time involved with cultural activities within the tribe. She had applied to the high school for extra credit in languages for studying Paiute dialects, and was one of the few younger members of the tribe who was nearly fluent in the language. Rudy knew that the only way he could sell university attendance to Ben would be to somehow convince him that Brenda would be able to maintain her ties to her culture while learning the workings of the "outside" world. He wasn't at all sure it was a case he could make.

The Avenger pulled out the third of the five one-time cellphones he had bought, and made the call. He then moved closer to the small rise in the desert outside Big Pine, until he saw the legend on the side of the building. He sighted through his scope on the word "Tribal," which was just above the windows of the one-story building. He quickly fired four shots, slid the rifle back into a case he had rigged onto the back of the bike, jumped on the bike, and headed toward the river. As he went over the wooden bridge across the river, he threw the cell phone in, and headed south.

Rudy got the first call, and he almost wished he hadn't. Shots had been fired at the Big Pine Tribal Offices, and they came immediately after a threatening call had been received at the tribal headquarters. The caller had simply said if the tribal patrol kept driving around, the next shots would be at them. He had added a few choice epithets about the Indians and what was happening to their "squaws" while the men were out on patrol.

The tribal leaders in Big Pine were furious, not knowing whether to blame the anonymous killer or the same hotheads who had shot at the Mexican workers in Bishop. And as the local law enforcement guy, Rudy took the brunt of their anger. They told him off, using some choice Paiute curses, English, and a few ancient Anglo-Saxon words thrown in for emphasis. They threatened to pull out the patrols, and Rudy's response telling them about finding the gas can got nowhere in calming them down.

Liz and Rudy met with Howard as soon as they got into the station. Howard had called Liz earlier and told her that she needed to come into the station and ignore what the state guys had said—he wanted her back on the case. Her role in working with the tribal patrol on the gas can find was a plus that balanced her supposed offense, which no one in the OCSD thought was serious, anyway. And actually flushing out the guy out at the firing range a few hours before the shots were fired at Big Pine was the best lead they had yet that the guy was working the east side of the Valley. So she was back on the job.

The new shootings at the tribal offices had gotten everyone worried. Howard had been at a meeting with the Sheriff that started at 6:30 that morning. He began briefing Liz and Rudy before he even sat down. "Sheriff is off the wall on this one. It's not bad enough we have some nut killing people—now locals are going after locals. And now he's going to have every human rights group in Southern and Northern California after us. And probably some of them are going to come over from Nevada just to make sure we aren't burning any crosses. All because some of the local bums decided to show that they live here and the Mexicans don't."

Rudy sat back in his chair, unsmiling. "I'm trying not to think that this takes the heat off the tribe for now, but I'm just not making it work." As Howard started to point at him, furious, Rudy quickly added, "I know, I know—it's bad, very bad. It means that if this guy was trying to get us to start fighting with each other by what he did to Finnerty, he's succeeding on a whole new level now."

Liz jumped in. "Rudy's not saying it's better—we all know it's gotten worse. But what are we going to do? What came out of the meeting this morning?"

Howard answered, "Sheriff is going to go along with the Board of Supervisors and call a community meeting. They had been resisting that, but now they think they've got to do it to let some steam off. Four days from now, Thursday, at the fairgrounds. Maybe we can get some of this out in the open and start building some backfires. That was the Sheriff's word—some backfires."

Rudy and Liz left Howard and went back to Liz's cubicle to go over the logistics of where they had found the gas can and where the chase had happened at the firing range, so they could mark it on the wall map.

Liz's office was sparse and functional, with a few exceptions. She had pictures of Paul and the girls up on one wall, a picture of her father and her brothers at her graduation from the Riverside Academy, and a signed poster of Diana Taurasi playing for the Phoenix Mercury.

They finished with the map, and found themselves with some down time waiting for Howard to come back to them. Rudy leaned back in Liz's extra chair, faintly smiling. Liz decided to risk a personal question,

"You close to someone, Rudy?"

"I was, at Fresno State."

"What happened?"

"She wanted a different life, in a different place."

"And so you did what?"

"Graduated and came home."

"Yes, but you're changing the subject."

He looked over at her, tilted his head back, and slowly shook his finger at her, mock scolding. "Didn't you ever read in your multicultural psych class about never asking an Indian a direct question?"

"Missed that class."

"You sure did. You don't do indirect so good."

"Nope."

Rudy waited, then said, "You know, I've figured out that you should be related to the pitcher."

"What pitcher?"

"Nolan Ryan. I know that's your last name, but you could have been named after him." He was getting at something he wanted to reveal in his own time, and Liz was going to wait him out.

"I follow football and basketball," she said, gesturing to the poster, "not baseball. Game's too slow for me."

"Nolan Ryan was a pitcher who threw about a hundred miles an hour. Threw it fast, almost always. Got most of them in for strikes, got a lot of strikeouts. But some of them damn near sailed over the backstop. He wasn't always in control, 'cause he threw hard, all the time—never let up." Then he was quiet, just staring at her, still smiling.

"Meaning what? I come on heavy? I sometimes miss?" Liz was irritated, but knew Rudy was trying to make a point in his own roundabout way.

"Something like that."

She looked at him, and came back at him as quietly as she could. "Why do you get to judge me like that?"

"Because you sometimes hit the target dead center in a way most of the rest of us are too cautious to try for. Because you have the guts of a bandit. Because people telling you the truth would not be the worst thing in your job right now."

It was as strong a declaration of support as Liz had ever gotten from a co-worker, and she was shocked at how much it touched her. No one but Paul had ever told her so bluntly that she was good at the work, and Rudy's earlier warning made it all the more powerful.

"Thanks—I think."

"You're welcome."

Howard came into the room, in a hurry, pointing at Liz. "Nolan, the deputy you ran into at the gun club, that kid Lucas, just called. He found what the guy on the bike was doing. Go on up and check it out. Looks like this guy is trying to start another fight."

As Liz walked out to her car, she gradually realized how deftly Rudy had changed the subject to her peculiarities, and away from his. She murmured an oath at how skillfully she had been manipulated, and drove away.

CHAPTER 41

Liz got on the radio and Lucas gave her the directions, which were to a site back up in the Whites about three miles north of where they had seen the motor bike. When she got there, Lucas had pulled his cruiser off the road and was standing next to a pile of lumber. Once Liz got out and walked over to it, she could see that it was a sign that had previously stood on the fenced property that ran from the dirt road back up into the Whites. Liz looked around and then figured out where she was—it was the old Kyle Ranch, which she had just read something about in the *Register*.

A sign had been erected where the dirt road led onto the fenced property, announcing the land gift as a memorial to the original owners, who had held the land in the family for 140 years. That was what the sign had described, in grateful words from the regional land trust to the Kyle family for their permanent gift. It was a magnificent property, including a volcanic cone that rose 100 feet above the desert floor, a stream that ran in the winter months, and a small meadow where the stream widened and was fed by an underground spring. It had escaped the federal expansion of the Forest and DWP land purchases because the owners were too stubborn and the property was too far from the River to matter much.

The sign had been sawed off at its base, cutting through both of the 2x4 supports that held it up. Then the sign had been defaced by running the saw across the letters and slicing off the corners in a random set of cuts.

A note on a large piece of cardboard had been weighted down by an ammunition can similar to those that were used at the firing range. The note read, *Hey, Plant Lovers: Take your pupfish and your stinking wilderness bills and clear out of this Valley forever. You are the polluters—your fences pollute so we can't shoot. Let us use the land as it was meant to be. Only God can preserve the land. Signed, Sportsmen of the Public Lands.*

Lucas said, "Seems like he tried to make it look like the gun club or somebody like us did this."

Liz said, "Sure does. Down to the ammo can. If we hadn't seen him on the bike, somebody else would have discovered this, and it might have worked. Nice work, Lucas, and thanks for staying with it. See if you can get a crew out here to look for prints and check for tire tracks."

Lucas gestured to the dirt road where it turned and headed south. "Found some tire tracks over there—about the size of a motor bike, but a pretty big one. Fits with where we saw him south of here."

"Look around some more and see if he threw the saw away somewhere near here—he may not have wanted to be riding around for long with a power saw on a motor bike. Maybe we can trace it."

"Will do."

Liz drove away, watching Lucas out of her rear view mirror as he began to quarter off the area for his search. She knew the print team wouldn't find any prints, because the guy was certain to have used gloves. She liked the kid, even if he was a hot rodder on the chase. She remembered being that new to the job, and felt a lot older than the kid, and looked forward to getting home to see if Paul could melt away some of her early twinges of middle age.

CHAPTER 42

After the meeting with Howard and Liz, Rudy drove back up to Bishop and pulled into the parking lot at the Crossroads Café. He had finally caught up with Max Chatham, the vice-chairman of the Bishop tribe. Max had been one of his quiet sources when the formal leadership of the tribe refused to speak with him publicly. He had known Max for a long time, had gone to school with and dated his sister for a while. Max was a very aggressive attorney who represented the tribe in the casino dealings with the County and the state.

Rudy had heard that Max was also known to take care of his own extended family, several of whom had jobs with the tribe, the casino, and other tribal programs. Max had an Indian mother and a white father, which sometimes weakened his ability to make things happen within the tribe, and Rudy had heard that he sometimes tried to make up for it by doing deals with everybody he could. Rudy worried that Max would not want to talk with Rudy about the killings for fear that it would jeopardize the autonomy of the tribe.

But Max wanted to talk about something completely different.

After they had reminisced a while about family, Max got to it. "I want to talk to you about some development ideas that might be good for the tribes in the Valley. Some new things have surfaced in the past few months."

"Why me?"

"Because you know people in the county government and have some idea how they work."

Rudy frowned. “Don’t put me in the middle here, Max. That happens to me on the job all the time, and I don’t like it from you anymore than I do from them.”

Max was quiet, studying Rudy. Max wore his hair in a braid, which Rudy suspected was his way of compensating for his law degree and his mixed heritage. Then he spoke, carefully. “I won’t middle you. But this is big, Rudy. For the first time we could go in with the big-money developers and make some serious cash for the tribe.”

“*We* could? The whole tribe could, or you and your relatives could?”

“We all could.” Max was irritated at being challenged, but he still wanted to make the sale, and he was trying not to lose his temper. “These people want some of our land, we control it, and it’s worth millions. Rudy, we’ve talked for years about a real scholarship and housing fund for kids who commit to coming back here to work. This is it—this is the chance to build that. How can you be against that? Plus, you’ve talked ever since you got back from Fresno about how bad you think the casinos are for the tribe. This is our chance to get out from under those crummy gambling deals and get back to our traditions.”

“The casino rips off addicted people and makes money off their addictions. It’s got nothing to do with our traditions.”

“Rudy, look, I agree with you, but we can’t replace something with nothing.” He laughed. “And ripping off addicted people sounds like the traditional American economy to me. The only difference is that people out there,” he waved vaguely toward the south, “are addicted to big-screen TVs and new cellphones every six months instead of slot machines. So two-thirds of the whole American economy depends on people buying stuff they don’t need—isn’t that the definition of addiction?”

Rudy was getting impatient with the debate. “What’s the deal you’re talking about—and who’s proposing it?”

“Let me fill you in. Some of this is tied into the water wars, and some of it’s brand new—it’s more about energy than water.” He paused and said, with a more pleading look than Rudy was used to seeing from Max, “Can I tell you some things and ask you to keep them between us for now?”

Rudy was curious what could be so important, and still didn't see how he figured into it. But he decided he wanted to know more and couldn't walk away from such an offer. He nodded. "I'll agree not to repeat it to any one without your permission—as long as there's nothing illegal about it."

"Deal. It's completely legal. But it's still very confidential." He paused, and then began explaining. "Rudy, there's been a battle building up for years to get our backing for some new development projects in the Valley, and no one knows how it's going to turn out. In the past, on any given issue, we decide case by case where we'll go—whether we'll line up with the greens or the greenbacks—the environmentalists or the pro-growth, pro-business people. Remember that court fight down at Little Lake between those private hunters and the energy company, fighting over draining the lake? The tribe down there got into the middle of that one, and I helped them, because the land that the hunters are protecting from the energy people has petroglyphs and sacred sites on it. On the Owens Lake court cases, we've been with the greens from the start, because the arsenic winds were poisoning us for decades. We've helped the greens, because our land rights and tribal sovereignty made their case a hell of a lot more appealing to the feds, and sometimes to public opinion, too. But you know that sometimes we've been on the economic development side of the argument with the developers, because we needed the jobs.

"Now this one, with the developers trying to use our water rights to make themselves a buck—we're right in the middle of it, too." Max went on to fill Rudy in on the conversations with Fred Bancroft and the energy companies that Fred was representing, and explained what was being offered to the tribes if they signed on to the development agreements.

Rudy was still unconvinced. "You said it's a battle for our backing. Sounds to me like it's more a battle for our soul. How can we sell out on our land rights for energy development that will pollute all over this Valley? You ever see the size of those smokestacks at the Four Corners?"

"Rudy—this is geothermal—you see that steam all over the Valley? It's not from burning coal—it's steam! It's energy that's already here."

"I just hope it's not burning up our future," said Rudy. Then he cooled down, starting to think about what Max had said, and remembering his talk with Janet Fourtrees. "You're right—I hate the casinos. You know there are people from tribes all over the country that are starting to realize how much gambling destroys our way of life. It's a lousy way to make money, even as small as the casinos are here in the Valley—so far. People all over Indian country are starting to agree. But are you saying this is a better deal, or just the latest hit on the federal smoke machine? And how much do you trust Fred Bancroft?"

Max continued explaining the deal and how it could benefit the tribe. He said he trusted Fred, as Rudy made a mental note to check Fred out himself. Max's final argument was one Rudy had never heard before, but made sense. "Rudy, Harvard did a big study of Indian development projects all over the country, and what they concluded was that what makes it work for tribes was not the land, not the resources on the land—but the quality of the tribal leadership. Which is a polite way of saying some of them have crummy elected leaders who are just looking out for themselves and hiring their own families, and some have better leadership. You've heard the stories about the tribes down south and their casino deals. There's a tribe down there on the river that has it all—their own land, right on the river, full title, no questions. But they haven't been able to make a casino and tourist development work because they just keep fighting among themselves. I *know* that, Rudy, and I don't want to be like those tribes. I want us to do it right—I know we've had our own stupid family power struggles in the past, but it's got to end now. This is too big to play games over. Once they catch this killer and things quiet down, a lot of this development stuff is going to take off. And I wanted you to know about it."

His tone was almost pleading at this point, and Rudy could see that he was trying to convince both Rudy and himself that this was truly something new and that he could get the tribe to agree to change its leadership style. Which, Rudy realized, would probably be a good thing for Max, too.

While he was listening, Rudy kept quiet about what he had heard from Janet about the casino investigation. He suspected Max already knew about it, and had planned part of his move away from casinos toward the new development as a direct result of the scandals that were about to break. They talked some more, neither convincing the other, but both agreeing to keep talking.

As he walked away toward his cruiser, he realized that Max had gotten what he wanted, which was a line into the law enforcement community and Rudy's reaction to the whole idea. He wondered what he had gotten.

And then as he headed toward Big Pine, part of the answer came to him. He picked up his cell phone and dialed Max. "Max, Rudy. Thanks for the lunch. I meant to ask you—what's the status of the tribe's scholarship program right now?" He listened to Max's answer and briefly described his niece Brenda's qualifications, then thanked Max for looking into it.

Rudy knew that his phone call came at a price, and that he had entered into the carefully woven net of obligations and debts that his request would set off. But he wanted Brenda to have a shot, and he only felt a small tug of guilt at crossing the line of non-interference. Then he began to calculate how he could deal with Brenda and his brother.

CHAPTER 43

The next morning, Rudy stopped by *Dos Aguilas*. He had breakfast there sometimes, because it was across the street from the Bishop substation and he liked Cecelia. At one point he thought Cecelia was trying to get him interested in her daughter, but no sparks seemed to fly when they met and Cecilia had the wisdom to leave it alone.

Rudy enjoyed the food at Cecelia's place, along with the warm colors and the international flavor of the interior. As he settled in, Cecelia came over and took his order. She turned it in and then came back to his table.

"What you doing these days, Rudy? I hear you're assigned to the team going after the killer. What an awful business, huh?"

"Yeah. We're getting closer, but this guy is nuts and smart all at the same time." He looked out the window for a moment, then abruptly asked her, "Cecelia, do you know Fred Bancroft very well?"

"Fairly well," she said, in a very cautious way. Rudy picked up on her tone.

"What do you think of him? Is he trustworthy?"

"I'm not sure. He's a good businessman, definitely. But I've seen him cut it pretty close when it comes to paying people fairly, if you know what I mean."

"Under the table."

Cecelia nodded, not wanting to verbalize her charges.

"He's been talking to the tribe—just between you and me. And the question of whether he can be trusted has come up."

"I wouldn't want to be quoted, Rudy—I have to get along with everybody. But if it were my people, I'd be very careful. Fred does things for his own reasons, never for somebody else's."

"Thanks. That's sort of what I was worried about. I'll pass it along without letting anybody know we talked. Wouldn't want to ruin of any of your business."

"Appreciate it; let me get your food."

CHAPTER 44

As Paul was beginning his lecture, he glanced up and saw the movement out among the students, and then the derisive expression. He dropped his books, hard, on his own desk, and took five quick steps back to the far row of desks. He leaned way over into the face of a now-startled Rex Richards. "You roll your eyes in my class when I say Manzanar—you roll your eyes at me?!"

"No sir, I was just..." he faltered and fell silent, looking down at his desk.

"Out—get out of my classroom now and don't come back until you learn some respect."

He had lost it, but it was one of the subjects he cared most deeply about, and he would not apologize for his ferocity. For Paul, Manzanar was so close to 9/11 and the immigration wars that he could not moderate his passion. He intended to make them feel what it meant to lock up the Japanese, and to feel the greater shame of knowing the contribution some of those internees made as warriors.

As Paul saw it, Manzanar was about the ugly mixture of bigotry and fear and war that sometimes plagued the country he loved. And it was also about the 2500 volunteer soldiers enrolled from those ten camps where Japanese-Americans were locked up. More than 100 of those volunteers had come from Manzanar alone in 1942, a few months after they and their parents had been locked up behind barbed wire on the worst land that LA Water and Power owned in the Valley.

And for Paul, it echoed down to today, in the 37,000 immigrant soldiers who had ended up in American units in the second Iraq war, dozens of whom were not citizens, dozens of whom had been killed and were then declared citizens—the hard way.

Paul had read the two great books about the Japanese–American troops in WW II, *Just Americans* and *Silent Warriors*, and thought of Manzanar in the same mental sentence as the 442nd Regimental Combat Team—the most decorated combat unit in the War. Those soldiers, including the "Manzanar 100," had bought and paid for the right to say that Manzanar was a huge mistake. And no smart-mouthed high school kid sixty-plus years later was going to question Paul's right to tell the story.

He took a deep breath and said "Who knows about the 442nd regimental unit?"

"Sir, that is a famous unit in World War II, made up of Japanese-Americans, some who signed up from Manzanar."

It was one of the Paiute students, one who had never spoken up in class before. Duane something, Paul couldn't remember his last name and didn't want to look down at the chart. The boy went on. "Sir, with all respect to what happened at Manzanar and the 442nd, there is a long tradition of Indians fighting in white men's wars. My grandfather fought in Morocco, Algeria, Tunisia, Italy and Germany. And there were fifty Oneidas with Washington at Valley Forge."

Duane, Paul now remembered, off-balance, had come to him early in the semester for an extra credit project to boost his final grade. He had been advised by the college liaison staff at the high school to get the best possible grades in his final semester, because he had been waitlisted at a CSU campus. And Paul had agreed, without much enthusiasm, that it would be acceptable to do a project on Paiutes and the military. This was the payoff of that work, Paul now realized.

The boy continued, "Long before the Navajo codetalkers in World War II, Paiutes were codetalking in World War I. You can look it up in Mr. Chalfant's book, page 90," he gestured to the pile of books Paul kept on his shelf, "even though he said rotten things about Paiutes in the rest of his book."

Paul was delighted, not at all concerned that his Manzanar story had been eclipsed for the moment. He was being out-historied by one of his own students, and he was having a hard time hiding his joy.

"You're right, Duane. The story of Manzanar does have something to do with others excluded from American life. Paying for full citizenship in the currency of military valor isn't how we should settle the question of who deserves to live here –but it counts. It counts when people who have been wronged by their country still choose to defend it when it is threatened. It counts a lot.

"General George Marshall, the general who commanded all the armed forces at the end of the war, said the 442nd was 'the most decorated unit in American military history for its size and length of service.' The next time you drive past that guard tower alongside 395 south of Lone Pine, you think about those words—and you also think about what Duane has reminded us of here today." Paul was ready to wrap up the military volunteer part of the story and move on, but then he saw that Duane's hand was still up.

"Duane?" He quickly looked down and saw that the boy's name was Duane Callison.

The boy was not done, and Paul marveled at his clarity and the guts it took to keep after the subject. "Mr. Nolan, we think that if you are going to talk about Manzanar that way, you should talk about Fort Tejon at the same time. One thousand of us taken against our will away from our homes and locked up, just like the ten thousand at Manzanar."

He fell silent, looking at Paul with a challenge, knowing he was right but not certain how Paul was going to react to the final comment. Paul could sense without looking at them that the other Indian students were also watching, and at the same time he felt the scorn building up from other parts of the room.

Paul waited a moment and then responded. "Duane, you nailed it again. The forced march to Fort Tejon that we talked about a few weeks ago was the Paiute Trail of Tears, and it took away the freedom of those people—your ancestors—just as much as Executive Order 9066 did for the California Japanese. And when they were marched south to Fort Tejon, on their way to a relocation camp, they walked right past Manzanar, right past the place where eighty years later, another relocation camp opened."

He continued. "I want to make sure that you all understand Manzanar and who was there. Some of them were college kids, like some of you will be in a few months. They were enrolled in colleges all over Southern California in 1942, and the police went in and rounded them up, and put them on buses and drove them up 395 and dumped them at Manzanar." He was pacing, ignoring the ones who were staring because he had become so intense. "Imagine you're in your college dorm and there's a knock at the door and 24 hours later, you're standing with the rest of your family with one suitcase for all your stuff, in the middle of the most barren desert you've ever seen, and these huge mountains are looming back there and it's March, and it's cold, and you've lost everything you valued.

"Executive Order 9066 did that. Never forget that. We got it wrong, and we must never forget that we got it wrong. We must never make a mistake like that again. And so when you drive past Manzanar, you should bow your head and remember what happened there. Not just about the Japanese, but about all those we locked up because of who they were, not what they did. Feel sad when you drive past that little entry gate and the watch tower. I used to drive by there with my father," and he paused, trying not to let his voice fill with the emotion he always felt when talking about it, wanting so much for them to get his meaning, and not just his passion. "And he would get angry and once or twice he even choked up as he tried to tell us what it meant that our country, which he loved all his life and had served in the Army, had made such a big mistake. You see, he had gone to school with Japanese-American kids down South in Elsinore for a few years when my grandfather worked down there. And my dad could never accept that his friends, guys he played basketball with, had been locked up for four years by his government. It made him sad and angry every time he drove by there—and it should make us sad, too." He stopped, wanting to make sure he could get the next part out without his voice breaking. "They called the camp newspaper *The Manzanar Free Press*!"

A hand went up on the left side of the room, which Paul recognized as belonging to one of the likely UC attenders—Eddie Michaelson. "But Mr. Nolan, what does Manzanar have to do with the Valley? It happened from outside, it was imposed on the Valley, they lived down there by themselves. They came, they were here for four years, and they left."

Paul paused to make sure he was clear. "Good question, Eddie. Let's look at it a little harder. Manzanar has power today because it shows us something that we don't want to see. What happened here was enclosure, exile, and isolation. It shows the power of a people with deep culture to overcome that isolation. And it shows the terrible uses of the power of the dominant culture when it feels threatened, when we become afraid. It shows how frightened we can get sometimes of other nations and cultures. And it reminds us that we sometimes let politicians make very bad decisions because we get scared.

"Let me be more blunt. Maybe Manzanar is about reservations. Maybe it is about some of our more recent history. It is definitely about whether we learned anything. Remember the Santayana quote we started this course out with? Who remembers?"

Predictably Mitch McLellan's hand went up, Paul nodded, and Mitch said, "Those who cannot remember history are condemned to repeat it."

"Yes! That's what Manzanar is about." Then, knowing he was possibly speaking the riskiest words of the entire semester, he added, "Guantanamo. Abu Ghraib." He paused, and then threw his curve. "Today, Manzanar might be about Muslims."

Jack Cunningham, one of the core Baptists, could not contain himself. "No way, Mr. Nolan. Those Muslim guys are killers, we should dump them in the ocean, not lock them up. That's not anything like Manzanar. Sure, that was wrong, when we look back on it. But these guys killed 3000 Americans on 9/11, and some of them are trying to blow up our troops every day. Suicide bombers, scum of the earth. Kill 'em all and let God sort 'em out, I say."

Paul grimaced, and went right back at Cunningham. "Actually, that's what a few of our ancestors said about the Indians. Look, let me be clear here. I have no problem locking up and prosecuting the kind of people we locked up at Guantanamo and in Iraq. They're evil people—most of them. But when we throw away their rights to a fair trial—including the ones that are American citizens—then we have forgotten our own history and how hard we fought to get the Bill of Rights. Either you have those rights when you are a citizen, or you don't. Manzanar is about how we treat people who live in this country but who somehow frighten us. They were *citizens*—they were almost all American citizens."

He waited for a question, and when there wasn't one, he decided to let it lay. He asked the class "And now let's wrap it up. Who knows what comes after Manzanar on the road north?"

And again, Duane got it first. "Independence, Mr. Nolan. After they were at Manzanar, they got their independence back." And Paul knew that should be the absolute last word. He had ignored what was probably still the majority sentiment in the room—though he hoped not—in his effort to tell the story right and to try to make the connection. And a few of his kids had made the connection, and he thought that was enough for one teacher on one day.

Paul sat and graded some papers, cleaned up his classroom and headed out the door. But as he walked into the hallway, he heard yelling from around the corner, in a part of the second floor that he could not yet see.

As he came around the corner, Paul saw Duane Callison being held by the collar of his jacket by a bigger kid and repeatedly banged up against a row of lockers. Distantly, Paul realized in some corner of his brain, as he ran toward the scene, that it was the same set of lockers where years ago he had confronted Liz's tormentor.

He heard the guttural curses of the attacker, a stocky kid whose name Paul forgot, but who had been in a US history course Paul taught two years ago. As he got closer, he heard the muttered message aimed at Duane: "I hear you're in there showing off, trying to make the rest of us look stupid, huh, boy. You trying to make us look stupid, boy?" With each phrase, the bigger kid was banging Duane into the lockers. Paul remembered his name; it was Jud Mills.

Once Paul got to the end of the hallway where it was happening, he grabbed Mills by the arm and spun him around, as Duane slipped away to the side. Paul was lithe and well-muscled, but he could tell the kid was considering swinging on him. Paul leaned over into the kid's face and whispered, "Don't do it; not only will you get expelled, but I will kick your sorry ass if you lift a finger. Turn around and get the hell out of this building. Now!"

The kid looked at Paul with already-dead eyes, and smiled. "Sure, Mr. Nolan. I'm out of here. Just making sure little man here knows who he is." And he turned his back on Paul and sauntered down the stairs and out toward the parking lot.

Paul brought Duane back to his classroom, and started trying to get through to him.

"Do you know the crab story, Duane?"

"No." He was looking out the window, expressionless, ready to be done with the conversation before it began, either frightened into submission by the older thug or going mute as a tactic to stop Paul's questions.

Paul went on. "It's a sad story black teachers tell a lot, and often it's about black kids. But it can be about kids from any group. Sometimes if you put a bunch of crabs in a bucket and one tries to get out, when it gets up near the top, the others reach up with their claws and pull it back. It's about making sure that no one tries to get ahead in a way that shames the group. It's a vicious thing, and it is wrong." He stopped, wanting to get through and afraid he was failing. "Do you understand? You did a good job in my class with that special project, a fine job. You honored those men who fought for their country and their heritage as warriors—you did a good job, Duane. And no misbegotten bully like Mills should make you feel you did anything wrong."

But the kid had shut down, and Paul knew he was not getting through. Duane was at a crossroads as surely as Brenda Warland was, and Paul felt culturally impotent to do anything about either of them. Duane had marked himself as a stand-out, and in doing so had crossed some line of resentment patrolled by a few of the Indian kids. Paul had no idea how many of them felt they needed to enforce the boundaries of mediocrity, but he hoped it was just a few. And they had targeted Duane in a way that might be temporary, until he got the strength to resist, or might last for the rest of his life. Paul told himself he needed to do all that he could to help Duane get past it, and promised himself to call Rudy Warland for advice.

CHAPTER 45

The next night, all hell broke loose when they found the third body at one of the most famous places in the entire Valley, the Alabama gates of the Aqueduct. This was the location which had been the target of the first dynamiting episode in 1924, so it was being watched closely. Four DWP officers had been patrolling that area in DWP trucks, because it was such an obvious place to make a statement.

At about midnight, the patrol heard a terrific blast in the direction of the Gates. All four of them ran off down the grade to see what the noise was. When they got back, the body was there, and they thought they heard a vehicle heading back up into the foothills on a dirt road. They chased it in their trucks, but there were dozens of roads, they saw no lights on any of them, and it was very cloudy, with little moon breaking through the cover.

The body was that of a retired DWP employee, Roger Nilsson, who lived in Olancha. Like the other two, he had been shot once in the head with what looked like a .22. He had worked for the City for thirty years, retired at 55, and lived with his wife in a doublewide off 395. Through her tears, his wife told Liz the next day that Roger had gotten a call to meet someone to talk about some land they were interested in buying.

When the patrol went back to the Gates, they found a small explosion had damaged the walls of the Aqueduct slightly, but it was obvious that it had been intended to cause more noise than destruction. Downstream a few hundred yards they found the remnants of a small raft that had been used to hold an explosive charge set off by a remote device. It had been a perfect diversion, relying on the vivid history of the Gates as the site of the 1924 blast to convince the guards that it had happened again.

When Rudy interviewed all the DWP workers in the area, he came across one possible hit. Ricardo Swift had been working by the Aqueduct that morning, and he told Rudy that he took a break at noon to eat his lunch, walking up toward the Sierra foothills, where he could see a mile or so in either direction. He had seen a man riding what looked like a motorcycle near the aqueduct, but over on the 395 side of it, so he assumed it was someone who had unloaded the bike from a larger vehicle.

When Rudy went to the area where Swift said he had seen the bike, he saw fresh tire tracks going from a pullout on the west side of 395 up into the area below the Aqueduct. The tracks were small and narrow, as if made by a motorcycle of some kind. The rider had circled around the area several times, obviously watching the Gates from different angles. Rudy wondered if the killer had been casing the spot where he had decided to leave the body. And he remembered Liz's report about the motorbike they had chased up by Big Pine.

The media were now going wild. There were TV trucks with satellite dishes in every town in the Valley, from national cable stations as well as the LA and Reno stations. The shots fired at the Big Pine tribal offices had gotten into the news, released by the tribe to make sure everyone got the point about their being targeted. The land trust sign being sawed down was not yet in the news, but it was sure to be picked up and would feed still more speculation about whether one person was doing it, or whether battles had broken out between different factions in the Valley. The media, of course, favored the second explanation because it was more spectacular.

The TV crews were taking full advantage of all the landmarks in the Valley—the views of Whitney from Lone Pine, Manzanar, the Eastern Sierra Museum, the Aqueduct, the County Courthouse. Standup interviews or updates were being taped repeatedly from these and other locations. The tone of the coverage was one part speculation about the motives of the killer, one part rumors about which local groups were attacking other groups, and one part commentary on how obviously the local law enforcement team was out of its depth, with the state or the feds about to take over—depending on which agency had leaked most recently to the reporter doing the story. But the pressure was increasing by the day, and the Sheriff was going to have to react.

Back at the station in Independence, Howard and Liz met with the Sheriff, who wanted to be briefed before the community meeting in two days.

The Sheriff was irritated well beyond his tolerance level for the usual amount of political interference, and he was taking it out on his troops.

"Three homicides and you guys have nothing," he yelled at Howard and Liz. "Nothing!"

"No, Sheriff, we don't have nothing," said Howard, ungrammatically, his own level of frustration building. "We know how the guy is getting around, and we think he may be finished if we can believe the note he left."

"Great! So he's done and we look like crap. And I've got about fifty phone calls over there," waving at his desk, "from LA TV stations, the feds, and half of the top brass at DWP. They want to send a regiment or two more of LA cops up here and someone even talked about the National Guard. But we should tell them we've got it all under control here because maybe this invisible guy is finished killing people on our watch?!"

Like most rural law enforcement officers, Michaels' nightmare was having outsiders descend on his fiefdom. More than most of his counterparts in other counties, Michaels had learned the hard way how to negotiate through the minefields of federal and state agencies who could barely agree on the time of day. But there had never been three serial killings in the County before, and he knew he was about to lose control.

He ended the meeting with Howard's team abruptly, wanting to make calls to all the other agencies likely to have a problem with the latest killing. The LA DWP was at the top of his list.

At the weekly interagency meeting the next morning, the Sheriff took a sharp departure from the past sessions. After discussing the latest killing—which had embarrassed the DWP security forces greatly, thus quieting Holland down—the Sheriff said "As bad as this is, here's what really worries me. If this guy wants to stir up serious trouble, he's not going to keep popping people off one by one. He's going to try to hurt us with the biggest explosion he could set off. And folks, we're a few weeks away from having 30,000 people show up in Bishop for Mule Days. This bastard could make it very hard on us with one phone call to the LA Times threatening to set off a bomb or two at the parade or the fairgrounds."

From the far side of the table came two muttered comments: *Oh shit*, and *he's right*.

The Sheriff heard the second comment: "You bet I'm right. This county's population goes up about 150% for a few days, and that's a pretty fat target. Plus—if he wants to hurt all of us and he knows this Valley as well as he seems to, he knows how much we count on that piece of tourist business this time of year. He can put a multi-million dollar hole in our revenue with very little effort."

"So what are we going to do?" asked the regional BLM manager.

"We're going to think about changing the way we do Mule Days, the business folks are going to tell us we can't do that because they'll lose a ton of money, then we're going to ask them for extra funding for a lot of overtime for a lot of troops. And we're going to watch the crowd carefully and cross our fingers."

"We'll authorize some overtime, Terry." the district manager for the California Highway Patrol said. "I'll get some heat, but everybody down South has read about this and they'll know why we're doing it."

"Thanks," said Michaels. The CHP guys were local, usually, and they got it much sooner than the outsiders.

Afterward, once the agency representatives filed out, the Sheriff had a quick wrap-up with Howard, Liz and Rudy. He made sure the door was closed and then said, "That was partly real and partly to keep people out of my face. I have no idea what's going to happen if this guy goes public with a threat to Mule Days. The handlers and show people will all be here—people who work with mules are nearly as stubborn as the mules. Not a good idea to tell them not to do something. And most of them are armed, so I'm more worried about somebody getting nervous and shooting another mule handler than I am about this guy wearing a vest and taking out the crowd.

"I don't think that's his style, anyway. A guy who shoots people one by one and leaves their body carefully in a special place does not seem to be the kind of guy who blows himself and a bunch of other people up. But I do think he'll try to mess up the crowds, and we may lose a lot of business. So let's talk about how we're going to handle coverage. Then I'll call the other agencies with armed troops and see what we can get beyond the CHP offer."

The Avenger had carefully hacked into a county computer in Independence and used it to send out emails to each Southern California newspaper and TV station, using a master list he had downloaded from the Associated Press. The message was simple: "Tell your readers and viewers that if they are planning on coming to Mule Days in Bishop this year, they'd better wear a flak jacket. Could be an explosively good time this year at the fair! Signed, The Avenger."

And the media spotlight brightened still more.

CHAPTER 46

The *Viejos* group gathered at Ernie's again, and decided to map out each of the incidents they knew about from the media or their own sources around the County. They laid out the eight incidents–the three killings and the other provocations that were likely carried out by the killer—on a map.

Ernie looked at the map and said, "This guy is playing us like a violin. He is doing everything to get us to fight among ourselves." He jabbed the map at Bishop Creek. "He killed Finnerty to make it look like the tribe was involved." Another jab east of Big Pine. "He took shots at the Big Pine Tribal offices to make it look like somebody was getting back at the tribe. Probably was setting that up when he saw my lights and took a shot at me." Jab at Manzanar, another at the Aqueduct. "He tried to bring up all the old feelings about Manzanar, and he is trying to get LA DWP into it and restart the water wars by tossing the dye in the Aqueduct and then dumping a body out there." A final jab in the center of Bishop. "And I'll bet he was the one who left the note in that bar in Bishop that got the shots fired at the Mexican construction crew. And now we hear about the gun club guys spotting him and then the land trust sign being sawed down."

Sam said quietly, "It's the faults."

Ernie snapped, "It's whose fault?"

"No—it's the faults in the Valley. He's exploiting every broken place you have here, the way an earthquake is worst at the old faults that lie beneath the surface."

Ernie was quiet for a moment. "Hemingway was wrong. He said we're all broken and afterward we're stronger at the broken places. That's crap—afterwards it hurts a lot *more* when you get hit at the broken places. In fact, it can be damned dangerous to get hit there." Then he said, "There's this guy Paul Nolan, who teaches history in Bishop, knows the Valley very well, family has been here as long as ours. Maybe we should bounce some of this off of him."

Sam looked at his watch. "School's over. Call him."

They reached Paul at school. "Paul, this is Ernie Scott. I have you on speaker here, OK? Some friends and I have been doing some unofficial work on these killings, and we'd like to come show it to you and get your reactions."

Paul quickly responded, "So why are you talking to me—why not Liz or the Sheriff?"

"Because we think it has a lot to do with the Valley's history, even beyond what the note said, and we think you may be able to help us flesh this out."

"OK. But with the agreement that we go to the Sheriff—immediately—with anything we come up with. And I'm going to tell Liz before we do that."

Ernie said. "Sure. We'll come to you. Where's your classroom?"

The three older men made quite a picture as they strode into Paul's classroom the next afternoon, carrying a large artist's case. They sat down in three chairs pulled over in front of Paul's desk. Paul recognized Sam Leonard's name from his Pulitzer publicity and his Mexico coverage on NPR, and had met Bill at some school meetings held in Lone Pine.

Paul started out. "I'm not sure this is a good idea. I mentioned to Liz that you guys were coming in, and she said she hoped you had something good. So show me what you have." His eyes lit up when they pulled out the map they had mounted on a posterboard with push pins at each of the five incidents and the three killings. Ernie spread it carefully across three desks they had pulled into a triangle.

Ernie took the lead, showing Paul each of the points and then laying out the theory that the killer was trying to provoke more killings. "Sam calls it the fault theory."

Sam shot back, "Ernie saw it first—his CIA training."

Paul gave Ernie a strange look, but got their point. "Sure—the faults under the Valley, the fights and tension among groups in the

Valley." He paused, looking at the map again. "I think Liz and the Sheriff's people see this, but maybe not in the same pattern. This guy is trying to get us to do his work, to start going after each other. He's poking at our weak spots, it's why he dumps the bodies where he does, and it explains the other stuff he's starting to do."

They talked about it some more and then Paul called Liz. She wasn't happy about it, having told Paul he should let it alone, but she agreed to try to set something up with the Sheriff for the next morning.

Ernie, Sam, and Bill arrived at the station in Independence at 8 am. Paul had stayed in Bishop to teach class, after a fairly tense conversation with Liz the night before. As they came into the Sheriff's conference room, Liz tried to keep herself from judging them based on their appearance. It was not just that they were carrying well over a century and a half of mileage—it was their confident air of older guys who hadn't exactly dressed up for the meeting.

Ernie Scott was in a fatigue shirt that had definitely been through at least one war. Sam Leonard had on a white Mexican *guyabera* shirt that managed to cover his tall frame. And Bill Solomon wore a paisley vest over his denim shirt that could easily have been borrowed from the prop room just before the saloon scene in a B Western.

The three made their presentation to the Sheriff, Jack Howard, Liz, and Rudy, with Ernie doing most of the talking, then stopped, waiting for reactions.

Jack Howard spoke first. "Who have you talked to about this?"

They looked at Liz, and she felt a sudden heat at the same time as everyone else in the room.

Ernie answered. "Paul Nolan."

"Anyone else?"

"No, sir."

"And what you have, you got from the public accounts of what happened—from the media, not from any of us." He said it without looking at Liz, but he didn't have to.

"That's right."

The Sheriff spoke up, offering a combination of credential-reviewing and smoothing things over. He spoke to Ernie first, smiling at their history. "Ernie, been a while since we've sampled your cigars and listened to Callas do *Traviata* out on your porch." Then he got serious. "As I recall, you have some investigative background."

"A long time ago, and a long way away."

"It seems you still know how to put the pieces together."

He turned to Sam. "Your work is well known, Mr. Leonard. It's a pleasure to have you up here for a while. And Bill, I haven't been down your way for a movie in too long a time—let's do that again soon."

"Love to have you, Sheriff."

Michaels leaned back in his chair at the head of the conference table. "Now if you three were just three old guys who cooked this up over too much beer, we'd thank you and send you on your way. But your past records are impressive, and you may have helped us see some things we didn't catch at first. We are greatly obliged to you, and I'd like to ask you to serve as informal eyes and ears for us as we go on through this thing." He paused, "There are one or two new pieces of the puzzle that aren't public yet that make your theory even more plausible."

Ernie spoke up. "Thanks, Sheriff, we'd be glad to help any way we can. We all love this place, and we hope you get this bastard before he does any more damage."

"Well, from what you've said, it's the damage we may do to each other that matters as much as what this SOB has done. That's what we're going to go to work on now."

Bill Solomon had been quiet, but now he spoke up. "Sheriff, one more thing, as Columbo used to say. Years ago we went out with a camera crew and made a map of every dirt road within forty miles of Lone Pine that would be a good shot for a car chase or a horse chase. I've got that map—it shows trails that no one else has ever written down. If this guy is using something like an ATV or dirt bike to get around, that's where he's doing it. There's places where the trails go under 395, in cuts they made for wildlife and water, so you can get from the west side to the east side without ever using the highway. There's also a lot of trails along the east side of the Valley, up against the Whites and the Inyos. So you might look at dirt trails all the way down to the county line below Little Lake, because we used a lot of those for shots. I think those trails are mostly still out there."

"Thanks, Bill, we'll check it out."

As the meeting was breaking up, the Sheriff motioned to Howard who went back into the room and talked briefly to the Sheriff, looking up at Rudy as he spoke. The Sheriff moved away, and Howard left the room and walked over to Rudy, motioning him aside. "Sheriff wants to talk to you. Just go and answer his questions. It's not a problem."

Rudy was sure it was a problem, but walked back into the room which was now empty except for the Sheriff and himself. The Sheriff motioned to a chair up toward the head of the table and sat at the head.

"I want to talk to you, Warland. Howard says you've been a big help on the case. Says the elders have been tough to get through to, but that you've tried hard."

"Yes, sir. We've got some communication, sometimes indirect. I'm also in touch with Max Chatham and some deals he's trying to pull off."

"I've heard about some of those deals. I appreciate what you're doing. I know you get stuck in the middle sometimes, and I want you to know I haven't forgotten the talk we had when you were starting out. You've done what I asked, and I admire your guts for hanging in there."

Michaels looked away at the window and was silent for a few moments. "When we catch this guy, it's very important that we smooth things out with the tribes. We all—people on my side of the table, anyway—take things for granted more than we should. I think I can get the Supervisors to move further, and if these new jobs Max and Fred Bancroft are talking about are real, it's going to affect law enforcement in this county a lot. So I'd like you to work directly with me when this case is over and give me some advice on what we need to do to move things with the tribes forward more than a few inches at a time. Will you do that?"

Rudy said, "Sheriff, that's fine with me. The heat I'm taking is nothing new, and I really think the tribal patrols have paid off. There may be some flak about this state investigation, though." Through Howard, Rudy had briefed the Sheriff on his contacts with Janet Fourtrees, and the Sheriff had encouraged him to work as an informal liaison with the state. "They may end up with several dozen people out of work if the state finds problems at the casino, and that will be tough right now with tourism for the summer affected by the stuff going on up here."

The Sheriff nodded. "We've already talked to the Chamber about a big tourism ad campaign down South as soon as we catch this guy, so we don't lose much this summer. But I know it might hit the rez harder than the rest of us if the casino gets cut back or closed. Let me talk to Fred Bancroft about any front-end jobs he may know of on his development deals. And you talk to Max. And Rudy, do everything you can to keep an eye on things out at the rez. I'm worried about some of those young guys getting out of control. That's all we need."

Rudy agreed, and left. Then the Sheriff called Howard in. He quickly explained what he had said to Rudy, and then went to the second set of problems that were keeping him awake at nights.

What worried the Sheriff even more than the Mule Days problem was the magnetic effect the media coverage might have on outsiders—as well as the possibility that some of the most unsavory locals would get fired up by the killings. The 2005 murder of a local resident by a Paiute had been a frightening time for a few weeks, marked by a supposed note from "the KKK" that had dredged up some painful history of racism in the Valley. Earlier, in the 1980s and early 90s, there had been sightings of supposed Klan members, and a militia group based further south had conducted some operations in the High Desert for a few years. The Sheriff had kept a very close eye on those groups, knew their members, and was not at all reluctant to press the DA for longer sentences to take them out of circulation.

The groups had since disappeared, but the Sheriff had authorized two deputies to work quietly to stay in touch with the law enforcement teams in Southern California that had been monitoring Minutemen activities along the border. The construction site shooting was especially troublesome, because it might attract some of the Minuteman types, given the certainty that some of the workers involved were undocumented.

At the same time, the Sheriff knew that there was a loosely identified group of young men from the reservation who had plenty of real and imagined grievances, and were not inclined to see the point of peacefully debating them. Feelings were also high among some of the older Valley residents about the recent victories of the environmental groups, and he worried that the destruction of the land trust sign might have the effect of rekindling some of those attitudes in ways that could lead to counter-reactions.

As it became more obvious what the killer was doing in probing the tensions of the Valley at their most sensitive points, the Sheriff wondered how long he could keep the lid on.

Driving back up to Bishop after his meeting with the Sheriff, Rudy knew he had been let further inside the workings of the real power systems of the Valley—further than he usually got. As always, his feelings were mixed. He resented being used, but he was honest enough with himself to admit that he was glad it was him and not someone else who was the channel. And he knew he had just seen at closer range than ever before just how powerful the Sheriff was, with ties to the supervisors and the business leaders that placed him at the exact center of the networks of political and economic power. Rudy was glad Michaels was a Sheriff who didn't ignore the tribes or see them as just part of the problem. And he was glad the Sheriff wanted him at his side. But the question he still kept asking himself was what good it would do.

Rudy passed through Big Pine, and as he drove, for some reason he thought about Estelle Thomaston. Estelle had been Rudy's girl in their senior year, and after he left to attend Fresno State, she rebounded quickly and badly and ended up in a terrible marriage to a computer game addict. The guy was rumored to live on meth for days at a time trying to build up points in online fantasy war games. When Rudy started his job with the OCSD, he had asked about her, and found that Estelle had three kids and was in constant trouble with the county child welfare agency.

Three years ago Rudy had visited her singlewide home, deliberately out of uniform, on a weekend. He had heard that her husband was locked up again after getting into a fight at a local liquor store. He visited her out of a tangled set of motives, wanting to see if he could help, wanting to see how bad off she was, angry at her husband and wondering if erasing him off the rez with a long-term prison sentence would make Estelle's life any better.

But he left the trailer feeling worse than he had when he entered. Estelle was non-responsive, barking at her kids as Rudy tried to talk to her. She merely grunted when Rudy offered her help and suggested that she go to the tribal social services agency. He saw the large computer monitor set up over the bed in the back of the trailer, with a stack of electronic games piled up on the bed. And he left wondering which addiction was most undermining the family he had just seen—meth, online games, or a downward spiraling lifestyle.

As he left Estelle's place, Rudy thought of the dozens of Paiute families' homes he had visited up and down the Valley that were pin-neat, with flowers in the front yard and vegetables in the back. And at the same time, he looked around at the near-caricature he saw around Estelle's home—wrecked cars up on blocks, sagging roofs of carports, refrigerators lying on their sides. In his head, he knew there were many more white families living in such squalor, from Pearsonville all the way up to the Sherwin Grade. But in his heart, he felt shame at what he saw as he drove down Barlow Lane that day.

Whose fault was it? As he came closer to Bishop, Rudy thought about the briefing for the Sheriff by those three old guys. He remembered their theory of the faults in the Valley and how the killer was deliberately probing each of them to create more havoc. But *whose* fault?

Or did the faults go so far back in time, so deep in the Valley itself, that it was useless to figure out where one began and another left off? Like the fault maps geologists created, with dozens of little lines drawn on the surface that represented large gaps in the earth's thick crust lying many miles beneath, invisible, and so tentatively understood, that the mere lines on a map were almost meaningless. Because once you looked up from the map, you still had no idea which of the hundreds of lines was the most likely to fracture, and so you could only submit to time and resign yourself to waiting for the next one, making sure that you were ready, certain that another great shaking would come someday and that it would test all who lived through it.

Heading back toward his office, Rudy made a short detour, hoping to get a lift from another trip down Barlow Lane. And then, as he came around a corner, he got what he was looking for. Straight ahead he saw the new Head Start Center, where he knew that sixty Paiute preschoolers were getting a great early start on their education, in a brand new "green" building that used the latest technology to save energy and give the children and their families a fine place to start their journeys into learning. He could see some of the children out in the fenced yard of the center, playing on the slides and swings. And he drove on, offering silent hopes for the futures of those children.

CHAPTER 47

"Dale, this has gone too far."

Sitting at their breakfast table, Fred began talking without anger, which made it even harder for Dale, because he was stating facts, and she knew there was no way she could deny them. So she decided to meet him halfway instead of trying to talk her way out of it. But in the back of her mind, she kept hearing the words of one of her fellow addicts in a group session ten years ago: *I'll say anything to get the next fix—I'll even promise not to do it again.*

"All right. I screwed up. What do you want me to do about it?"

"I want you to put back what you lost, and I want you to work for it this time. I'm not going to just give it to you. And I want to take over your checkbook for six months or so."

That hurt. Dale had never had money of her own, and having a spending amount that came with no questions asked had given her a good feeling. But she knew it had also been how she got into trouble. And she realized, as she considered Fred's "offer"—which she knew was a well-worded ultimatum, not an offer—that he had not yet said that she had to stop gambling.

"How am I supposed to work for it? I don't have a job, and you said you never wanted me working for the firm."

Fred said, "I was mistaken. I was worried that you'd get bored making coffee and having to do what I told you. But now paying this back is more important. I'll pay you a thousand a week, and we'll see if you've earned back any of that after twenty weeks." He stopped and looked at her with a mixture of affection and frustration. "Dale, I'm on the edge of a bigger payoff than we've ever seen—a payoff that will remake this Valley. And I could use your help making it happen. But it won't happen if I am spending my time wondering where you are and what you're going to do next. I want this deal to go through for us, babe. I want us to get some time away after this comes together and go to some of the places you've always wanted to go. Italy, Greece, Egypt, Brazil—we could do that if this comes together. But I need to give this my full attention, and not worry about you getting into trouble again and having to bail you out. And I'd like to have you helping me, if you want to."

Dale was off-balance. She wondered what had moved Fred away from the stolid, business-obsessed mindset that had made him so boring to her over the past few years. But she knew this was the best deal she was going to get. And then she also remembered, painfully, that when Fred had come out of the few therapy sessions they had done together, he told her that he agreed with the counselors when they said he was an enabler who had let Dale fall into the pit of her addiction. And with his next words, he confirmed it.

He leaned forward. "This is probably our last chance, babe. Your last chance to get clear of this stuff, and our last chance to put ourselves back together. I don't know what else I can do." And then he reached out and took her hand, trying to get through. "It's not the twenty grand you lost. It's that I won't ignore it any more."

She knew he was right. And all she could say, with tears beginning to come, was. "I know, I know. I'll do it. I will." And as he stood up to hug her, she hoped she meant it.

CHAPTER 48

No one remembered where the idea for a Valley-wide community meeting first came from, but the Sheriff and his crew knew it was going to be painful. The County Board of Supervisors had told the Sheriff that they favored having the meeting only if the Sheriff would guarantee that "there would be no problems." The Sheriff, who was elected countywide, represented the whole county, not just one of the five supervisorial districts. And so he wasn't all that polite in telling the Board that there was no way he was going to vouch for 20,000 or so people who included some certified nut cases. He said he would have all the available deputies he could find, and they were welcome to ask for local police as well.

But despite the Supervisors' anxiety, the meeting was scheduled. It was held in the biggest indoor room in the Valley, the Charles Brown Auditorium at the fairgrounds. They had crowded nearly a thousand chairs into the building, and they were nearly all full ten minutes before the meeting began, with people still milling around outside the doors.

As Liz drove up with Paul, they saw more than twenty Sheriff's and police cars surrounding the building. Even though a few of them were just parked there to look like more officers were there than were actually on duty, Liz knew that it was deliberate that all the light bars were on and blinking while people were arriving. Liz and Paul took their seats in the back so Liz could stand along the side of the room once the meeting began, visible in full uniform.

The Sheriff stood up and walked up to the front of the room. Everyone could see that there were ten uniformed officers with sidearms and clubs within a few steps of the rostrum where he was standing, and several dozen more around the room.

The Sheriff waited for quiet, and then said, "Evening, folks. We have some serious problems that we need to talk about, and we're going to do it the right way. Anyone who wants to start yelling when it isn't their turn to speak will be asked once to sit down, and if they don't get the message, they will then be escorted from the room by my deputies. There is enough rotten stuff going on out there," he motioned toward the door, and then lowered his voice, leaning into the microphone, "*and we aren't going to bring it in here.*" He smiled, and asked, "Any questions?"

There weren't any, yet. The Sheriff gave a 10-minute briefing, using a map on the LCD projector to show where the three victims had been found, the same map Liz had used when briefing the interagency team a week earlier. The map also showed the Aqueduct, the reservation land, and the boundaries of the National Forests. Someone had gone to some trouble to add in the historic markers—all fifteen of them, from Olancha to Bishop.

Howard had told Liz and Rudy that afternoon that heated negotiations had gone on about who was going to be allowed to speak after the Sheriff and before the floor was thrown open. The planning team had finally agreed that the Chairman of the Board of Supervisors, the Chairman of the Bishop Tribal Council, which was the largest of the four reservation groups, Cecelia Flores, on behalf of the Owens County Hispanic Council, Rob Morrissey from the Owens County Business Council, and Elaine Carpenter, who had been selected by the Ministerial Council. The local Assemblywoman had been asked to speak as well, but she had to attend an emergency session at the legislature in Sacramento. The state and federal agency representatives and the DWP had all wanted to speak, but the Sheriff pointed out that having people talked at for more than an hour probably wouldn't make for a very pleasant meeting, and he had promised to call on the representatives during the open floor session.

The Chairman of the Board made wholly predictable remarks about how everyone had to stand together in a crisis and how violence wasn't the answer, seating himself with a great, palpable sense of satisfaction that was shared by no one else in the room. Then Eddie Turnower rose and looked around at all the attendees with a faint smile.

He began, "I represent the Bishop Tribal Council, with our respect to our brothers and sisters in the other three tribal councils in the Valley. We are glad to have been asked to help find the evil one who has killed three members of the community. We are here to talk about who is harming us, all of us. But to deal with that honestly, we must talk about the harm done before this evil man began.

"Because one of those killed was a man who said evil things about our people, some people blamed us. Now we have seen that the killer, whoever he is, has also tried to harm us by shooting at the Big Pine tribal offices. So no one should believe any longer that anyone from the tribes has done this thing." He paused for a long beat, and then went on. "We have endured many attacks in the past, and we will endure more. Who stole this land first? We had territorial rights, and you ignored them. We dug the first canals in this Valley thousands of years ago, and planted the first orchards, and you took them and drove us off the land."

At that, a faint *Oh, sit down and stop complaining* came from the back rows. Turnower stopped and glared the room into silence, as three deputies, including Rudy, quietly moved a few steps toward the seated members of the audience.

Turnower went on. "Then *you* owned the land, and then the DWP overpowered you when they got the water rights that they wanted. And now *you* are crying." He paused and looked around the room with disdain. "Be glad the DWP does not march a thousand of you across the desert to Fort Tejon."

Then he softened it with a wide smile. "Now if you will forgive me, I want to tell a story that some of you may have heard, but it seems like a story we all need to think about here tonight." He tipped his head back and began a kind of recitation, telling a story he had obviously told many times before. "When NASA was preparing for the Apollo Project to the Moon, the astronauts went to a Navajo reservation in Arizona for training. One day, a Navajo elder and his son came across the space crew walking among the rocks. The elder, who spoke only Navajo, asked a question. His son translated for the NASA people: "What are these guys in the big suits doing?"

"One of the astronauts said they were practicing for a trip to the moon. When his son relayed this comment, the Navajo elder got all excited and asked if it would be possible to give the astronauts a message to deliver to the moon. Happy to get some free publicity, a NASA official accompanying the astronauts said, "Why certainly!" and told a staff person to get a tape recorder.

"The Navajo elder's comment into the microphone was brief. The NASA official asked the son if he would translate what his father had said. The son listened to the recording and laughed for a long time. But he refused to translate.

"So the NASA people took the tape to a nearby Navajo village and played it for other members of the tribe. They too laughed long and loudly, but also refused to translate the elder's message to the moon. An official government translator was summoned. After he finally stopped laughing, the translator relayed the message, which said, "WATCH OUT FOR THESE ASSHOLES—THEY'VE COME TO STEAL YOUR LAND."

The audience was hushed for a second, and then it exploded in three very different directions. All the Paiutes started laughing so hard they almost fell out of their chairs, and one elder had to be helped out of the room after a coughing fit. Elaine Carpenter and several dozen members of the audience tried unsuccessfully to control their own laughter, and then let it go. But many of the rest of those in the room just sat and glared at the Sheriff, as if Turnower's "speech" had been his fault.

The Sheriff never cracked a smile, but those on his team who had worked with him longest knew how hard he was working to keep from it. Finally, as the room died down, he said, "Thanks, Eddie, for those words of wisdom. Many of us may have a different perspective on what is going on, but all of us are going to listen tonight."

But before he could introduce the next speaker, Earl Latham, the father of one of Paul's students, stood up and said, while glaring at Turnower, "I know one thing. I know that if Finnerty were alive he'd say that nothing that happened at Fort Tejon or Wounded Knee or anywhere else entitles you to run casinos that prey on gamblers—people with addictions as bad as the alcoholism that plagues your people." And he sat down, to applause from at least half of the audience, a few muttered oaths, and one shout of "and keep your damned beer cans off my front lawn."

The Sheriff stood up, glared in the direction of the outburst, and said "Thank you, Earl. Now I'd like to ask Rob Morrissey from the Business Council to say a few words."

Morrissey, a well-tanned, early 40's man looking as if he had just stepped out of a board room, began by thanking the Sheriff, the County Board, and everyone in attendance. He then proceeded to tell everyone what they already knew—that the tourist business in the Valley was down and would stay down if the murders were not immediately stopped and if any further violence happened, "no matter who causes it, no matter who starts it." His remarks earned dutiful applause, but little enthusiasm.

The Sheriff then called on Chris Carter, a retired DWP supervisor who lived in Lone Pine. Carter was tall and white-haired, with the lean, worn look of a man who worked mostly outdoors. Carter began slowly. "I worked for DWP for thirty-five years. Some of us are hated, because we come in here and we're what they used to call flatlanders and we throw our weight around too much. And some of us get tolerated pretty well because we try to walk lightly on the land, and respect the locals, and truly want more green in this valley. *Lots* more green, to tell the truth. We went native a long time ago, only most of the locals never noticed it. But they sure know it down South at the Headquarters—they don't trust us any farther than they can throw us. They say it happens in the Foreign Service all the time, and it used to be the reason cops on the beat in cities got rotated away from the same places after a while. 'Going native'—a funny thing to call it when the real natives have been here a few thousand years longer than any of us.

"But I'll tell you something I learned working up here for all that time, before I retired. Whatever happened back in the 1900s and the teens and twenties, when you all say the land was stolen, included enough bad faith and betrayals on *both* sides to make sure that not too many of us here can go around preaching to the others. But over the last twenty years—and you aren't going to like to hear this, some of you—you'd be a damned sight worse off if it hadn't been for DWP."

The loud cries of "BS!" stopped him, but only for a moment—"because of the law, and because of the courts," he stopped, trying to keep himself under control, "and because some of us love every inch of this blessed Valley as much as any of you, and have worked a lot harder than most of you to keep it from getting any more raped than it already has been. And we have to find this guy, and stop what he is doing to divide us even worse than we already are. He is betting that we hate each other so much that it will blind us from seeing what we share."

Then it was Cecelia's turn. She rose, patted Rosa on the arm without looking at her, and made her way up to the front. The Sheriff nodded at her, and she began talking in a low, intense voice. "Most of you know me. I'm Cecelia Flores, and I own the *Dos Aguilas* restaurant. A lot of you have come in for a meal, and I appreciate your business. And all I really want to say tonight is two things. First, some of us have been here longer than you think. Second, we are all in this together, *whenever* we got here.

"You may be thinking that I'm going to get up here and talk about those workers who were shot at here in town, and how hard they work, and how they shouldn't be treated that way." She paused, letting her words percolate through their suspicion. "But I don't need to say that. There isn't a single person in here that hasn't already seen these workers around town, and you have already made up your mind about them. Some of you hire them, and some of you ignore them, and some of you wish they would take their kids out of your schools and go home. But what very few of you know is that the first Mexicans who came to this Valley were here long before most of your ancestors—except the Paiutes, of course. Mexicans were doing the dirty work in mines in this Valley and all over Eastern California from the 1860's on. Cerro Gordo was discovered by Mexican silver miners from Sonora, and half of the miners here in the 1870 census were from Mexico, not from San Francisco or the East. And as some of you know, my husband was related to the miners who dug those first mines, and he died in one of them."

She stopped and looked at the audience, some of whom were trying hard to ignore her. "I apologize for the history lesson, and I know Paul Nolan," she nodded at him in the back of the room, "can do this much better than I can. But some of you seem to think we all just got here from Mexico last week. We have been here for a long, long time, and we love this Valley just as much as you do. And those who are recent arrivals came for the same reasons most of you did—to make a good life for their families. If they break the law, they should be sent back home. If they work hard—for you, in most cases—they shouldn't be shot at. What happened to those two men who were shot is terrible, and we don't want any more shooting—at anyone. And that's all."

As she made her way back to her seat, she heard scattered applause, and then some more. She smiled to herself, knowing she had done as much as she could. She had made them listen, and maybe made them think a bit. And maybe the next time one of them heard a neighbor kid bragging about how he was going to go out and rough up some of the Mexicans, someone would say "Ah, leave them alone, what did they ever do to you?"

And as she sat down, she saw Jim Scott who was applauding her with a big smile, and she wondered if she was going to have to suggest that Rosa invite him up to Bishop for a big dinner where she could check him out further.

The next speaker was Tom Newell, a former school board member from Lone Pine, a local businessman who had invested well in projects around the Valley and in Southern California and had spent twenty years on the school board as a widely respected voice for quality education. He had been an advisor to the DWP and to other state and federal agencies in the Valley, and occasionally traveled to Sacramento and Washington to testify on Valley issues.

"I want to talk about change. Now folks, we may all be thinking that things don't change up here too much. A little growth, a few layoffs, but not much change. And maybe that's how it's going to stay for a long time.

"But somehow, I don't think so. I think a lot of what is happening in the rest of the country is going to start to happen here. You know, we're not really immune from energy problems and deficit problems and the problems faced by the rest of the country, just because there are fewer of us and we live further away from things. And if I'm right, and we're in for a lot more change than we have seen in a long time, then we are going to have to work even harder at getting along. And if we don't, then all the important decisions are going to be made by outsiders, because we couldn't get our act together, and they will have to step in and do it for us."

He smiled and asked "Now who the hell would want that?" He waited for the chuckles and "hell no's" to die down. "So the hard work begins after we quiet things down. The Sheriff and all his helpers," gesturing to the uniformed officers lining the walls, "are going to catch this bastard. But when they do that, we aren't going to have anybody else to blame for the problems in this Valley. It's going to be up to us—all of us." He looked at the crowd for several seconds, then sat down.

By now everybody in the room knew that the Sheriff was running the show. He had tried to choose speakers who would have a calming message, despite Turnower's comments, knowing that he was going to get a lot of flak from some of those attending the meeting. His plan, as he explained it to Howard while they were driving up to the meeting, was to "stroke 'em and soothe 'em," in hopes that the softer messages would set a tone that would lower the level of the outbursts that were bound to come. He was making a bet that he could get away with a balancing act between needing to let off steam and hoping that most of the messages were more unifying than polarizing.

Pat Davidson stood up and made his way to the front of the room. He was a geologist with the Forest Service who had served on countless advisory groups up and down the Valley in his decades of service with the NFS. He was a well-known moderate, often able to find common ground between the extreme greens and the arch-conservatives. He rose slowly from his chair near the front of the room, and walked up to the podium. He began slowly, talking softly but using the microphone with the skill of a veteran of hundreds of community meetings.

"Here's what I know from forty years of walking around these hills and this Valley. In this place, this place which has been sacred to some of us, if we are open to the land, we can sense the larger forces that blow us around and sometimes shake beneath our feet. We, all of us, wherever we came from—across the Bering strait ten thousand years ago or up 395 in a rental truck last week—we are the little human things in this vast space of high and low places. The land is too large and harsh to care about us much, and so we must care for each other. That's all there is."

There was a brief hush, then scattered applause. The Sheriff stood up, ready for his wrapup, but before he could begin, a heavy-set, beer-gutted man stood up. Pete Crosby had worked in construction for thirty years, until he fell off a ladder and broke his arm in three places. He lived on disability and beer, and was an amiable feature at several of the Main Street watering holes.

Pete said, in a low, near-growling voice, "I've heard a lot of nice words tonight, some of 'em pretty fancy for people like me. Nice talk, lots of it. But here's what I know. Some evil S.O.B. is out there shooting people, and it will take all of us to stop him. All of us. And so anybody that knows or sees anything had better tell the Sheriff, or this thing is going to get a lot worse. And people will start shooting at each other, just because they're worried someone is going to be shooting at them. And that sure as hell wouldn't be good. That's what I know."

The Sheriff rose again, saying "Thanks, Pete. Anybody else?"

Half way back in the audience, a hand went up and a man in a suit began working his way down the row toward the aisle. It was Wilbur Rostovich, the minister from one of the small churches in Independence. The Sheriff frowned, remembering a story about how disruptive the minister had been in a recent interfaith meeting held in Lone Pine.

"Thank you, Sheriff. I wanted to speak tonight because I keep hearing an undercurrent here, and I'm not sure I like it. The message here seems to be you folks all go on home and stop worrying, because we've got it under control. Sort of like you're saying, you simple folk just leave it to us big shots."

He paused and watched for some nods, and got some. "Well, that isn't going to work. This guy is killing people, and the vengeful wrath of God needs to come down on him and maybe on some of us, too."

There was a snicker from the back of the audience, and Rostovich wheeled around quickly. "You want to laugh at us? You want to call us fundies? You want to look down your nose and think of us as simple-minded, uneducated trailer trash? You go right ahead, friend. But you are talking about half the people in this Valley—maybe more. And those people you think of as simple-minded are out there obeying the law, and staying away from hard drugs, most of them, and raising decent kids, most of them. And we are getting tired of this killer giving all of us a bad name, and if you all—" he gestured to the deputies and CHP officers around the walls of the room, "don't catch this guy soon, then some of us are ready to go out ourselves and start locking up anybody who is not where he belongs."

He paused, and looked around the room. "Some politician recently—I forget his name—called people like us 'bitter.' Maybe, maybe so. But if we're bitter it's because we are getting tired of being lectured by people like all of you who've been up there at the front tonight. Not you, Sheriff, you understand us most of the time. But some of you talk like we have no clue and you need to tell us what is happening. Well, we know what's happening. This is becoming a dangerous place to live, and that is not why we moved up here and that is not why we stay here. And we are going to do what we have to do protect our kids and our property." He stopped, and pulled a piece of paper out of his pocket. "These are the names of fifty men from our church and others like us who will go out on patrol every night until we catch this guy. We hear you have some patrols from the rez, and maybe that will work—and maybe not. We're going to come see you tomorrow, Sheriff, and we want to know what you are going to do next."

He sat down to thunderous applause from more than two-thirds of the room, and for the first time the Sheriff looked uncomfortable. But the meeting went on, for another hour. Some of it was close to Rostovich's threats, and some of it was closer to the softer remarks of Carter, Davidson, and Cecelia. And there was some yelling, but things quieted down after the yelling each time, and Liz finally felt that the Sheriff's careful staging of the initial remarks, combined with the physical presence of armed and uniformed officers, had kept the lid on.

Finally the group appeared to have run out of steam. The Sheriff rose and began slowly, thanking everyone who had spoken, then thanking people for keeping it under control. Then he waited for silence, waiting longer than people felt comfortable with, and then began again, speaking slowly, with intensity.

"It seems to me, listening here tonight, that this evil bastard, whoever he is, has shown us some of the fault lines in the Valley. Not the ones that run under the Valley, but the ones that divide us, all of us who live here. And we will get through this only if we remember that we have more that unites us than what divides us."

He paused, and then added, "Let me ask you all a question to think about, if you would. You can all read the papers, and you watch TV. You know what's going on, even before these killings. We're still disagreeing about a lot of things in this county. The water wars aren't over, the immigration wars aren't over, and some days it looks like the Indian wars aren't over, either."

He stopped and looked out at the crowd, and then asked, in a softer voice, "Do you people just want to keep fighting *forever*?"

He went on. "We still have all these fault lines—who sold their land to DWP and who didn't, who was here first, who deserves to work here and live in this county, who's new and who lived here longest. We have all these stupid little fractures where we are broken or hurt or just suspicious and a little paranoid. And either we build on those things we agree on because we live in this amazing place—or we are just a bunch of animals trying to get more than all the other animals." Then he stopped. "Which do you want to be, folks?"

Holding the silence as a master politician or preacher sometimes can, he waited, and then broke the tension. "Now I want to ask Elaine Carpenter to give us a kind of benediction here."

Elaine walked up, ready for the invitation after the phone call she received from the Sheriff that afternoon. She waited a moment and then pointed casually at Paul, sitting on the aisle in the back. "We were talking in the youth group last Sunday about some of the maps Paul Nolan has been showing his students. Those maps showing all the states in red or blue, depending on who they voted for? Red for Republicans and blue for Democrats, red is conservative, blue is liberal. But Paul did an interesting thing with those maps, something that taught his students a real lesson, from what they were telling me. Those maps are made up by state, so if a state is Dem, it's all blue, and if it's Republican, it's all red. But Paul changes it. He switches the map down to the county level. And then he changes it based on shadings of red and blue, to show that in a lot of places it is 60-40, or 45-55, or even

51-49. And guess what—*most of the map turns purple*. Not all red, not all blue, but purple."

She paused again, letting it sink in. "That's what we need to work harder at—seeing the purple. Seeing where we come together, not where we're opposed to each other. Seeing how close together we are, even when we do disagree.

"You know that song we all learned in school—that song we all know? It doesn't say 'red mountain majesties, above the fruited plain.' It doesn't say blue mountain majesties. It says *purple* mountain majesties. And that is where we live, and that is who we are. And as the Sheriff said, we just have to work harder at seeing it. May God help us with that task."

The room was quiet, for longer than Elaine thought possible. She wondered if she had missed it, if they were past hearing her. And then, from the back, came a ripple of applause, which became a small wave, and then a torrent of noise. She heard some loud Yeses, and even a few Amens. And she said a fast prayer of thanks, and knew some of the hard part was over, though she was not yet done. She still had a sermon to preach, but that could wait for Sunday.

As Elaine drove home, the moon was nearly full, and she could see the Sierra clearly as she headed west up Yaney Street. And suddenly, with a pang of loss, she remembered a recurring conversation she had with Ed.

For Elaine, driving was sometimes worship. Ed had laughed at her, kindly, as she explained her ideas about driving as worship.

"Down South, when I was in seminary, I realized that most of the time you drive around and you deliberately turn part of yourself off, so you won't see the gray streets and the concrete overpasses and the ugly strip malls. So you won't get frustrated and go crazy about the traffic creeping along, and the bad drivers, and the mean ones that cut you off and never let you in from the on-ramps. You just deaden yourself to it.

"But up here, when you drive to the store, to your job, to a meeting, to church—especially to church—if you are not feeing sorry for yourself or mad at someone, if you are open to what is around you in such abundance—you can't help but be filled up with a sense of Creation all around you. A horse in a field up against the mountains, clouds coming in bunched together, blown by a strong wind, the volcano cones rising up out of the middle of a flat desert—it's Creation. I would hate to get to a point where I don't see that any more. Where I don't even look for it any more. And I think a lot of people up here get like that.

"Sometimes when I get up in the pulpit I want to stand there for five minutes—long enough to get their attention, and just point out the window and yell "LOOK!!" And then sit down."

And as she pulled into her driveway, she was tired, and grateful that the only task that lay ahead that night was accepting the unending love of a good dog, her friend Dulcinea.

CHAPTER 49

The three *viejos* were out on Ernie's front porch. After the meeting at the fairgrounds, they felt good about how much their ideas had penetrated into the discussion. Their cigar-aided, beer-enhanced conversation moved on to speculating about what would happen next.

Ernie spoke up. "I sure liked how the Sheriff and Elaine Carpenter handled all that red-blue stuff. Makes you think about the rest of the country."

Sam said, "You know all this polarized politics stuff is crap, right?"

Ernie looked uncertain and asked "What do you mean?"

"Polarization is something the pols and the media are selling—it's not real. Every study done over the past ten or twenty years concludes that we're all still pretty much in the middle. It's just that the extreme people out on the edges are getting better at getting the spotlight. The way the media works now, the story about the middle can't sell enough papers or TV ads. So they write about polarization. And then those idiots in Congress who got elected from lopsided districts think their district is all that counts—so they play to the voters in their primaries, and we elect more screamers and fewer moderates. The Republicans have pretty well cannibalized all their moderates, and now the Dems are trying the same thing. And money follows purist passion—there's not much money in moderation."

Ernie nodded, "It's very hard to be a moderate and not seem naïve. The centrists all look like namby-pamby balancers—'on the one hand, on the other hand.' It is so damned satisfying to get your rocks off and pretend that all the truth is on one side. But it almost never is."

Bill chimed in. "But who wants to seem naïve? And up here, in tough-guy land, where you can still see the shadow of John Wayne riding around the corner if you look in the right places in the Alabama Hills—ain't too many moderates around these parts, pilgrim."

Ernie said. "But what about all the hot button issues—abortion, race, affirmative action, immigration? We're supposed to be totally divided on those, right?"

"Not if you ask the right questions. On a whole series of questions—immigration, rights for gays, aid to the poor—the difference between the so-called red states and the blue states is only 3 or 4 percentage points. Very smart lady, Republican to the core, Mary Matalin, said on Meet the Press a while back 'America is not red or blue. America is mostly purple.' She got that right. Middle ground solutions always get big majorities, as opposed to polar slices of public opinion." Seeing his chance, Sam struck. "Polar bares the truth about how small the fringes are."

"That's pathetic—I hate writers who try to make puns. But then where does all this polarization talk come from?"

"Like I said, it helps the media. Ernie, no one reads the newspapers any more except old farts like us. They've got to jazz it up as much as they can to beat the TV people. The Internet and all those blogs just make it worse, with millions of people spending their time reading what they already agree with, their minds getting narrower and narrower. And the politicians play to their base when nobody else shows up to vote."

"It's our fault."

"Not exactly. Our generation still votes more than anyone else, way disproportionate to our size in the population. So we get more stuff, more benefits."

Ernie smiled. "I like that part."

Sam said, "Yeah, but wait'll you see the intergenerational battles we have in a few more years about whether we can afford all the health care we're going to need, not to mention those two nice checks they send you every month for federal retirement and Social Security. It'll make racial politics look mild in comparison."

Ernie laughed. "My motto is 'dementia relieves.' When you can't remember where the pain comes from, sometimes the pain just fades away. But look, this intergenerational fighting will finally get all the younger ones voting, right?"

"Almost certainly. The sleeping giant will wake up."

"And vote to pull out our feeding tubes."
"Very likely—unless we be nice now."

CHAPTER 50

Jim Scott felt as if he had magically returned to being 17 as he opened the car door for Rosa. She had succeeded in forcing him out of his favorite routines, the smooth, easy banter that got him by so well with the great majority of his prior conquests. At one point he told Ollie, amazed, "She really wants to talk, and it's not all about her, and it's even sometimes about what's happening in the world!"

He had decided to invite her to drive up to The Restaurant at Convict Lake, one of the finest eating places between Reno and Los Angeles. He had suggested they escape the Valley for at least one night, away from the tensions that had broken out into the open. And Rosa quickly agreed.

She was wearing pressed jeans and a colorful blouse scooped enticingly down across the tops of her breasts. Her hair was partly up, gathered in the back with a silver clasp. He asked her where she had gotten it.

"My cousin Maria gave this to me. She wore this on the March."

"Wow. Piece of history there."

"Yes." She paused, wanting to tell him more. "I'm going to go visit her in Mexico in the spring semester. They're letting me take an advanced anthropology course because of the courses I took at Cerro Coso." She paused, watching him. "I think I may go work with her after I graduate." And then she told him about Maria's work with the *indigenas*, the dozens of native groups in Mexico that were among the poorest of the poor. She waited for his reaction, hoping he would be able to understand.

Jim smiled and gently covered her hand on the table. "You'd be great at it, if that's what you want to do." Then, wanting to lighten it up and at the same time tell her what he felt, he asked, "Don't suppose they have any old trucks down there that need fixing, do they?"

And Rosa, filled with joy at his response, leaned forward and said "I've heard that they have *thousands* of them, all needing repair. Sad, forlorn old trucks, needing tender attention from a handy *gringo*." And then she gave him a smile that promised more than Jim dared believe possible.

They ate dinner, talking about UCLA, the classes Rosa was going to take, and Jim's travels. Jim eased into the evening after a while, realizing that she was as interested in him as he was in her. And then as their dessert came, he said, "I reserved a cabin."

Deadpan, she answered. "I've always heard those cabins are full of spiders."

"Not this one, it's the newest one. Want to see?"

"Sure. Let's take dessert and sit on the porch."

It was a newer building, standing at the top of a hill that overlooked the lake.

After they had watched the moon over the lake for a while, Jim said, "If we stay the night, will your mother kill me?"

Rosa laughed softly, reached for his hand and said, "If we don't, I might." Then she added, "Besides, my mother needs training in getting used to my being gone, and this will be a short preview for her."

They moved toward each other and then walked slowly, arms around each other's waists, into the bedroom. Though it would be their first time, Jim felt an ease with Rosa, knowing that being together would not be a hurdle to get over, but, in the words of a Neruda poem she had taught him, becoming a single river.

But then, as they began making love, for all his feelings for Rosa, he was also feeling each of his years, as well as the double shift he had worked beginning at 3:30 that morning in Lone Pine. And just as his anxiety began to affect him, he felt a new movement, both of them moving together, taking over his own body, with a rolling that went on and on, and then became sharper and stronger, exciting both of them as their bodies and the bed and the whole building seemed to be rising and falling in surging waves.

And then, a few seconds after his own explosion and hers, they both realized what had happened was a major geological accompaniment to their lovemaking, in the form of an earthquake. Later, they verified on the cable news it was a 5.1 "centered in the Convict Lake area."

Rosa recovered first, and said, laughing, "I wonder if we caused it."

Jim answered, "I don't know. I just hope it doesn't spoil us for next time. It may be kind of hard to pre-schedule it as well as this one. What was it Hemingway said—did the earth move for you?"

Rosa snuggled into him and said "Oh, *yes*. Now I know, oh man of the world, that you will never forget *our* first time."

Jim said, arm around her shoulders, face deep into her long flowing hair, "Not likely, *querida*."

CHAPTER 51

"So over in American Literature, what are you people reading these days?

Blank stares, then Emma Pinson quietly spoke up. "Huckleberry Finn, Mr. Nolan."

"Huck Finn, eh? Who said that was the greatest American novel?"

More blank stares, then Emma again, even quieter this time, lest she stir up envy among some of the other college-bound students. "Ernest Hemingway."

"Yep. And it was written by a man with a little bit of Owens Valley history in him."

Watching carefully, he saw what he hoped for: five, maybe six sets of eyebrows moving upward with interest. Continuing, he started into the core of his lecture.

"Today, we are going to talk about the mines and how they have defined the Valley. And we'll get around to Mark Twain, too. Of course, it all begins with the land again, the geology, and the fire and ice. Because you get gold and silver, and other things worth digging out of the ground, when the land gets all crumpled up against itself.

"The mines were what destroyed part of the Paiute way of life here, because they made Owens Valley too profitable to pass up. At first, it was the cattle that were driven through here, and all the supplies going up to Aurora, and later Bodie. But then, we had our own mines, just north of the Valley at Mammoth, then east of Owens Lake in Darwin and Cerro Gordo."

He had turned on the LCD, which was projecting a map of the mining towns—ghost towns, today. "How many of you have been up to Bodie?" Twenty or so hands went up, while the ten who were left tried to look bored as if they knew they hadn't missed anything important.

"No one knows how to create gold, or how it is created." He stole a glance at Fundie Row, and they were smiling quietly, because *they* knew how it was created. "Alchemists tried for centuries, and modern physicists have tried, but no one has ever done it. We know gold samples have been found that are dated to be three billion years old." No glances needed now, since he already knew the smiles had flashed into frowns. "And new research suggests that microbes have something to do with the formation of gold. So maybe gold is a living element. But in this valley, it has been the cause of hundreds of deaths, maybe thousands."

More eyebrows rising, since even in their video-enhanced world, death was a draw. Paul went on. "Miners in the late 19th century lived alone on the side of a hill, often in holes that were more like a cave than a house. And they weren't exactly patient people; most of them didn't get rich, and the ones that did were sometimes the ones that were ready to take it from the others. They took it any way they could—at the point of a gun, or by getting to an assay office with a claim that couldn't be protested by its original owner, since he had died of a broken neck when he was pushed down a hundred foot mine shaft.

"Stagecoach robberies, holdups, wagon trains of gold and silver bars being highjacked on their way to Reno or LA—it all happened right here in this valley. At one point there was so much ore being mined east of Owens Lake that it paid to run a steamship across the lake—and there was one, for three years in the 1870s, running from Keeler to Olancha.

"And Cecelia Flores was right in what she said in the community meeting a few nights ago. Many of those early miners were Mexicans, who had learned to mine silver in Sonora, and migrated up here when the big gold and silver strikes started in the 1840s and 1850's."

"Yeah, but none of that makes it OK for illegals to sneak across the border and come up here to live off welfare." It was Jack Latham again, and Paul was torn between admiring the kid for having the courage of his—or his father's—convictions and wanting to shut him up for fear he would spark another explosion.

"I'd welcome your facts on that after class, Jack, since illegals, as you call them, aren't eligible for welfare." He stopped, resetting. "All right. Back to Mark Twain. He wrote a book about living in this part of the country, called *Roughing It.* He was living in Aurora, Nevada, when Bishop was first settled. And Mark Twain clearly went through the Owens Valley more than once while he was working in the silver mines in Nevada. He wrote about it in *Roughing It,* which has a long section on Mono Lake. Amazing guy who grew up on the Mississippi, became a miner and journalist in the California and Nevada silver fields, and wrote most of his books in a house in Hartford, Connecticut. New England and the Eastern Sierra—you can't get much further apart than that.

"And finally, we need to fit in the Civil War here. The Civil War was fought a long way from California, but its tensions were felt right here. Lincoln only won 32% of the popular vote in California in the 1860 election. The mines got all tangled up in the Civil War; the Union needed the silver to pay for the war and all the munitions, and the Confederates in California tried to keep that from happening. There are still traces of the tension here in the Valley. The Alabama Hills were named by Confederate sympathizers, after a confederate gunship that won a battle early in the Civil War. Soon after, Union supporters in the Valley adopted the name of the U.S.S. Kearsarge, a ship that sank the Alabama, and named the peak, the pass, and a lake after the Kearsarge. The troops at Fort Independence were all California Volunteers, Union supporters who never made it to the East but got stuck on guard duty in California."

Paul pressed to wrap up the lecture, because the day was turning warm, as late May days sometimes would. And warm days brought their own problems.

Paul was faithful to his wife, and would never dream of becoming involved with anyone else. But it was May, and it was getting warm, and over Paul's twelve years of teaching high school, the pre-summer and summer outfits had become skimpier and skimpier. As a normal male human being, Paul was having problems. He thought of them as The Temptations.

The problem was that there was just nowhere to *look.*

For six hours a day, a flowing sea of adolescent flesh moved in front of him, jiggling, bouncing, and bulging. As spring warmed into summer, he found himself using visual aids more and more often so he could get his laser pointer up to the front of the room and move as far away as possible from the front row. He wondered if they knew what they were doing—he supposed they did—when the least clothed girls sat in the front row. He even imagined that there was some kind of unspoken game going on, in which he would lose points if he were caught staring at some of the sweet, swinging cleavage on display.

So he grasped his laser, faced the front of the room, and hoped for summer's respite from all the bounteous, barely restrained flesh arrayed before him.

He had once mustered his courage to ask Liz what he should do, and after she stopped laughing at him, she said "Look at them, stare if you want—that's what they want, so look! Don't drool, but show that you appreciate a fine pair, even if it's in a really slutty outfit."

But it was advice that he was too uncomfortable to take. So he faced the board and the maps and tried to look everywhere but at the smoothly curving wonders of the world.

CHAPTER 52

Liz and Rudy were tired after another long day, and when Liz asked Rudy if he wanted to stop off and get a beer, he agreed. They walked into a Main Street bar that had a semi-shady reputation, but also a very convenient parking lot behind it, which made it an easy place to have a quick beer.

As they sat down in a booth, an overweight guy at the bar turned and watched them, then elbowed his friend and said, loudly, "Whoa, look, Earl, Tonto and Hiawatha."

Rudy said "Let me…" But Liz had already slid out of the booth and walked quickly across the room to the bar. She got up next to the drunk and pointed to him, "You said what to me? You called me *what*?"

Enjoying the attention and too drunk to pick up on Liz's full anger, he drawled, "I was talking to the chief, hon. Back off."

Unhappily for the drunk, he was tipped back a bit as he sat on the bar stool, so when Liz flashed her hand forward, grabbed the front of his belt and jerked him up, the entire bar stool came out from under him and he hit the floor. He lay there shaking his head for a few seconds, and then came roaring to his feet. "What the hell do you think you're doing?!"

"I'm knocking you on your ass. You spoke disrespectfully to an officer of the law. Do you want to go home now or do you want to spend some time in jail?"

He shook his head again, then pushed away the hands of his nearest buddy who was softly telling him *not now, she means it, let's leave, Bobby.* "Not the last you hear of this, babe."

"You'd better hope it is, trashman."

He left, hitting the door with both hands and cursing as he exited with his sidekick. As Liz returned to the booth, she saw Rudy half-grinning but trying to look serious at the same time.

"Lots of people in here, Nolan. This may get back to Howard. Thought he told you to go easy."

"Bastard was disrespecting us. We work our butts off and we come in here and have to listen to that bullshit?"

"No, but there are a lot of ways to handle it without the guy ending up on his ass. Liz, I decided a long time ago, the first time they call you Tonto or Chief, you let it go. After that, you draw the line."

"Maybe. I draw it differently."

"I noticed. Let's hope Howard agrees if he hears about it."

And he did hear about it, but he didn't agree. Bobby and Earl managed to find someone in the bar with more standing with the OCSD than they had, and whoever it was called in a complaint. Howard called Liz in to his office the next morning.

"Nolan, you've decided we don't have enough problems—you're going to go around knocking guys off barstools? What are you *thinking*?!"

She shot right back. "He was disrespectful and it was a room full of people who were watching him do it. I gave him a chance to back down, and he insulted us again."

Howard studied her for a moment, as she raised her chin a bit, as if ready for a punch. "Always the chip on the shoulder, Nolan. You went after the Governor's guy—fine. But it cost you. Now you go after some loudmouth drunk. You know, Nolan, you're going to have your hands full if you choose off every loudmouth drunk in this County."

He stopped, watching her frown, while keeping quiet. "Now listen. You are coming back on line. You are going to keep your mouth shut. You are going to do exactly what you are told or you will be demoted to the worst job in this department." He paused, and looked at her intently. "Nolan, we are going to salvage you, despite your worst instincts. Understand?"

"Yes, sir."

"You will continue working with Warland on this case. We're getting closer, and we need you. Don't flake out on us, Nolan. And try not to knock anyone else off barstools." He shook his head. "Maybe you should take up boxing or something."

PART FOUR:
THE NET CLOSES

CHAPTER 53

After Liz's talking-to from Howard, the three of them met to go over the forensics. Howard spoke up. "No surprise—all three shot by the same gun, a .22. Looks like the guy knows how to shoot—all three head shots."

Rudy said, "He's either cocky or stupid, using the same gun. Like he wants us to know it's him. He wants us to know we can't catch him."

The phone rang, and Howard grabbed it. "Tell me," he said quickly. He listened and then said "Check it out and call me." He looked up as he replaced the phone. "We may have caught a break. One of Rudy's patrols from the Lone Pine reservation found an RV that has been parked down in Pearsonville on one of the RV pads. They had checked out that map that Bill Solomon gave us—the old trails that the movie companies used—and they found some trails going around Little Lake to the east, all the way down to Pearsonville. So they went into the RV park and asked this guy if he had anybody renting who was in and out over the last few weeks. The manager said a guy from down South rented the RV space a month ago, and then disappeared. No one has been near the RV since then. They called it into the substation in Olancha, and Joe Ricks is going to go look at it."

"Maybe it's the guy's base of operations," said Rudy.

"That's what I'm thinking. Meantime, let's go over the times and places map again. We've got to see if the pattern makes more sense if you put an RV into the picture."

Liz was still smarting from her chewing–out, and for once, decided to stay quiet.

An hour later they got the follow-up call. Howard took it, asked a few questions, and then said "Thanks, Joe, we'll be down there as soon as we can get a warrant. Watch it and don't let anyone inside."

He turned to Liz and Rudy. "Guy who runs the place said he hasn't seen any sign of the guy who rented it last month. Started to make him suspicious. Said it's rented by a guy who comes up every year from Glendale or Burbank or someplace down there. He has a motorbike on the back of his RV and goes off into the hills twice a year, spring and fall."

"How old a guy?" asked Liz.

"He says maybe late twenties. Only sees him coming and going at night—guy has been coming up for five or so years but does everything by mail. Keeps to himself. But this time he disappeared."

"Maybe our guy," said Liz.

"Maybe. Let's go check. Call and make sure the Judge is in his chambers." He turned to Rudy, and said "You call the tribal leader down there, and you tell him they did a helluva job picking up this lead."

They got the warrant, and headed off in Howard's cruiser.

When they got to the RV campground, they parked blocking the front gate and walked over to the manager's office. He came out of the office when he heard the car, and told them he had no keys to the RV. They walked past the mostly empty pads to Ricks' patrol car, which was parked with the motor running next to an RV. It was a 34-foot Tioga, in good shape, with a bike rack on the rear bumper. Ricks stepped out of the car and said "Nothing, no signs of anyone since I called."

The lock was easy to break with the tool kit from Howard's car. Liz went in first, gun hand out, all by the book. No one was inside, and the RV looked uninhabited. There were a few cans of juice in the fridge and some cereal and soup in the cabinet over the stove. A bookshelf over the bed held some books on the Valley. A map of the Eastern Sierra hung on the wall in the bedroom, and fishing gear and two coats were on hooks in the closet. They found a late model portable computer and a printer in the cupboards over the sink. A radio scanner sat on the table next to the kitchen counter. The dishwasher had two glasses and a bowl in it.

"Guy is a sort of neat freak," said Rudy.

"Yeah. For a guy," said Liz. She picked up some papers from the printer's out-tray, and was startled to see her own picture. The guy had printed out an online newsletter from the OCSD that had a picture of Liz in a group receiving an award. She pointed it out to Rudy and Howard, and Howard grunted. "He's been trying to figure out who's looking for him. Guess we should assume he's listening in to all our calls on that scanner."

Howard had his cellphone out and called Independence for fingerprint coverage. "Be sure to take the glasses and bowl from the dishwasher after you take photos of the inside—we may be able to get some DNA. And run the plates on the RV through the DMV."

Then he called the Sheriff to give him an update. He put the phone down and gave Liz and Rudy a strained smile. "Terry sounds happier than I've heard him for a week. He wants us to get on this RV fast and let him know as soon as they get the prints back."

They ran the plates on the RV and quickly got the name Brent Dobson, at an address in Glendale. Rudy called the Glendale police, who said they could check out the place in a few hours, promising to call back as soon as they had gotten there.

The print run turned up nothing. The guy had never been arrested and didn't have a passport. The DNA would take two more days from the Bureau of Forensic Services in Sacramento, even with a top priority from the CHP and the DWP pushing for it. And DNA was a long shot because the guy had no arrest record.

They did get a partial lead on the motor bike, however. The tracks leading from the RV were good enough for them to be able to match it with a Honda 250 CC motor bike—the biggest made. And the real lead was trailer tracks—the bike was pulling some kind of trailer, maybe one big enough to hold a body.

When the Glendale police called back, they said there was B. Dobson listed at the address, which was a second-story rental unit in a nondescript apartment building. Rudy explained what would be needed to get a warrant linked to the killings, and the Glendale team promised to get right on it.

Rudy and Liz were sitting at the Independence station, reviewing what they had. Rudy went over the pieces. "The gas can that led us to the motorcycle, the RV in Pearsonville, spotting him up in the Whites—we may be finally closing in on this bastard. And Howard says the Navy is going to let us use three spotter choppers for two days, together with a recon plane that is going to take a picture of every inch of the Valley. Those guys can blow up a photo to see a one-foot rock if they want to. One run at noon and an infrared one at midnight. If a guy is out there on a motorcycle, we're going to find him."

CHAPTER 54

With the leads finally coming in on Brent Dobson, the team began to put together a picture of who he was and what was motivating him. Later, a journal found in his last underground shelter filled in more of the pieces. He had made entries every day up to his leaving to go into Bishop for the Mule Days parade, apparently thinking he could return to the shelter later, after he escaped from the Valley.

Dobson's parents had separated when he was two, and his father took a job as a night supply clerk job at a warehouse so he could be with his son. His father explained his mother's absence by saying she had decided to move "back East," but when he was twelve, he had gone through his father's papers and discovered that she was in a mental institution in northern California.

Dobson had learned to make his world work by replacing his anger at his mother with rock-solid reliance on his father. In fact, his father was devoted to him, and poured into Brent's upbringing all the emotional energy that his wife had rejected. Teased in school as the kid without a mother, Brent had few friends. He was a good student, interested in history and how mechanical things worked.

His hatred for the Valley dated from the day of his father's death. He was fourteen, and he and his father had been riding their ATV on their way up toward Onion Valley. His father was showing him how to ride along the ridge of the foothills when a tire popped and the ATV flipped. His father was thrown off the vehicle and down a steep grade into a rock, where he was killed instantly. The boy had been unable to climb down to his father's body, and waited nearly a full day before a car came along and another day before the ambulance crew could recover his father. Those two days seared in his brain a hatred of all

Owens County officials and those who lived in the Valley where his father had been lost to him. He needed an object for his anger and loss, and the Valley and its residents became that object. And he became what he called The Avenger.

When his father died, his world collapsed. He left high school in South Pasadena and after a year, his grandparents found him living in a group home, placed as a delinquent minor after he had been caught stealing food. They gave him a small apartment over their garage in Burbank, and he finished high school there. Once he realized they would keep him in spending money, he reached an agreement that they would finance his studies at Glendale Community College. He got his AA and began working in a sporting goods store. He was very good with tools and equipment, and developed special skills in working with bikes and motorbikes. From his years roaming the desert with his father, he also became very interested in survival equipment. He frequented shooting ranges, learning to fire a high-powered rifle.

Fueled by his father's death and his aptitude for history, he read everything he could about the history of the Valley, filtering all of it through his belief that the Valley had cost him the one human being who cared for him. In his reading, he began to see undercurrents, re-shaping them in his mind into the evil strains that he saw in all of the Valley's tangled history. Every time he read about a slice of the Valley's history, whether it was the Indian wars, Manzanar, or other events, he turned it into further proof that the people who had lived there must be punished for their history of transgression.

It was all laid out in the journal, in neat, small handwriting. The "evil places" became for him the physical sites where evil had been done. He only saw what was wrong with the Valley's history—he was blind to the rest of it. He hated the Valley, but he knew more about its history and how to get around it than 90% of the people who lived there. He read and read, and gradually built a half-real, half-imagined chronology of violence and exploitation, working toward the time when all he had learned could become weapons aimed at those he had come to see as the evil-doers.

While they were still looking for him, the team had sent everything they had on Dobson to a forensic psychologist who worked in the Attorney-General's office. She had read through the file, and sent them a report explaining that sometimes a trauma like Dobson's father's death can trigger a mental and emotional warp that can bring out deep-seated anger. Dobson, the psychologist speculated, had a genetic tendency toward his mother's schizophrenia, which his trauma and isolation after his father's death had ripened into full paranoid disorder. He needed someone to blame for his father's disappearance from his life, and the people of Owens Valley became that target.

Twice a year he came up to the Valley and compiled a map of all the backroads and old trails along both sides of the Valley. He learned how to dig into the desert and make a shelter below ground; once he got offroad, he was invisible. He could walk for miles and used the bike to get around after he set up the van as his base of operations. He had altered the bike so it was almost completely silent, with an ordinary exhaust muffler that he had welded to a container of water that cut the sound down. If you were ten yards away you could barely hear the bike.

He had located several bases of operation, mostly in the Owens Valley, but had another over in the Death Valley region. The journal made clear that in his extended study of the Owens County area, Dobson had read everything he could about Charles Manson, who had set up his bizarre "family" in the Death Valley region. Manson had predicted a race war between blacks and whites, drawn from the most apocalyptic views of the 1960's. Dobson had set up one of his bases near where Manson had lived, infected by some of the same hate-fueled ideas, and pondered Manson's methods, slowly concocting his own plans for dividing the people of the Valley from each other and fomenting armed conflict.

Dobson was careful to change his appearance as he built his bases of operation around the Valley. As police reconstructed his earlier years, they found pictures of him in his grandparents' effects in a trunk in his apartment. He was tall, but thin, looking gangly as a teenager and lankier as he aged into his twenties. He had sharp features, with a nose that had outgrown the rest of his face and hair that lay flat on his head. His skin had never completely left adolescence behind, and was mottled and patchy. He shaved irregularly, usually having a two- or three-day beard. He wore different hats and caps, hid behind dark glasses and sometimes used wigs and goatees to vary the shape of his face.

He had continued his "research" for years, diverting all his anger into an attempt to master moving around the Valley and understanding its tangled history and geography. Finally, the year he turned twenty-five, he felt he was ready to put The Avenger's plan into action. Both his grandparents had died, and he was completely alone. They had left him some money that he used to buy and equip the RV. He had stocked each of his bases with enough supplies for a week, so that he could move up and down the Valley without using the main roads or running the risk of being seen.

One of his final preparations was to set up a wireless Internet connection in the RV, which he used to research the Valley's law enforcement methods and staffing. He had ordered a codes book from a law enforcement supply house, so he could follow most of the radio broadcasts among the deputies, the CHP, and the local cops, using his scanner.

Once he knew who was on the team that was trying to catch him, he had located Rudy's and Liz's house, and had spent some time observing both. He had noted that Liz's girls were there with the sitter after school, and that Paul often stayed late at the high school.

CHAPTER 55

The next morning, Howard and Rudy walked into the conference room at 9 to join the briefing on a conference call from the Navy spotters. The team from the Sheriff's office and most of the other agencies on the case were all there. Everyone sat down at the stroke of nine and began listening carefully to the Navy briefer. He was using both audio and a remote video shot projected on the conference room wall. They could see hundreds of photos blown up into a composite of the whole Valley.

The Navy briefer, a young lieutenant named David Matthew, ran through the background of what they had done with the Marine choppers and the Air Force's C-130 recon plane, and then brought up a new slide. He said "This is the one you're going to want to check out. We have some guys stationed here who know more about the rocks in Afghanistan than the Afghans, and they interpreted these shots for us. They say this shot"—the camera showed a piece of desert that started with a wide shot east of 395 and north of Lone Pine and zoomed in on a dirt road with a clear overhead shot of a motorbike—"is the one you want to look at."

Everyone in the room leaned forward, trying to make out the rider, whose face was blurred, even with the astounding resolution that showed he had on a red plaid shirt and boots. He wore no helmet, and there was no windscreen on the bike. The rider seemed tall, but it may have been the angle of the photo.

"Maybe just a dirt biker," someone said.

"Not out there," said the DWP cop who had been leading their security team in the southern half of the county. "He had to cut a fence to get in there, that's all DWP land—and it's totally fenced off."

"Now watch this," said the Navy guy. "This is a sequence of pictures taken about a minute apart."

They could see six pictures in a row of the guy on the motorbike, dust trail rising beyond him. In the seventh, the dust was still in the air, but the motorbike had disappeared.

One of the BLM guys asked the briefer, "Can you get us the coordinates of the place where he disappeared?"

The Navy briefer pushed a button and said "They're on the screen now, sir."

The BLM guy pointed at the seventh shot. "I think I know what he's doing. He's got a survival hole out there—some of those guys can dig into the desert and live there for weeks. We pay people to train BLM staff in these survival techniques. Look, there are some tracks going off the main trail into the desert over here." He pointed to a spot where the bike had left clear tire tracks, which disappeared about fifty yards from the trail.

Liz turned to Howard and said "That's how he disappeared up at the shooting range—he had one of those dug-out hideouts up there, too. This guy has been planning this for a long time."

The Sheriff pushed back from the table, and started pointing at people. "Call the Lone Pine station, take the DWP people," gesturing at them across the room and getting a quick nod in response, "get out there, use the GPS coordinates, and surround the place. If the guy is there, I want him, no shots unless you have to. Shoot the bike first, I want to know what this guy thinks he's doing and if you guys perforate him, it won't happen. Go!"

As the room cleared, Rudy looked at Howard. "We haven't heard yet from the Glendale police on the warrant—want me to push them?"

"Push them, hard. And do it from your vehicle—I want you out there where they spotted him."

So he did, and later that afternoon he received the call. He forwarded the information to Howard immediately. They had gotten into the apartment, found some ID for Brent Dobson, some camping gear, topographic maps of the Valley and an operator's manual for a Honda 250. Howard knew they were getting closer, because now they had a name, they knew how the guy was moving around, and they had him spotted at a specific location.

At the coordinates they were given, they found what the BLM guy had predicted. A seven foot deep ramp had been dug out, with a motorized lever system triggered by a remote that lifted an aluminum plate placed across the top of the hole. The plate was covered by dirt and plants, which had been placed on top of some kind of glue applied to the top of the entire plate. All the guy needed to do was ride up to the hole, click the remote, slide the bike into the hole, and drop the cover, probably taking less than thirty seconds from open to closed. The enclosure had dry food, blankets, a flashlight, and a crude periscope that looked up through a piece of sagebrush. If you were standing ten feet away, it looked exactly like the rest of the desert.

But the hole was empty. He had left. They knew who he was, and they knew where he had been. But they had lost him. Howard called the Navy and asked for the choppers to try to spot him, but they had gone back to China Lake and wouldn't be up until the next morning.

Brent Dobson sat in another hole three miles away in the foothills of the Inyos, watching through a small periscope. He had known they were coming an hour before they got there, from what he had been able to hear on the scanners he used, even though it had been in code. And now he knew that the choppers he had seen the day before were not on a routine patrol, but were looking for him and were dangerous. So he was back to traveling at night, which was fine with him. He was going to collect some things from his base and then head back up to Bishop for Mule Days.

CHAPTER 56

The next day, Jim Scott was sitting with his father and Sam Leonard on Ernie's front porch, making plans to meet for a meal in Bishop after the Mule Day parade. Gingerly, Ernie asked, "I hear you have a new lady friend."

Jim was silent and then said "Dad, she's different. I worry about the age thing, but she really has her act together. She's going to do big things, someday. Before—with other girls, that would have turned me off. But now I want to help her do it, somehow."

"You know that Sam knew her cousin in Mexico?"

"That's what Rosa said. What's she like, Sam?"

Sam leaned back with a faraway look. "Jim, she's like no one I've ever met. If there were twenty of her out around the world in the countries of the South, the next fifty years would go a lot better. She is that important."

"Rosa wants to go down there to see her. Maybe work with her for a while."

Ernie said, "Great food and great people down there, son. You let me know if you need any help." And then he shut up, remembering Sam's advice and how many times he had tried to tell Jim what to do, with no results other than to make him angry.

"Thanks, Dad," said Jim.

It was the kind of cryptic conversation between father and son that Jim had endured all his life, but with a subtext that was somehow very different. This time, he was talking about a woman he loved, and changes in his life that were bigger than any he had ever made. And he knew his father was trying to help him without telling him what to do.

After he left, Sam and Ernie looked at each other and smiled. Sam said, "You did good, dad. You didn't push him."

Ernie said, "Thanks. I wonder if they're going to make it. She sure sounds special."

"She must be. You know, they have some of the odds with them, Ernie. They're different, these kids. Somebody calls them the millennials—Rosa's generation. And one of the ways they're different is they just don't think about race and culture they way we do. They intermarry a lot more, because the options are so much a part of their lives. In the Census, nearly 5% of the state's population checks the multi-racial box. The only state with a higher number is Hawaii. And if you ask kids in schools to identify themselves, one in five kids in some districts selects 'other.' In lots of those California schools now, the old categories just don't work any more. What's Asian? Chinese? OK. East Indian? Pakistani? Persian, Iraqi, Afghan? Kids from families who came here from the Middle East, who make up a growing chunk of the public schools, aren't going to check Asian—they don't think they're Asian at all. So they check 'other.'"

Sam added, "I guarantee you, if Jim and Rosa make it work, the fact that she's Latina and he's Anglo will be one of the least important problems they have."

Ernie nodded. "She's a lot younger than he is, but I have a hunch she's going to be a big part of what helps him finally grow up."

Not everyone agreed with Sam, however. Later that day, Jim was talking about Rosa to his pal at work, Ollie.

Ollie asked, "She's Mexican, right?"

"Uh, yeah."

"How do you feel about that?"

"What do you mean?"

"Being a different race, you know."

"What do you mean, a different race?"

"Well, they're different."

"No, they're not. She's just knock-out gorgeous. Plus, she's smart as hell."

"Smarter than you? You want to get into that—a woman smarter than you?"

And Jim answered, with a wide grin on his face, "How else you ever going to learn about life, Ollie?"

That night, Jim and Rosa went out for dinner again, in a restaurant in Lone Pine that Jim knew well. Rosa had driven down after classes, and had picked Jim up at his small house off Main Street in Lone Pine. Jim had bought the house after he returned from the Gulf War, and had fixed it up with the predictable big-screen TV, spare furnishings, mostly tending toward second-hand, and a wall of books that surprised Rosa.

"You read all those?" she asked.

"Nah, they're just for decoration. I like the green ones, especially."

She smiled and poked him. "It's OK if you read them, Jim. I like a guy who can read."

"Well, teacher lady, I'm up to the sixth grade readers that they let me have over at the school when they're done with them."

"It's *OK*." She walked over and looked at the titles. "Big emphasis here on Louis Lamour, I see. Some Michael Connelly—somebody said I had to read his stuff before I go live in LA. And a shelf here of Robert Parker, with some T. Jefferson Parker thrown in. Lots of mysteries. Oops—here's the works of F. Scott Fitzgerald. Afraid you're getting a little too high-brow for me." She paused, and gave him a mock frown."Hey, Jim—ever read any books by women?"

"Uh, yeah. Sue Grafton? Except she wrote a really bad book about the Valley, so I stopped reading her. I read a great one a while ago by someone called Wiggins, about a photographer. Fine book. Elizabeth George? Dark, very British books by a lady from Huntington Beach. And I like J.A. Jance's Arizona books."

"Your father got you reading, didn't he?" Jim had tried to explain his father to Rosa, without much success, and had mentioned his books filling the doublewides.

"Yeah. Though we don't read the same stuff."

"No, probably not. My mom and I don't either, but she always had books around the house, and I got the message that it was something you can do and enjoy. And then I had this teacher..." She got a faraway look. "I had an English teacher when I was a freshman who really got to me. She was reading a poem to us one day and she stopped, because she was starting to cry and couldn't go on. She asked one of the other kids to finish it. It was about a little boy who grows up. She had a son who must have been thirty then, but that poem just got to her. That lady had been working with books all her life, but this poem really moved her. It was the first time I realized that words had that kind of power."

"My dad gave me some of that, but the message came along with some other stuff I never really understood."

"Like what?"

"Well, he's into a lot of stuff I don't understand. Opera and stuff like that."

"So? Nothing wrong with opera."

"No, but he has these really bizarre ideas. He gets all worked up about Beethoven's string quartets, too."

"Never heard of them. What are they?"

"I couldn't begin to explain them." He laughed, softly. "One time he went off on a wild tangent trying to tell me about how important the silences in the quartets were."

"The silences?"

"Yeah. See," he said, "that's the kind of weird thing he gets enthusiastic about. The silences!"

Rosa smiled, and said lightly, "That doesn't sound weird to me. Sounds typically male. Making a big deal about silence."

Bill and Ernie and Sam had continued talking and drinking after Jim left. After a while, the talking became influenced by the drinking.

They had been talking about how people would react if Dobson were caught, and then Bill said to the other two, "You know, we're all pretenders up here. Some of us are pretending that we can escape LA. Some of us are pretending that we're legal workers and citizens. Some of us are pretending that there won't be a Big One that will shake hell out of our homes or kill us. Or that the volcanoes up here aren't live and will never erupt. Or that the snows will keep coming and global warming isn't real and the rivers and lakes won't dry up one day."

Ernie began singing, off key, "Oh yes, we're the Great Pretenders—pretending that we're doing well…"

Bill continued, speaking over the feeble attempt to sing. "That's why I love the movies so much. They *admit* they're just pretending."

"Pretty profound, Bill."

But Bill was on a roll. "And we're still pretending that we don't have all this old history up here of trying to rape the landscape and kill each other off."

"Real cheery, Bill. You're drunk."

Bill quickly replied, "Yes, but as Winston Churchill said to the woman who told him the same thing, 'Madam, that's true, but you're ugly. And the difference is that in the morning, I shall be sober.'"

Sam said, "With that, I shall take the extra bedroom, and you, Sir Winston," he said to Bill, "you will take the couch, and I would also recommend some aspirin. Good night, fellow *viejos*."

CHAPTER 57

Brent Dobson wanted to go back to the RV one final time to collect the things he would need for Mule Days. He realized it might be watched, and parked his bike over a mile from the RV yard, walking in as slowly as he could to see if anyone was posted at the RV or in the yard. After sitting beneath a cottonwood for an hour, he had seen no movement at all in the yard, and moved up behind the RV, listening for any sound within.

There was none, and he moved up to the door and slowly opened it. The RV was empty, but as he closed the door, he heard a soft clicking noise that he knew was not part of the door mechanism. Certain that the door was alarmed with a remote sensor of some kind, he moved quickly to collect the items he had come for, tossed them in his backpack, and was out the door within sixty seconds. He ran out to where he had hidden the bike and pushed it for two or three hundred yards, then stopped and listened again. Hearing nothing, he kicked over the motor and rode off.

The tribal patrol that had been monitoring the sensor placed in the door arrived five minutes later. They had alerted the CHP to watch the 395 as soon as the sensor was tripped, but they all knew by that time that Dobson was on the backroads, probably on the east side of the Valley again.

They'd missed him again, and when the Sheriff heard about it, he cursed the size of his county and the judgment call he'd made about leaving a unit at the RV yard. He'd considered a full stakeout but he had played the odds, thinking that Dobson would not return to his base. So the electronic unit on the door had been the compromise—and he'd lost the gamble. But he knew he might get a second chance as Dobson moved up the Valley, and he sent out a second alert.

The alert had been picked up by a BLM security team working out by Keeler. They had borrowed some high sensitivity sound detectors from the Border Patrol when they were first placed on duty in the search for Dobson, and they had planted four of them across a mile of old trails. When they heard the Sheriff's alert, they gathered around the monitoring unit and watched the four lights that were tracking each of the detectors. The lights were all on—which meant no sound had been detected.

The team quietly did the math. If Dobson headed north within five minutes after the signal went on in the RV, moving at 25-30 mph, he'd hit the first of the detectors in ten or twelve minutes. They went silent, standing beside the monitoring unit with their two trucks parked facing outward toward east and west roads. They were tense, starting to worry that Dobson had gotten by them again or gone up the west side.

Then the third light began blinking, and all three members of the team held their breath. They stared at the monitor and then at a map they had set up under an infrared light, and saw that the third detector was about two miles south on a trail that would run within two hundred yards of them.

"Move out, no noise," the BLM unit commander said. Then he clicked on his radio and said softly, "Alert—suspect detected moving at checkpoint Red/East."

The third light had come back on, and as they packed their weapons and searchlights into their trucks, they assumed Dobson had headed past the detector on his way north. Then the detector light started to blink again.

"Shit!" said the unit commander. He's turned and headed south again—he heard us or something. Hurry—let's get out on that trail!"

They had known Dobson was monitoring the Sheriff's radio from what they had seen in the RV, but they hadn't factored in the BLM link. They stopped to listen for the sound of the bike, but the desert was silent. After half an hour, they knew he wasn't coming that way, and the team packed up and left.

The Sheriff had always known that there was a downside to having compatible radios used by all the units, and when he criticized the feds for their fragmented system, he thought to himself that the downside was a big one: when the security on the network was broken, the whole network was open to an outsider. And that is exactly what had happened.

Dobson knew that the law enforcement coverage coming after him would expand and intensify, and he'd prepared tactics for every possible response. This one had worked. He decided it was time to leave the crowded southern part of the Valley and head up for the north—which was even more crowded, but was where he could hide in the middle of the Mule Days events. So he carefully headed northeast on an old mining trail that wound up into the Inyos before it swung back down into the Whites. He'd beaten the stupid cops again, and his confidence was sky-high.

CHAPTER 58

The church service was somber, reflecting the anxious mood about the killings. Liz and Paul sat in their customary place, but Liz was not really all there. As she sat, feeling mostly dutiful and tired, she let her mind go blank for a moment, trying for a small respite from the day. Jessie had been especially difficult to get ready for Sunday school, and Liz was worn down by the struggles over breakfast, room cleaning, and clothes, on a day when she longed for rest.

And then, gradually, she began to hear the music, which was being sung by a pretty good soprano, one of the high school girls. It was familiar, though at first she couldn't place it, because it was usually performed at another time of year. And then she looked down in her lap, where she held the program, and read the words to the aria that was being sung:

> He shall feed His flock like a shepherd; and He shall gather the lambs with His arm, and carry them in His bosom, and gently lead those that are with young. (Isaiah 40:11)
> Come unto Him, all ye that labour, come unto Him that are heavy laden, and He will give you rest. Take His yoke upon you, and learn of Him, for He is meek and lowly of heart, and ye shall find rest unto your souls. (Matthew 11:28-29)

And then she could not see any more, for her eyes had filled with tears, and they were spilling down her cheeks and dropping gently onto the page, in such abundance that she quickly reached into her purse for a tissue.

"Gather the lambs…and ye shall find rest." Such a peaceful image, and so different from the killings that had filled her mind for the last few weeks. Jennie and Jessie were her lambs, and she offered a quick prayer for the help she knew she needed to give them what they needed. Handel's timeless music had gotten through some of her well-defended layers, and had penetrated deeper than she usually let the girls' problems go.

Her tears had stopped by then, but not before Paul and their next door neighbor, Sara Davids, had noticed and leaned forward looking at her questioningly. And Elaine, sitting up near the altar, noticed as she looked down that Liz was wiping her eyes.

Elaine started her sermon slowly but resolute, looking at each face, knowing she had an uphill climb and only fifteen minutes to get there. "I suppose this should be a Good Friday sermon, but the timing of all this has not synced very well with the church calendar. So today we need to take stock, because what has been happening in this Valley has the potential to touch all of us. Each of these bloody, bloody episodes has uncovered a piece of ourselves, our tortured history, that we would just as soon forget. It has shown us a side of ourselves that we mostly do not want to see—that was uncovered by these sad, terrible events. But sometimes *you have to lift the rock up, so you can roll the rock away.*"

She paused, knowing they were not with her yet. "What does that mean? It means we cannot be one with Christ, we cannot roll away the rock from the tombs where we have buried our own best selves, our better angels, unless we lift up the rocks we use to cover up our worst selves. We lift up our own rocks when we look beneath the surface of our lives to what truly matters. We have to face the ugly facts of our bigotry, our hatred of the other, our pathetic inability to see the human face of those who look different than us or pray to a different conception of God. This is what we hide under our rocks, because that is where such narrow thoughts belong, not out in God's own sunshine."

A few nods, a lot of frowns. So she had to make it even more concrete, to bring it home where it would hurt some more but meaning would be clearer. "When these killings began, we all hurt, and we all hoped it was not someone who lived here, didn't we?" She waited for the nods, and then went on. "We wanted it to be an outsider, so we didn't have to blame ourselves. And we still don't know, but the saddest thing is the signs that we have already lost some of our own community by taking sides in this thing. And it may be that the most diabolical thing of all is that that is exactly what the killer wanted us to do—to start fighting each other. We fell back on the old debates—who got here first, who took the water first, who controls the politics and the economics. We fought among ourselves—we couldn't blame LA or the tourists or the government any more, because we were so divided.

"And if that is what the killer wanted us to do, then he has won. But if we put it back together, if the twenty thousand of us who live in this Valley realize that the blessings of living here include all those who live here with us—*all* of them—then we will have conquered the evil done by this man.

"Let me close by telling you a true story about Billings, Montana. Billings is a place that is a little like this Valley. In December 1993 a Jewish boy in Billings had taped a paper menorah to his window, in celebration of the Jewish holiday of Hanukah. When a brick was thrown through his window, the community was shocked. And then a local campaign began that they called "Not in Our Town." Churches handed out paper menorahs, and the newspaper printed a menorah for people to cut out and tape in their windows. There were only about fifty Jewish families in Billings at that time—and it is estimated that 6,000 menorahs were in windows within days of the incident. It is a great story, because it is about what a community can do when ugly and evil things happen.

"We don't need a symbol like the menorah. What we need is to remember that our symbols are out there in the mountains and the skies, in the high desert and the rivers and lakes. We see our symbols every day, as in Scripture, when the Psalmist says "I will lift mine eyes up unto the hills, from whence cometh my help.'

"Let us lift our eyes up, and see our mountains, those purple mountain majesties, and see our neighbors, too, and know where our help comes from. Amen."

And as she greeted the departing congregation at the door, she was surprised once again when the publisher of the local newspaper stopped and asked her permission to use her sermon notes for a piece he was writing for the next week's issue. It was the first time that had ever happened, and as she agreed, she wondered how her words would seem in that setting, going out to a much wider audience than her usual congregation of a hundred or so. She hoped they would help.

CHAPTER 59

Max Chatham and Fred Bancroft had asked for a meeting with the Valley Chamber of Commerce. They knew they were going to run into opposition, but they wanted to pre-empt some of the flak by allowing the group of businessmen to hear first-hand what they were proposing. They had discussed it at length before the meeting, prepping at Max's house out on the reservation, and neither of them had any illusions about the support they would find in the group. At the last minute, Max suggested that Fred bring Dale along. And Fred quickly agreed, because Dale had already begun to make herself an active part of the team.

Three days before the Chamber meeting, Fred had a big problem. He had been going back and forth between Max and the energy company from Texas that was interested in geothermal power in the Valley, and the energy company had finally given him the terms of what they wanted to do. Fred had originally told Max that the tribe could be equal partners in the deal, but the Houston firm had insisted that the deal was off if they could not be majority owners. Fred sat down at dinner with Dale and updated her. She was not happy.

"You promised Max? You implied it, even? You're wrong to go back on that, then, Fred, and you have to march your butt out there and tell him you know you were wrong and put the deal back together."

Then she looked as angry as he had ever seen her. "In gambling, if your word is no good, you leave the game. Even an addict knows that, Fred."

He was stung, realizing that their roles had suddenly reversed—he was the one out of control, acting dishonorably, and she was arguing for playing it straight. "But the Houston guys will pull out. I've worked with them for a year on this thing. They'll pull the plug and my commission will be peanuts—or even nothing.

Dale fired back, "Then it will *be* nothing, and we'll find another partner. If this is a good deal, Fred, then somebody else will buy into it. Hell, I've heard you talk about this for hours and you've convinced me—can't you convince another big company that this is worth doing?"

"Maybe."

"Then let's go to work and figure out who the next investor could be. But we're not going to screw Max—we're the ones that live here, and we're not going to crap in our own nest. We need their sovereignty rights, but we also need to do the right thing. For once, the best deal is the right thing, Fred."

And they went to work, and carefully reviewed the brochures of the five firms that had done the most with geothermal projects in the U.S. in the last decade. They finally stopped working at midnight, having selected three companies in rank order of those most likely to buy in.

By the next day, Fred had lined up a new partner, which turned out to be a firm that he had originally considered and rejected because it was Canadian. But with the dollar imbalance, the Canadian firm was better off than the Texas firm. Fred called them, and they readily agreed to becoming minority partners with Fred and the tribe, assuming Fred and Max could get the local approvals. Will had done some magic with the spread sheet and pulled a lot of detailed information on the new company off the Internet, and the deal looked better than ever.

Fred realized that Dale had set him on a new direction, and a better one. He hoped he could do the same for her.

At the Chamber offices, in the large conference room, Fred started out after the introductions. "We appreciate the chance to talk with you all. We think some things are going to change in the Valley, and wanted to get your reactions to how we think we should respond.

"Development in this Valley has been uphill for a long time. The developments that have been proposed have run into problems about who owns the land, and then when that gets cleared up, the Sierra Club and Friends of the Inyo and all the other local conservation groups have raced off to court and slowed everything down. And we've gotten to where we take that for granted, and some of us even like it, because it means things stay the same, and we're already here, and we feel protected from change.

"But now the winds are changing, and the only question is whether we will sail with those winds or be blown away by them. You want a different metaphor? There are three or four tides headed our way, and we may not be too good seeing them coming, because it's been a long time since tides ran through this valley. But they are coming."

As he looked out at their faces, trying to gauge his effect so far, he saw disbelief, skepticism, and, most of all, complacency. He bore down, trying to make his case.

"Listen to what will happen next:

"Four things are going to change in Washington, and they will all affect this Valley for years to come. Some of it is obvious, and is already happening. Some is coming more quietly, but is still inevitable. First, the feds are broke. They have a ten trillion dollar deficit, and until now, there has been no serious plan for reducing it. But the new people can count, and they are going to have to cut that deficit in half to regain international credibility for the dollar. So they are going to do what any of us do when the business runs dry—they're going to sell the assets they aren't using. And that means land, and they have a lot of it. They've been selling federal land in Nevada for years"—he paused for a few nods from heads of companies who did a lot of business in Nevada—and he got them. "And now it's going to start here."

"Second, they're going to get serious about Indian economic development, because the new administration has figured out that the worst poverty in the nation is on reservations. Partly because the evangelicals are going after the poverty issue, partly because it's right." He stole a look at Dale, glad he didn't have to fudge on that issue. "And, partly, it seems, because there are a few Puritans left in Washington in both parties—and they hate gambling. And the only way to counter casino expansion is with serious economic development, aimed at both residential development and energy projects that bring new jobs."

He continued, "And that brings us to the third thing—the feds are going to try to find a few million new green jobs, working on any kind of energy that doesn't have to be shipped here from countries that hate our guts. That's a national security issue now, folks, that's no longer just an environmental issue or a jobs issue.

"So that means energy that isn't about oil." He gestured out the window to the Sierra. "Would you rather have a nuclear plant out there or a geothermal plant?

"Now I know you are thinking that the Sierra Club and all the rest of them will go berserk and stop all this because it involves some new construction. But stop and think—when have the environmental groups ever been able to stop the federal government and the sovereign Indian nations when they get their act together—and when national security is on their side of the argument?" He turned to Max and said, "Max, your turn."

Max stood up and began. "We believe in respecting the land," then he smiled, "and we were green before green was in. But we also believe in earning a living instead of just getting a check. And some of us are convinced that gaming is wrong, and that good jobs are the only way to escape it. And energy that comes from the land is good. In fact, geothermal is best, because it disturbs the land least, and leaves the least residue. We estimate that the energy development and the residential development that comes with it can create at least a thousand new jobs in the Valley—and we know we can fill one third of those."

He waited to make sure they were following, and then he made sure he went back to Fred's points again. "Fred's right—the red ink in the feds' budgets and the green movement for cleaner energy are all going to mean a lot more jobs up here eventually."

A rancher from Lone Pine spoke up. "Are you saying the whole tribe agrees with you? You speak for all of them?"

Max answered, "I don't yet speak for the whole tribe. We've had exploratory discussions, just like this meeting today. But I believe a majority of the tribe will agree, and I'll stake my future as a leader of the tribe on it."

The head of the CHP division was next. "Nothing is going to happen up here until they catch this guy." A chef at the finest restaurant in the Valley, Aaron Jacques, added "Business will not pick up, and housing won't pick up either, until he's put away for good." The owner of a local car dealership, a stunning brunette whose family had sold cars in the Valley for almost a century, said, "And if they don't, the credibility of our law enforcement is going to be zilch. And nobody is going to want to invest up here."

Fred came back into it, nodding in agreement. "That's right, Janet, but they *are* going to catch him. I've heard the feds are in it, the Navy is involved, and they are getting closer. And then we can start calming people down when we see it was just one nut—if that's what it is."

He continued, watching them closely for reactions. "But what is even more important than catching this bastard is realizing what else is at stake here, if we are right about what is going to happen next. Because we are going to lose control if we don't get ready.

"Here's the thing: nothing will happen here that *we* will be able to control unless we get our act together. The feds and the people that work for them have tons of money and years of political contacts. They have the lawyers that can put it all together. And they'll tie us up in court and beat us every time if they can, picking us off one by one again. They'll sell what they want, to whoever they want, unless we have a plan that we agree on and will fight for—together.

"And it is going to be just like it was a hundred years ago. We all know some of the people in the Valley sold to LA, some held on and fought it. But we were fighting against each other as much as we were fighting LA. And in the end, nearly all of us lost. If this guy makes us fight each other all over again, then we'll lose again. And if we don't get our act together after we catch him, we're still going to lose."

Fred was starting to lose it himself, sensing that he wasn't getting through to some of them. "Don't you *see* that? We have a chance to put all of the pieces together—what the tribe needs, what the developers want, the water and the energy that the whole state needs—and we are going to screw it up because some jerk comes up here and starts shooting a few people and we all start fighting again. Didn't you hear the Sheriff at the meeting?"

"Maybe, Fred, but the greenies will never let it happen." It was Rip Beasley, one of the rock-ribbed conservatives in the Valley, a retired Army colonel who was rumored to bankroll several conservative causes in California almost single-handedly. "They'll sue your ass off if you try to build anything out here."

Fred bore down, trying to make them see it. "That's why we have to do this in a way that gets the new development and the green causes and the energy all rolled into one set of linked projects. What we're trying to say is that the Valley's best hope is to become a green enclave—which will cost money at first, but will be more sustainable in the long run. We could be a laboratory for the five million green jobs and the billions of dollars of technology that this country needs to get OPEC's feet off our necks. We've got to stop sending oil money to countries that hate us—and this Valley is where we can show the way.

"And that gets to the fourth thing. We're going to build more houses up here—the only question is whether they will be green or cluttered crap like all the other resort tracts all over the West. The airports are bound to expand, both in Lone Pine and up here, as the short-hop low-fuel planes start getting used more. And we're going to have the energy development, and they're going to keep selling the land off. And we've won most of the water wars."

He laughed, trying to lighten it up. "You know that old saying: 'Be sure to flush, LA needs the water?' Now—unbelievably—in May 2008 the Mayor of LA announces they are going to start recycling sewage to convert to drinking water! It's all different now—the river is almost completely off limits to LA, and they know it. Orange County has been recycling millions of gallons of waste water for years, and now LA's going to be doing it. They've got no choice."

"So the only question is whether a ton of new people are going to come along with all the land sales and energy development, and how ugly it will be if they do. Folks, none of us want Victorville North up here, but that's what we're going to get if we're not careful."

Fred saw the looks of distaste. The Victorville area had exploded, becoming an archetype of lower-cost housing sprawled across the desert, and he knew the reference would hit home.

But Beasley wasn't backing off. "Sounds good, Fred. But let me tell you why it's a crock. Number 1, this Valley is in the middle of the most earthquake-prone region in the continental U.S. The 1872 quake was the biggest ever to hit anywhere in the US. The biggest, ever. And no one is going to license anything that goes down into those faults and starts screwing around with the water table or the thermals. I can get fifty scientists here tomorrow to tell you why that is a dumb idea, and the feds will be just scared enough to go do it in Arizona or someplace else.

"Number 2, the greens have got the courts so screwed up out here they could stop somebody who tried to build a new one-seat outhouse. Not happening. I don't know where you got the idea that they would come on board.

"Number 3, nobody who lives here now wants anybody new coming in to mess up the landscape. We're just like anybody else, but we've got more land—and we're going to pull up the drawbridge because we're already in the castle. And to hell with anybody new who wants to come. That's what property rights are all about. Those things aren't going to change—they just aren't."

Fred was building up for his counter-punch, but Max put his hand on Fred's arm, and then Dale spoke up. "I know all of you want to think about what we've said, and we aren't going to push for a decision today. We just wanted to brief you on what we think is going to happen, and get your feedback." She paused, for emphasis and lowered her voice a notch, to a level Fred couldn't help but notice sounded a lot more seductive. "We also wanted to make sure those of you who might want to participate get plenty of advance notice. How about we come to the next regular meeting in a month and give you all a chance to kick this around some more?"

It was the perfect defuser, delivered with Dale's classic Western businesswoman flair, combining charm, skillful redirection, a slightly too-tight white blouse, and a world-class smile. The group quickly morphed into a gaggle of bobble-heads, nodding nearly in unison, and the meeting was soon over.

Max and Fred walked out with Dale a step ahead of them, and as they paused to get used to the afternoon sun on the porch, Fred said, "Nice save, babe. I was getting a bit hot there at the end, and your cool-off was perfect pitch. Thanks." And he took her arm, as Max added, "Wow, Dale. That was perfect, just what they needed to hear. You basically told them they could get on the train or not, but it was going to leave with or without them. But then you sweetened it. Great wrapup." He laughed. "I was all set to go into my routine about the Geysers thermal plant being built right on the San Andreas fault, but that's probably not our best selling point."

And Dale told herself, as they walked to the car, that while it might not have had the full tingle of a full hand, stepping in and making the meeting come out right brought a definite tingle. And she squeezed Fred's arm closer to her.

CHAPTER 60

Sitting in his apartment in Big Pine after the day in Independence, Rudy was angry with himself, because he was having a hard time putting the pieces together. He was tempted to take it to Liz, because they had been working together so well and seemed to be getting someplace the other day with their brainstorming about the killer's motives. But he knew he wasn't ready to go to her with the pieces that affected the tribe so directly—and those were the pieces that weren't adding up.

Rudy had heard the presentation on "the faults" by the three wise men, as Ernie, Sam, and Bill had been labeled around the Sheriff's office. He knew the law enforcement team was going to catch up with Dobson in the few days or so. They had figured out what Dobson was doing. But Rudy couldn't sort out the overlapping agendas and how they might affect the tribes.

He had made a rough chart that now included five points of a pentagon: the casino investigation, the tribe's water rights, Max's proposal for new energy development, the investors Max had mentioned, and finally, the killer. He had added the investors without knowing who they were, but was certain that Max would not be going as far as he had without some assurance that serious money was on the table.

The killer belonged in the picture for at least two reasons, as Rudy saw it. Until he was caught, the media circus around the killings would dominate news out of the Valley—and any development in the Valley would suffer. Second, Rudy figured, the killer's efforts to pit the Valley's residents against the tribes were certain to weaken any move toward wider tribal land rights, at least politically, if not legally.

Rudy rose from his arm chair and paced across the small area that served as his living room. He had taken the apartment as one of the few places available in Big Pine where he could live temporarily when he first got the job with the Sheriff's Department four years ago. Strictly speaking it was not an apartment, but a very small two-room house built in the furthest corner of the back yard of a larger home. In theory, he was saving for a down payment on a home. He was determined to stay in Big Pine, and the land that he wanted on the east side of town was not for sale yet. He wanted to live next to the small area that made up the Big Pine rancheria, but not on it, in the middle of all the family feuds and questionable land titles.

He was used to small living spaces, and except for the horrified looks he occasionally got from friends and female companions he brought back to the apartment—though there had been very few of the latter over the past few years—he was content with the "temporary" arrangement. He had furnished the place with more of the native baskets and weavings that he had in his office, and had a late-model desktop with an Internet connection linked through the cable station in Bishop. His only other indulgence was a high definition flat-screen TV, linked to all the satellite networks he could buy, which he permitted himself because of his still-strong addiction to college and pro football.

The phone rang. It was Janet Fourtrees, the investigator from the Attorney-General's office. She apologized for calling him at home, but said she was going to be in Bishop in a few days and wanted to check in with him. She said she couldn't talk about it on the phone, but her team had uncovered some more problems that she needed his reaction to, and wanted to set a time to see him as soon as she got into town.

Rudy said "Sure, let's get together. I'd like to get your reaction to some economic development stuff that's going on over here. Energy ideas that one of the guys from the tribal leadership has been kicking around. He says it would be so good it would just make the casino stuff fade away."

"Did you say energy ideas? What kind of energy ideas?"

"Some kind of geothermal project that the tribal leadership—one guy in the leadership, anyway—has been talking to developers about. Why?"

Janet's tone became much more intense than when she was talking about the casinos. "The Yurok tribe has worked on geothermal projects for ten years. It's become a very big deal for us, lots of geysers up here.

I should give you the names of some of our guys who are doing this. It's real, Rudy, it's how we're going to stop depending on Middle East for energy."

"You're really into this, aren't you?"

"I wanted to be an engineer but pre-law looked more interesting. And I've been looking ever since for ways to combine the two. Renewable energy deals seemed the best way. We can't beat the casinos with nothing. We could be in on the future—or we could just keep ripping people off. That's not a hard choice for me. The technology is changing all the time, and the cost of oil makes it work. Investments that were too expensive five years ago pay for themselves fast, now that oil is so high and the country is waking up from its oil addiction."

"You sound like you're excited."

"I am, a little. I want to come see…see what is going on there."

He caught the pause, wondering if she was going to make a more personal remark. And then he decided to risk it. "You actually look a little excited in the picture of you I saw online."

"What picture?" She was clearly surprised, but Rudy did not hear any anger in her tone. More like amusement, he thought.

"There was a picture of you in some tribal meeting."

"You Googling me, Paiute man?"

"Something like that. Wanted to know who I was talking to."

"Well, then I guess it's OK to tell you that I went to law school with Edna Davies."

He was amazed. Edna had been a close friend at Fresno State, maybe his closest non-dating friend among the small, close band of Indian undergrads.

"So, you're saying you know something about me."

"Yeah, a bit more than a picture, I guess."

She was teasing him now, knowing that she had more cards than he did. Edna had spent many a weekend drinking with Rudy and some of his football friends, and knew Rudy from a time when he was lonely and willing to tell his friends about it. Edna had been a sisterly support to him, at times almost a confessor. So Janet knew a lot of it, the loneliness, the aggression in football, the shyness with women. Rudy felt naked, but then he felt clean, too, because some of the games he was used to playing with women were needless if she had talked to

Edna. She was holding a psychological X-ray of him, and he wondered if she liked what she saw.

Despite his instincts to leave it alone, he *had* Googled Janet after he spoke to her the first time and found two pictures of her on the Internet. She looked tall, compared with the others in the group picture he had found, with long hair that she seemed to wear in a braid. Her face reminded him of pictures he had seen in pictorial reviews of the Northern Plains nations, proud, angular, but with a faint smile that softened her features.

And then she took the next step, hinting at what she was considering. She asked him, "Tell me about your job."

"I like the work, but sometimes they use me as sort of a go-between." He paused, wondering how much he should reveal. "I'm not sure it always works."

"Takes a strong spirit to do that. To hang on to who you are while they use you that way. To know when it's the right thing for the people and when they're just using you."

"Yeah. Some people in the tribe are pretty sharp with their words when I come to deal with them. Lots of apple talk."

She said, "I get some of that, the work I do. I have to come down on tribal leaders when they screw up with the gambling. I get a lot of that, actually."

"You seem strong enough to take it."

"Yeah. I am."

Then Rudy was certain that he would see her and be drawn to her when she came. He said, "OK, then let's get together when you are over here and we can talk about it some more." They set an appointment that sounded to Rudy, hopefully, like part date and part meeting.

After indulging himself in some daydreaming, Rudy shook it off and began trying to integrate Janet's news about the casinos into what he already knew. He was certain that Max Chatham was aware of the investigation, which he assumed would make it easier for Max to make the case within the tribe for non-casino economic development. If the tribal leaders who were tied up in the casino were going to get some bad publicity, it would help Max's cause. And if the latest strife in the Valley meant that it would be a good time for a new image of the tribal leadership to emerge, Max might have himself in mind. Rudy suspected Max may have been angling for a larger role in the tribal leadership, as well as a piece of the action on the investment side. And it struck Rudy that Max's approach to him might have been about lining up support from neutral parties like Rudy and others who had not been wrapped up in the casino.

But Rudy also knew there would be a huge battle as soon as the outlines of Max's proposal surfaced. The energy, water, and environmental groups would all go to work on each other in the media, and the interests of the tribes were likely to be submerged in the crossfire.

So Rudy went on musing about the economic pieces, trying at the same time to get his mind off the picture of Janet Fourtrees. And then the phone rang again.

It was Paul Nolan.

"Rudy, how you doing? I hear from Liz that things are getting pretty warm for you guys, and I won't take much of your time. But I wanted you to know I'm going to try to talk to Brenda tomorrow at school about college. She's missed some of the deadlines, but I talked to some people at Berkeley and at Santa Cruz and UC Irvine and they are very interested in her."

He paused. "Rudy, I don't want to be too heavy-handed here. But she has real gifts, man. Maybe you have to do this non-interference thing. But I don't. I can get in there like all of us culturally insensitive types and mess things up and maybe do some good along the way in my own clumsy, Eurocentric way." Paul was making fun of himself, partly, and at the same time telling Rudy that he was going to step in and try to do the best thing for Brenda.

Rudy said "You ought to do that, man. I appreciate it." Then, to take the tension off a notch, he added, "Even white men sometimes get things right."

Paul went on to tell Rudy about the Duane Callison episode. "What should I do about that? And about Mills?"

"That is so wrong, man. But I got some of it, too. Even with football I got some of it. A little kid like that, it's a hundred times worse." He paused. "Only thing I can tell you is watch out for the kid in the few weeks you have left and tell the other teachers to watch out for Mills. And maybe I'll run into the guy and let him know he's being watched."

Paul thanked him, and they ended the call.

CHAPTER 61

Elaine Carpenter had aged gracefully into a minister who deserved the title, who knew how to ease her congregants' lives. She could smooth over hard spots and remind people just where their better instincts had been mislaid, buried in years of neglect and battles with low wages, high prices, and the seductive distractions of bodies and bottles. Elaine saw all that, and, as much as a Protestant clergy member could, helped those who wanted a confessor's gentle, accepting words to ease the way to forgiving themselves, as the first step on the way to the harder work with those they had harmed. She ministered to their needs, and she was good at it.

But some were easier than others to approach. She had gotten to know Liz Nolan gradually, realizing that Liz was wired tightly and knowing from earlier work with law enforcement people that Liz was unlikely to open up beyond a bit of conversation after church and at an occasional adult ed session. Elaine had no idea what Liz's basic faith tenets were, wondering if the Irish background she and Paul shared meant a Catholic upbringing, but feeling that she was probably unwilling or unable to go too far into her faith.

Paul had been much more open, bringing the girls for baptism and enrolling them in regular Sunday school. When Elaine learned that Paul and Liz's daughter had emotional problems, she suspected that Liz probably was handling it differently than Paul, and began trying to conjure up an excuse to talk with Liz. And then, when she saw the effects of the solo on Liz at the Sunday service, she had instinctively decided that it was time to risk a rebuff from Liz, and called her to suggest coffee some day after work. They met in late afternoon, at one of the quieter coffee places on Bishop's Main Street.

After some light opening chat about each other's day and the weather, Elaine referred casually to something Liz had said about work and her role in trying to catch the killer. "You're quite the tough guy, aren't you?" She smiled, trying to soften the label.

"It's a pretty tough job. I do it well." Then, not liking how boastful that sounded, Liz added, "…most of the time."

"I'll bet you do." She waited, then asked. "Can I ask how your daughter is doing? Paul said she was having some problems."

Liz, surprised and troubled by how quickly her emotions were triggered by Elaine's kind question, blurted out, "She's better. We're trying some meds that the doctors down south said she should try. It helps—some of the time." As she spoke, Liz was anxiously casting around for an excuse to leave. She knew that talking honestly to someone who truly cared about how Jessica was doing would let loose a whole sea of emotions that she didn't want to deal with then and there. She liked Elaine, but Paul was the only one she had ever talked to honestly about Jessie, and her despair was too near the surface to share with Elaine.

Then Elaine said, "It must feel like you have lost control sometimes. Parents want to do all they can, and then something like that comes along and you know you're not completely in charge. You want to protect your kid any way you can, but some biochemistry that's no one's fault keeps doing scary things to your kid. Must be hard." Lightly, she reached out and briefly patted Liz's hand as it lay next to her coffee cup.

And for the second time in a few days, Liz let go. She could not raise her head, but she let the first tears just drop, then reached for a napkin to wipe her eyes.

"Good thing I never wear eye makeup," she sniffled. "Tough guys never wear eye makeup."

"No, they don't," said Elaine. "But they get to cry when something sad happens, and they get to ask friends for help. And they can ask God too, if they want."

And the conversation went on from there, much easier for both of them than they had imagined, Elaine knowing when to let Liz set the boundaries and when to push a bit, staying away from all those issues she had learned to distance herself from in seminary with the joking clinical label of "the FOO stuff"—family of origin. Elaine saw that Liz was sad enough without going into her family history. And for all her sadness, Elaine knew that the toughness was a large part of who Liz was, and suspected that it had come in very handy at some points in Liz's life.

And Liz felt a part of her load lifting as she talked about Jessie, opening up just a bit, but more than she ever had, and promising herself that she would be talking with Elaine again.

CHAPTER 62

Fred had decided to test his marketing offensive on a sometimes friend, Nick Jamison. Nick had been the leader of the local environmental and conservation movement, either as its designated chairman or financially behind the scenes, for as long as it had existed. He was from an old Valley family, and had both the finances and the credibility to press for environmental issues that might not have gotten a hearing otherwise. He won some and lost some, but always had a seat at the table, and some projects had never happened because of the anticipated reaction from Nick and his allies.

When Fred had placed solar panels on some of his apartment buildings, Nick had given Fred an award at the annual banquet of the local conservation trust. But later, a much less pleasant confrontation had grown out of Fred's determination to develop some of the land along the expanded lower Owens River. So Fred knew that Nick was a critical player, and had decided to surface some of the energy development plans before Nick read about them in the local paper.

Nick had obviously picked up some of the details already, but he stayed quiet and let Fred present his proposals, using the same rationale he had used at the Chamber meeting. Fred wrapped up his pitch with an attempt at humor.

"So, Nick, how do we keep the greens from throwing their same old monkey wrenches into the works every time someone tries to bring a few new jobs up here?"

Nick answered, unsmiling, "Don't mess the place up and no wrenches need to be thrown."

Fred blinked, seeing that Nick was not going to make it easy. "That's fine if that means your folks will not automatically oppose these ideas."

Nick waved Fred's comment away. "We don't automatically oppose anything, Fred. We look at it and we compare what the land and the Valley would be like after the new ideas get carried out, and then we compare it to how things were—or how they ought to be, in the case of restoring the river flow."

Then he stopped talking and just looked at Fred for a few moments. He started up again, slower, as if he wasn't sure Fred would understand what he was saying.

"Let's say you're right, Fred. Let's say the feds and DWP are going to sell some land—a lot of land. And let's say there is in fact a way to get to some serious geothermal power, not just a few vents around the Valley. And let's say Max and his friends persuade most of the tribes to go along because they'll get some real jobs out of it." He paused, letting his stipulations sink in. Then he lowered his voice and increased its intensity: "The problem is—*it's all illegal.* What you're proposing breaks at least fifteen environmental laws—for openers."

Fred shook his head, frowning. "That's not how our lawyers see it. Max has done a lot of work with tribal lawyers around the country from some of the tribes that have already gotten into alternative energy projects. The sovereignty thing is a big card, Nick—and you know it."

Nick nodded. "Yes, it is, and for good reason. We've all screwed the tribes for almost four hundred years, and we're a long way from balancing the scales. But," and Nick was now pointing his finger at Fred, "we don't have to do it at the expense of the land they revere. And we aren't going to go green with solar and geothermal and at the same time screw up all that hard work we've done for years fighting to get water back in the river. We didn't do all that just to set up some huge solar plants or geothermal plants that would pollute the river again, just as it's starting to grow out a little along the banks. Heat like that brought up from that far down doesn't always make things so great up on the surface. We'd want some serious environmental reviews."

Then he changed the subject. "Fred, I hear they're about to catch up with this nutcase who is killing people. Sounds like he's been deliberately trying to get some of us mad at the rest of us. We heard what happened to the sign that the land trust just put up out by the Kyle ranch. We've spent some time worrying about how deep these divisions among all of us are, and some of our leaders have been thinking about the Valley and where we could work a little harder to carve out some agreements. So I'm going to keep listening to you—but I want to make sure you keep listening to me."

He paused, and went on. "We may even want to talk about some kind of dialogue where we would keep talking about this in an organized way, bringing the tribes in and DWP and the feds and everybody else with a stake in it. Maybe we could try it that way before firing off press releases and unleashing the pit bull lawyers. Maybe we could even get Max to suggest some ground rules that come from the way the tribes make decisions like these, working for consensus carefully, taking time to listen to everyone, instead of all our bloody rules and laws messing things up."

He continued, "Fred, I've seen some strange things lately around here. A Supervisor running for re-election recently said the Valley ought to be about solar power, geothermal, and European tourism. Of course, he had to throw in mining, talking about the price of gold lately. That's all we need—some more holes in the hills."

"But three out of four ain't bad," said Fred.

"No, it's not. Fred, here's where I agree with you. If we wait for Washington and Sacramento to solve this thing, they'll screw it up from here to eternity. But if we can put together a process here that respects the land and the law, we might just come to an agreement that the feds and the state would have to honor, because we worked it out here on the ground, where it matters." He smiled. "I heard you were over at the Chamber earlier this week talking about what you called 'Victorville North.' Well, you're right—none of us want that. So if we can put this together, and spend the time it deserves, and make sure the tribes are true equal partners and are not just getting bought off again—there is no end to what we might be able to get done. It will be uphill, but sometimes you can make an uphill road smoother."

It was the most hopeful thing Fred could have imagined Nick saying, though the shrewd businessman side of him heard no concessions on the issues. But even a midway point in exploring the disagreements might be a start, Fred realized, and as he shook hands with Nick at the end of the meeting, he was cautiously hopeful.

And then, as he drove home, he had a distantly familiar thought, one he had not felt for a long time: he wanted to hurry home to tell Dale about what had happened and get her reaction.

CHAPTER 63

Rudy parked and got out of his cruiser. He had waited until the end of the day, trying to find a time when he was likely to see Jud Mills away from the school. Someone had told him that Jud and his friends hung out at the liquor store on Line Street and sure enough, they were there, five of them, leaning up against the building.

They started whispering and snickering as Rudy got out of the car and began heading toward them. He made sure he didn't give them any reaction to their disrespect.

"Jud, got a minute? I'd like to talk with you."

"What about? I didn't do nothing wrong."

"I didn't say you did. I'd like to talk to you."

Now it had become a contest between Jud's not wanting to yield to Rudy and not wanting his sidekicks to think that he was scared. So Jud pushed off the building and walked slowly over to Rudy.

"What?"

"I hear you were hassling Duane Callison at school the other day."

"That little wimp? Why, did he call you and complain? I didn't hurt him—I just told him to remember who he is."

"That's not really your job, Jud. You need to leave Duane alone from now on." He paused. "I'm pretty sure I'll hear about it if you bother him, so don't. OK?"

"Yeah. Maybe. Maybe you'll be hearing from my brother, too."

"That'd be fine, Jud. You tell Hank to call me if he wants; I'd be glad to let him know what you're up to." Rudy saw the look of fear and surprise cross Jud's face and knew he had scored. He suspected that Jud had only told Hank Mills his version of the Duane story, and now Jud was worried that the bullying side of it was going to come out. Fighting was not a bad thing among men in the tribe, sometimes, but unfair fighting was frowned on as unmanly.

Rudy walked back to his car and could hear Jud trying to repair his standing with the rest of the boys. He knew he would hear from Hank fairly soon.

The call came sooner than he expected. That afternoon, he was leaving his office when the phone rang. It was Hank. Rudy had steered clear of Hank, who had graduated several years before Rudy, and who was actually Jud's half-brother. He was involved in several shady enterprises and had, Rudy knew, served time in state prison for drug dealing.

Hank got right to it. "You threatened my brother, Warland?"

"No, I did not. He was beating up a kid a lot smaller than him, Hank. Half his size. With a bunch of other guys standing around backing him up. Not so brave."

There was a pause, and Rudy knew Hank had not heard this version of what had happened. So Rudy pressed. "I have no quarrel with you or with Jud, Hank. But he needs to leave that kid alone. Duane Callison did nothing to bother Jud."

"He shot his mouth off in class. Trying to show the rest of them up. Jud was just putting him in his place."

"He was manhandling the kid, Hank, and that's bullying, and that's against school policy and state law. And he'll get arrested the next time it happens."

Hank snorted. "Maybe we can settle this, you and me, if you can take your badge off some time."

"Maybe. And maybe you'd like to put on some gloves and work out with me at the gym down in Lone Pine some time."

Rudy was not a boxer, but he had worked out with the boxing team at Fresno a few times and knew he had enough speed and reach to embarrass Hank in front of whatever witnesses they would both bring to such an event. Hank weighed about 250 pounds on a 5'7" frame and usually had one of his thugs do his fighting for him.

"Screw it—I'm not dancing around some stupid ring with you. You leave Jud alone and he'll leave that little pipsqueak alone."

"That works for me." Rudy rang off, knowing he would need to keep an extra eye out for Hank but that Jud was in at least as much trouble as Rudy was.

PART FIVE: THE END GAME

CHAPTER 64

Dobson headed north to Bishop. He knew that the town would be full of Mule Days celebrants during the week leading up to Memorial Day, and he planned to take full advantage of it as he continued his havoc. He suspected the Navy flights might have infrared detection, so he had rigged up a heat shield that might dissipate some of the bike's heat signal. He rode the bike north at night into an area outside town, along Line Street where the Owens River crossed the street, and hid it in some brush. He walked the two miles into town, arriving the day before the Mule Days parade. His next "action" was going to happen along 395 just north of the fairgrounds, and he headed that way.

As he walked, Dobson replayed each of the three shootings over and over, trying to squeeze all the revenge he could out of the look on each of the victims' faces in the last few seconds after they saw his intent but before they actually registered the impact. Finnerty's had been too fast, he realized, but he had hated Finnerty more than the other two, who were really accidental victims, in the wrong place at the wrong time—or the right time, from Dobson's view.

Washburn had been his first, and as the beginning of his revenge, he was still Dobson's favorite. His death had set the whole plot in motion, whereas Finnerty and Nilsson had merely shown that he could kill any time he wanted and that he was completely in control of events in the Valley he hated so much.

The Mule Days event had blossomed into one of the biggest tourist draws of the year, stretching over five days, and attracting as many as 30,000 people into Bishop. It drew politicians from all over eastern California. The featured events were a parade down Main Street, a rodeo at the fairgrounds north of the downtown areas, country music in the fairgrounds, and six parking lots set aside for RVs and horse/mule trailers. The locals advertised the parade as "the longest running non-motorized parade in the U.S."

The Sheriff, the Bishop police, and the CHP had had several meetings to consider canceling Mule Days in light of the killings, but decided that they needed to go ahead with a sign of normalcy. So they gave the green light, with the understanding that extra police would be on duty, along with the DWP force and the added state officers. So far, the crowds had been noticeably lighter than in recent years, but there were still thousands of people in town. Banners were stretched across Main Street, concession stands were set up along the Main Street parade route, and three flatbed trucks were backed up to side street intersections with the parade route, rigged with platforms for videocamera operators and the local cable station.

Dobson arrived on Main Street early in the morning as the parade was setting up. He had sown another seed of disruption the day before, and had stayed overnight in a small storage shed behind one of the downtown businesses that had been "locked" with an easily picked padlock. He went into a coffee shop for breakfast, knowing that he would easily blend in with the crowds, able to go anywhere he wanted in town. He assumed that by now they had his driver's license picture posted, but he had been careful when having it taken to grow a mustache and wear his naturally dark hair long. Before his last trip north he had shaved off the mustache and cut his hair very close, dying it blonde. He kept a long-billed cap on, managing to cover much of his face.

By this time, Dobson was certain that over the next week or so, he had no better than an even chance of escaping from the dozens of officers and civilians who were looking for him. From what he could pick up on the local radio and a few overheard conversations, he could tell that his actions had split the Valley in just the way he had hoped, setting fire to some of the vengeance he had worked so hard to achieve in his father's memory. He had been ready to die, but as his plan worked out, he had begun to believe that he might be able to escape. He had gradually developed a plan that might improve his odds of escape, and he was ready to carry it out after his final disruption at Mule Days.

Dobson rose to leave the coffee shop, left a ten for the meal and a tip, and noticed an older man who was waiting to pay his bill. He thought he remembered seeing the man somewhere, maybe on television, but not recently. But the name escaped him, and he quickly exited to the street and the crowds waiting outside for the parade.

Sam Leonard watched the tall, thin young man who had kept a cap on his head through his entire meal, and wondered why he was moving so furtively. In forty years of journalism, Sam had learned to observe people, and he knew something was not right with the young man. But he didn't make the connection with the events around the killings in the Valley. Sam walked outside and headed for the corner where he had agreed to meet Ernie Scott. They planned to watch the parade and then get together with Jim Scott at Cecilia's café.

Cecelia had negotiated another truce with Rosa, in part because she needed her to help run the concession stand at the fairgrounds during Mule Days. So they were loading their truck together and pretending that they hadn't had another tense conversation about Jim Scott. As they worked, Cecelia replayed her conversation with Rosa last night. She remembered her part of it with pain, aware that she had over-reacted badly, and seeing from Rosa's softer response that she was determined to spend more time with Jim. Cecelia remembered Jim's reaction to her comments at the community meeting, and began to formulate her apology and an invitation for Jim to come to dinner.

Fred and Dale Bancroft had made a Memorial Day tradition of watching the parade from the second story of a friend's motel on Main Street. They had joined with their friends for the past ten years, ensuring them a much better view of the parade than most spectators had on the sidewalks. Dale brought the chips and dips, Fred brought the beer, and they had tacitly agreed to set aside their cautious attempts to work through Dale's recent losses and Fred's attempted betrayal of Max—at least for the day. The day brought back some good memories of earlier years when they had attended the parade, and Fred settled back to enjoying himself and to being with his friends and his wife.

Jim Scott parked behind his favorite hangout in Bishop, a bar that catered only to locals and was uniformly hostile to outsiders. He planned to have a morning beer and then watch the parade and catch up with Rosa. It was a bar defined by a great story Jim had heard told and retold a dozen times. Two women who had a permanent relationship ran a small clothing store on Main Street, and after work they would sometimes stroll over to the bar and have a few drinks. One evening two men from Southern California who were similarly inclined toward their own gender stopped their car at the stoplight, and noticed the women entering the bar holding hands. They parked their car, and went into the bar. Within thirty seconds or so, they were quickly escorted outside by a large bartender. When they protested that "you let those women in your bar," the bartender scoffed and said "Them? They ain't queer—they're local."

Elaine Carpenter stood with her youth group, which had a float in the parade. She had spent an hour trying to steer fifteen units worth of raw energy and adolescent hormones in the general direction of useful activity, deciding who would sit where on the float, who would walk, and how the driver was going to see the road through the greenery wrapped around the front of the truck. She loved the challenge of working with the youth and seeing them eventually come up with something productive, but this was one of the times when she most missed Ed, who had a quiet, joking way of working with teens that was much less jumpy than her own attempts to corral them. Which was a fitting image, she realized, as she found herself downwind of the mules that would walk ahead of them in the parade.

Howard had assigned Rudy and Liz to watch the parade, and had gone back to the Bishop sub-station to deploy more forces to cover the rest of the events. The interagency circus had subsided somewhat, as everyone realized that thousands of temporary residents in town would offer new possibilities for trouble. The town was covered block-by-block along Main Street and the major side streets, with teams of twos and threes, and every agency was participating fully. The Bishop Police, the CHP, and the OCSD had the lead, with private DWP cops and some feds filling in behind them.

So Liz and Rudy were working the parade, walking up and down Main Street together, letting people see them armed and in uniform. Liz had left the girls at home with the sitter, having promised them a trip to the rodeo and entertainment that night. The girls were jaded, having seen several parades in their lives, and not at all interested, as Jessica put it, in "another parade with a bunch of stinky mules." Marilyn McGill was available to watch them, so Paul had decided to grade papers at school while Liz worked the parade.

At their morning conference, Liz had speculated that Dobson was unlikely to show up at Mule Days, but Rudy pointed out that he had been unpredictable throughout the whole tangled history of his vendetta against the Valley. So they were on the lookout for him as they moved through the crowd along Main Street. As they walked, Rudy briefed Liz on the latest phone call he had gotten from Howard.

The day before, a message had come from the Bishop casino, intended for the local cable TV station. It was clearly marked as having been written on a computer at the local casino. It said "*Finnerty was the first; beware to those who disparage our Nation. The Ghost Dancers will ride again! Stay tuned.*"

The station was sitting on the story for a day, at the Sheriff's request, but they were going to run it in 24 hours if they couldn't get any additional information that it was phony.

When the call came in, Howard had asked Rudy to go check out the casino. It was a delicate assignment, and Rudy knew he was deliberately going alone because of the sensitivities. A few years ago, the Sheriff's forces had gone into the casino to investigate some reported welfare fraud by employees of the casino who were working while receiving welfare. The raid had gotten ugly, and the casino security forces had kicked the Sheriff out, who came back the next day with bolt cutters and took files for all the casino employees, not just the alleged fraud cases.

Because of the thorny tribal sovereignty implications, the case had actually gone to the U.S. Supreme Court, after battles in district court, and the Sheriff was partly vindicated. But it had led to even more suspicion on both sides, and Rudy ended up getting caught in the middle every time he ventured onto the reservation on any official business. So he moved very carefully whenever he was asked to play the role of designated inspector, which he disliked, but understood to be part of his deal with the Sheriff.

Rudy arrived at the casino around 3 pm. As he entered, the casino was a brightly-lit scene of constant sound, the legendary ka-ching of the slot machines, punctuated occasionally by the plopping sound of coins dropping into containers designed to amplify the sound to the maximum, the quieter murmur of card games as dealers relayed their tallies of wins and losses, and the background buzz from the coffee shop as early afternoon customers rehearsed their recurring stories of conquest and misery. The tough California smoking law was not in force in the casino, based on its sovereignty, and the prohibition of alcohol seemed to have the effect of redoubling smokers' addictions, so the tobacco smell wafted into the casino and added to the air of decadence.

For mid-afternoon, a surprising number of people half-filled the room. Six people sat in the coffee shop, maybe twenty were at the tables, and another dozen or so were seated in front of the slots, nestled up against the flashing machines, cups of coins at their elbows. With staff, there were at least fifty people visible in the casino.

Rudy could quickly pick out the role players who work in every casino—waiters, dealers, uniformed security guys, undercover "watchers." He looked for the security cameras and spotted only two, angled down at the poker and blackjack tables, which Rudy suspected still left half the larger room uncovered.

The head dealer—Rudy could tell by the placement of her table and the confident look and half-smile she gave him as he walked in—was finishing up a round of blackjack. She swept up the cards and chips, offering a lingering view of her low-cut blouse, and focused on Rudy. "Need to talk to me?"

"Yes, if you've got a minute. Not official, just talk. I'm Rudy Warland."

"Ruth Montero. Let me check out for a while. Andy doesn't like us to be away without backup. Sheila can cover for me."

Andy Thornton was the casino manager, and he and Rudy had a strained relationship. Andy had been one of those who had singled Rudy out for ridicule when he made clear he was going on to college, and neither of them had forgotten their confrontations in high school. Rudy knew there were bad feelings, and he and Andy had stayed away from each other as much as possible.

But Rudy was going to have to talk to Andy to find out what had happened, so the session with Ruth was going to be a warmup. She came back and sat down in one of the booths across from Rudy. She was an improbable blonde with mostly Hispanic features, and, Rudy noticed, great hands with no rings. She saw him looking at her hands and gave him a slow grin, moving one hand slowly over the other. "Is this about that creep who's shooting people?"

"Partly. Has anyone been hanging around here who looks strange—who might have gotten to the computers here?"

She looked over at a wide mirror hanging too far above the room to be anything other than a one-way window. "You'd have to ask Andy, but there was a guy in here yesterday who said he was doing an audit or something with the computers." She half-turned to the window and did a quick hand signal with three fingers, then a fist, which Rudy assumed was a summons. Within thirty seconds, Andy came out a door underneath the mirror.

He was civil, friendly enough to keep the conversation moving. He confirmed that they had been "security audited" by a firm out of Reno that had sent the guy Ruth mentioned. The guy took a few hours and checked the security filters on all the computers used at the casino. Andy described a tall, young-looking technician who obviously knew a lot about the machines and had credentials from the company the casino had used before, so Andy let him go ahead and check the equipment.

Rudy explained, watching Andy carefully. "We think he sent a message from here. We think it might be the guy who did the killings. Looks like he is trying to start fights between groups here in the Valley. We don't want you to talk about this to anyone." Andy was nervous about having the casino's computers used without authorization, and he quickly agreed to stay quiet, and Rudy left.

It had to be Dobson. Rudy called Howard. "He's in Bishop, and he went to the casino to use their computer. The message fits the guy's pattern—he tries to get one group pissed off at another, and now he's working the Finnerty angle again."

Howard quickly ended the call, telling Rudy that he was going to call the TV station and tell them the email had been another of Dobson's tricks. He was confident he could pressure them not to release it once they saw what Dobson was doing.

As they walked along Main Street, noticing the extra uniformed presence along the parade route, Rudy said to Liz, keeping his voice low, "I think he's here. We picked up his trail in Pearsonville and then outside Lone Pine, he goes to the casino, and now Mule Days gives him cover for whatever he is going to do next."

"I don't know," Liz answered. "This guy is a loner. We've got thousands of people here, which is not his scene. He's OK when he's holed up in some rathole out in the desert, not walking down Main Street with lots of people around him. What's he going to do next, anyway? We know he hates all of us, blames us for his old man's death. He wants us all to start fighting among ourselves, like Elaine and the Sheriff said at the meeting. So what's he going to do next? Where the hell is he?"

Dobson's downloaded pictures of all of the deputies from a newsletter published by the Sheriff's Department enabled him to recognize both Liz and Rudy as they walked by him. He knew from the scanner that they were part of the team assigned to find him. He felt a rush as they went past him and turned into the City Park where dozens of arts and crafts booths had been set up along the stream that ran through the park. Briefly he thought about following them, and then he realized that would be a risk beyond even his sizable appetite for thrills. But having seen them, he realized that they were watching for him, and he began thinking about a way to neutralize them.

CHAPTER 65

An hour went by, full of visiting politicians, bands, baton twirlers, floats with waving kids—and hundreds of mules. Then the parade was over. Liz and Rudy moved on over to the fairgrounds. As they entered, they saw that the Sheriff had lost an argument to the organizers of the event, because there was no body scanner set up at the gates. The Sheriff had argued that it would be safer, but since the fairgrounds was actually owned by the state, technically the Highway Patrol was in charge of the site. The company that operated the fairgrounds concessions had lobbied for no scanners out of fear that it would remind the crowd what had been going on in the Valley. It was the last thing they wanted if people were going to loosen up and spend money. And the CHP had agreed.

The crowds definitely seemed smaller than Liz remembered from the year before. But the familiar smells of popcorn, fry bread, and overcooked hot dogs fit in well with the merchandise in the booths they were walking by as they moved toward the grandstand: raffles of ancient cars, backpacks, carved materials, T-shirts, and cowboy hats. Lines wound out from most of the booths, as customers waited patiently to buy their souvenirs and food. The atmosphere was relaxed, a welcome relief from the tensions of the last few weeks.

Liz murmured to Rudy, as they walked through the crowd, which was getting thicker as they approached the metal stairs leading into the western side of the grandstand, "Watch for somebody who's watching us."

And as soon as she had said it, she saw what she was looking for. A tall, fairly thin man with a cap who was holding a canvas bag had been staring at them from the first row of the grandstand, quickly turning away when Liz stopped scanning the crowd and stared back at him. "Rudy, look at that tall guy over there. Remind you of the aerial shot the Navy guys showed us?" She looked over at Rudy, but when she looked back, the guy was gone. "He was right over there, come on." And she started walking fast, not wanting to cause a stir in the crowd, but not wanting the guy to get away. She assumed he would go down the stairs on the right of the grandstand, and headed there with Rudy hurrying behind.

But when they got there, the guy had disappeared. They half walked, half ran down the ramp leading up to the grandstand, and then raced around the corner to a concessions area behind the grandstand. But they saw nothing but mules and their handlers in the corrals to the east of the grandstand area. The corrals were set up along the far edge of the fairgrounds, running along Highway 395 over to an area where 395 and US 6 came together, which locals called "the Y."

To the west, behind them, spectators were beginning to file into the grandstand, but it was still an hour to the rodeo kickoff parade, and the crowd was still building, moving slowly, munching on their corndogs and fry bread.

Rudy pointed to the corrals and said "He's headed over there, it's darker and he can hide better behind the mules and the trailers. Let's go, call it in." As Rudy began running, Liz cursed her slowness, but knew Rudy could get there faster than she could, and clicked her radio to raise the dispatcher. Panting as she tried to follow Rudy, she gasped out "Possible sighting in fairgrounds area, Nolan and Warland following suspect. Send assistance to corrals east of the grandstand over by the Y."

As she came around a corner of the corral area, she almost ran into Rudy, who had stopped and was looking intently at a group of mule handlers who had gathered in a cluster. One of them was standing apart from the others, and was slowly moving to the far side of the group so that the handlers would be between him and the officers.

Rudy said "If that isn't him, it's a guy who's acting very weird. Let's split up and try to scare him out of there."

He moved off to the right, motioning with his left hand that Liz should move around to the other side of the nearest corral. They had moved about twenty steps apart when the group of handlers dispersed and headed toward the grandstand area. Liz could no longer see Rudy, and as she stood up on the lower rail of the metal corral to look around, she suddenly saw a spark jump off the top rail and heard a loud metallic ping where the spark had been. She ducked down below the top rail, clicked on the radio, softly said "Shots fired, Nolan in corral area," and stayed low as she bent over and moved slowly toward where she had last seen Rudy. She could hear the sirens, and wondered if that would flush the guy out into the open.

Later, when he heard about it, Bill Solomon inevitably said to someone, "That reminds me of the scene in *Gunfight at OK Corral* when they are firing at each other from behind the cows in the corral." Having seen the movie, Rudy had to agree—when the cows moved, the gunfighters moved, and that was just how it was playing out. There were only six mules in the pen, but they had sensed the shots and the intruder, and were braying and moving nervously to the far side of the corral. Rudy had heard the ping of the first shot at Liz, and then heard what had to be a second shot plow into the trailer right behind him. Clearly Dobson had a silencer, and obviously he wasn't afraid to fire at them. Rudy maneuvered slowly, knowing Liz was headed back toward him, and then saw her. They moved together this time around to where the shots seemed to have come from, hearing the sirens growing louder all around the fairgrounds.

But when they got around to where he had been, and the other officers from the local police arrived, there was no one there. They searched an area that ended up on the far fence where the fairgrounds bordered 395, and found a place where the fence had been cut. Dobson had been there, and he had gotten out of their net. So they sent out foot patrols in the surrounding blocks, while at the same time putting out all points warnings on every highway he might use to leave the area. Ten or fifteen minutes went by as the area was closed off, but Liz and Rudy were both afraid that Dobson had gotten out of the net.

Liz was angry. "Dammit—we had him. Wonder what he was going to do here if we hadn't spotted him?"

Later, Liz's question got a chilling answer. The forensics team that was trying to find some trace of Dobson came across a bag with three flash grenades. It looked as if Dobson had planned to throw them into the crowd at the grandstand, which would have caused panic and probably some serious trampling and deaths. If Liz hadn't spotted him, it could have been the most deadly incident of all.

CHAPTER 66

And then Liz got the worst phone call of her life.

Her cell rang, she saw a "restricted caller" label on the caller ID, and debated answering. But she went ahead and clicked on. "Liz Nolan, who is this?"

There was a pause and then a very soft voice came on, saying "This is the guy you are looking for, Liz Nolan. You and your people are making it uncomfortable for me, so I am going to have to change my base of operations and get a little more aggressive. I hope everything is OK there on Fowler Street at your house. You might want to check, though." And then the line went dead.

Liz felt a dagger in her heart. Fumbling at first because her hands were shaking, she dialed the house. After ten rings she knew no one was going to answer. She called Paul, but realized he was still at school and often turned his phone off when he was grading papers. She called out to Rudy, hoping he was following her, and raced across the fairgrounds to the patrol car and her home just six blocks away.

She burst in the front door and found Marilyn McGill unconscious in the rocking chair in the front room, with a trace of blood on her temple. She checked to see that she was breathing, then raced upstairs to the girls' rooms. They were empty, as she knew they would be.

Rudy had managed to catch up with her at the fairgrounds and leapt in the car at the last minute. He was standing in the front door, calling Howard and letting him know what had happened.

And then Jennie walked in the front door, tears running down her face. "Mama, a bad man took Jessie. He took Daddy's car, and then made me get out and said he only needed one of us. He hit Mrs.

McGill and made her go to sleep." As she finished, the words were coming out in spasms, punctuated by her sobbing.

Marilyn McGill was conscious by the time they got her to the hospital, which was only a few blocks away, and the emergency room doctor said she had a mild concussion and should stay there overnight. Paul had raced home from school and kept Jennie occupied with television. Once Marilyn had been wheeled off to a room, Liz and Rudy walked outside to see Howard and three other deputies there, along with two of the CHP detail.

Howard quickly brought them up to date. "We've got road blocks up north and south, but he may have gotten by us. We posted it on the Amber Alert all over the state. If he goes back into the offroad areas, we're going to have to use the Navy's infrared equipment, and they've got a flight taking off in fifteen minutes or so." He looked hard at Liz. "How you doing?"

"I'm OK. We're going to find her. I know we're going to find her." She was flat, with almost no emotion. Howard looked worried, but behind Liz's back Rudy motioned to him and he nodded to Rudy when she looked away. She was on the phone to Paul as the car pulled away from the house, now with a look of raw pain on her face that Rudy could barely watch.

When they got to the Bishop substation, Rudy took Howard aside a few steps away from the group. "Jack, I think this guy is going north; he knows we are all over his place down South. Either that or he's going over Westgaard into Nevada. But I think he wants to move fast and I think he's going north."

"Makes some sense." Howard looked at his watch. "He's got about an hour on us, maybe a little more, based on when he took those shots at you two at the fairgrounds. The Bishop force will watch the streets and roads around the city. Move on up Sherwin with the CHP cars out front. Watch the old road, too. Maybe he'll stop, with the kid with him. Maybe you'll have to follow him into Nevada—they're watching at the state line and all the way up to Reno. Take Liz with you, but watch her. I'm going to ask her if she wants to go home and she'll say no. So watch her."

Howard was dead right with his prediction about Liz, and as she got into Rudy's car, she asked him, furious, "What the hell made him think I was going to go home and sit by the damned phone?!"

Rudy answered softly, "He wanted to give you the chance to be with Paul and Jennie, that's all. He knew you would want to keep after Dobson, but he wanted to give you the chance."

CHAPTER 67

As he drove north, Dobson began to doubt that taking the kid had been such a good idea. For one thing, she was likely to slow him down. For another, she was weird, sitting on the far side of the front seat and softly singing a song he thought sounded like "If only I could have a puppy, I'd call myself so very lucky." But she kept singing it over and over, never getting to the next line. He decided she was retarded or something and wondered if he could drop the kid somewhere. It had seemed like a good idea to steal the cop's own kid as a hostage, but now he wasn't sure.

And then he heard a soft beeping sound. Looking down at the dashboard, he saw a fuel tank light flashing. The damned car was almost out of gas! He cursed, and Jessie came out of her reverie and frowned at him, saying "We're not supposed to say that word."

"Shut up, kid."

"We're not supposed to say shut up, *either*. You're in a lot of trouble, mister. My mom is a cop and she is going to arrest you and lock you *up*! You'd better take me home, right *now*. I want to see my momma."

As he raised his hand to swipe at her, Dobson suddenly had a mental image of himself sitting on a rock crying. He lowered his hand to the steering wheel, and started looking for a turnoff where he could get another car.

CHAPTER 68

Irene Pinsky had moved to the Valley from London in the 1950's, when land was cheap. She was a skillful negotiator, and she ended up owning millions of dollars worth of property around Round Valley, at the northern edge of Owens County.

She had bought land off the Old Sherwin Grade Road, along the Lower Rock Creek Road, and built an astonishing architectural testament to the mountains—a building constructed with an open view of the Sierra and the Whites out its front and back sides. She had brought in special strengthened windows so that the soaring vistas of both ranges could be seen through broad expanses of glass that made the mountains seem a few hundred yards away.

She had deliberately built on the last few acres in Owens County before the county line at Boundary Road. When she first arrived in the Eastern Sierra, she had been in negotiations with Mono County to the north, but something had gone wrong, and Owens County ended up the winner.

She had named it the Palmer's Green Inn, and only those who knew London well understood why she had imported a name from the old East End of London. Elaine Carpenter had met her soon after moving to the Bishop area, and had become a good friend.

Irene had never fished in her life, but she could describe lake and stream trout and lures for hours. She had a board with lures on it that she fished up from the depths of the lake with a huge magnet somebody had given her, and she must have had thousands of them.

After living that long in the Valley, she had had won the respect of nearly everyone who lived in Owens County. She wore her years well, with classic features on a small frame, and a voice and manner that recalled Audrey Hepburn at her most gamine. But beneath that porcelain exterior she was tough as nails. She had had to be, carving out a small empire in country as raw as the Eastern Sierra had been in earlier decades.

Yet for all her toughness, she had a very soft spot for children. In the afternoons, she ran an informal reading group for some of the children, which she had organized as an afterschool program for the children after their bus rides down to the Round Valley School. Elaine had visited her a few times while she was sitting with the children in a small classroom area that she had made out of a corner of the hotel lobby. Watching her read to them, encouraging them to pick out words themselves, Elaine saw that Irene was a gifted teacher. A small tributary of Rock Creek ran through her property, and she had widened it to build several enclosed fishing holes for children who stayed at the Inn.

One night Elaine sat with her on the wide porch of her log-cabin residence adjacent to the Inn, where she lived in the summer—she stayed in Florida and the Caribbean in the winters. Elaine asked her why she had bought the hotel, and why in such a godforsaken place, compared to London.

Irene was quiet, and then answered, softly, "Because of the bombs."

"The bombs?

"Yes. I was in London as a child in the Blitz, and then they evacuated us, and we lived in the countryside. And then they moved us back and we were there when the V1s and V2s came down. It was terrible, and random, and unforgettable. And I never again wanted to live in a place that was crowded enough to be worth bombing." She looked around for a full minute, at the stream flowing by her front porch, the Sierra, the sky and stars overhead, and no more than five lights from houses out across her secluded part of the Valley. "This seems to fill that bill, don't you think?"

CHAPTER 69

As they approached the Sherwin Grade on 395, Liz was watching the Old Road out the left side of the back seat. Suddenly she shouted, "Stop—I think I see our car." She had spotted a car that looked like Paul's Escape parked on the east side of the Palmer's Green Inn. They slowed and motioned to the following CHP cars, waving them to go on past and then radioing them to cut back at the Rock Creek turnout so that they could not be seen from the hotel.

When the cruisers had all arrived at the bottom of the road up to the hotel, staying out of sight of the front windows, Howard motioned the team over to his command car and squatted down. "Check around back for other cars, and put a team back there. Check doors and passageways—we need to know all the exits when we go in. Now let me get the Sheriff." He picked up his cell phone and speed dialed a single digit, turning away from the group to talk.

The team crept up to the outer wall of the hotel, careful not to expose themselves through the wide glass front wall of the building facing the Sierra. Pines were planted closely together along the front of the hotel, and provided ample cover as the team moved. Two other officers had crawled out and placed disabling puncture strips under the Escape's front wheels in case Dobson somehow got past them and tried to drive away. The two shooters on the team had maneuvered around, trying to get a sniper's angle through the window of the lobby, but the front desk where they thought Dobson was probably standing was off to the side and out of the line of sight from the front windows. They tried to raise Irene Pinsky on the hotel phone, but no one was answering.

As they waited, Liz knew they would not let her go in with the first wave. She would ask, and Howard would turn her down. For Liz, the inaction was as bad as her worry about Jessie. Action was everything to her, movement defined her, and she kept pushing down her memory of the Bonds incident when she had to act suddenly, decisively, to recapture the control she had almost lost. But here the control was gone, again, and she felt a nearly physical pain to have to trust others with her flesh and blood.

Rudy was assigned to lead the first team, and he took Liz aside and said quietly "I'll get her. They'll go for him, and I'll get her out of the way. I promise you."

Howard came over to her. She was standing by the cruiser, parked behind the dense row of trees that screened the hotel from the old road to Rock Creek. "The Sheriff agrees we've got three choices, but he wants to go in now and forget the other options. You do not have a veto—but I want to know what you think before we make the call. The second choice is to tell Dobson we're here and try to talk him down. But he's got at least two hostages in there and it could be a long time."

Liz asked, looking up toward the front of the hotel, "What's the third choice?"

"We wait until it gets a lot darker and try to sneak up on him for a disabling shot. But then we run the risk that he gets away with her even if we have the place surrounded. He ties her to the car or something as he drives out, and we have a very messy chase scene with blown tires and Jessie in the car."

Howard stopped, looked at his team as they checked equipment, and then turned back to Liz. "One other thing. Sheriff knows the lady who runs this place. Says she's very steady and won't go soft on us. That helps." He waited for Liz to say something, and watched her carefully.

"I want to go in with the first wave."

Bluntly, Howard said "No way, not going to happen that way."

She said, eyes closed, "All right. Do it. Go on in now. Have Rudy in the front—he told me he'd go in first. Do it."

Liz stood watching the team adjusting their flak jackets and checking their weapons. She thought of Bonds again, and she thought of her father, and then with great clarity, she thought of Jessie. She felt in her pocket. She had grabbed a T-shirt of Jessie's as she ran out of the house, knowing without wanting to think about it that the K-9 unit dogs might need it to track her. She raised it to her face, smelling pure Jessie: soap, bubble bath, little girl smells, conjuring up all that Jessie was, her enthusiasm, and how much she sometimes needed Liz. She closed her eyes for a moment, then opened them, shoved the shirt back in her pocket, and started walking.

She headed over to the backup truck where there was a pile of flak jackets, slung one on without buttoning it, and said, to no one, "Screw this. That's my kid." And then she started walking toward the front door.

Howard had his back to her, and Rudy was the only one on the team who saw her start walking past the group pressed up against the wall just outside the front door. He broke from the group and said, walking quickly backwards in front of her "No, Liz, it's more dangerous this way. Don't go in." But she kept walking, her 9 now out and in her hand. For a second, Rudy thought he should grab her and stop her, but he knew Liz well enough to suspect that could be even worse for Jessie—and for Liz. He stopped and let her walk by, and then frantically motioned the rest of his team up to follow her in on his signal. He pulled out his own sidearm and moved up next to the window beside the front door.

Inside the hotel, Dobson had a short leash around Jessie's neck, with the leash taped to his left arm. He was holding a gun on Irene as she stood behind the registration desk. Jessie had a strange look on her face, and to Irene it seemed as though the child was in a trance. Five minutes before, Dobson had burst in the back door of the hotel and had forced Irene to give him some food from the hotel kitchen. He made Irene order the small hotel staff into a guest room on the far side of the ground floor.

Dobson said, "Now that I've eaten your swill, I need money and I need another car. You've got three minutes to give it to me before I cut this brat." He pulled hard on Jessie's arm, causing her to stumble forward.

Irene said with icy calmness, "There's no need for that. I'll get you money and you can take the shuttle van. There are the keys," pointing to a set of keys hanging by the desk.

Dobson quickly grabbed the keys and asked "Where's the van?'

"Just outside in the back, it's through that door." She motioned to a door on the other side of the room from the registration desk and began walking around from behind the counter to Dobson. "I'll get you some money."

As Dobson turned toward the back door, the front door of the lobby swung open.

As Liz walked in the front door, gun drawn, Dobson wheeled and raised his gun, dropping the leash he had around Jessie's neck. Before he was able to train his gun on Liz, two shots were fired. The first was Rudy's shot, aimed through the side window into the ceiling, intended to distract Dobson as the first wave of deputies rushed in a few steps behind Liz and the second wave broke in from the back of the lobby. As the first shot registered with Dobson, he turned his eyes away from Irene toward Liz, and Irene pulled out a .22 target pistol she had been holding under the counter and shot Dobson in the temple from less than six inches away. He slumped to the floor, his gun dropping onto the carpet.

Irene and Liz reached Jessie at the same time, putting their arms around the child, turning her away from Dobson's body. Irene unfastened the leash and threw it on a chair by the registration desk, as Liz began walking Jessie away from the lobby, down a hallway to the dining room. Irene caught up to them and walked beside Jessie, talking to her in a soft voice about some books she wanted to show her.

Howard came over to Rudy and the team, shaking his head and looking at Dobson in a pool of blood as the team called for a meaningless ambulance. "We lucked out."

"Yeah, but that Pinsky woman was fast."

"Liz is still Liz."

"Yeah. All guts, all the time. This time it worked out. One person coming in might have been a better play than rushing the bastard."

"Yeah, but who knew we had a sharpshooter already inside?"

"Good thing. Another tough lady." He watched Irene as she continued reading to Jessie, who was now in Liz's lap in one of two big arm chairs that had been pulled together in the dining room.

Rudy answered, "Tough and very fast. I figured I was going to get winged and then someone else would get him. But she had him down before I even got in the room."

Once Irene had disengaged from Jessie and Liz, Howard drew her aside and asked her what happened. She said, as though speaking to someone who was somewhat dense, "I killed him. He was hurting a child, so I killed him. Will there be anything else?"

Howard asked her, slowly, "And he was pointing the gun at you, it looked like he was going to shoot you?"

She realized that he was coaching her, and said, with a frown, "Yes, it was self-defense, if it needs to be. But it shouldn't *need* to be. He was hurting a child, he was a moral leper, and he needed to be killed." She stopped, giving deliberate emphasis to her next words. "I am rather an Old Testament kind of person, you see."

She was doing what people who knew her well called her "being Queen routine." But this time she was deadly serious. She could be haughty, imperious, curt, and arch—all at once, as though she were true royalty.

Howard said, "I don't think there will be any problem. I assume that gun is registered, ma'am."

"Yes. The Sheriff bought it for me and registered it himself."

"Fine. You did the right thing, ma'am."

"Yes, I know," she answered with a trace of impatience. And then she walked back to where Liz was sitting with the child, picked up the book, and resumed reading to her. She was animated, with a gentle lift in her voice that calmed the child as she sat leaning back into Liz's arms, blinking her eyes, wanting to sleep but not yet wanting to miss any of the marvelous story. Watching her, Liz remembered and was grateful for what she and Paul sometimes thought of as Jessie's powerful "erase button"—her ability to move past her flashes of emotion, settling into to a quieter place of her own making.

When the story ended, Jessie was almost asleep. Nestling deeper into Liz's body, she said slowly, "When he took me, Mama, I just made it into a story. I knew you would come get me. I knew it would turn out OK in the end, because that's how I made the story end. You and Daddy told us we can make happy endings if we do the right thing, so I knew it would be OK."

And so, Liz thought with immense gratitude, Jessica's creative gift, the grace of the scale-balancing talent that came with the mania, had gotten her through. As Jessica continued to chatter about it, processing it, Liz realized that her imagination had somehow insulated her from the horror of being with Dobson.

As she walked out to her car with Jessie, Howard motioned to Liz. "Just a second, Liz. Rudy can take Jessie." Jessie stumbled a bit, and Rudy gently swooped her up and carried her over to Liz's cruiser.

Howard said quietly, "Liz, you could have really screwed this up."

"Maybe. But I'm just not made to watch somebody else try to take care of my kid when I'm here. So do what you have to, Jack. I've got Jessie back, so I don't care." Then her voice softened. "I know you needed to do it by the book, Jack. But I just needed to go after her—I couldn't watch it."

She walked away from Howard, knowing he was done talking to her for the moment, and went over to Rudy, who had tucked Jessie into the cruiser and wrapped a blanket around her. "Thanks for carrying her. I just...I just couldn't do that non-interference thing, I guess."

"You did great, partner." Rudy patted her on the shoulder, and opened the door for her. "You were a warrior for your kid. You did great."

Liz started to get into her car, and then stepped back out, saying to Rudy, "Watch her for a minute more—I never thanked Irene."

She walked back inside, glancing at the tablecloth that now covered Dobson's body. Irene Pinsky was standing behind the counter, looking as if she had just come on shift on a normal day.

"I never thanked you. You were amazing. You made it all work out." And Liz gave Irene an awkward hug.

Irene responded, "I was glad to help. That is an amazing little girl—I could tell she is very special. You must bring her back one afternoon for tea." She had a twinkle in her eye that Liz caught, marveling at the composure of the remarkable woman.

A few days later, after everything had calmed down, Paul finally asked Liz about what happened at the Palmer's Green Inn, and he almost wished he hadn't. He had been told that she disobeyed Howard's orders and walked into the lobby while Dobson held Jessie hostage, and could not understand why she would have taken such a risk.

As softly as he could, he asked her "Why did you do it that way?"

Liz looked at him and said, simply, "I thought he would shoot me and then they would shoot him and Jessie would be OK."

And they never talked about it again. But Paul thought about it over and over, marveling that Liz had been so clear-headed about being killed for her child. Painfully, he admitted to himself that in her place, he would have still been trying to think his way out of the problem long after the threat was over. And he knew once again that as much as he loved Liz, as close as they were, she had a deep, instinctive core of pure action that he would never penetrate.

CHAPTER 70

A week later, Paul went up to the front of the room and wrote on opposite sides of the blackboard, covering the whole front wall: *Takings* and *Leavings.*

He began slowly. "Is it the land or is it the people? We talked about Robert Frost before. Remember? He said the land was ours before we were the land's. But the land was here long before old Zenas Leonard came poking through here in 1834 with the Walker expedition. It has been snowing up there in those blessed, fantastic mountains for thousands of years, even before the Nuumu got here.

"Yet the people made the land serve them, until finally they took so much from it that it could not give back what it had provided so readily before. And then the taking became evil, taking the water, taking the minerals, taking the planting lands from the Paiutes. Taking so much that the land could no longer give back enough." He wrote under "taking" the phrases: "The Paiute land and irrigation system," "the water that goes to LA," "Manzanar."

"And sometimes what is taken is invisible, a tiny bit of chemicals in your brain, taken away through changes we still don't understand, but without those chemicals, a child or one of you can't stop yourself from making bad decisions or losing control."

Catching himself, he saw a few glances across the aisle and raised eyebrows and realized he had gotten too close to the story of Jessie to be able to talk about brain chemistry in the abstract. So he veered away, going back to the main part of his wrap-up.

"So we need to fill in the taking part," and then he moved to the other side of the blackboard, "and we need to pay attention to the leavings part, too.

"Lots of people leave this Valley. Many of those we have been talking about in this course left. Sam Bishop left to live in San Jose. Mary Austin left—abandoned her disabled child here, and went to live in a treehouse in Carmel and then in New York. Richard Owens, whom John Fremont named the Valley after, never even got here. Most of the miners left when the mines played out. And the Army left the forts behind when they moved out. The Japanese left gladly, leaving behind the years stolen from them."

Then, softer, wanting them to hear the next part as their own story, not "history," he began again.

"They left, and so will some of you. More than two hundred of you will graduate from high schools in this county this year. And nearly half of you will go on to college, 4-year or community college. Some of you will go up the hill to Cerro Coso, and some will leave. And some of you will stay here, or go into the service, or go south and try to find a job down there.

"And part of your own future and the future of the Valley will hinge on what happens after that. It's not just whether you will come back to live and work here, though that's part of it. It's whether this special place and the history of this place will stay with you, or whether you will leave it behind, too.

"Some of you will leave and come back only on holidays to visit your families. But the best of what is here travels well, and some of you will take it with you. I've had the chance to watch many young men and women like you go off into the world, into military service, and careers, and raise families all over the nation and the world. And what some of them take with them is a simple code, a way of life, not needing to live near a Nieman-Marcus or a super-mall, wanting blue sky and trees and water and willing to do some work to keep wherever you live clean and clear.

"And for those of you who stay, the place may keep on working its magic, or it may just become just part of the numbers in the background of your lives, a zip code and an area code. And that would be a loss, to be surrounded by all this outrageous beauty, and to stop seeing it and take it for granted. Leaving without returning is bad. But taking it for granted, whether you stay here or leave and come back, is bad, too."

He leaned forward across the desk, wrapping up now, knowing he would never see many of them again. "So *don't* take it for granted. This *is* a special place, a great place to live, and that psycho killer helped remind us of that, by distracting us for a time with what divides us from each other instead of what we share here. Takings and leavings will go on forever, but try to take some of the best of the Valley with you if you leave. Take the openness, and the love of the land, and the respect for God's creations. Take the balance we achieve—most of the time—as we come from so many different places to live here with those who got here first and those who got here a few weeks ago. Take all these things, all these blessings with you on your journeys. Godspeed."

They sat for a few moments, most of them knowing he was trying to do a lot more than finish the course. And some would ponder it, and some would dismiss it, and some would just forget it. But he had done his best to make them understand, and some did. And as they rose to leave, a few of them stopped by his desk to thank him. As the last ones left, he watched them go, wondering about the rest of their lives.

And then, having done the work he was given to do that day, Paul closed the door to the classroom behind him and headed down the hall, bound for home to see Liz and Jessie and Jennie, to comfort and be comforted by his family.

EPILOGUE

Liz took two weeks off to make sure that Jessie and Jennie were all right, helping them adjust to the end of their school year as Paul wrapped up his own teaching for the year. She had asked to be assigned to work with Rudy out of the Bishop sub-station, and Jack Howard had assured her it would go through, telling her he was sorry to lose her on the headquarters team.

Liz spent the two weeks of leave talking with Jessie's teachers and joining two Internet groups of parents of children with bipolar conditions. She scheduled a trip to UCLA during the summer to see some of the specialists she had originally seen when Jessie was first diagnosed. Somehow, she hoped, they were going to find a combination of therapy and medication that would level out Jessie's peaks and valleys. Jessie showed almost no effects of the kidnapping, but Liz and Paul feared a delayed reaction.

Liz and Paul made plans to use some of the savings her father had given her for the girls' education for a family trip. The four of them had made a dinner-table game of deciding where they would go, with the choices finally boiling down to Hawaii, Alaska, or France. Jessie was holding out for France, based largely on a book of impressionist paintings Paul had given her. Jennie, ever the practical second child, wanted to go to Hawaii because it was much closer to their home.

Paul planned to use part of the summer to turn his lectures into a long monograph on the Valley that he could use the next time he taught the course, and that he hoped would eventually become a book. He had begun working with Rudy to connect some of his lectures with the youth programs on the reservation that were run by the Indian Education Resource Center.

And Liz had set some time aside to keep her conversation with Elaine Carpenter going, uncertain where it would lead, but knowing that it had become an important connection for her. Going after Jessie had taught Liz that she was always going to act when she felt pressure, but beginning to talk with Elaine had also shown her that caring for the girls and being with Paul were going to take something beyond pure action.

And she could not help but hear her mother, somewhere, saying, "Now Elisabeth, sometimes, you just need to stop and think. *Stop, and think*. And it's OK to have feelings, too."

Two days after the shoot-out, Janet Fourtrees had arrived, and Rudy met her and took her to dinner. She was even more alluring than her photo, and when she admitted how detailed her conversations had been with his friend from Fresno State, he was secretly pleased that she had asked about him. She told him that the investigation was proceeding, and that the tribal leadership had been notified that an inspection was being sought through the Attorney General's office. The Supreme Court case about sovereignty of the casinos had been invoked, but it looked as if there was enough steam behind the investigation to overcome any legal action that the tribe might attempt. While the state had backed away in the earlier case from supporting a Sheriff who was going after a little welfare cheating at the local level, when it was state revenues that were being diverted—however small—the state got very serious. Janet said she might have to stay in the area for at least a week, and Rudy began planning his campaign.

Rudy had heard stories about couples from different tribes who had not been able to put their lives together because they could not break their ties to their own tribe and the culture that went with it. Some of the saddest people he knew were so-called urban Indians, who had been forced to trade their ties to their own reservations for a job and a career somewhere else. Some made it work and made new lives, but others ended up confused, wherever they were, because they were no longer in a place where they knew *who* they were. And as he thought about leaving the Valley, he felt a sharp ache, and he knew it would not be easy for him and Janet to be together.

Rudy also set aside some time in the summer to be with his brother and Brenda, because Brenda had been late-admitted to UC Irvine and was going south for the summer to attend some orientation courses. She was excited, and Paul's intervention had meant that the heat for interfering had been directed at Paul—which was fine with Rudy and, he knew, with Paul as well. And Brenda's father Ben had traveled down to Irvine with Brenda and had met the staff at the excellent American Indian Resource Program, finally beconing assured that Brenda would not be leaving behind her ties to the rest of her life.

Elaine Carpenter, encouraged by the feedback on her sermon and her remarks at the community meeting, had begun editing a collection of her sermons. She had pulled together all her sermons about the Valley, and realized she had given nearly forty sermons on the Valley's history and geography over the eleven years she had been a minister in Bishop. So she began reviewing them for a compilation that she supposed a few parishioners might buy. The Dodgers were narrowly hanging on to first place in their division, and her nights were well-programmed.

Elaine had a painful conversation with a congregant who was trying to come to closure with what had happened with Dobson and the events surrounding his death. The member, Mary Benson, was a long-time member of the church whom Elaine, despite all efforts at charity, had never been able to warm up to, since she was a classic half-empty negaholic. Mary's summary of the whole episode was "It was random, then. All of this was random and none of it makes sense."

Elaine was angry, and exploded back, "No, Mary, it was not. What that idiot did was random, but what we did to respond was deliberate. We did the right thing, after almost screwing it up and setting off a dozen little wars. But we came to our senses, and people from all over the Valley worked together to keep things on track. It was *not* random!"

The remark had set her off, striking at the center of her philosophy, where she cared most about her work and her life. For Elaine, life may not be predictable, and God's purposes may be unfathomable, but what could be controlled should be. She knew the Niebuhr quote appropriated by AA asking for the serenity to know the difference between what could and could not be controlled, but she was enough of a reborn Puritan to believe that when humans *could* exercise discipline and seek control—they should make the effort.

Memories of what had happened at the three evil places had been powerfully renewed by the deaths of the victims placed there. But Elaine hoped that the responses of at least some of the residents of the Valley had balanced the evil that Dobson had tried to deepen by his probing of the faults. The assets beneath the surface of the Valley, like those among the people who lived there, lay dormant, not yet fully tapped, but capable of lifting up some healing to balance the evil.

And yet the faults remained. They would open up again one day. And Elaine knew that she and the people of her congregation and the whole Valley would again be tested in their decency and resolve, as they decided once again how they would respond to each other and to the natural world that surrounded them with such beauty and such risk.

Fred and Dale Bancroft had begun reorganizing their office, and Dale had come up with several ideas for marketing the new "green" condos on the river. She had been handling the discussions with Max Chatham about the tribal role in the energy development projects, as well as the discussions with Nick Jamison and the environmental groups. Fred was delighted at how well she managed the difficult negotiations. One night Dale confided to him that now that she understood the energy deal with the tribe, the feds, and DWP, she saw it all as a big gamble that could pay off for them—or not. Fred cringed slightly at her wording, but said he hoped she was saying that her love of risk was fitting into the business. And Dale said yes, that's what she hoped too.

Jim Scott and Rosa Chavez had packed her car for the trip south to UCLA, where she had enrolled in summer school to get a head start on upper-division credits. They had talked about when he would visit and when she would come home, agreeing to a pre-Thanksgiving trip he would take south before she came home for the long weekend. Rosa knew that it was the first of what might be many negotiations on who visits whom and where to live. She knew that traveling to Mexico in the spring semester to see her cousin Maria was likely to affect the rest of her life, and Jim's. And Jim knew that he would need to do things he had never done before, to try to be a constant in her life—to be reliable. Ernie and Sam had come to say goodbye to Rosa, and afterward Ernie had gruffly told Jim that he had set up an account that Jim could draw on for expenses for the travel south, with the condition that Ernie could come and visit them with Sam in Mexico while Jim was visiting Rosa. And Jim accepted the gift and the condition gratefully, even looking forward to being with his father in a foreign country, where he was certain he had a lot to learn—both from Rosa and from his father.

And Cecelia had mostly succumbed to their being together for a while, beginning to like what she had seen of Jim and at the same time, thankfully realizing that Rosa would have weeks of being apart from him, immersed in her new world, able to fit Jim in if he still made sense to her. And she began in earnest the long task of letting her daughter go, knowing Rosa would return on her own timetable, full of her own life and loves, and beginning to leave her own mark on the world.

Sam Leonard headed south to visit his daughter and finish his series on the forgotten history of Southern California. He had enjoyed his stay in the Valley, as he always did when he visited Ernie. But he looked forward to returning to Mexico and connecting with Jim and Rosa—and possibly again with Maria Chavez.

As the summer warmed the Valley and continued to melt the last of the winter's snows still clinging to a few northern mountainsides, Paul began to think about his book. He had set aside some time to write, negotiating carefully with Liz and the girls for the time it took, cleaning out a writing space in the workshed in the back yard, trying to get enough sleep at night to enable him to rise early and work before dawn, then walking down to the Black Sheep to get some spoon-standing-up coffee before Liz and the girls were awake.

Somehow, he knew, the book would have to begin with a parade. Starting with the first Nuumu clans coming into the Valley ten thousand years ago, it would feature Zenas Leonard, John Fremont and Richard Owens, Sam Bishop, Lieutenant George Evans and his troopers, Pablo Flores and the rest of the Cerro Gordo silver miners from Mexico and the Chinese miners, Winnedumah, Chief George, Joaquin Jim, the basket weavers, Mary Austin, Mark Twain, William Chalfant, the Watterson brothers, Fred Eaton, even William Mulholland and the thousands of anonymous workers who dug the Aqueduct. The operators of the Owens Lake steamboat company, the founders of the company that built the narrow gauge rail line up the Valley. The riders of the Alabama Hills, Tom Mix, Gene Autry, Hopalong Cassidy, and Marion Morrison—known as John Wayne. The brave warriors of World War II who marched out of Manzanar and the ten thousand they left behind. The legal warriors who had finally fought Los Angeles to a standstill, the conservationists who used laws in a different way to preserve precious land and water in the Valley.

He would need to show all of them parading through history, marking the Valley with their faith and their works, some disappearing forever, some leaving deep and lasting signs that they had come to the Valley. And with the imagined parade beginning to wind its way through the pages of his book, he went off to his writing with an open-hearted joy.

THE END

AFTERWORD

This novel imagines current events that have mostly not happened in the Owens Valley, against the backdrop of history that definitely did happen there. The Valley's history is as fascinating as its landscape, and I have long wanted to try to capture some of both. Starting with my own family's move to Bishop in 1958, we have had ties to the Valley for over a half century. After graduating from high school in Bishop, I never lived in the Valley for longer than a year at a time, but I have visited it for many years as a non-resident lover of the place.

This book probably began gestating sometime in the mid-1950's, when I first asked my father what the little building with the oriental roof was doing out in the middle of the desert after we had just passed through Lone Pine on a camping trip to the eastern Sierra. He explained Manzanar briefly, and I went back to my book.

But then, a few weeks later, playing basketball with some eighth grade classmates, I remembered my dad's explanation, did some arithmetic, and asked one of the kids who was playing if he knew what Manzanar was. He gave me a funny look, said "We lived there," and turned and shot the ball toward the hoop. I have never forgotten how hard it was to accept that he was one of the ten thousand people who had been relocated to Manzanar just because his family was Japanese. At that time, in the eighth grade, he and his brother were two of the smartest kids and best athletes in our school and their older sister was an outstanding student in the high school where my father was the principal.

The next time we drove by Manzanar, it had a face: the faces of the Nakai family. And then I knew my country had done a terrible thing.

I want my children and grandchildren—and maybe a few more who come across this book someday—to be true patriots. And so I hope they will, in the words of my favorite patriotic song, believe in an America where we must continually ask that "God mend thine every flaw."

The later ingredients of this novelistic stew included a growing dislike for the television and print media's simplistic cant about "red and blue states," ignoring the possibility of purple at the intersection of communities. The over-done red-blue divisions of our national politics are most meaningless at the local levels, in the small towns of this vast nation, where there may be lots of red attitudes and some blue ones as well, but where consigning your neighbors to such a box forever is just another kind of bigotry.

And so the sometimes purple skies and peaks of the Sierras seemed to me a good vantage point from which to view "purple communities"—places that blend red and blue in more ways, with more decency and understanding, than we sometimes give ourselves credit for having. The Billings, Montana story related in the book also moved me deeply, and that is underneath some of the book, too.

No Valley resident nor anyone else is responsible for my interpretation of events, but I did receive a great deal of help and guidance for which I am very grateful. My brother Ted and sister-in-law Pat have been very patient over the years with my questions, and as local residents with strong community ties have helped me understand cross-currents far deeper than my own visits could fathom. Brother Terry drew on his years of law enforcement in Mono County for some fine advice. Other members of my extended family read the manuscript and had very useful comments. I had an excellent local editor, Annie Kellner, who thoughtfully suggested alternatives to some errors of fact and interpretation. Carma Roper of the Inyo County Sheriff's Department was very helpful with some background information on the County and the Department's operations. Any errors of fact, and obviously all interpretations, are mine alone. I have occasionally moved things around a bit for dramatic effect; I didn't invent any new geography, but I slightly relocated a few sites. All of the characters, of course, are imagined and are not intended to resemble anyone living or dead.

My written sources are many, and I should thank the owners and staff of that great natural resource of the Eastern Sierra, Spellbinder Books in Bishop, where there was always a new book to pick up and unfailingly friendly booksellers. Major sources included *The Story of Inyo* by W.A Chalfant; *Deep Valley: Guide to Owens Valley* edited by Jeff Putnam and Genny Smith; Rebecca Fish Ewan's *A Land Between*; Mary Hill's *Geology of the Sierra Nevada*; Mary Austin's works *The Ford, The Land of Little Rain*, and *Lost Borders;* the fine books about Japanese American soldiers in World War II—*Just Americans* by Robert Asahina and Jack Wakamatsu's *Silent Warriors.* On water, *The Great Thirst* by Norris Hundley, Jr., *Western Times and Water Wars* by John Walton, Robert Pearce's revisionist *The Owens Valley Controversy and A.A. Brierly*, Nadeau's *The Water Seekers*, and Abraham Hoffman's *Vision or Villainy* were all useful.

In writing about "purple politics," I've drawn on Morris Fiorina's *Culture Wars? The Myth of a Polarized America* as well as the Brookings Institution's two edited studies of polarization in politics.

Kirk Mitchell's Dee Laguerre novels, especially *Deep Valley Malice*, were a further inspiration. The Harvard Project on Indian Economic Development publication *The State of the Native Nations* and Charles Wilkinson's masterful *Blood Struggle* gave me some useful background on recent economic and casino development on Native Americans' lands. Also helpful were *Sand in A Whirlwind*, by Ferol Egan and *Genocide of the Mind*, edited by MarilJo Moore. Louise Erdrich's works were a somewhat intimidating benchmark. Peter Dreier of Occidental College wrote a review of casino gambling expansion in California that provided useful background. *Mayflower* by Nathaniel Philbrick was a reminder that both sides of the country have some very dark history.

I am greatly indebted to Kathleen Fox of the National Indian Child Welfare Association, who suggested I read Rupert Ross' remarkable book *Dancing with a Ghost.* The explanations of Native thinking and feeling were very helpful in brightening the inevitable opaqueness of my own Eurocentric view of Native people. Traveling and working with Nadja Jones, also of the NICWA staff, were wonderful experiences that added to my understanding. A generous conversation with Kris Hohag in Bishop was immeasurably useful in getting the perspective of a remarkable Paiute college student. Diana Meyers Bahr's *Viola Martinez: California Paiute* was a wonderful resource.

The geothermal speculations are nearly all taken from recent newspaper and online accounts of what is actually happening in California—some of it in the Valley. Geothermal economics rises and falls, but in the hard economic times in which I write, all that heat underneath is a tempting power source. You can get a lot of arguments among economists and energy experts about geothermal power and desalinization, which figure in the plot of the novel. From a layperson's perspective, we are in for more of both, however much they may cost at the moment. And I've read enough to believe that betting on alternative energy is a better gamble than staying with oil—unless you're willing to argue for major nuclear expansion or deeper involvement in oil nations' politics.

Some additional perspective came from a long-ago dinner in Bishop in the late 1950's, where I found myself at a table with Otis Chandler, then publisher of the Los Angeles Times. He was in Bishop on a good will tour of some kind, in which a group of high school seniors had been assembled as an audience. At that time I had no idea of his family's history with the water wars and their impact on the Owens Valley, but I vaguely remember naively predicting great growth for the Owens Valley in the decades ahead. Chandler's non-committal response makes a lot more sense now than it did then.

Sam Leonard came back into this one for a bit part, after his larger role in my first novel, *Like a Single River*. I like Sam, and I thought he might have a good perspective on the Valley from his earlier role in an imagined set of events in Mexico and California.

The Faulkner quote is from *Requiem for a Nun*.

A final word about the politics of the novel. Some writers believe politics has no place in a novel, while others believe the purpose of the novel is to make us see and make us act. For me, politics comes into that somewhere. And of course a novel is a place where we can construct a world that should be, whether or not it may exist today.

A portion of the profits from sales of this book will be donated to the Indian Education Resource Centers in the Valley and to the Eastern Sierra Land Trust.

Sid Gardner
Irvine/Bishop/Havasu
July 2009

Printed in the United States
By Bookmasters